THIRST

An Alex Graham Novel

Katherine Prairie

Stonedrift Press Ltd
Vancouver, Canada

Published by Stonedrift Press Ltd.

First Canadian edition

This is a work of fiction. All of the characters, places, organizations, and events in
this publication, other than those clearly in the public domain, are either products
of the author's imagination or are used fictitiously, and any resemblance to real
persons, living or dead is purely coincidental and not intended by the author.

Front cover image: Bespoke covers
Illustrated map: Margaret Kernaghan

Stonedrift Press Ltd.
P.O. Box 14308, Granville Island P.O.
Vancouver, BC V6H 4J6

www.stonedriftpress.com

Library and Archives Canada Cataloguing in Publication

Prairie, Katherine, 1958-, author
Thirst : an Alex Graham novel / Katherine Prairie.
Issued in print and electronic formats.
ISBN 978-0-9949377-0-4 (paperback).--ISBN 978-0-9949377-1-1 (epub)
I. Title.
PS8631.R35T55 2016   C813'.6   C2015-908122-X
                                             C2015-908123-8

Printed and bound in Canada

For Bill

"The security of the United States and Canada is uniquely linked by proximity and a long history of close collaboration between our two governments. Today's announcements reflect our commitment to cooperative action to protect and safeguard both nations' vital assets, networks and systems, as well as the shared responsibility to protect all citizens from cross-border crime and terrorism."

— *U.S. Department of Homeland Security Secretary Janet Napolitano, July 14, 2010 announcing the Canada-United States Action Plan for Critical Infrastructure*

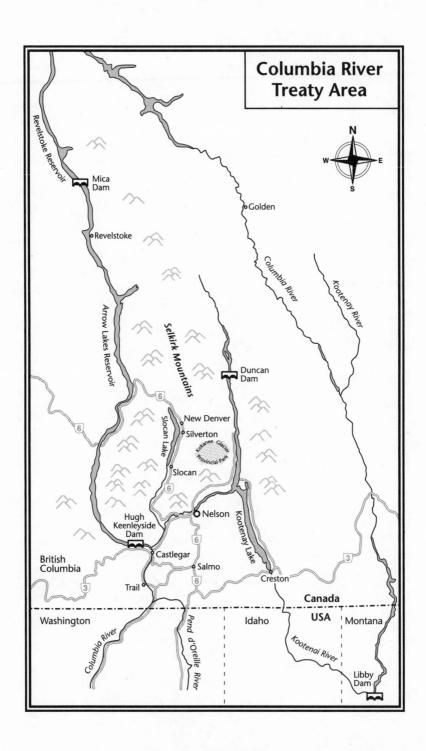

1

ALEX GRAHAM KNEW when to be afraid.

Her pulse quickened at the distant low-pitched whistle that warned of yet another rising wind gust far above her tent. She held her breath and listened for the sound to die off, for the wind to settle. But a mournful howl signalled the wind's plunge over the jagged granite peaks into the narrow valley she called home.

Eyes tightly shut, she clenched her sleeping bag tight beneath her chin. Massive boughs shook as the high-speed downdraft lashed at towering evergreens that lined the lower reaches of the steep rock face. The rattle of thousands of aspen leaves whipped into frenzied movement betrayed the wind's push across the valley floor.

It wouldn't be long now.

She buried her head deep in the down-filled mummy bag, every muscle tense. The wind blasted against the tent with the force of a freight train. Rope that strained to hold the fibreglass tent frame in place vibrated — then failed.

The tent wall flattened against her shoulder, pinning her against the nylon floor. Stale sweat and unwashed clothing odours tinged each shallow breath in her suffocating cocoon. She pulled her knees up to her chest to create more space near her face, but it wasn't necessary. Its energy spent, the gust vanished and the tent wall rebounded.

She pulled her head from the sleeping bag and took a deep, cold, pine-scented breath. The wind would return, but her tent, staked and still secured by multiple guy lines, would hold. For now, she could relax. She tugged at her t-shirt, forcing it down over the top of her

sweat pants. Turning onto her back, she stared up at the ceiling, listening to the gentle rustle of leaves. With luck, the windstorm would
soon ease. Until then, one too many close calls in weather like this
would keep her from sleep.

She shivered at the all-too-recent memory of an emergency helicopter landing forced by hurricane conditions in the harsh, unforgiving
Arctic. For forty hours she and the pilot had hunkered down against
biting winds until the weather lifted enough to risk a harrowing flight
out to Yellowknife. The story about the heroic pilot and the thirty-
year-old geologist in his passenger seat passed quickly throughout the
isolated northern community, bringing an uncomfortable amount
of attention her way.

She tried to keep a low profile in a cut-throat profession where
the winner claimed the right to mine gold, silver and other lucrative
metals and the loser moved on. Once word of her interest in the
remote Arctic region became known, North-Mineral swooped in
with a team of geologists. Within days, they laid claim to what should
have been her gold mine. She lost out.

At least this time she could escape by road at any time to New
Denver or one of the other small towns that dotted the southern
British Columbia landscape. And none beyond a trusted few would
ever learn of her project here in the Kootenays.

But she didn't plan on going anywhere. Not yet.

Her stomach growled. She glanced over at her all-weather jacket
hanging from the back of the canvas chair next to a desk piled high
with notebooks and maps. No doubt there'd be a chocolate bar or
two stuffed into the pockets. But to get there, she'd have to cross
more than eight feet of cold nylon in her bare feet. Instead, she buried
herself deeper in her sleeping bag.

The crunch of gravel drew her attention. Propped on one elbow,
she listened for the thud of a hoof or the snort of a bear. One heavy
footstep, then another, advanced swiftly toward her tent. It sounded
like a bear, but it moved faster than she expected. And it was headed
her way.

She reached down alongside her sleeping bag and slid her hand around the smooth wooden rifle stock. Her finger curled against the trigger, she disengaged the safety mechanism.

The footsteps stopped. Barely breathing, she watched the opposite tent wall for the moonlit shadow of the intruder. But a faint orange glow rather than a bulky shape appeared.

A flashlight? She stared at the spot near the tent floor and tightened her grip on the rifle.

Flame burst through the tent fabric.

Fire!

She let go of the gun and tugged hard on the sleeping bag's zipper. With the bag only partly open, she kicked her way free of its embrace. She grabbed the gun and crawled toward the tent door. With her free hand, she pulled at the tent zipper, but it refused to give way.

A quick backward glance into the tent made her heart pound. The pungent smoke that burned at her nostrils blanketed the tent interior in a grey haze. Black scorch marks stretched high up on the tent wall as the growing fire licked at the fabric.

She dropped the rifle in front of her knees. With a firm grip on the bottom edge of the tent door, she jerked the zipper free. Fresh, cold air rushed through the tent door. She sucked in a deep breath, but the flames also drew strength from this new source of oxygen.

From behind her came the roar of the fire, and she twisted back. The blaze had leapt to the crude plywood desk, where it now gorged on the rolled maps. A cloud of fiery, burned paper fragments swirled above flames that also raced up the tent wall and fanned out along the floor. The flame-resistant fabric bought her some time, but soon the desk itself would ignite and her backpack and duffel would be next.

She needed that backpack. Her GPS and computer held weeks of valuable data. But could she reach it before the flames did?

Above the crackling fire, she heard the howl of a swelling wind gust. If it descended into the valley, she'd have a minute at best before the tent turned into a fireball.

Now or never.

Turning her head to the open doorway, she took a deep breath that only made her cough. She tried again and this time sucked in a lungful of cold, clean air. She grabbed her hiking boots and threw them outside. Then she covered her mouth and nose with the neck of her t-shirt and crawled back into the smoke-filled tent.

Acrid smoke stung her eyes as she neared the flames. Heat from the all-too close blaze now consuming the wooden desk burned at her face. She could go no further.

With her left hand, she reached for the pack. Pain hit as flames lapped at her arm, and she jerked back. So close. She stretched her hand toward the pack again. This time she caught one of the straps of the backpack and hugged it to her chest.

She turned and crawled toward the door, both dragging the pack and pushing at it with her knees. At the door, she flung the bag free of the tent and snatched up the gun. She clambered to her feet and thrust through the gap into the darkness beyond.

In one swift motion, she ripped the t-shirt away from her face and then rammed the rifle into her shoulder. The fire was intentional. *Who's out here? And where is he?*

With the muzzle pointed at the dense evergreens, she fought to keep the rifle steady in her shaking hands. Her back to the fire, she slowly circled the tent, each step against the hard ground painful to her bare feet.

At the crack of a breaking tree branch, she spun to her left. The yellow firelight thrown from the blaze revealed nothing near the tent. Beyond in the dim moonlight only the outlines of tall spruce trees against the ink-coloured sky were visible. She scanned the line of trees. Her eyes settled on a dark void, an opening she knew led to a narrow path through the tangled underbrush.

There. That's where he has to be.

Her shoulders heaved with each breath. She stood motionless, watching for movement. Above the gusting wind, she heard only the roar and hiss of the fire as it tore through the tent's contents. Its heat burned at her back until the red-hot flames forced her to take a few steps forward. But her focus never wavered from the sliver of darkness between the trees.

She spun around when a loud crack came from behind her. Her desk now collapsed into the flames fuelled the fire. Black-grey smoke, foul with chemicals, poured from the blaze that greedily fed on the tent and its contents. In another few minutes, only ash would remain.

He tried to kill me.

Against the raging bonfire, she was clearly visible, and there were a thousand places for her attacker to hide. She found her hiking boots and rammed her bare feet into them as she slung the backpack over her shoulder. Sharp pain jolted her, and a quick glance at her left arm revealed angry red skin.

She stared at the scorched skin. Either adrenaline or shock kept the pain at bay. It wouldn't last.

She had to move.

After quickly lacing up her boots, she ran toward the 4x4 truck, now her only shelter. The doors were unlocked and the key was in the ignition, an old habit that promised a quick escape. But as her hand grasped the door handle, she stopped.

If I have easy access to the truck, so does he.

She peered into the driver's side window of the truck and checked the front and back seat. She took a deep breath. One white-knuckled hand gripped the rifle while she flung open the back passenger door with the other.

Her eyes swept across the rear seat of the truck. Empty, except for the gear stored on the floor.

Back tight against the side of the truck, she crept to the rear of the vehicle with her rifle raised. Eyes directed into the darkness, she stretched her left hand back to grab the hatch. She forced in a deep breath and squeezed the handle until she heard a metallic pop.

Both hands back on the rifle, she spun to face the rising hatch head-on. The dark interior came into view, but it revealed only the vague shapes of her equipment.

Wind pounded the truck, and she looked back at the fire. The powerful blast of air sent billowing smoke and ash high into the clear night sky.

Her breath caught in her throat.

Drones! If the American pilots in some far-off U.S. city who controlled these sophisticated unmanned surveillance aircraft hadn't spotted the smoke yet, they would soon.

She had to put this fire out. Now.

With one trembling hand tightly clenched around her rifle muzzle, she leaned the gun against the 4x4's fender. She threw the backpack into the truck and hauled out the fire extinguisher.

With each hurried stride toward the fire, pain flashed down the arm that cradled the heavy canister. Unwelcome hot tears spilled from her eyes, blurring the flames that fed on the last of her belongings.

As near to the fire as she dared, she blanketed the fiery threat in white foam until the canister was emptied. Wisps of smoke rose from blackened ash untouched by her efforts, but she could do no more. She flung the extinguisher to the ground and ran back to the truck.

She barely broke stride to grab her rifle and slam the hatch closed before she jumped into the truck. The engine roared to life, and with her foot heavy on the accelerator, she raced down the rugged back road.

2

HAND ON THE dark-stained banister, RCMP Constable Nathan Taylor looked up to the second floor, where the warm yellow glow told him his daughter was still up. Not bothering to turn on the hallway light, he climbed the carpeted stairs toward her room.

From the top of the stairs, he saw Olivia in her pajamas, sitting at her desk with both legs hugged to her chest. She looked so small and vulnerable that he wanted nothing more than to scoop her up into his arms and hold her close. But his little girl was a teenager now, a young woman about to graduate high school, and she would only squirm in his embrace.

Where did the years go?

A creaking floorboard in the hallway betrayed his approach, and she snapped shut the lid on her notebook computer. But not before he saw the face of a man on her screen for a brief moment. A young man, but not a face he recognized.

"Liv, who was that you were talking to? It didn't look like one of your usual friends."

He leaned his six-foot-four, two hundred and twenty-pound body against the door and wrapped his hand around the doorknob. She swivelled the chair away from the cluttered desk to face him.

"Just somebody I met."

She pushed her long blonde hair behind her ears. He remembered when she used run to him at the breakfast table, ribbon in hand, asking him for braids. Not anymore.

"Where?"

Instead of answering him, she tucked her hands under her thighs and swung one leg back and forth as though keeping time to some unheard rhythm.

She's hiding something about this boy. "Is he someone from school?"

He prayed she hadn't met him online. Nothing scared him as much as the unseen men who trawled Internet chat rooms for their young victims. Predators who stole lives.

"Don't get all paranoid on me, Dad. He's not a bad guy. Why do you think that every guy I meet is out to hurt me?"

"I'm a cop. It's what I do. And you're changing the subject. Who were you talking to?"

"A friend of Michael Walden's."

"Walden?" He gripped the door handle hard, his knuckles white from the exertion. His brown eyes narrowed. "I didn't think you even knew the dead boy."

"Of course I did. He was in some of my classes."

"But you never mentioned him before. So why is this guy calling you now, almost a year after Walden's death?"

"He wants to do something to honour Michael at graduation. That's all." She turned her head away from him and picked up a pen.

"You're kidding, right?" He stared at her hard, waiting for an answer. But she said nothing and he pushed. "The school isn't going to let you do anything to honour that boy."

"Michael was a hero," she said softly. Her gaze never wavered from the blank notebook in front of her, which left him staring at her rigid back.

"A hero? He was no such thing. He was a terrorist!" Dropping his hand from the doorknob, he balled it into a fist. "You know as well as I do that he was caught with explosives at the dam. If he had lived, he would've been convicted."

She threw the pen onto the desk and swung the chair back around to face him. The anger in her brown eyes betrayed her response before she said a word.

"He wasn't a terrorist!" she shouted. "He was doing what the rest of you should be doing. Fighting back."

"Against the dams? Liv, there are better—"

She snorted. "You think Michael died protesting a dam? He was at war with the U.S. Army."

"An army that wouldn't be here at all if the Mica and Keenleyside dams hadn't been bombed in the first place. Do you understand how critical those Columbia River dams are to the United States?"

Three dams: the Duncan, Hugh Keenleyside and Mica in Canada, and a fourth, the Libby dam in Montana. Together they controlled the raging Columbia River, preventing floods and fuelling the electricity-producing Grand Coulee dam and other powerhouses further downstream. Enough power for the Pacific Northwest and much of California. International cooperation at its best, until expiration of the Columbia River Treaty loomed and the Mica dam was bombed. Now all of the dams on the Columbia were jointly secured by U.S. and Canadian forces. And all were targets.

She shook her head. "They shouldn't be here."

He threw up his hands. "And Walden figured if he bombed the Keenleyside dam a second time, the Americans would go home? Olivia, that's nonsense. None of the soldiers — Canadian, American — none of them are going anywhere until the threats stop."

"You don't get it, and you never will." She rolled her eyes at him and turned away again, this time grabbing a textbook from the pile on top of the desk. With a flick of her wrist, she slammed the cover open and roughly flipped through the pages.

She was right. He'd never understand how Michael Walden or those who followed in his footsteps thought their tactics would force the Americans back across the border. They conveniently forgot that agreements announced by President Obama and Prime Minister Harper long before the first bomb exploded, paved the way for the cooperative defence of critical assets by the two neighbouring countries. That U.S. troops had been welcomed by the Canadian

government. But he wouldn't win an argument on the subject with
Liv. Not tonight.

"Look. I have to leave for work in a few minutes," he said as he
checked his watch. "I don't want to fight with you."

Olivia stared at the page in front of her, dead-still. She looked up
when the lights flickered but returned to her book without comment.
In the silence, the scratch of tree branches driven against the windowpane by the gusting wind filled the room. The wind was picking
up. No doubt there'd be a power outage before the night was over.

There was a time when she would have looked to him for reassurance in a windstorm like this one. He glanced around the small
bedroom where she spent so much of her time these days. The Harry
Potter books and posters had long been taken down, replaced by
college course calendars and nature posters. It was the bedroom of
a young woman, not a girl. At least she was home tonight. One less
thing for him to worry about.

He tried again.

"Liv, please."

She pushed a set of ear-buds into place, shutting him out completely. As she ran her fingers over the smooth surface of her smartphone, he finally retreated to the hallway.

"Did I hear you and Liv arguing?" Jess asked as he walked into
their bedroom. Pillows stacked behind her, the latest Steve Berry
title in hand, he knew his wife, wrapped in her favourite chunky
blue sweater, would be up for hours. The life of a cop's wife. Twenty
years of nights filled with worry, made worse since his assignment
to the Integrated Task Force. She'd tell him that she fell asleep not
long after he left the house, but her tired blue eyes always betrayed
her. And he loved her all the more for the lie.

"She was talking to some friend of Michael Walden. When I told
her what I thought of Walden, she got angry."

Jess put down her book and patted the quilted duvet beside her.
He squeezed onto the bed beside her and slipped one arm behind
her, gently closing his hand around her narrow shoulder.

"She's not speaking to me now." He brushed her blonde hair aside and kissed her forehead. He caught a faint floral scent as his lips touched her smooth skin, a remnant of her favourite perfume. "I didn't even know she knew Walden. Did you?"

"He was by the house once or twice I think, but they weren't close," she said with a shake of her head. She leaned into his shoulder before she continued. "She went to his funeral, you know."

Along with thousands of others from the Slocan Valley. The event marked the beginning of a string of protests that kept him working overtime for days, tightly controlling the crowds marching through the streets of Nelson. In the early days, the protestors had been peaceful. But as the months passed, weapons and Molotov cocktails had replaced placards. And dynamite had become the bullhorn.

"Do you think she's caught up in this nonsense? She actually thinks Walden is a hero. Can you believe she said that?"

"You're worked up over nothing," Jess said as she brushed her cheek against his rough hand. "She's a smart girl."

"She may be smart, but she thinks she knows everything. What does she know about politics?"

"What I know is that we've got nothing to worry about. You have to trust your daughter."

"With everything that's going on—"

"Especially with everything that's going on," she interrupted. "You can't control her every move. So just let her know you trust her to do the right thing, and she will."

"Just like that?" Nathan asked with a snap of his fingers. Nothing was that simple when a teenager was involved.

"Just like that." She ran her fingers over his shirt collar. "Are you heading in early?"

He nodded. "Something's up. Got a call to meet a military patrol in the Valley up near New Denver."

3

WITHOUT TAKING HER EYES from the road, Alex cranked the heat up as high as it would go. But it did nothing to stop the shivering.

Spruce boughs whipped at her bumper as she drove tight to the trees lining the side of the narrow road. Jolted in her seat by shock absorbers strained by the rough surface, she gripped the wheel hard. In the yellow beam of her headlights, a massive tree trunk rose up in front of her, and she cranked the steering wheel to avoid it while turning into yet another curve that came up fast. Too fast.

This time she wasn't as lucky. Her front bumper scraped against a rough tree trunk as her front tires left the road. She eased up on the gas and threw her weight into the turn. Her back tires sent up a spray of gravel from the soft shoulder of the road, and the truck swerved violently but regained the rutted road.

She floored the gas pedal and checked the rear-view mirror again. There was only one way out of the valley, and she was on it. If he gave chase, she couldn't miss him.

The sound of her tires as they ground against the loose gravel of the road filled the night. She would have heard a car drive up this road, despite the howling wind. Fear stabbed at her gut. Her attacker had probably hiked into her campsite.

For the past week, she had trekked the mountain ridges without seeing anyone. But it didn't mean she was alone up here. The Slocan Valley had long been the haven of those who sought to escape from society. Some lived in near total isolation deep in the woods, shunning all social contact. Would they hunt down and murder an intruder?

The smooth black pavement of the highway up ahead reflected in her headlights. Easing up on the gas, she brought the truck to the end of the gravel road and stopped just short of the intersection. A quick check in both directions revealed a deserted highway, and in the rear-view mirror there was only darkness. She was safe here. For the moment.

She squeezed her green eyes shut and rested her forehead against the soft black leather of the steering wheel. Tears threatened as pain, pushed aside in the race out of the mountain valley, now exploded in her arms. She switched on the interior light and turned both of her forearms up into the dim beam. Bright red skin ran the length of both arms. From the blisters on her left arm, she knew the burns were serious. Yellowish fluid oozed from broken skin near the edge of her watchstrap.

Eleven thirty. An hour ago, she lay tucked in her sleeping bag, heedful of the storm. If she'd been asleep, she'd be dead. She swallowed hard.

This time the wind had saved her life.

With shaking fingers, she tugged at the watch strap buckle and gingerly slipped the leather from her wrist, leaving a pale reminder of its steady presence. Her thumb circled the scratched cover of the simple white-faced timepiece, a graduation gift from her father eight years ago. A gift from one geologist to another.

She stuffed the watch into the pocket of her sweats and got out of the truck. From the cargo area she grabbed the first-aid kit and hauled it back to the cab. There she tossed the kit's packaged supplies onto the passenger seat beside her until she found a small packet of painkillers. She ripped it open and swallowed the two white ibuprofen pills without water. Exhausted, her adrenaline-fuelled energy depleted, she leaned her head back against the seat and closed her eyes.

She couldn't give in.

None of this seemed real. Had she stumbled onto an illegal marijuana grow-operation? The Kootenay region was the source of high-quality marijuana known as "B.C. bud," and her remote location made an ideal grow-op location. With big dollars at risk, a grower might do just about anything to keep his crop from prying eyes.

But murder?

Digging through the dumped first-aid kit contents, she retrieved a large bandage and pulled the edges of the paper package apart. Pain flashed through her arms, and she dropped the bandage. Tears ran down her cheeks unchecked until she brushed them away with a trembling hand.

She threw the first-aid kit on the seat with such force that the last of its contents spewed onto the floor. It was impossible for her to treat her own burns. There was no option but to head for the hospital.

It was risky. She'd run into military patrols along this section of road before, soldiers piled into canvas-topped trucks and armed to the teeth. But there was no going back.

The highway that lay in front of her was the only major road serving the Slocan Valley communities. Not far to the north lay New Denver, but at best, the small town would have a walk-in clinic with limited hours. The hospital in Nelson was a better choice, but that meant at least a half-hour drive south through the Selkirk Mountains.

Can I make it?

No choice. A call to 911 would bring more than an ambulance. The joint American-Canadian military force guarding the area would be notified, and a lengthy interrogation was sure to follow. If they were satisfied she posed no threat, they might let her go, but it was just as likely she'd be arrested. Either way, the military would shut down access to the area while they investigated the fire. She'd be cut off, unable to continue her work.

Her eyes darted to the rear-view mirror, reassured by the blackness behind her.

At least at the Nelson hospital she could get help without revealing her campsite's location. But the military controlled the small southern British Columbia town, and she'd be walking into the heart of the conflict over the Columbia River dams.

The lights of a northbound car on the highway broke the darkness. Parked this close to the intersection, her truck could easily be spotted. She glanced at her soot-covered reflection and took a hard look at the strewn contents of the first-aid kit. *Damn.* Even if she somehow managed to hide her burns, a military patrol would be suspicious.

She had to move.

Switching off the interior light, she punched the start button and stepped on the gas. A quick southbound turn put her onto the highway before the car reached the intersection. As the distance between the cars closed, her headlights revealed the distinctive markings of an RCMP cruiser, and she relaxed. The cop wasn't likely to pull her over. Still, she watched her rear-view mirror until his red tail lights were out of sight.

Her eyes trained on the centre white line and nothing else, she drove down the highway toward Nelson, the last place in the world she wanted to be.

4

THE TIGHT BEAM of his headlights caught the looming hulk of military vehicles parked across the dark, wind-swept highway. He resisted the urge to slam his heavy boot against the brake pedal of the truck. Instead, he eased the speedometer down and slowly approached the roadblock that severed the highway.

A line of khaki-uniformed men moved forward, their steel rifles held ready. Among them, stood a lone RCMP officer in blue, the bland working uniform of a federal police force more famous for its scarlet full-dress serge.

Of the hundreds of perimeter roadblocks he'd crossed, only a handful of low-level soldiers typically manned the barricade. The Mountie's presence warned of something other than a routine stop.

His grey-blue eyes darted to the rear-view mirror. The empty gun rack mounted on the back window wouldn't raise suspicion. He whipped his head sideways and scanned the seat and floor beside him. Only his black backpack now rested in the front cab. The duffel with its bundled sixteen-inch dynamite sticks lay safely hidden, awaiting pick-up.

My hands.

He rubbed his palms against his jeans, knowing it wouldn't help. He'd worn latex gloves while working with the dynamite, but a simple swab would reveal any trace of nitroglycerin residue that clung to his skin.

Fifty yards still stood between him and the barricade of jeeps. His hands clenched around the steering wheel. He checked the rear-view mirror. No headlights. He could swing around, retreat from the roadblock. If the military were just turning cars back, they might forgive the move. *Acceptance without argument.* A common enough reaction among locals beaten down by months of martial law.

Unless these soldiers were looking for something — or someone.

Betrayal?

He slammed his hand against the steering wheel. If some coward had gone to the cops, avoiding these soldiers did nothing to keep him out of an interrogation room.

Except. Unless the cops had a recent description of him, they'd be looking for a man with a greying beard and brown, shoulder-length hair. A man with forty more pounds on his five-foot-ten-inch frame. A man who no longer existed.

He might yet escape.

Ten feet from the barrier, he rolled to a stop. The burly cop stepped out from the protective line of soldiers, his eyes locked on the truck.

His hand slid over the door rest. Fingertip on the window control, he waited, listening to the scuff of boots against the hard pavement. Until the cop stood, a mere arm's length from the door, flashlight held high.

Window rolled down a crack, he turned to face the cop who controlled his fate. A cop he recognized. The Mountie who'd grilled Diane and him countless times in their darkest days.

He clenched his fist, forcing his fingernails painfully deep into his palm, fighting back the anger. Fighting to keep emotion out of his face. His eyes.

Breathe.

"We'll have to ask you to turn around, sir. No traffic allowed through here for another hour or two," Constable Nathan Taylor announced.

He watched the cop's breath, steamy in the cold night air. Waiting for more. But without another word, the army's puppet stepped back. Either Taylor hadn't recognized him, or he didn't care.

It didn't matter. Truck gear slammed into reverse, he stepped hard against the gas pedal, sending the truck roaring back from the cop and his rifle-bearing companions. Gravel spat from beneath his tires as he whipped the steering wheel hard left and hit the highway shoulder. *Easy.*

His eyes darted to the rear-view mirror, to the line of men watching his retreat, until the darkness swallowed the navy-jacketed cop.

Now what? He forced air into his too-tight chest. The barricade blocked his only route home. His only route to safety.

Ahead of him, the dark highway that linked Nelson to New Denver appeared empty. But that didn't mean a patrol or second barricade wasn't up ahead. He had to get off this road.

In his mind, he pictured this section of highway along the Slocan Lake, a route taken so many times before. A campground. A side road. Both lay nearby, but in this windstorm his would likely be the only vehicle parked there.

Drones. He stared into the night sky. There was no way to know if air surveillance had been stepped up. Not without knowing what had drawn the military this deep into the Valley in the middle of the night.

The gentle slope of a driveway appeared in his headlights. A farmhouse. A gift.

Foot light on the gas pedal, he steered off the highway onto a narrow driveway. He watched the dark-windowed house for the twitch of a curtain, the glow of a light as gravel crackled beneath his tires. But the howling wind masked his approach.

As close to the house as he dared, he cranked the steering wheel over, sending the front end of the truck into the trees on the north side of the driveway. Branches scrapped against the passenger side of the truck, but he pushed forward until the truck rested just inches from a massive tree trunk. Only then did he shut down the engine. The truck, dark red and tucked against the trees that lined the driveway, would not easily be spotted. And air surveillance would read his heat signature as just another occupant of the house. He was safe. For now.

He yanked off his baseball cap and ran a sweaty palm over his shorn hair. That barricade, set up just before his turn-off, meant trouble. A raid of one of the handful of houses on that side-road. His road.

Shit! He slammed his fist against the steering wheel. In a few days, there'd be nothing for the cops to find. But a raid now, tonight, would destroy everything.

The wind howled, echoing his rage. He stared through heavy branches that whipped across the windshield into the darkness, knowing he was trapped here. Helpless. Until the soldiers dismantled their barricade and he could go home.

Only then would his fate become clear.

5

THE TALL, SLENDER emergency room nurse who entered Alex's treatment bay introduced herself simply as Susan. A tight smile beneath a boyish haircut made clear this blonde's no-nonsense attitude. But the bright-blue plastic watch with its playful cartoon character hinted at another side to this thirty-something nurse beyond the hospital walls.

"So tell me how you got those burns." Susan propped a sneakered foot up against one of the bed rails and dug an electronic tablet out of her pocket.

"My tent caught fire." Saying the words aloud sent a shiver through her. She pulled the thin hospital-issued blanket tighter around her shoulders.

"Your tent? How'd that happen?"

Her hand gripped the edge of the blanket. *Keep it simple.*

"Must have been my lantern."

"You were using a kerosene lantern? In this wind?" Susan shook her head and continued without waiting for an answer. "I'd say it's time to invest in new equipment. Something safer."

She watched the nurse enter a note into the digital medical chart. For better or worse, this lie was now the official story.

With a small flashlight pulled from the pocket of her maroon scrubs, Susan checked Alex's nose for singed nasal hairs or soot and then examined her mouth and throat.

"You breathed in a fair bit of smoke. How long were you in the tent after it caught fire?"

How long had it been? It seemed like forever, but it couldn't have been more than a minute or two.

"I was out of there pretty fast."

"Not fast enough, my dear. These are serious burns."

Susan clipped a pulse-oxygen monitor to Alex's right index finger before wrapping a blood pressure cuff tightly around the bicep of the other arm. Alex squeezed her eyes shut, expecting the worst with the first puff of air squeezed into the cuff.

"Just relax. The cuff is far away from your burns. It's not going to hurt. Now tell me, was anyone else at the campground injured?" she asked while watching the monitors.

"No. I was the only one there." Alex stared at the expanding cuff, as she spoke.

"I can't say I'm surprised. It's pretty early yet for camping. I didn't think the campgrounds were even open yet. Where were you?"

Alex looked up to find the woman's hazel eyes trained on her. Her heart pounded wildly, and she forced a shallow breath. She needed a believable answer. And fast.

"I wasn't actually in a campground. I was in the backcountry near Kokanee Glacier Park." Close to the truth, at least. She'd spent weeks in and near the spectacular British Columbia provincial park as she investigated abandoned silver mines high in the Selkirk Mountains. But last night's campsite had been far removed from the park itself.

"Can't say I see the appeal." Susan shook her head. "I'd much rather be home in a warm bed, especially in weather like this. You did know about the storm, right?"

Alex nodded. She braced for another question, but Susan popped her stethoscope earpieces into place. No doubt the cold metal diaphragm held against her pounding chest betrayed her fear. But if her inquisitive caregiver suspected Alex's racing heart rate was due to anything other than the painful burns, she said nothing.

"Let's get you over to the sink."

She leaned her elbow into Susan's extended hand and set her bare feet on the cold floor. Nausea threatened as she struggled to stand on wobbly legs.

"I've got you. Just take it slow."

The woman's strong arm kept a tight grip around Alex's waist as they shuffled together over to the sink. The stream of cold water flowing from the faucet doused the searing pain that had steadily intensified since she fled the fire. She could have stayed there forever, but the nurse directed her back to the bed all too quickly.

Left alone in the treatment bay, Alex closed her eyes and rested her head back against the narrow bed. The worst of it was over. There'd be no more questions. The doctor would treat her burns, and she'd be out of here.

She glanced down at her wrist before she remembered that her watch sat buried in a plastic bag on the floor. The steady hiss of oxygen came from somewhere nearby. She stared at the thin grey-striped curtain that offered the only privacy to patients in the emergency room. Although she heard only muffled conversations from the nursing station down the hall, there could easily be other patients behind the curtain on either side of her.

The rush of rings against a metal rod announced the man in blue scrubs who entered through the front curtain. At least this doctor looked like he'd been out of school for a while.

"Ms. Graham? I'm Dr. Keenan. Let's take a look at those burns."

From a wall-mounted dispenser just above the small bedside cabinet, he pulled a pair of latex gloves and fitted them over his slender fingers. Perched on the edge of the bed, he examined the angry red skin and blisters clearly visible below the short sleeves of her hospital gown.

"What happened?" he asked.

"I told the nurse already." *Hell. Don't these people talk to each other?*

"I'd like you to go through it again with me, if you don't mind."

She pressed her lips together in a hard line and then recited the same lie about the lantern. Unlike the nurse, this man didn't question her story. She was in the clear.

"Second-degree burns. You're lucky. It could have been much worse."

Stethoscope in place, the doctor instructed her to take a series of deep breaths while he listened for rales or wheezing in her lungs. When he was done, Alex watched as he stood near the foot of the bed and quietly entered notes into her electronic chart.

"Ms. Graham—"

She interrupted, "Alex."

"Were you in the perimeter?" he asked.

Stunned, she simply stared at him. This wasn't a question she expected to hear. Not from him.

"You're aware of the five-kilometre restricted zone on either side of the Columbia River and alongside all major highways?"

The perimeter. Three miles of controlled territory insisted on by the American military and agreed to by the Canadians. A zone she couldn't avoid.

When she nodded, the doctor continued, "I'm under orders to report any incident within that perimeter to the army."

Her mind raced. If a military drone had spotted the fire, police might check the hospitals for burn victims, but she wasn't going to make it easy for them.

"I wasn't in the perimeter. There's nothing to report," she said.

Silence hung between them. He stood completely still, the only movement the steady blink of his blue eyes.

"Okay." He nodded and flashed the first smile she'd seen since he entered the room. "I'll give you something for the pain, and then I'll treat those burns."

He removed his latex gloves and threw them into the stainless-steel waste bin in the corner of the room.

"By the way, was the fire out? In this wind, it wouldn't take much for it to spread. Do we need to call the fire department?"

"No. I used a fire extinguisher on it before I left. It's out."

"There was no one with you?"

"No." She watched the smile fade from his face.

"Let me get this straight. You were alone. And with these burns, you put the fire out and then drove to the hospital. Why didn't you just call 911?"

"I don't know. Shock, I guess."

At the answer, he cocked his head to one side. *He doesn't believe me.* She held her breath and waited for his next question.

But it never came. He parted the curtain with a practiced slip of the wrist and disappeared.

She heard voices beyond the curtain, but she couldn't make out any of the conversation. Maybe she should just leave. Go to one of the clinics and try again with another story.

No. If she left, they'd be even more suspicious, and soldiers would track her down from the information she had freely given to the hospital when she arrived.

She knew the risks when she had set up camp just inside the perimeter. But from what she'd seen, the military patrols north of Nelson were concentrated on the sections of highway that ran directly alongside the Columbia River. Occasionally, they travelled the back roads, but in the more remote areas, they depended primarily on U.S. military drones.

Drones. Those unmanned aerial vehicles were a constant threat. But while their infrared cameras might pick up a heat signature from her body, she counted on the pilots who monitored the aircraft's video feed to ignore such a small threat so far from the Columbia.

No doubt her dad would chastise her for not staying well out of the way of politics and its enforcers. After more than eight years of fieldwork, much of it in countries with unstable political situations, she knew better. But this was Canada, her home, and she'd let her guard down.

The soft squeak of a sneaker heralded the return of the nurse. Susan set a blue paper-wrapped package on the bedside table and then handed Alex two white tablets.

"These aren't going to put me to sleep or anything, are they?" Alex asked as she stared at the pills resting in Susan's palm.

"You'll probably feel sleepy, but it's not a sedative. It'll help with the pain."

If the police arrived, she'd need a clear head. But the promise of relief from the searing pain trumped her fear. She popped the tablets in her mouth and swallowed them with water from a small paper cup Susan handed to her.

She leaned back against the bed, watching Susan slip a short-nailed finger beneath the masking tape of the package. Her stomach churned when the nurse pulled back the blue paper to reveal sterile medical instruments, gauze and gloves. Alex hated needles, and this looked a whole lot worse.

Her breathing quickened with the return of the doctor. Susan slipped past him through the curtains as he slid the lone chair over to the bed. He slipped his hands into sterile gloves without a word and positioned her left arm on the bed, forearm exposed, before he picked up a pair of forceps. She cringed as he caught the edge of a piece of loose skin from a broken blister with the forceps and reached for a small pair of plastic scissors.

"I expected that to hurt," she said with the first snip.

"It shouldn't. The skin I'm removing is dead. There's no feeling in it."

At the sound of heavy boots in the hallway, she jerked her head towards the front curtain. At least two men headed this way. The footsteps drew closer. He must have called the police.

The curtain wall to her right shifted. Low voices followed. A woman greeting her sons. She looked back down at the brown-haired doctor who worked his forceps along the edge of a blister. Maybe this doctor was on her side after all.

"How long have you been here in Nelson?" he asked.

"I arrived two months ago. I've rented a house, but I spend most of my time in the mountains."

"I'd be inclined to skip the camping for a while and sit back with a good book and a glass of wine instead. Maybe some chocolate."

She smiled. He was charming, she had to give him that.

"From your boots, I'd say you're not camped out in the mountains just for the fun of it." He tugged at a piece of skin. "Prospector or geologist?" he asked without looking up.

She glanced over at her scuffed leather boots in the corner, where the chair had been. This guy didn't miss much.

"I get paid a lot of money to be discreet," she said.

"Geologist, then. Prospectors don't usually get paid." He grinned. "I can't say I've met many women doing that kind of work. Are you after gold or silver?"

"My client—"

"I know, I know. You can't tell me. It seems to be the one thing everyone heading up into those mountains has in common."

Nelson had its share of prospectors, amateurs and pros alike guided and encouraged by the Chamber of Mines. Like her, they kept their ideas and their whereabouts secret.

"It must be tricky working out there right now. Does the military give you much trouble?"

"The roadblocks are a nuisance." Beneath the blanket, she picked at the bottom edge of her cotton t-shirt. "But once I'm in the mountains, I don't see any soldiers. Just a few more helicopters."

"Sort of like it is here. Inside the hospital, it's more or less business as usual. A few more reports to file. More meetings. But outside that door. Well, you've seen them. The army vehicles. The soldiers. It's better now than it was, but I'm not sure I'll ever get used to seeing American uniforms."

It wasn't a distinction that mattered to her. Every soldier — Canadian or American — patrolling the Valley was a threat to her.

"Done." He set down the forceps and stood. "I'm going to cover the burned area with artificial skin. Since you spend so much time outside, I want that wound well-protected, and the artificial skin will speed healing."

"How long will it take for my arms to heal?"

"Probably two weeks or so for the left arm, a little less for the right. But you should start to see improvement in a few days." He smeared cream over the burns and wound soft, white cotton gauze around her arm. "You should know that some of the deeper burns near your left wrist are probably going to scar."

Her arms and legs bore scars from the inevitable slips and falls that came with years of scrambling over rocks. Most came with fond memories of mountain-climbing adventures with her dad, but these new scars, visible to all, would tell of attempted murder. She shifted her legs beneath the sheet.

"Let's see that right arm." He gently cradled her arm in his hand and spread cream over the burns. "I'll give you a few oxycodone tablets to help you get through the night and tomorrow. I'm also going to give you a codeine prescription that you should fill in the morning. No driving with either of these meds."

She shook her head. "Not possible. I have to get back to work, and that means driving. I'm going back into the field tomorrow."

She felt sure he was going to lecture her, but nothing he could say would change her mind. Especially not when the military could shut down access to the Slocan Valley at any time.

He didn't answer her. Not at first. "I don't recommend it," he said with his eyes on the gauze he wound carefully around her arm. "But if that's your plan, then you can take ibuprofen instead. Be prepared though. It's not likely to give you much relief. Your arms are going to hurt like hell for the next couple of days."

He entered a note into her chart and took a few steps towards the hallway. One hand on the edge of the fabric curtain, he stopped and turned back to her.

"I'm not sure exactly what happened out there, but be careful. I don't want to see you back here."

So he didn't believe her.

But he hadn't reported her either.

6

SEATED AT A DESK near the nurse's station, Eric Keenan watched the geologist's uneven walk past the nurse's station toward the ER exit. Damned if he knew exactly what had happened to her. Not that it was his concern. He'd asked the perimeter question demanded by the military but he refused to interrogate his patients.

"Eric, there's a patient in bed one that you need to take a look at right away. Laura Bennett," said a voice from behind him. One glance at Susan English's serious face was all it took for him to close Alex Graham's file and turn his full attention to this ER nurse.

"Bennett came in complaining of vomiting and diarrhea a couple of days back. I checked, and you treated her. She's in worse shape. Heart rate was fifty-five at triage, and her oxygen level is at eighty-nine percent on room air. I've started an IV and O_2 already and put her on a monitor."

He pushed back his chair and hurried over to the critical care room with his tablet gripped in his hand. The room's curtains were pulled back, allowing a clear view of his patient as he approached the narrow bed.

The harsh white fluorescent light from above the bed exaggerated Laura Bennett's pale white skin and the unflattering dark circles that surrounded her eyes. The middle-aged woman made no attempt to push back the strands of dark blonde hair, damp with sweat, that had fallen across her forehead. A hiss of air, and the black blood pressure cuff wrapped around her arm inflated automatically, updating her blood pressure on the monitor above her bed.

"I'm Dr. Keenan. I treated you when you came in two days ago. Still not feeling well?"

He checked her vital signs on the monitor. Thin grey cables that snaked beneath the blanket recorded a heart rate of only fifty-two beats per minutes, well below the normal range of sixty to eighty beats. But her heart tracing, the record of each beat that pulsed through her chest, looked steady and normal.

"I thought I'd be feeling better by now, not worse." She paused and took several short, rapid breaths before continuing in a weak voice. "It's difficult to breathe."

With the monitor showing blood oxygen levels of only ninety-one percent, he wasn't surprised. Reaching over the head of her bed, he doubled the flow of oxygen delivered directly into her nasal passages, from two to four litres per minute.

"Are you still vomiting?" he asked.

She nodded. "And the diarrhea hasn't let up. Even with just tea and toast."

He perched on the edge of her bed. "I'm going to do a quick check of your lungs. Can you lean forward a bit?"

With one hand against her back, he gently assisted her into an upright position. With effort, she drew in a deep breath while he listened to her chest. He didn't like the crackles he heard. They meant fluid-filled lungs. His mind went quickly to a diagnosis of congestive heart failure, pneumonia or ARDS, adult respiratory distress syndrome.

"Any fever over the past few days?" he asked, even though her chart indicated a normal temperature.

"I don't think so. I'm drenched in sweat most of the time, but I don't really feel warm." Her voice faltered.

She clutched a tissue in one trembling hand and dabbed at the secretions running from her nose around the prongs inserted there. As she raised her hand to her face, the IV tubing curled across the surface of a blue vein bulging from the translucent skin on the back of her hand.

"Have you taken any pain relievers like acetaminophen or ibupro-fen?" he asked. With pneumonia, he'd expect a fever ,but she might have suppressed it with an over-the-counter remedy.

"No. I don't really have any pain. And I'm not sure I could have held it down anyway."

Her chart listed no existing medical conditions. He checked her age. Just forty-one. Patients her age and younger could suffer from heart failure, but it wasn't common.

"Is there any history of heart disease in your family?"

"No," she said, shaking her head. "My parents are both healthy."

He looked at the monitor again. Her oxygen blood levels were up to ninety-four percent with the increased airflow. Still low, but better. He moved to the nurse's station just a few steps outside the critical care room.

"Susan, can you run an ECG on Bennett and set up the ultrasound machine? And let's get a bedside X-ray in here."

There was no way his patient was leaving the ER, even for a short trip down the hall to the X-ray department. In her chart, he requested a full cardiac and abdominal blood panel and scanned the long list of available lab tests before requesting a few that might help pinpoint a diagnosis. With that done, he picked up an ABG kit and headed back to his patient.

"I'm going to take an arterial blood sample. It will give me a measure of the amount of oxygen you have in your blood. I have to turn off the oxygen while I do this," he said as he leaned over and closed the valve. "But I promise I'll be quick."

Seated in a grey plastic chair pulled close to the bed, he mentally ran through the necessary checks for an arterial puncture. Once satisfied, he pulled on a pair of sterile gloves and swabbed the area at the base of her hand first with Betadine, and then alcohol. With a solid grasp on her left hand, he bent it back and then uncapped the syringe.

"Take a deep breath," he said. When she complied, he plunged the needle deep into the radial artery at the base of her wrist. Bennett winced at the painful jab, but under his firm grip, she couldn't move her hand away from the needle.

"Sorry about that. I know this procedure's a bit nasty." But at least he was good at it. Unlike some doctors, he rarely missed the artery on the first try. This time was no different. Blood spurted into the collection tube he attached to the needle, filling it quickly.

"All done." He positioned a sterile four-inch square gauze bandage on the puncture site and pressed his thumb against it. With the other hand, he capped the needle and set the blood-filled tube on ice. "Susan, let's get that sample off to the lab." In fifteen minutes, her blood work might give him the answers he needed.

He smiled at Bennett. "I'll keep pressure on this for five minutes, then you can get comfortable." He leaned over and with his free hand once again adjusted the oxygen valve, restarting the flow at its previous level of four litres per minute.

Hand gripped around his patient's wrist, Eric stood to let an unsmiling technician into the room with an ECG machine.

When the ECG strip started printing, Eric looked over the technician's shoulder at the results. Bennett's heart rate was still low at fifty-nine beats a minute. But the normal morphology trace generated by the ECG told him her heart was functioning properly.

"Is my friend here?" Bennett asked.

"Your friend? Is she in the waiting room?" Eric asked.

"No, I don't think so. She took the dog out for a walk. I have to feed him now," she said, her lips pressed together in a hard, determined line.

Mental confusion or lack of sleep? It was difficult to tell. He looked over at Susan, who discreetly shrugged. The technician backed out of the room, giving Eric access to the bed.

"Have you ever had an ultrasound before?" When she nodded, he continued. "Then you know that other than the chill of the gel, you shouldn't feel anything."

He squirted clear, conductive gel onto the ultrasound transducer before gliding it into position against her ribs. With upward pressure, he adjusted the device until the monitor displayed a good angle of the heart. The strong, rhythmic pumping action of her heart muscle reassured him. He wasn't a cardiologist, but her heart looked good.

He checked the monitor and saw that her oxygen levels were down again. Her numbers hovered too close to the ninety-two percent threshold below which respiratory failure was likely. She needed more oxygen.

"Susan, I'd like her on a non-rebreather." He turned back to his patient. "Ms. Bennett, have you travelled out of the country recently?" She shook her head. "No."

He was relieved. At least it probably wasn't the latest avian flu originating in China, H7N9. And not Ebola or another of the nasty diseases he'd seen so often in his work in Africa.

Susan stepped past him and moved over to the head of the bed. "I'm going to replace those nasal prongs with an oxygen mask." She pushed Bennett's damp hair back and unhooked the tubing wrapped over the tops of her ears before removing the nasal cannula.

Eric stepped out of the bay, making room for the large portable X-ray machine squeezed into the small space by a technician. He checked the monitors while he paced outside her room. The ER was busy, but until she was stable, Bennett would get his undivided attention. As soon as the X-rays were done, he moved back to his patient's bedside.

"You told the nurse that you were fine until a few days ago. Anything different in your routine over the last week or so?" he asked while he reread her chart.

"Nothing. The usual stuff. Working mostly. Walking the dog." Her voice sounded muffled from under the mask that now covered her nose and mouth.

"Your chart says you're a psychologist. Do you work in one of the professional buildings here in Nelson?" he asked, wondering if this was chemical exposure.

She shook her head. "No. I have a small practice based out of my home near New Denver. Most of my patients come from the small communities in the Valley."

He was relieved that these answers seemed coherent. But nothing she said gave him any further clues.

"I'm feeling dizzy." Her voice faded.

He watched the colour drain from her face. The monitor alarm sounded, and her heart rate dropped to forty beats per minute. Symptomatic bradycardia.

"Give her 0.5 milligram atropine now!" Eric ordered when Susan ran into the bay with a crash cart.

The nurse immediately injected half the contents of a preloaded syringe of atropine into one of the IV ports. Eric watched Bennett's pulse rate rise on the monitor, finally settling at sixty. Colour was returning to Bennett's deathly pale face, and her closed eyelids fluttered. His patient was stable. At least, for now.

What is going on with this woman?

His runners squeaked against the tile floor in his rush to his computer. Perched on the edge of his chair, he scanned the orders and notes entered into Bennett's electronic chart during her last visit. Her white blood cell counts had been high, but her blood panel was otherwise unremarkable. He had suspected gastroenteritis and ordered IV fluids to treat her dehydration. She was given dimenhydrinate for the nausea and sent home.

What have I missed? His worst fear. To lose a patient he could have saved. Unwelcome memories of a young woman who had recently died under his care flashed briefly before he pushed them away.

Not this patient. Not this time.

A click of the mouse brought up her X-rays. Her lungs were wet, but there was no evidence of consolidation. So she didn't have bacterial pneumonia. Viral pneumonia was still a possibility, as was ARDS or sick sinus syndrome. But the fluid in her lungs could also be caused by her slow heartbeat, and it would ultimately lead to heart failure if left uncorrected.

Not on my watch! This woman, in a fight for her life, needed every advantage, no matter how small. And that meant aggressive treatment, even without a clear diagnosis.

"Susan, let's get her started on IV levofloxacin and BiPAP." With antibiotics onboard and bi-level positive airway pressure to flush fluid from her lungs, he upped her odds. But would it be enough?

"Get a set of pacer pads on her just in case. And administer 0.5 milligram of atropine if she has symptomatic bradycardia again."

Eric picked up the phone and called the ER department of Kootenay Boundary Regional Hospital. Bennett needed to be in an intensive care unit, and that meant a transfer to the larger regional hospital in Trail, almost seventy kilometres away. When Dr. Steven Banks came onto the line, Eric rattled off a summary of Bennett's vitals and treatment in staccato medical shorthand.

"Steve, we have a serious windstorm blowing here, and the critical care transport team has told me it could be a few hours before a helicopter can deliver her to Trail."

"Is she stable enough to transport by ambulance?"

His grip on the phone tightened. Waiting was a gamble, but so was an hour-long ambulance ride.

"I don't think so. I'm going to keep her here and wait for the helicopter."

"Okay. Call me again when she's in the air."

Eric eased the phone from his hand and stared at the long list of patients on the tracking board behind the nurse's station. On such a busy night, he'd just committed himself to caring for a critically ill patient. He ran his fingers through his hair.

Only the next few hours would tell him if this decision would keep her alive.

7

FINGERS WRAPPED AROUND the edge of the truck door, he eased the metal close enough to the frame to douse the interior light. Wind-rattled leaves muffled the sound of gravel crushed beneath his heavy boots. He stared up at his two-storey house, its curtains drawn. Soldiers, if they'd been here, would have found nothing in the house. His eyes shifted to the oversized steel building, as tall and long as the house, that stood at the end of the driveway. The workshop was another matter.

Another few days and he'd be in the clear. But in the local café, he'd heard rumours of an armed resistance against the U.S.-Canada military force. Too many rumours. And among his neighbours, an ex-commando with access to enough weaponry for every man and woman in the Valley who wanted to join the fight. The marine wouldn't escape the notice of military intelligence.

Neither will I.

With each careful step down the driveway toward the steel building, he scanned the yard. Moving branches cast shadows along the fence-line to the left of the house. But if the cops hid in wait there, he'd never spot them. Not in the dark, not at this distance.

Feet planted firmly in front of the narrow door, he looked up at the security sensor mounted above the door frame. Armed and operational. *But it could have been reset.*

The windowless wall in front of him offered no hint of what lay within. With one last glance behind him, he plunged his key into the deadbolt and swung the door open. He reached for the light switch, flooding the workshop in fluorescence that hurt his grey-blue eyes.

He squinted against the light, scanning the fully-loaded shelves and the workbench. Everything looked as it had when he left.

Swift steps took him to the twelve-foot-long wooden workbench centred on the polished cement floor. There, quick taps of the computer screen icons brought up the security system status. No alerts.

His vibram-soled hiking boots thudded loudly with each stride toward the front door. He yanked open the top drawer of a small cabinet and pulled a handful of .22 calibre bullets from a half-empty box. These he stuffed in the right front pocket of his jeans before he grabbed his rifle.

He zipped his grey fleece jacket tight against his chin and stepped out into the windstorm that had dogged him all night. The door slammed behind him, locked on contact with the metal frame. Still, he rearmed the door sensor with his key fob before he stepped into the driveway.

He peered into the driver's-side window of the cargo van parked in front of the workshop, pulling hard on the handle. Locked.

Cold wind blasted at his face. He darted for the sidewalk between the house and the workshop. Here, sheltered from the wind, he slowed his pace, careful with each step along the uneven cement walk that led to the back twenty acres.

His rifle jammed into his shoulder, he peered around the corner of the house. He aimed at shadowed movement, his pulse racing until he realized that it was nothing more than fruit trees beaten down by the wind.

He tramped over the wet grass to the greenhouse. The door handle gave way under pressure. A door that should have been locked.

His rifle raised, he pushed the glass door open. He crept along the centre aisle between two rows of wooden benches crowded with potted plants. Only when he reached the end of the forty-foot-long domed structure did he lower his rifle.

He retraced his steps, moving quickly now. The wind had subsided, dropping the yard into quiet stillness. His boots thudded with each hurried step to the house, to the back stairs.

Standing at the door, he deactivated the alarm and then slipped the key into the lock. At the click of the deadbolt, he flung the wooden door open and raised his rifle.

The dark kitchen stood empty. He stepped slowly across the linoleum floor into the living room at the front of the house. Hands wrapped tight around his weapon, he slunk past the sofa and chair. He studied the clutter of unread books, newspapers and maps on the coffee table. It looked undisturbed. But there was no way to know.

The wall at his back, he climbed the creaky stairs to the three upstairs bedrooms. Each step along the worn carpet confirmed he was alone. Still, in the front bedroom, he inched the floral curtains aside and stared into the darkness. The emptiness did nothing to reassure him.

They're coming.

The only question was when.

8

ALEX BOLTED UPRIGHT in bed, startled by the urgent whine of a siren. For a moment she thought she was still in the emergency room, but the quiet calm of the dark room told her otherwise. After almost a week of sleeping on the ground, the comfortable bed in this rental, a small house perched high above Nelson, was welcome. But its proximity to the hospital meant late-night sirens, an annoyance discovered anew each time she returned here for a night or two.

She threw back the down-filled duvet and swung her feet onto the bare hardwood floor. At the window, she lifted the fabric shade and peered out. Below her, the town of Nelson nestled against the edge of Kootenay Lake looked peaceful. In the dim streetlight, nothing moved except for trees forced into motion by the wind.

The blue glow of the alarm clock on the bedside table gave the time as 4:15 a.m. Just three hours since she'd slipped into soft cotton pajamas and surrendered to drug-induced sleep. But the fierce, throbbing pain dulled by the potent narcotic had returned, and another dose was another hour away.

Turning on the lamp, she rummaged through the dresser until she found her wool sweater. She eased its cabled sleeves over her bandaged arms before gently tugging the oversized pullover over her head.

Smoke. She could still smell it. No doubt her clothes heaped in one corner of the bedroom floor bore most of the blame. But a quick sniff of a handful of hair confirmed her contribution to the charred stench that filled the small room.

Her feet soundless on the carpet, she headed for the bathroom. In the harsh light, her green eyes looked like dark pools in the pale, soot-smudged face reflected in the mirror. With a comb, she tugged at the tangled mess before she gave up and tucked the long, brown strands behind her ears. With a wet face cloth, she gently wiped her face clean, relieved to find no evidence of burns beneath the black dirt.

She'd been lucky last night. It was time to find out if her good fortune extended to her computer.

Before she reached the bottom stair, her nostrils stung from a foul chemical odour that emanated from her scorched backpack. Crossing the living room floor to the front door, she bent down and picked up this sole possession pulled from the fire. She cradled the pack tightly against her chest, careful to avoid shifting its weight to her injured arms in her walk to the kitchen.

She dropped the bag onto the seat of one of the wooden chairs and turned it from side to side. Save for a gaping hole in one wall of the bag, the rugged fabric remained intact, although blackened by the flames. She prayed the same could be said for its precious cargo.

Papers and binders covered the kitchen table, and she pushed some of these aside to make room for the computer she pulled from the backpack. She opened the lid and pressed the 'on' button, watching the black screen for signs of life. A moment later, she heard the familiar clicks and whirs of the hard drive. At least it still worked.

She checked the document folders and opened a few of her key files. Reassured, she dug into the backpack for the handheld GPS unit. The colour screen came up almost immediately on the unit and displayed her last entered location. Her cell phone and mobile gas detector joined the list of gear spared in the fire, but there her luck ended.

A fragile charred edge cut across the bottom corner of the hard-bound notebook. She slipped a fingernail between two pages near the centre of the book, gently prying them apart. The brittle paper crackled as it gave way to reveal handwriting and drawings obscured by brown stain. With time she could replicate the map from the GPS data, but the thoughts and ideas jotted on these pages were lost. *Damn.*

She set aside the notebook and unzipped the front pocket of the backpack, from where she retrieved a small bottle of perfume and a lipstick from the same luxury brand. When she opened the black lipstick case, she found not the red tapered stick she loved but a messy lump melted and reformed by the heat.

The small cardboard box she next pulled from the pack bore the scorch marks of an encounter with the flames. She took one of the six cartridges out of the box, running her finger along the tapered brass-coloured surface of the sleek, lethal package. If just one of these bullets had exploded in the fire, she might not be sitting here.

None of this makes sense. She walked over to the counter and stared out the small kitchen window above the sink into the darkness. The windstorm that howled with rage in the mountains was quieter here, but no less damaging. In the backyard, overturned pots and a swirl of garden debris littered the grass beneath tree branches thrashed by the wind.

She turned away from the storm. Standing with her back against the hard, cold edge of the granite countertop, she stared into the brightly lit kitchen. A glance at the stove's digital clock and a quick calculation gave the time in Tanzania as midafternoon. With luck, her dad would be in his tent handling paperwork. She reached for her smartphone and pulled up his number. Finger positioned over the call button, she hesitated.

Her dad would tell her to leave, that no project was worth her life. This despite the fact that he had risked his life in far-off countries countless times. She couldn't just walk away. Not this close to a prize that would make her dad proud.

She dropped the phone on the table and headed for the living room. Remote in hand, she turned on the TV. On the screen, an overenthusiastic chef expertly minced onions to his own running commentary.

The last time she'd prepared anything more demanding than a steak had been Steven's birthday, more than a year ago. Just before their relationship ended. Since then, none of her few dates, squeezed in between too many overseas projects, had moved beyond the restaurant stage.

She switched the channel to a *Mad Men* rerun and turned up the volume before dropping the remote onto the sofa. Back in the kitchen, she started the kettle before scrounging through the freezer for a plastic container filled with cookies bought at a Nelson bakery a few weeks ago. With two chocolate espresso cookies set out on the counter to thaw, she returned the stash of sweets to the freezer, the only place they survived her long absences from the house. And she intended to be gone by morning.

From the floor rack sitting against the kitchen wall, she grabbed a rolled map of the Nelson area and unfurled it on the dining room table. While she dropped heavy, tattered leather beanbags on each corner, she eyed the dozens of red-lined properties that had brought her into the military-controlled Slocan Valley.

Four months back, she'd taken an intriguing call from the widow of her friend and mentor, Baxter Donnovan. The lanky six-foot-tall geologist, a friend of her dad's, had been a frequent guest in their Calgary home in her youth. But it was only after she moved to Vancouver for university that she really came to know the man.

And she missed him sorely. They had met at least once a month at his favourite pub in downtown Vancouver, to talk geology and politics. But it was more than that. Tears blurred her vision as she ran her fingers along the Baxter's red-lined mining properties on the map. With her dad away so much of the time, Baxter had become a surrogate father of sorts, a favoured uncle, someone she could turn to for guidance, especially here in the Slocan Valley.

Unlike her dad, Baxter never left Canadian soil in his hunt for precious metals. Instead, the unorthodox geologist endlessly trekked the mountains of British Columbia, hammer in hand. Silver. Gold. He'd found plenty of both in the Slocan Valley, and over forty plus years he'd amassed an impressive number of claims, known locally as the Donnovan properties, as his legend grew.

Like Baxter, Alex believed the Cordillera mountain range that dominated this part of British Columbia held a silver deposit larger and richer than anything yet found. The ever-elusive mother lode. And Baxter's wife, Sylvia, a stunning grey-haired woman she'd met only a handful of times, was giving her the opportunity to prove it.

The kettle clicked off, leaving only the voices from the TV in the room. At the kitchen counter she poured boiling water over an Earl Grey tea bag and stared out into the darkness. Over coffee in Sylvia's modest Coal Harbour condo, the two women had shared their memories of Baxter, laughing at some of his crazy adventures. But then the conversation turned unexpectedly to business, and Sylvia quietly offered Alex a discounted price on Baxter's mining claims. Alex had nearly dropped her coffee cup in shock. But as Sylvia explained, her late husband would be thrilled to have Alex take over the reins.

A unique opportunity, but an expensive gamble even at the discounted price, given that many of Baxter's claims were based on little more than a hunch. She'd asked for time to evaluate the properties, but with looming claim expiry dates, Sylvia had been able to give her just three months. After that, the childless widow would sell the properties to the highest bidder. A tight deadline under any circumstance, but even more so given the tense political situation in the Valley. And some of the Donnovan properties fell within the perimeter, an added complication.

So far she had successfully avoided the soldiers who zealously guarded this restricted zone, but tonight's fire might have changed everything. She couldn't count on the doctor not to report her burns. Especially if the military showed up at the hospital.

The fire was no accident.

She clutched her arms to her chest, fingers dug deep into her wool sweater. Only a tight circle of trusted people knew she was in the Slocan Valley, and none of them, not even her dad, knew her exact location. Tony Germaine, the owner of a small mining company, MTC Resources, had provided the perfect cover when he asked her to investigate several old abandoned Slocan Valley silver mines. It kept word of the pending sale of the Donnovan properties quiet, a necessity if she hoped to claim any adjoining properties without competition. And it meant she could surprise her dad with what could be the deal of a lifetime.

She wasn't ready to leave. Not yet.

Finger on the map, she traced a path along a creek near two of the Donnovan properties and followed it down to the main highway. A nearby valley with access from an old logging trail offered a promising new campsite location just outside the perimeter.

A sudden bang jolted the house. *What the hell?* She hurried to the living room window, but the darkness beyond revealed nothing unusual.

She jammed her feet into her shoes, opened the front door and ran out into the night.

9

"THE WHITE BUILDING just blew up!" Susan slammed the phone into its cradle.

Dr. Eric Keenan swivelled his desk chair around to face the busy nursing station. "How many injured?"

"No idea yet." She thrust a plastic sample bottle into the hands of a hovering nursing assistant. "Danica, take this to the lab and tell them it's a rush." When the young woman hurried off, Susan turned back to Eric. "Every ambulance is down there. We have to start clearing beds."

He eyed the electronic patient tracking board. Five or ten minutes from now, casualties might be headed into this already busy ER. And with no sign of the storm easing, the demanding care of a critical patient remained in his hands as well. At least Susan and three other good nurses were on duty with him.

"How many explosions in the past month?" he asked in a voice too loud. "Three or four out at the dams. Another two here in Nelson. A half dozen American soldiers dead, three injured in the school bombing, one at the library." He shook his head. "This madness has to stop."

"These bombers are going to give up any time soon. Not until the military leave." Susan grabbed a medical chart another nurse handed her. "And there's no sympathy for the Americans. Not after everything that's happened."

She surprised him. He didn't expect her to spout the rhetoric too often heard in Nelson. Not a nurse who'd dedicated the last fifteen years of her life to saving lives. But he wouldn't risk their friendship with an argument.

Susan jabbed a finger up at the patient tracking board. "Labs are back on beds six and nine, and there's a new patient for you in bed two. Name is Gary Barlow. Complaining about the flu."

He knew a Gary Barlow. The owner of one of the local organic grocery stores, a friendly guy who knew more jokes than Eric thought possible. With luck he'd clear the man quickly and free up a bed. But not until he'd checked Bennett's blood work.

Her arterial blood gas sample showed low levels of dissolved oxygen, but everything else was normal. *Damn.* He ran a hand through his hair. He didn't need a blood test to tell him what he already knew. What he needed was a reason for her condition, and he wasn't finding it here.

Two quick strides brought him to Bennett's bedside. His eyes went immediately to the monitor. Her heart rate hovered at fifty-nine beats a minute, and her blood oxygen levels remained above ninety. No change from his last check five minutes earlier.

Her red-rimmed eyes turned to him. Eyes that begged for reassurance, the one thing he couldn't give her. Not without a diagnosis.

"I know it's hard in this place, but try to get some sleep." He rested his hand on her shoulder. "I'll be back soon."

Next door, he pulled back the curtain to the exam area to find a man he recognized perched on the edge of the bed.

"Hey, Doc."

"Gary Barlow. What brings you into my ER in the middle of the night?"

"I've got a pretty bad case of the flu. Been throwing up for days, and everything hurts. I tried some of that flu stuff from over at the drug store, but can't say it helped," Gary said.

"When did it first start?"

"Well, I've been tired for a few days now. Hard to get up in the morning. You know me, down to the store before the sun's up. And

I didn't feel much like eating. That got Melissa fussing and making soup and all for me."

Eric chuckled at the comment and shook his head. He'd met Gary's wife, and he could well imagine that she'd left her husband no choice but to allow her to nurse him back to health.

"But then I started throwing up. That's when Melissa went to the drug store. God, that stuff she gave—"

"Code blue! Bed one!" Susan shouted.

Bennett. Damn.

He spun on his heels and sprinted to the critical care room just behind the four nurses of the ER. A feeling of dread rose up in his chest as he closed in on the whine of Bennett's medical monitor alarm.

His eyes immediately went to the monitor. Her heart rate was down to forty. Damn. He grabbed a pair of gloves and wriggled them on.

"I administered one milligram atropine. No response. Patient is now unconscious. Time is 0431 hours," Susan said.

Another of the nurses performed CPR, the rhythmic pumping of her hands working to keep fragile hold on a life slipping away.

"One milligram epi," he ordered.

He watched the monitor while the syringe preloaded with one milligram of epinephrine was injected into the IV tubing. No change. Oxygen blood saturation was just eighty percent. *Too low.*

"One milligram epi administered," Susan said, echoing his order. This and every other action in the crowded room, meticulously entered into Bennett's electronic chart by a nurse dedicated to the task during a Code Blue response.

He grabbed a box of intubation supplies and started setting everything up. One of the nurses ripped off Bennett's BiPAP mask, anticipating his needs.

Moving to the head of the bed, Eric cradled Bennett's skull in his right hand and gently tilted her head up and back. He opened her mouth and used his left hand to insert a laryngoscope, watching the image of her vocal chords transmitted by the scope onto a small screen.

He eased a large, flexible endotracheal tube into her throat and watched it slip past her vocal chords into her trachea on the screen. He removed the introducer wire and blew up the cuff.

"I'm in," he said as he moved aside.

Immediately, a nurse attached a bag valve mask to the open end of the ET tube and started squeezing air into Bennett's lungs.

"Two minutes is up," Susan said in a loud voice that rose above the chatter and equipment. Every two minutes, another check on the patient's vitals.

"Check rhythm and pulse," he said.

"Heart rate is thirty, and there's a faint pulse," came the reply.

"One milligram atropine. Dial up the pacer," he ordered.

Susan turned up the voltage of the pacer machine. Small electrical currents pulsed through the pacer pads attached to Bennett's chest, prompting her heart to beat. He watched the monitor for signs of pacing spikes, evidence of connection between the pacer shocks and the heart muscle, but found none.

"No capture," he said. *Damn.*

"Two minutes."

Chest compressions were halted. He stared at the monitor. Sinus brady at forty-five. *Too slow.*

"What did we give last?" he asked.

"Atropine," Susan said.

"One milligram epi and resume compressions," he said.

CPR compressions restarted. Susan immediately injected into the IV port the vital medication that might turn this patient around.

No change. *I'm losing this battle.*

"I'm going to float a pacemaker. Give me a central line kit."

Adrenaline coursed through his body as he gave the order. He had just minutes to thread a slim pacing wire into a large vein and wait for her pumping blood to deliver it into her heart. Only then could he send electrical pulses directly to her failing heart.

A sterile kit was set on the rolling table next to the bed by one of the nurses. He poured antiseptic over Bennett's chest and put on fresh gloves before quickly draping the area below her collarbone with sterile paper.

"Two minutes."

CPR was halted. Heart rate was thirty.

"Another round of atropine," he ordered.

He inserted a needle below her collar bone, walking it into the right subclavian artery. Blood spurted into the barrel attached to the needle when he pulled back on it. He was in.

"Heart rate is now forty."

Finally, a step in the right direction. But not enough.

"One milligram epi." He removed the barrel from the needle and grabbed the guide wire assembly from the kit.

At that moment Bennett started to seize. Her arms and legs flailed wildly against the hard hospital mattress. A foul smell filled the room, a warning that she'd lost control of both her bowels and bladder. Her eyes deviated to one side.

"Great, not what we need," he said.

He stood helpless, waiting for the frenzied movement to stop. And when it did, the monitor showed nothing but a flat line. Her heart had stopped.

"One milligram epi. I'll take over CPR." His hands replaced those of the nurse. He pumped hard against her chest, his focus on the monitor.

"Two minutes."

He lifted his hands just long enough for a vitals check.

"No pulse."

"Another round of atropine and epi." Even as he gave the order, he knew it was hopeless. But he'd give her this last fifteen minutes. This last chance.

At each two-minute mark, he had only a few seconds of rest before he slammed his hands against her chest once more. His arms and shoulders burned. But his patient's heart refused to beat.

He stared into her lifeless eyes, their pupils fixed and dilated.

"Give me the ultrasound." He squirted a mound of gel onto her chest and ran the ultrasound transducer through it before he passed the instrument over her heart. A futile search for signs of cardiac activity.

"It's over," he said. "Time of death 0512."

His last duty to his patient. A record of his moment of failure as a doctor.

"Shit."

He tore off his gloves and left the room without another word. Even though he knew that his patients were often the most critical in the medical system, he expected to win every time. When he lost this high-stakes game with death, he agonized over his actions, unable or unwilling to accept that some patients couldn't be saved, no matter what he did.

At the nursing station, he stared up at the patient tracking board. A full house and no doubt a crowded waiting room beyond the emergency room doors.

He wouldn't fail again.

10

HEAT BURNED AT Alex's face as she stared at the flames that consumed the six-storey building.

Chairs and desks hung at odd angles over the edge of gaping holes where windows and walls once stood. Wind swirled through the offices, carrying paper and other detritus out beyond the building, and then dropped it haphazardly onto the growing jumble on the manicured lawn.

An RCMP officer pushed past her and ducked under the yellow tape. His radio crackled with voices, but the thundering spray of water drowned out the words. She watched him rush over to a group of uniformed men huddled beside an army jeep. At their centre stood a tall man with enough hardware on his olive-drab jacket to make clear his senior rank.

The military is in charge.

She caught sight of a red sweater and a single running shoe, on the wet grass, reminders that the chairs and desks that dangled precariously over a broken concrete and steel edge would have been occupied by people in just a few hours. The thought of anyone trapped in the red-hot flames sent shivers down her spine.

Three green-canvas trucks screeched to a halt in front of her. A platoon of men, dressed in camouflage fatigues and armed to the teeth jumped to the pavement.

Glass shattered, sending a roar of flames through a top-floor window. A booming voice sent men thundering past her toward this new threat, and the soldiers surged forward.

"Back! I want all of you back now!" came the command, reinforced by a human chain of rifle-bearing men.

The large crowd moved back as one. No one dared to disobey. She squeezed herself through onlookers until she stood at the outer edge of the crowd.

A gust of wind sent icy water spray over the crowd, making her wish for something warmer than her fleece. But it was all she'd found in the front closet when she rushed out of the house and jogged down the hill to the fireball that lit up the night sky.

It was foolish to be here at what was likely a terrorist attack. But she remained rooted in place, unable to draw her gaze from the wreckage.

Dense black smoke burned at her eyes and throat. Coughing, she huddled, her back to the wind.

"You okay?"

Alex turned to face the middle-aged woman beside her who'd spoken. "Yeah." The single word croaked out between coughs. When she finally caught her breath, she added, "Man, I sure hope there's no one in that building."

"There are a couple of ambulances over that way." The red-head pointed with her chin, keeping her hands tucked deep in the pockets of her purple knee-length down jacket. "But there shouldn't be anyone in the White Building at this time of night."

"The White Building?"

"You're not from around here then. Nelson City Hall. The B.C. provincial government. They share this place. It's painted white, so it's called the White Building. Total lack of imagination." The rosy-cheeked woman shook her head, sending the large tassel on her knitted hat swinging.

A cheer erupted from the crush of people tightly pressed against the yellow tape. The bark of orders came from within the army of men up ahead. *A rescue?* She stood on her toes, searching for answers between bobbing heads.

Gloved hands pointed to her right and she swivelled around. Fuelled by a powerful wind gust, flames had leapt to a towering evergreen tucked too near the neighbouring court house. Firefighters scrambled into position in front of the century-old stone building and sprayed a torrent of water onto burning branches.

Laughter rang out beside her. She searched the faces of nearby strangers, all turned in the direction of this new fire front. Their smiling faces told her everything she needed to know. They cheered for the destructive force of the fire, not the heroic efforts of the firefighters.

Nelson attracted its fair share of tourists and transients, many of them lured by the promise of easy drugs in a town known for its illegal marijuana trade. Not this time. Many of these people had come to join a war.

Time to go. To escape this madness before the soldiers turned on them.

Ahead of her, a cop tried to push his way through the crowd, but two young men blocked his way, both refusing to move. The burly RCMP officer shoved one man aside and then stood mere inches from the other with his feet planted in a wide stance.

The crowd went silent. Under the menacing stare of the cop, the bearded man in his torn army-surplus jacket seemed unfazed. Head thrown back, he glared up at the lined face of the cop, defiant.

"Leave us alone!"

"Judas!"

"Fuckin' traitor!"

The shouts came from voices behind her, from men and women made brave by the anonymity of the crowd. Other voices echoed the taunt. Until a low murmur, filled with anger and hatred surrounded her. All of it directed at the cop.

But the cop didn't react. The two men stood unmoving until the young challenger pulled his ungloved hands from his pockets.

What the hell is this crazy guy thinking? She tried to take a step back, but the press of bodies prevented escape.

Slowly the cop brought his right hand up to his waist, to his holstered gun. His other hand reached for the radio secured to his shoulder. One word from him would bring soldiers thundering into the crowd.

Her heart raced. She felt suffocated by strangers, so close now that they touched her shoulders and back. Instinctively, she hugged her bandaged arms to her chest, a move intended to protect her injuries. A fresh round of searing pain hit, but she held her arms close as her neighbours pressed in.

And then it was over. The bearded challenger dropped his chin and stepped aside. A hand slapped him on the back, and the murmur of quiet reassurance rose from those nearby. The grip of the crowd loosened. A gap formed.

Only then did the cop raise his cell phone.

Pictures. *Hell!* The last thing she needed was to be associated with this mob. She dropped her gaze, but it might not have been soon enough.

A muffled blast shook the ground. All eyes turned to the west. *The dam.*

11

"DOMINIC PETRELLI. FIREFIGHTER. Age twenty-four. Minor smoke inhalation. Vitals are stable."

Paramedic Jason Reynolds rattled off this report without pause as soon as Eric was within earshot of the treatment bay. Eric stood at the curtain, giving the well-known ambulance medic and his junior partner space to manoeuvre their gurney into the small room. A quick lift and Petrelli, fully decked out in protective clothing, lay on the hospital bed.

Susan squeezed into the room and pulled an oxygen mask from the wall. She removed the nasal cannula, slipped the mask onto their patient's soot-covered face and reached back to the wall to start the oxygen flow. Then with Jason's help she raised the head of the bed and eased the heavy coat off the first responder.

"There's another firefighter on the way," Jason said as he rolled the gurney past Eric. Tonight there were no hockey updates or humorous stories from the EMT, only a tight face that told of a long, difficult night. "Second ambulance should be here in a minute or two. I'm heading right back out."

"How many injured?" Eric asked over the rip of Velcro as Susan readied the blood pressure cuff.

"Not sure, Doc. It's a mess out there. The wind is making it tough to control the fire." The paramedic gave Eric a tired wave and left.

Eric stepped into the room and introduced himself to his patient. He'd treated others from the fire department in his ER, but this man, who didn't look old enough to be out of high school, was new to him.

"So what happened?" Petrelli started to lift the mask from his soot-covered face, but Eric held out a hand. "Keep that on. I can hear you just fine."

"There was an explosion at the Bonnington Dam," came the muffled answer.

"The dam?" Eric looked over at Susan. "We heard it was the White Building."

"That was earlier. The dam was bombed about a half-hour later. Pretty big explosion this time, too. It took a while for us to put out the fire that started in the trees and—" A violent coughing spasm shook Petrelli.

"Try to relax. Take a few sips of breath," Eric directed. He watched his patient carefully until the cough eased.

Petrelli rested his head against the bed. "Except for this cough, I'm fine. But you know how the chief is. So if you just give me the once-over, I'll get out of here."

"You're not going anywhere until I'm satisfied you're okay." Eric smiled and placed his hand on the man's knee. "You know how those firefighters are. They downplay their symptoms."

Petrelli grinned. "Not me. I promise."

"Now, how many times have I heard that?" Eric laughed. "Full workup before you leave my ER, I'm afraid. Relax and enjoy the break."

Eric slid the curtain closed as he left the room. At the nursing station, he entered orders into Petrelli's chart and then headed for Gary Barlow's treatment bay.

In the hour since he'd last seen Gary, beads of sweat had collected in the deep wrinkles of the man's forehead. The grocer's blue hospital gown bore dark, wet stains along his chest and underarms. Clear signs of profuse sweating, diaphoresis. Eric checked the medical chart but found no fever to explain this symptom.

Gary grabbed the vomit bowl from his lap and held it under his chin. For a long moment, neither man moved.

With a heavy sigh, Gary dropped the empty basin into his lap and leaned back against the bed. He wiped a tear from his cheek. "Man, do I feel lousy."

Eric studied his patient's red-rimmed, watery eyes. Eyes that showed signs of excessive tearing, or lacrimation.

Damn. Damn. Damn. How could I have missed it?

SLUDGE. Every medical resident learned this mnemonic, and another, DUMBELS, to remember a distinctive set of symptoms that pointed to just one thing. Organophosphates. Pesticides that paralyze and suffocate their victims to death.

His eyes darted to the monitor. Gary's heart rate looked good. At least for now.

"Gary, how long have your eyes been watering like that?"

"Started yesterday ... maybe the day before. Must be allergies." The bear of a man wiped away tears with his rough hand. "I'd take something, but I don't think it'd stay down."

Allergies could be the cause, but he wasn't convinced. Not with the vomiting and diarrhea. Symptoms he shared with Laura Bennett. But on her he hadn't seen anything like the tears that ran down Gary's face. His chest tightened. Or had he seen and dismissed her tears as nothing more than the emotion of a frightened woman?

He stared down at his tablet, knowing the answer wasn't there. Seven years out of residency, he shouldn't have made such a rookie assumption. Wouldn't have made it. But that meant either he had missed the lacrimation symptom, or it wasn't there.

How the hell were they exposed to pesticide? He shifted from one foot the other. Suicide might explain Bennett, but Gary wasn't the kind of man to take his own life. Accidental exposure had to be the answer. He refused to consider the alternative.

"You okay, Doc?" Gary asked quietly.

"Just thinking. Do you have a garden?" he asked. The grocer furrowed his brow, spurring Eric to add, "I know it's an odd question. Humour me, Gary."

"You'd think I'd have a big garden, seeing as how I run the market, but truth is, I don't have time." He ran a rough hand over his tear-stained cheek. "Melissa does a bit. Tomatoes mostly."

A third victim? His heart skipped a beat. "Is Melissa sick too?"

"No, she's fine. Is there a flu—"

Eric interrupted him. "I'm going to order some blood work, and we'll talk after the results come back," he said, quickly leaving the room. Unless he wanted a second code tonight, he needed to get a handle on what was happening with Gary. And fast.

Perched on the edge of his chair, Eric did an online search for organophosphate toxicity on the Medscape site. Most of it confirmed what he already suspected, but he was surprised to see that eating *Inocybe* and *Clitocybe* mushrooms could trigger many of the same symptoms.

He pulled up the number of a local expert in mushroom identification who offered on-call services to the ER department. Phone to his ear, he hesitated. Spring was the wrong time of year for mushroom poisoning cases. Not only that, in such patients the symptoms disappeared within a day, and Gary had been sick longer than that. So had Bennett.

He dropped the phone into its cradle. No matter how much he wanted to believe otherwise, everything pointed to organophosphate pesticide poisoning. And depending on how much of the pesticide Gary had been exposed to, the grocer was running out of time. He sprang from his chair and headed back to Gary's treatment bay.

"A few more questions. Have you been out picking vegetables or fruit from any of the farms nearby?" he asked.

"No. Nothing." Gary ran his hand across his wet forehead. "We buy all of our fresh veggies and fruit at our market."

"Any problems with ants or other insects around the house?"

"What are you getting at, Eric?" Gary shifted his legs under the thin blanket.

"Your symptoms suggest pesticide exposure."

"Pesticide? We don't keep that kind of stuff at the house. Wouldn't expect to run into it at the market either." Gary crossed his arms over his chest. "None of the organic farmers who bring stuff to us would use pesticides. I'm sure of it."

"And you haven't shopped at any of the other grocery stores in town?"

Gary shook his head. "There's not much we need that we can't get from our own store."

"Well, so much for that theory." Eric turned to leave and stopped before he got to the curtain. "Gary, do you know Laura Bennett?"

"Sure. Nice lady. She's been a customer of ours for years."

He gripped the curtain edge. "Have you seen her recently?"

"Took some groceries out to her place a few days back. She was pretty sick, so I did her a favour. Did I catch something from her?"

"Let me do a few more tests. I'll be back."

He hurried over to the nurse's station, where Susan sipped what had to be her sixth cup of coffee of their overnight shift.

"Susan, administer 0.5 milligram atropine to Barlow, please," he said, entering the order into his chart. "And ... keep a close eye on him."

Gary's oxygen levels were well above the threshold for the moment, but that could change in an instant. If Gary had been exposed to a pesticide, Eric needed him started on an antidote immediately. He wasn't going to wait days for confirmation through blood cholinesterase levels. Better to be proactive he thought, and get a head start on neutralizing the toxins coursing through Gary's body. But was he being proactive or was he overreacting because of Bennett's death?

No. These cases were too similar to be a coincidence. He hadn't ordered cholinesterase blood levels on Bennett, only the standard blood panels. Now he could only pass along his suspicion of organophosphate pesticide poisoning to the coroner for follow-up. He didn't intend to send a second case to the morgue.

He pulled up the pharmacy drug listings and scrolled through the list twice in a futile search for the antidote, 2-PAM. At the squeak of Susan's running shoes, he swivelled around to face her.

"How the hell do you find 2-PAM in this damn electronic pharmacy system?" he demanded testily. "I'm having a hell of a time. Why does everything in this damn hospital have to be so difficult?"

"I think it would be faster for you to call the pharmacy," Susan said in an even tone.

He closed his eyes and took a deep breath. *Focus.* He picked up the phone and dialled the pharmacy extension.

"This is Dr. Keenan in the ER. I need a dose of 2-PAM for a patient."

"Did you say 2-PAM? What's the generic?" the pharmacy technician asked.

"If I knew that, I wouldn't be calling you!" Eric snapped, giving into his frustration.

"Just a minute, and I'll check with the pharmacist," came the reply.

Eric stood up and paced the floor near the desk with the phone held to his ear. He checked his watch. Just about 6:00 a.m. His twelve-hour shift would end soon, but he wasn't going to leave without making sure Barlow was okay.

"Dr. Keenan? Kelly Markham here. I'm the pharmacist on duty tonight." A formal greeting from the woman he'd known for all of the three years he'd worked at this hospital. But he'd come to expect it. The intellectual redhead had decided from the first day they met that she didn't like him, and since then the two of them clashed on almost every front.

"We have 2-PAM listed as pralidoxime. How many patients are we expecting, and how soon?"

Damn. Without hesitation, she'd gone straight into disaster response mode. *Isn't that what we're all taught to do?* Prepare for the worst. And with organophosphate pesticide cases that meant major spills. Or the unthinkable. Bioterrorism.

"I have just one patient, and it's only a suspicion right now." He wasn't ready to share his fear that Bennett had been poisoned too. That he missed the diagnosis. Not with Markham.

"We have exactly one dose of 2-PAM here. I'm sending it to the ER now. And Dr. Keenan, if anything changes, I need to be your first call. To get more of the drug into the hospital will take time."

"Understood." Eric hung up the phone, thankful the by-the-book pharmacist hadn't insisted he report his tentative diagnosis to the military.

"Susan, order up emergency transport for Barlow." He wasn't about to wait for Gary to get worse. "When you've done that, can you check on the atropine stock here in the ER? Call up to Cardiology and ask how much atropine they have on hand too."

If Gary's condition deteriorated, he'd need all the atropine he could find.

12

"HEY, ERIC. I hear you had a busy night. Anything you need me to follow up on?"

At the sound of Dr. Lillian Sayer's voice, Eric swivelled his chair around to find the tall blonde in front of the electronic patient tracker board. He jumped to his feet and wove past a pair of fresh-eyed nurses to join her. *Shift change.* It was time for him to leave too, to hand off his cases. But if any doctor other than Lillian had shown up to relieve him, he would have stayed.

"Lillian, you're never going to believe it." He rattled off a rapid-fire summary of Laura Bennett's case.

"Organophosphate poisoning? Nasty." Lillian wrangled her long, wavy hair into a pony tail. "Could have been her heart, though. We'll have to see what shows up in the autopsy."

"Thing is…" He waited for a nurse to pass by before he continued in a low voice. "There may be a second case here now. Gary Barlow."

Unlike Markham, Lillian could be trusted. The attractive doctor had moved to Nelson from Vancouver not long before he had arrived here from Toronto, and the two of them had bonded over the challenges of adjusting to life in a small town. Both single, they'd dated a few times, but they quickly discovered that they didn't share many interests outside of the hospital. And so they'd settled for a tight friendship.

"I've arranged for emergency transport to Trail for Barlow, but we're at the mercy of the weather." He waved a hand through the air. "Again."

"I hear you." Her slender fingers touched his arm. "But Eric, if we have multiple pesticide poisoning cases, we have to call it in."

The ER doors swung open and a gurney rolled through, followed by a paramedic and urgent. Susan stepped past him, directing the EMT to their only empty treatment bay. He waited for the rush of feet behind him to move down the hallway before he spoke.

"Do you want to deal with the military on this?" he asked quietly. "I don't. Not until I'm sure there's a problem." He crossed his arms across his chest. "Bennett could've been a suicide attempt, sloppy gardening, anything. There's no obligation to report stupidity as far as I know. Barlow was at Bennett's house, so my guess is that he was exposed to pesticide there."

A new name flashed up on the patient tracker board. He held his breath, watching for details. Fearing another pesticide case. Relieved when *ortho* appeared next to the man's name. A broken bone, nothing more.

Lillian leaned in close enough for him to catch the faint scent of lavender. "You know as well as I do that it could be a spill. Accidental or intentional," she whispered. "I'll go along with you for now, but..." She locked eyes with him. "If another case shows up, we'll have no choice but to report it."

He'd seen the look before, and he knew that it meant Lillian would tolerate no further argument. "Fair enough. In the meantime, we need to get Gary's wife in here. He says she's okay, but you'll want to check her out just to be sure."

"Okay. And we need a list of places Barlow visited over the past few days. Just in case." She slung her stethoscope around her neck. "I know you think the pesticide is at the Bennett house, but we need to cover our bases."

"Agreed. Let's go see him. Full gown and contact precautions," he said.

Eric tried not to think about the fact that he'd touched Bennett last night, without the gowns, masks and sterile gloves he donned now. He prayed he wasn't about to become the next victim.

"What's up with the masks?" Gary asked when Eric slide the curtain aside.

"Gary, this is Dr. Lillian Sayer. I'm going off shift soon, and she's going to take over." He studied the monitor, thankful to see numbers unchanged from his last check just fifteen minutes ago. "You'll be in good hands. If I were lying in that hospital bed, I'd be asking for her." He glanced at Lillian, sure she smiled beneath her mask.

Eric expected a clever comeback from the man, but instead his pale patient lay quiet on the bed. He moved in close to the head of the bed, and Lillian followed.

"So here's what's happening." He folded his gloved hands together. "The masks and gowns are for our protection. The shower you had got rid of any pesticide on your skin, but it can still show up in your sweat or your tears, so we have to be careful."

He saw fear in Gary's eyes. His voice calm, he tried to reassure the man. "We caught this early. I'm starting you on an antidote for pesticide poisoning, and if I'm right, then you should start to feel better soon. And as soon as the weather lifts, we're sending you over to the hospital in Trail."

"Can't I just stay here?" Gary wiped sweat off his forehead with the back of his hand. "Melissa can't be driving over to Trail to see me."

It was a concern raised by most of the patients they sent to Trail and an even bigger concern for those sent further west to Vancouver. He hated separating patients from their families when they were at their most vulnerable. But he didn't have a choice.

"I know it's hard. But if you've been exposed to a pesticide, you're better off in the bigger hospital." He didn't mention that Gary might soon need the constant monitoring available in an ICU to save his life. "Where is Melissa right now? I'd like her to come in so we can check her out. Make sure she hasn't been exposed too."

"Melissa? You mean I might have made her sick?" Gary squeezed the edge of his blanket tight.

"Let's not jump to any conclusions. You told me that Melissa has been feeling fine. We just want to make sure she stays that way, okay?"

Lillian jumped into the conversation. "In the meantime, it would be helpful if we could figure out where you might have been exposed. A farm maybe?"

"A farm?" Gary shifted his legs under the blanket. "We're out to all sorts of farms in the Valley. We check on the farmers who sell stuff through the market, you know? But they're organic farms, mostly."

"It would help if you could give us those names." Lillian pulled her tablet from the pocket of her white coat.

Gary crossed his arms over his barrel chest and stared at Eric. "They're all good people. I don't want to get any of them into trouble."

"Trust me, Gary. We're not trying to cause trouble for anyone," Eric said. "But if there's a pesticide spill out there somewhere, and you happened to run into it, then others might too. We just want to check it out."

Gary sighed. "Okay, soon as the store opens, Emily can get a list of our local suppliers. I'll go through it and try to figure out which places I went to this week."

"Any chance you can get that list now?" Eric tried to keep his voice neutral, but even before Gary spoke, he knew he'd failed.

"You're starting to scare me, Eric. Just how bad is this?"

Eric rested a gloved hand on Barlow's leg. "We just don't want to waste any time tracking this down. See what you can do to get that list faxed here to the ER. And give Melissa a call."

The doctors stripped off their protective clothing and disposed of it outside the treatment bay. "Maybe I should stay. At least until the 2-PAM is administered," Eric said.

"Eric, I'll take good care of him. He's stable, and I'll call you if anything changes. Now go home and get some sleep."

"No way. I'm going over to Bennett's place to see what I can find."

"That's crazy. You can't do that. Eric, go home. You've had a rough night. Just go home."

But he couldn't. He had to know.

"Call my cell." He spun on his heels and left before Lillian could say another word.

13

ALEX POKED THROUGH the burned remains of her tent with the barrel of her rifle. The only evidence of last night's violence lay in the ashes left by the fire.

Evidence. She glanced down at the spent fire extinguisher she'd foolishly left behind. The realization that her fingerprints on the metal canister would quickly be matched to those on file with her explosives license had led her back here. The last thing she needed was to waste time answering questions about a fire inside the perimeter, one she had failed to report.

What the hell happened here last night?

Her eyes focused on the path through the trees near her campsite. Last night, she'd aimed at that spot, waiting for her attacker to appear. *Would I have actually fired a bullet into him?* She wasn't sure. Bears were a common threat to her life in the field, and she'd used her rifle on them before. But even shooting a grizzly wasn't something she did easily. It was only when one of the massive shoulder-humped bears gave her no choice that she pulled the trigger.

She kicked at a charred piece of wood that had once held up a corner of her makeshift desk. Plywood and lumber from the local hardware store would replace the desk, but Tracey Caminski, their company manager back in Vancouver, would have to round up the rest of the gear. The petite mother of two toddlers, both boys, was the heart and soul of the team. Tracey kept them organized, supplied and safe, no matter where in the world the geologists found themselves.

Tracey picked up on the first ring, and Alex launched into a recap of last night's fire. She could well imagine Tracey's brown eyes narrowing and her easy smile dropping with each detail. But the unflappable thirty-five year-old made no comment until Alex finished.

"I assume you don't want your dad to hear about this?" Tracey asked.

"Not yet." She slung her rifle over her shoulder with a tight grip on the phone.

"I'll put together a complete set of gear from the warehouse and send it out this morning. The usual set-up, I assume?"

"Yep. Send out everything." While new camping gear could easily be purchased in one of Nelson's many stores catering to the outdoor enthusiast, she didn't want to draw attention to herself. Or the Donnovan properties. Not even Tracey knew these specific claims were on Alex's radar.

"And you'll need clothes too. I'll head over to your condo and fill a bag for you." Alex smiled. As always, Tracey had anticipated her needs. The two brunettes — the only women at Graham and Associates — had become fast friends when Alex first joined her dad's company eight years ago. To Alex, Tracey was as close to an older sister as she'd ever had. And the only woman in her life since her mom died five years ago.

"Can you throw in a new first-aid kit too?" she asked, staring down at the scorched grass.

"Why? Are you hurt?" Tracey anxiously asked.

Alex sucked in a deep breath and told her trusted friend about the burns.

"You need to come back to Vancouver until your arms heal and the police find the guy who started the fire," Tracey demanded.

"The police aren't looking for him. I didn't call them." She clutched the cell phone hard, anticipating Tracey's reaction.

"What do you mean you didn't call them?" Tracey practically shouted.

"You have no idea what it's like here, Tracey." Her mind flashed to the scene outside Nelson's White Building. The cops, the soldiers, the armed vehicles. "The army is here in full force. It's like a war zone."

"Doesn't matter. You need to tell them." Tracey's words were edged with anger.

In all the years they'd worked together, Tracey had never challenged her decisions. Not like this.

"And get arrested? I was camped in the perimeter, Tracey. It's not allowed."

"Then give them some other story."

"Like what? I barely managed a good cover story at the hospital last night."

"Then just come home. You need to get out of there."

Their conversation had morphed into something she'd expect from her dad, not her friend. She paced the gravel road that had taken her to safety last night, phone tight to her ear.

"Why would you risk your life for this project, Alex?"

The question shocked her. This was no worse than other tight situations Alex had manoeuvred successfully.

"You're being overly dramatic. I'll move my campsite, and that will be the end of it. I was probably just too close to a grow-op."

But even as she said the words, she thought it unlikely. Easy access to the road was part of the reason she'd picked this site, but it also made this location a poor choice for an outdoor marijuana crop.

"And what if it's something more?"

Was it? Her heart pounded at the thought of someone targeting her, hunting her.

"Let it go, Tracey."

"Well, at least let me send some help your way. How are you going to manage with those burns? The work will go faster if you've got help. And that means you'll be out of that hellhole sooner."

If last night's fire had been the work of some crazy guy living out here in the woods, he might try again. In broad daylight, she'd be safe enough hiking the mountains near this campsite. But without knowing why her attacker had tried to drive her out, even setting up base camp elsewhere offered no guarantee of safety overnight.

"Okay. Okay. Send somebody out with the gear this afternoon." She had to admit that she'd sleep better with some company.

"Good. Are you at the house in Nelson?"

Alex's grip tightened on the phone. Tracey wouldn't understand her need to return here today, not without knowing about the Donnovan properties and her looming deadline.

"Right." A lie, one of the few she'd ever spoken to her friend.

"Get some rest, and I'll call you with the flight details."

The call ended, she stared out into the blue sky that hung like a blanket over the narrow valley. She heard the throbbing beat of rotors long before she saw the helicopter.

Shielding her eyes from the bright morning sun, she stared up at the cloudless sky. The storm that had dogged her every move yesterday was gone, replaced by a calm spring day.

In the distance, a helicopter skimmed over a mountain peak. She checked for a sling attached to its belly, hoping for a glimpse of equipment. Mining equipment cinched into the netting often revealed a mine site's stage of activity, despite a company's best efforts to keep things quiet.

But the sleek black machine that approached was unlike those typically flying the skies in and around Nelson. Built and armed like a warship, this was not a practical working machine. There was no doubt in her mind that this helicopter belonged to the United States Air Force.

Hand tight on her leather rifle strap, she ran toward the trees and ducked beneath the protective boughs of an evergreen. Her truck was hidden from view only if they didn't get too close. If they saw it or the burned-out campsite and set down to investigate, she was in trouble.

Crouched low, she backed further into the trees. Pain seared through her arm when she pushed at a large tree branch, but she ignored it and heaved herself deeper into the underbrush.

Motionless and barely breathing, she listened to the rotor beat of the rapidly approaching helicopter. Her eyes darted to the path that ran through the trees not far off to her right. But there wasn't time for her to fight through the tangled underbrush to reach it.

Rotors beat the air overhead. She squeezed herself against the ground and tightened her grip on the rifle. Her only hope was to hide.

The roar of the rotors eased off ever so slightly. A moment later, she breathed a sigh of relief. They were leaving.

She eased herself upright with the help of a branch, wincing at the new round of pain the action brought. Carefully, she pushed her way through the trees into the open valley. Eyes shielded by her hand, she watched the helicopter until it was but a small dot high above the jagged peaks.

It was foolish to think she could work out here today. The soldiers in that helicopter were just the first of many who might spot this suspicious fire in the perimeter. *Damn.*

She quickly crossed the open ground to the charred mess. With one hand, she reached down and grabbed the fire extinguisher, barely breaking stride. Once at the truck, she threw the empty metal canister into the back seat and slammed the door shut.

I need to get as far away from here as I can. And if she was smart, she wouldn't come back.

14

ON THE HORIZON, an RCMP patrol car appeared, the first since Olivia had left Nelson for the Slocan Valley. She held her breath and watched the approaching car.

It's okay. It's okay. If a member of the small detachment recognized her, they'd wave, nothing more. There was no reason for her not to be out here on the highway. And if they stopped her, none of the men and women who worked with her dad would search her truck. The military patrols were the ones she needed to worry about. Not that they'd find anything. Not yet.

Olivia eased her truck into a right turn that took her from the black pavement of the highway onto a side road. She slowly drove down the dirt road, her eyes darting up to the rear-view mirror every few seconds, watching for the RCMP car. Even if the cops had seen her turn, it wasn't likely that they'd follow her down this road. Not at this time of day. Still, she'd practiced a story, just in case. Out to meet a friend for a hike. Took a wrong turn. Only if the cops asked would she give out Nicole's name. Her hand clenched the steering wheel. Nicole would cover for her, but only if she warned her first.

She jumped at the sound of an engine from up ahead. Seconds later, a dusty truck pulled out around a curve in the road. The driver corrected quickly to hug the left side of the road, giving the two vehicles just enough room to pass.

Even with her hair piled under a hat and her face concealed by a pair of dark sunglasses, Olivia was quick to pull down the visor and turn her head aside. But not before she caught a glimpse of the woman driving the truck. A woman who looked to be as nervous as she was to run into someone on this back road.

Not a cop. One of the things about growing up with an RCMP officer for a father was her instant recognition of police. For years, she'd played a game when people came to the house, guessing whether a cop or lawyer stood in their living room. She often missed the lawyers, but not the cops. There was something about their eyes. The way they scanned a room. And they never showed fear. When the soldiers arrived, she'd discovered that they did the same. They were cops of a sort, after all.

And the one thing she knew about cops was that you couldn't give them any reason to be suspicious. She'd become pretty good at giving her dad just enough information to make him think he knew what she was doing. Not lying, exactly. Just colouring the truth.

Of course, last night had been different. Taking the video call from Dylan had been stupid. All she had to do was wait for her dad to leave to be safe. But instead, afraid that there'd been a change of plans, she'd answered the call.

There was no way to know just how much of the call her dad had heard. She knew from his questions that he hadn't recognized Dylan. Had no reason to recognize him. Although she'd known Dylan since grade school, they'd never really been close friends. Not until after Michael died.

But rarely did her dad show up at her bedroom door without the creak of a stair giving his approach away. Had he purposely concealed his climb up the stairs? Or had she just missed the sound? Either way, she'd made a careless mistake.

And she knew better than to be drawn into an argument with him about the protests. The last thing she needed was to create suspicion. Not when it was her turn.

They had all agreed. Each of them would take turns retrieving and storing the bag, sharing the risk equally. The piece of paper with her carefully written name had been picked from the plastic container holding all of their names, save four. Those who'd handled the duffel before were excluded, as she too would be in future draws.

The location of the drop-point was known to all of them. There were no secrets. She was as important to the cause as any other member of their small group.

She passed what looked like the remnants of a fire. Someone had been camped here. Inside the perimeter.

The woman? So why did she burn her tent to the ground? It was stupid. It guaranteed interest from the military. She glanced up at the sky, knowing she'd never spot the drones.

Her sneakered foot slammed against the gas pedal. She stormed past the campsite, bouncing hard in the seat with each rut in the road. Once around the next curve, she was in the clear. Unless the woman called the cops.

Think, Olivia! If this was the woman's campsite, there was no way she would call the cops. Not with an illegal campsite inside the perimeter. But the military might already have this spot on their radar, and sent a team to investigate. Her heart pounded. *Maybe I should go back. Try again tomorrow.*

She stopped the truck, foot hard on the brake. She stared out the front window at the road ahead. So close. But it would take her at least fifteen minutes to get the bag. And she'd be on this back road, inside the perimeter, for another fifteen minutes beyond that. Too long.

She reversed the truck and spun in a tight circle. Carelessly fast, she roared past the campsite and bumped down the rutted road toward the highway. Heart pounding, she forced herself to slow down.

I took a wrong turn. I thought I was on the road to the trailhead. She rapped the steering wheel nervously as she practiced her story. And she'd tell the truth. That she'd been home in her own bed last night. That this wasn't her campsite. Her dad would back her up. He'd question why she'd been out here instead of at school, but she could handle that. She eased her foot off the gas.

She was probably overreacting. But she'd been told to trust her instincts. And she still had two days to complete her mission.

I can't be the one who leads the cops to my friends. The one who lets them down. Terry and Dylan trusted her. They'd convinced the group to let her in. Let her be part of the fight to set things right for Michael.

I won't be the one who fails.

15

ERIC STARED AT the laminated menu, knowing he should eat but hesitant to force food into his queasy stomach. He dropped the single page onto the plastic tablecloth with its faded rose print and pulled his cell phone from his back pocket.

No text messages. No voicemail. His finger hovered over Lillian's number. But if Gary Barlow's condition had changed in the fifteen minutes since they last spoke, Lillian would have called.

He clenched his hand around the phone and turned toward the smudged window edged with pink ruffled curtains. A small garden, green leaves sprouting from the black earth, filled a massive yard protected from the wind by dense evergreens. A reminder that the Slocan Valley was farm country, with millions of acres under crop. And a pesticide spill could be anywhere.

At the jingle of a metal bell, he swivelled around to find his patient from last night at the café's wooden door. Although she looked different in her street clothes, he recognized the geologist immediately.

Her eyes settled on him, and he found it impossible not to return her broad smile. She tucked her hair behind her ears as she walked toward his table, her hiking boots loud against the wooden floor.

"Burns from last night, remember me?" She smiled and held up her arms, although her fleece covered the bandages.

"Of course I remember, Ms. ... Graham, right?" She gave a quick nod. "How are your arms this morning?"

"They're okay. The ibuprofen helps. And it's Alex."

He hesitated for a moment, looking around the near empty café. He wasn't sure what would be worse, having her join him or them staring at each other across the room.

"Join me, please."

"Are you sure you don't mind?"

"Really, it would be nice to have some company." He set his phone on the table and gestured at the unoccupied seat across from him.

She dropped her tote bag before scraping the slat-back chair against the worn floor. "This is probably the last place I'd expect to find you, Dr. Keenan." She scanned the tired restaurant with its six tables and leaned in close. "Or is the food here so good that it's worth the drive from Nelson."

He matched her smile. "It's Eric. And I have no idea about the food. But hey, they've got the old classics. Omelette. Pancakes. It's hard to go too wrong."

She took the menu he offered. "Ah, yes. Bacon, sausages. Both dripping in fat, no doubt." She peered over the top of the page, her green eyes mischievous. "The sort of food doctors tell us not to eat."

He couldn't help but laugh. "If you only saw the food in the fridge of the doctor's lounge."

"So tell me, Eric, what are you doing in the Valley after a long night at the hospital?" She flopped the menu onto the table.

The question caught him off-guard. *What am I doing here?* But before he could come up with an answer for her, she filled the awkward silence.

"Sorry. Bad habit of mine, asking too many questions." She dropped her gaze to the table. But only for a moment.

"You're not out here prospecting, are you?" she smirked.

He chuckled and shook his head. "I'm trying to picture myself with a backpack hiking through these mountains. Trust me. It's not my strong suit."

Her eyes sparkled when she laughed. So different from last night, when those same eyes betrayed the pain of her burns.

"I take it you didn't spend much time camping as a kid?"

He shook his head. "I grew up in Toronto, and we had a summer cottage on Lake Muskoka." Elbow on the table, he rested his stubbled chin against his hand. "A proper bed, a kitchen, TV … we weren't exactly roughing it. My brother Matt likes to canoe, but for me it was all about swimming and tennis." Activities he told himself he needed but never seemed to find time for. Especially with his all-too-eager acceptance of every extra ER shift that came his way.

A rail-thin woman in torn jeans and clogs, the only waitress in the café, came over. The young woman scribbled out his order for toast, scrambled eggs and coffee while Alex asked for an omelette, bacon and orange juice.

"So what about you? Are you working near here?" he asked when the waitress shuffled away.

She nodded. "About an hour or so off the main highway. Outside of the perimeter," she added too quickly.

He saw her take a deep breath and right then he knew. *She was camped in the perimeter.* He wondered what would drive her to take such a risk.

Conversation stopped when the clack of clogs brought the waitress to their table with drinks. He added milk to his coffee, stirring it longer than necessary, searching for a safe topic, something that wouldn't make her uncomfortable. She saved him the trouble.

"Aren't you exhausted after working all night?"

"Coffee helps." He lifted his white mug. "I'd usually be catching a nap by now, but there was something I had to take care of this morning."

When he'd left the hospital, he'd been so sure of his destination. But once out on the highway, he realized the foolishness of his plan and pulled into this café. Lillian had been right. He couldn't just waltz into Bennett's house. And what did he hope to find? A bottle with skull and crossbones in plain sight? But he wasn't yet ready to give up and return to Nelson.

"You don't live all the way up here, do you?" She bit her lip. "Sorry. As I said, asking questions is a bad habit of mine."

"No. It's okay." He sipped his coffee, aware of her gaze. "I live in Nelson. Close enough to walk to the hospital." He set down his cup. "I'm up here trying to figure out how a patient of mine was exposed to pesticide."

The words tumbled out of his mouth before he could stop himself. He said more than he'd intended.

The staccato beat of clogs signalled the approach of their waitress, her hands beneath white plates piled with steaming food. A reprieve. But not long enough for Alex to forget what he said.

"Pesticide." Alex bit into a crisp slice of bacon. "Man, that's a tough one. It could be anywhere. Soil, air and water are all possible contact points. And it may not be recent. Some of those pesticides have a long half-life, and even years later, they're potent enough to do real damage."

Her comments surprised him. "It sounds like you know a thing or two about pesticides."

"Lots of chemistry in a geology degree, and I took a few classes in hydrogeology ... groundwater." She shook salt over her omelette and squeezed ketchup onto her plate. "You learn how to predict the groundwater path of a contaminant or work backward to find the source. Not my area of expertise, but I know enough to get by."

He leaned forward. *Maybe she can help.*

"Most of the time, it's easy. People show up in the ER because they've been careless. They don't bother with gloves when spraying pesticides. Or they load up their garden with the stuff and then start digging up weeds." He stared past her at a pair of jean-clad workers who clomped through the front door and gave a wave to their waitress before taking a table near the wall. "But I don't think that's the case this time. Not with this woman."

"Doesn't have to be her. You have to look at her neighbours too. She might have breathed it in if the guy next door was spraying his yard with pesticide. Or the farmer down the way sprayed his fields on a windy day. Most of them know better than that, but to be safe, I'd ask her if there's a farm nearby."

"I wish I could." He ran a finger along rim of his coffee cup, his eyes on his uneaten breakfast. "She died early this morning."

He watched her face change with this simple statement. No one really ever knew what to say when death entered the conversation, and she was no different.

In the emergency room, death was scripted. He followed a set of procedures, delivered a set speech to grieving relatives. And he waited for the in-hospital review to reassure him that he'd done everything possible. That he wasn't to blame. But it never made death easy.

"I'm really sorry to hear that." Her voice was soft.

His now-quiet companion fiddled with her fork as though searching for something more to say in the dull, scratched metal. Laughter from the newly occupied table filled the void.

"You mentioned water too," he said, changing the subject.

"Right. Pesticides can make their way into the water supply pretty easily. Rainwater carries pesticide applied to farm fields and gardens overland to rivers or downward into the groundwater."

"So it might be in the well water, and the people living next door to my patient might show up in the ER next." He pushed his plate aside, his appetite gone.

"Not necessarily." She swallowed a forkful of eggs. "Groundwater is complex. People often visualize it as a large, buried lake, but that's not right. The water is stored in spaces and cracks in the soil and rock, and those spaces may or may not be connected. Are you with me so far?"

He nodded, although he struggled to visualize what she was describing.

"Do you have a pen?" She pulled a napkin from the metal dispenser and took the pen he offered. "Let me draw it out for you."

A blue line stretched over the napkin. "Here's the surface. And below that, at some depth we have a layer of porous rock, a rock with lots of holes or voids." Two parallel lines appeared beneath the first, between which she added circular shapes of all sizes. "The water is in these holes, and it can move between any two holes that are connected. How well these holes are connected, something known as permeability—" She stopped and looked up at him. "Sorry, you probably know all about permeability."

He nodded. "Yep. Cell membranes. Blood-brain barrier."

"Same idea, I think. I'm afraid the last biology course I took was back in high school. Nothing but fossils since then. No blood and guts in anything dead for a million years." She grinned. "Anyway, if we have good permeability, then we have good groundwater movement."

She added curved lines to a napkin that was starting to look more like the artwork of a child than anything in nature. He brought his hand to his face to hide his smile.

"And if you have good groundwater movement, you have an aquifer. Usually these water-filled layers are confined by nonporous rocks or soil like clay. So you have to drill into an aquifer to bring the water to the surface. But it's not always easy to find the aquifer in the first place, because the clay layer doesn't have to be horizontal. I'm sure you've heard some people complain about having trouble finding a well on their property."

"Sure. They bring in water diviners and the like," he said.

"Don't get me started on the diviners. How you can detect water with a forked stick is beyond me." She shook her head and put down the pen. "Here's the bottom line. Two neighbouring properties might not share the same aquifer, but two homes that are a kilometre apart might. And contaminants can take a long time to travel within a single aquifer from one point to another."

Dread rose in his chest. Between the Bennett and Barlow properties in the Slocan Valley lay hundreds of homes. Thousands of victims.

"If I were you, I'd test her drinking water. It's a good first step. If her water supply is clean, then your pesticide source is probably elsewhere." She reached into her back pocket and passed a business card to him. "And if you do find something in the water and you need help, give me a call. As I said, it's not my area of expertise, but there are a few people I can put you in touch with."

His slim fingers covered the card. Had Bennett been exposed to pesticide? If he'd treated her successfully with 2-PAM, he'd know. He'd know whether to call in the military if her drinking water turned up contaminate-free. But now all he could do was wait for the autopsy, and that was several days out.

What have I done?

16

HIS TRUCK LURCHED forward into the narrow gap between him and the fender of a rusty sedan before he slammed on the brake. "Shit!" He pounded his hand into the steering wheel.

For twenty minutes, he'd been caught in this snarl of traffic that snaked back to the Nelson bridge. And now, up ahead, a barricade of army jeeps blocked all access from downtown streets.

But why? With each of the other bombings, he'd been able to park nearby and join the crowd who watched cops and soldiers sift through debris. But these roadblocks were set up almost a mile from the blast site. Further than necessary.

He glared at the American soldier who forced him into an unwanted turn. Hiking boot light on the gas pedal, he joined a long train of vehicles that crawled along a tree-lined residential street.

Cars crowded the curb, making it impossible to park. At the intersection, soldiers and their jeeps prevented escape from the prescribed detour, pushing him further from the blast zone.

As his truck climbed high above the town centre, his eyes darted to the rear-view mirror. But other than faint grey smoke that hung in the sky, he could see nothing of the damage. And no reason for the excessive Nelson lockdown.

Up ahead, another pair of jeeps forced him further south. At least if Nick had been caught up in this mess, he'd probably managed to reach the U.S.-bound highway. Unless soldiers stopped and searched those who tried to leave the city limits. His hands clenched tight around the steering wheel. It would be hours yet before he could be sure.

He was under no illusions about his driver's loyalty. Nick's years of illegal marijuana deliveries into the States made him the perfect patsy. The scratchy-voiced man didn't ask questions. Not about each load delivered to a Washington warehouse, nor his unseen boss. But if he were arrested, he'd confess all.

That had almost happened three months back when a soldier questioned Nick's phony paperwork. The wily thirty-year-old had managed to talk his way out of arrest, but the incident served as a warning.

The close encounter forced him to look for a way to protect the precious cargo Nick carried south across the border. His lips curled into a tight smile. It had been so easy.

Three successful trips followed, a fourth if Nick made it through safely today. And after one more load, the dope smuggler would be done.

He slammed his foot on the brake. Traffic came to a standstill at the t-bone barricade that forced drivers left, back around the city or right, to Highway 6. The balding driver three cars ahead of him poked his head through the window, shouting something at an unsmiling soldier. In an instant, a pair of men pounded to a stop in front of the van, their rifles aimed at the angry man.

Shit. Behind him, a bumper-to-bumper row of vehicles. And in the rear-view mirror, the steely glare of a driver ready to fight. Cold sweat dripped down his armpits at the threat of being caught in a confrontation. The last thing he needed. But the soldier stepped back, and the driver kicked his car into gear to turn left, back around the city.

Under the watchful eye of khaki-clad guards, he steered the truck right, heading for Highway 6, only to find that he could turn only south. That meant access to westbound Highway 3A, the road to Castlegar, had also been cut off.

The dams.

Out on the black pavement, clear of the gridlock, he slammed his foot against the gas pedal. A side road, unguarded, came up quickly on his right. He cranked the steering wheel hand and turned onto the gravel road. Alone on the quiet road, he slowed, snaking his way down the narrow rutted road to the banks of the Kootenay River.

It didn't take long before a column of smoke appeared high above the treed bank on the other side of the river. He checked the rear-view mirror. No traffic behind him. Past a cluster of homes, he parked the truck on the edge of the gravel road.

He stood outside the truck, his eyes on the empty road behind him. From somewhere off to his right, came the sound of voices. His chest tightened. Until he heard laughter. *Not cops.* Others like him drawn here by curiosity. He yanked the rim of his ball cap low and then reached across the leather seat to grab his backpack.

Pack slung over his shoulder, he followed a narrow path through the underbrush to the river's edge. Beneath large sweeping pine boughs, he dropped the bag at his feet and pulled a pair of binoculars from it.

He focused the lenses below the grey smoke, at the orange glow of fire barely visible behind the trees on the opposite bank. *A bomb.* Probably detonated just outside the heavily guarded gates that lead to the Upper Bonnington Dam.

Stupid fools. The soldiers would stand their ground. Die to protect the dams. And the government would quietly deem their deaths an acceptable loss.

No. To win this war, innocent civilians must be targeted.

17

ERIC REACHED DOWN for the newspaper, tucking it under his arm as he unlocked the front door. Setting his keys and the paper on the cluttered table in the entranceway, he used his foot to pry his still-tied running shoes off by the heel. He hung his leather jacket on the closet doorknob and headed straight for the living room.

He turned on the stereo, filling the room with smooth jazz. But even Diana Krall's sultry voice wasn't enough to relax him. Not today.

His mind raced with questions over Bennett's death. He'd replayed every detail of the case dozens of times, reviewing her symptoms and analyzing his actions. Each time he came to the same conclusion: he'd missed important clues that pointed to pesticide poisoning, clues that might have saved her.

At his antique burled oak desk nestled into the corner under windows that looked out at Kootenay Lake, he slid into a black leather chair. The clear, sunny skies gave no hint of the fierce windstorm that had kept Bennett in his ER last night. If, like Gary Barlow, Bennett had been airlifted to Trail, doctors there might have caught what he had missed.

Stop. Playing the "what-if" game served no purpose. He tucked the chair in tight to the desk and pushed aside magazines and mail that sat piled next to his laptop.

Eyes closed, he hummed along to a familiar song coming from the stereo, one he'd tried to learn to play. He glanced over at the saxophone perched in its stand next to the overstuffed leather sofa. The last time he'd held the instrument was when his younger brother

Matt had visited a few months back. The two of them, Matt on the guitar and him on the saxophone, had played long into the night, their music more out of key with each glass of wine. But since then the horn had sat quiet.

He flipped open his computer and brought up the Interior Health Authority website. Their current health alerts listed the usual *Listeria* and *Salmonella* outbreaks and a few relating to *Clostridium botulinum* — botulism. While serious, none of them produced the distinctive set of symptoms he'd encountered. Neither would the animal or insect transmitted infections of hantavirus, West Nile, Lyme disease or rabies, all of which listed as potential health problems at this time of year.

There has to be more. He turned down the stereo, picked up his cell phone and dialled the Nelson Health Unit.

Soft rock music broadcast from one of the local radio stations replaced the voice of the woman who had answered the phone. Phone tucked under his chin, he scrolled through his email, scanning for familiar names amidst the impersonal messages.

A young voice cut through the music. "Amy McNeil speaking. What can I do for you?"

"This is Dr. Keenan. I'm an ER doctor at the Kootenay Boundary Hospital." He pushed back his chair and walked over to the window as he spoke. "I've had two patients in the past twenty-four hours who may have come into contact with a pesticide. I'd like to rule out their drinking water as a source of the problem. Can you tell me how I might do that?"

"Do your patients live in Nelson or in the Slocan Valley?"

"Both homes are in the Valley, near New Denver."

"It will take me a few minutes to get into the system and look up the last set of reports. Do you want to wait or call me back?" she asked.

"I'll hold," he said. Her smooth voice disappeared, replaced by a popular song Eric hummed while he crossed the floor to the kitchen. He grabbed a bottle of apple juice from the stainless fridge and placed it on the granite counter. When McNeil came back on the line, he was just about to reach for a glass from the cupboard.

"The reports from the last month all look good, and there haven't been any complaints other than the ones related to turbidity that we always get at this time of year," she said while she clicked her keyboard. "When people start to see muddy water in their drinking glass, they usually call us. Sometimes we get calls about taste too, but those are less frequent."

Although McNeil sounded like a twenty-year-old, she delivered this report with the confidence that only came from years of experience.

"Would they taste a pesticide? Or maybe smell it?"

"You'd have to have a lot of it in the water before it would make a noticeable difference to taste. Same for smell, probably, although that might depend on the pesticide. The only sure way to detect pesticides is through water analysis."

"And your reports show the water supply is fine." He grabbed a glass and set it on the counter. Phone tucked under his chin, he twisted the juice lid open.

"That's good news, isn't it?" Her voice echoed her confusion.

"Of course. But it doesn't help me understand what's happened to my patients."

"Keep in mind that the locations you've given me probably rely on well water, so I can't say for sure that there isn't a problem."

He sighed. "Let's start again. Do you have any information about the current state of the drinking water supplied to my patients' homes or not?"

"I'll try to explain." The words spoken like a teacher frustrated by a difficult student. "The drinking water that runs from the taps in New Denver is regularly analyzed, and we get routine reports. But with well water, things are done a bit differently. The Ministry of Environment reports on the water quality from a set of monitoring wells that are located throughout the Slocan Valley."

"And you said that the water reports show no problems, so the well water is okay."

"Not exactly. The aquifers sampled by the ministry don't account for all of the groundwater sources homes draw their well water from."

He rolled his eyes. Getting a straight answer from this woman was impossible. He opened his mouth to ask another question but was interrupted by the melodic voice on the other end of the line.

"Dr. Keenan, it's more like an early-warning system for the Slocan Valley as a whole. Routine water samples from strategic locations give the general health of the groundwater." He poured apple juice into his glass while he listened to this practiced answer, delivered at a measured pace. "These samples are supplemented with groundwater reports required when a homeowner drills a new water well or a farmer expands an irrigation system."

"Let me get this straight." He dropped into one of the leather chairs tucked under a glass table. "There may be a problem, but you might not know about it except by accident?"

"I wouldn't put it quite like that," came the crisp response. "My advice is to send a water sample from the home of each of your patients off for analysis. It's the only way to be sure that their water supply isn't contaminated."

"Can you send someone out to get the water samples?"

"We'd need a warrant to do that. Just have the owner bring in a sample of water from their tap."

Eyes closed, he forced a deep breath into his lungs. *Stay calm.*

"Look. One of the homeowners is dead and another is seriously ill. Neither of them can bring in a water sample. You're part of the Health Authority, and this is a health issue. Isn't that enough for you to get involved?"

"We'd need more evidence of a problem before we could get a warrant to enter private property. You've got no medical proof it was a pesticide, and these two locations you've given me aren't exactly next door to each other. There may not be a link at all."

A lecture wasn't what he needed. His voice rose in anger. "You want proof to do anything, and without the water sample we have no proof. It's the most ridiculous thing I've ever heard of."

She didn't say anything immediately. *Have I pushed too far?* He took a deep breath. Although he hated to admit it, she was right. The only link between these two patients was their symptoms. But he couldn't let it go.

"We're not the bad guys here, Doctor. There are rules I have to follow."

He'd reached the end of the road with the Health Authority. He would have to try something else.

"Okay. I'll get a water sample. Now, can you log my call so there's a record of a problem—"

"Possible problem. We can't officially record a suspicion," she said.

He pressed his fingertips into his forehead. "Okay. Can I at least leave my phone number in case you get any complaints about water in the Valley?"

"I'm sorry, but we're really not set up to handle that kind of thing."

Damn. Another dead end. He closed his eyes.

"Look, the best thing to do is bring in a sample and have us test it. If something shows up, a warning can be issued for residents living nearby." Her voice softened. "The sample doesn't have to be in any special container or anything. A clean jar will work. And I can give you the name of a reputable company if you'd rather have someone go out and collect the samples."

"Go ahead and give me the name of the company," he said. He scribbled the details she rattled off onto the backside of an envelope. "How long will it take to get the analysis results back?"

"Most likely a week," she said.

"A week!" He dropped into a kitchen chair.

"I can put a rush on it, Dr. Keenan, but I'm not sure it will get done much faster." Her voice dropped to a whisper. "And if our water analysis shows even the slightest problem, we have to alert the military. You'll have way more control over the situation if you use a private lab."

"I don't need control. I need answers." He made no effort to hide his irritation. "And if there's pesticide in the drinking water, we're going to need the army.""

Before she could say anything else, he punched the end button and dropped his cell phone onto the table with such force that it skittered across the glossy surface.

Damn. This should be easy. Report a problem, take a water sample. Waiting a week just wasn't an option. He'd have to find another way.

His chair scraped against the floor as he pushed off and headed for the counter. The colourful Tekay Orchard label on the container next to his forgotten juice-filled glass brought him up short.

The locally produced fruit juice was one that the friendly Sunlight Co-op grocer lying sick in his ER had suggested he try. He checked his watch. Lillian had assured him Gary was stable when he called her an hour ago. At least now that the storm had passed, their patient could be airlifted to the hospital in Trail if his condition deteriorated.

He could call the military, report his suspicions and let them handle it. But despite what he'd told McNeil, he didn't want to involve the army. Not without something more than gut instinct.

Eyes closed, he sucked in a deep breath. The answer was out there but he needed someone to help him find it.

In the quiet kitchen, he stared at the dusty beam of sunlight that stretched across the table. The sunshine, a reminder that by now he should be sound asleep. *One more call.*

It took only a few minutes for him to connect with an engineer at the firm McNeil had suggested. But as he listened to a humourless man tell him that it would be several days before they could even send someone out for the water samples, he knew he'd have to find another way.

The geologist. She had said she had contacts. Did he dare?

He pulled Alex's business card out of his wallet. It read simply *Alex Graham, P.Geol., Geologist, Graham and Associates* and included a Vancouver address, several phone numbers and an email address.

She obviously ran her own company, and he wondered how many associates there were, if any. He dialled her cell phone, hoping she wasn't already deep in the mountains and out of touch.

"Dr. Keenan?" Her voice sounded muffled, distant. "I didn't expect to hear from you so soon. Is everything okay?"

"I'm looking for a bit of help, actually. Is there any chance you know of a company that might be able to take a water sample right away and test it?" He leaned against the kitchen counter.

"The lab I use works pretty fast, but they're in Vancouver. I don't know of a company here in Nelson that does that sort of thing. Why?"

He rushed through a summary of his phone calls. "A week is too long. I'm trying to get something faster."

"No kidding. Listen, I can get your samples run pretty quickly. Maybe in less than forty-eight hours. And since I'm up here anyway, I can take the samples before I head to the airport."

"Alex, you're an angel." He grinned like a schoolboy. "I'll make a couple of calls and arrange for you to get into both places."

"Not so fast."

His breath caught in his chest. He should have known this was too good to be true.

"I'll do this for you. Call it payback for taking such good care of me last night. But I want to be kept out of it if anything shows up. You don't mention my name. Not to anyone. You handle everything that comes up yourself," Alex said.

An odd request. What exactly what she doing in the Valley? He shifted from one foot to the other. *Can I trust her?*

Did it matter? Right now, she was his best hope. His only hope. "You've got a deal."

18

IT WASN'T UNTIL the second ring that Beth Chambers stole a quick glance at the caller ID. She fought down the urge to let the call go to voicemail and snatched up the phone.

"Beth, hi. I'm glad I caught you." The greeting spoken by Amy McNeil was without introduction, as it always was.

"What's up?" Eyes locked on the rows of numbers that spanned the computer monitor, Beth Chambers stabbed at the keyboard with her free hand while she spoke.

"I got a call from a Kootenay Hospital ER doctor about two of his patients. One of them died this morning and another is in serious condition. He's convinced they were exposed to pesticide, so he's looking for answers. Both patients are from the Valley, and their homes are supplied by well water. That puts you directly in the line of fire."

Beth glanced up at the open door to her office into the hallway beyond. Both doors to the offices across the carpeted hall remained closed, their occupants scrambling as she was to finish their budgets for a department meeting scheduled to start in less than an hour. Still, she left her chair and pressed her door closed before she answered Amy in a low voice.

"He thinks there's pesticide in the groundwater? That's crazy. Not a single water analysis has shown a contaminant in months … maybe years."

"I hear you. But this doctor isn't going away. I explained to him that the Health Authority's hands are tied. We can't just go into to people's homes and test their water. Not without permission. Anyway, he's pretty upset, and I'd bet my paycheque that his next phone call will be to the ministry."

Straight to me. As the only geologist on staff in the Kootenay Regional Office, all groundwater-related inquiries ended up on her desk.

Beth sighed. "Give me the addresses, and I'll take a look. Make sure we haven't missed anything."

Beth jotted the addresses on a scrap of paper and ended the call. She checked her watch. *Shit. Shit. Shit.* With less than half an hour before a department meeting guaranteed to take most of the afternoon, the last thing she had time for was a doctor on a wild goose chase. Her reports were mostly complete, but this last spreadsheet needed review before that meeting. The doctor's crazy suspicions would have to wait.

Her fingers on the keyboard, she tried to focus on the column of numbers displayed on the monitor but failed. She'd known Amy since high school, when the two of them would cut class and head to the mountains to snowboard. The popular blonde wasn't one to raise the alarm lightly. Not then and not now.

She sighed and with a click of the mouse closed her spreadsheet. Muffled laughter came from the hallway, and through the rippled glass sidelight she caught sight of a face turned her way. No one would question her closed door. Not with a budget meeting so close. But it also wouldn't stop someone from interrupting her.

The face disappeared, and she breathed a sigh of relief. With quick keystrokes, she pulled up the Slocan Valley reports and scrolled through the pages for the most recent water analyses.

Her mouth went dry. The last water quality testing completed for this survey area was dated six months back. She stared at the screen. An inquiry into the New Denver area was the last thing she needed.

Two months ago, with the cold winter weather finally lifting, she'd taken some unofficial time off instead of completing her quarterly water survey. Nothing ever changed, and she had intended to get back up into the area later to collect the samples. After that, she would simply slip a few extra samples into the pouch headed for the lab.

She'd done it before without a problem. Although all of the samples were logged, no one paid much attention to the dates and locations on the individual bottles. And if they did, she'd find an excuse. A missed sample found in her backpack. A mislabelled bottle. The guys at the lab weren't likely to question her.

But one of the local mining companies had brought in a watershed plan for approval, and she'd forgotten all about the missing survey samples.

Until now.

Could they actually hold her responsible for someone's death? She scanned the lab results for the last year, fingers twisting strands of her brown hair into tight coils while she read. Small shifts in values but nothing significant. Toxic chemical levels high enough to kill didn't just show up overnight, not unless there was a spill. With the military conducting their own environmental surveys, a spill would have been detected already. There couldn't be anything wrong with the water.

Her mind raced. She could copy the previous quarter results, doctoring the numbers just enough to make the values different. But did she dare? If new drinking water samples showed a problem, her boss would check all of the reports. Pesticides broke down into various chemical compounds over time, making it possible to estimate when the contamination occurred. She'd be fine if the pesticide spill was recent, but otherwise her boss, Derrick, would quickly figure out that the numbers didn't look right. He'd request a repeat analysis of the original water samples, and when they couldn't be found, he would discover her deception.

Shit. Hair twisted tight against her finger, she stared at the numbers on the screen. What she needed was another report. The biologist from the Department of Fish and Wildlife she'd met at a conference not long ago might take routine water samples. It was worth a call.

She scanned her contact list, searching for inspiration, smiling when she saw the name of Pam Shannon, a Department of Fish and Wildlife biologist. They'd met at a conference not long ago and she'd promised to keep in touch with the lively redhead. A promise that faded in the face of a schedule crammed with work and her son's after-school activities. These days she found it hard enough to find time for her husband.

After two rings, the biologist picked up. Beth kept the greeting short and plunged into her request.

"Pam, do you have any water quality reports from the upper Columbia River area in the last six months?"

"Why?"

"We have a crazy old guy who thinks his water is poisoned. You know how it is." Beth bit her lower lip and waited.

"Not another one. They believe either the Americans are stealing all of our water or poisoning all of it." Pam chuckled.

Beth breathed a sigh of relief. "So you're getting a lot of those calls too. It makes life interesting, doesn't it?"

"You can say that again. I've never heard so many crazy stories. I'm sure you've heard the conspiracy theorists too?" The slight lilt of a maritime accent still coloured Pam's voice, even after more than nine years away from Halifax.

"Right. The ones who are convinced the Americans are here to build new dams and divert the river."

Beth shook her head. Many locals believed the grandiose water diversion scheme known as the North American Water and Power Alliance (NAWPA) dreamed up in the late fifties and early sixties was about to become a reality. The plan called for dams on most of British Columbia's rivers, with water forced back into the Rocky Mountain trench, where it would join rivers diverted from Alaska to flow south into the United States. It had never gotten off the ground nor would it ever become a reality. Everyone agreed that constructing dams on four of the largest rivers of North America would be an ecological disaster that neither the United States nor Canada was prepared to even consider. Still, it played in the back of the minds of Canadians, stirred from time to time by well-intentioned environmental groups or those protesting bulk water exports.

"Well, I'm sure this is more of the same. But my boss likes to be thorough. So have you got anything on the water?" Beth asked as casually as possible.

"I'm surprised you'd think we have more information than your department has."

Beth rubbed her sweaty palms against her jeans. "I thought you might have taken a more recent sample."

"We don't take many water samples. That will change if the First Nations are successful in reintroducing salmon to the upper Columbia River basin, but right now we don't run comprehensive water quality checks."

"But you do run some water quality checks."

"Sure. Basic stuff mostly. Not as many measures as you take."

Shit. Pesticides probably wouldn't show up in a basic water quality test, but it was better than nothing.

"When was your last check?"

"Back about two months ago."

A flash of denim beyond the glass caught her eye. People were starting to head into the conference room.

"And no reports of problems in the New Denver area?" Beth asked as she pulled up her spreadsheet.

"Nothing. No, wait… There was a man who called awhile back about dead birds along the banks of some creek out there. But as I recall there wasn't anything there when one of our guys went out to check."

"Do you remember which creek it was?" Beth asked over the whir of the cranky old printer behind her.

"Give me a minute and I'll pull up the report."

Beth checked her watch. In less than five minutes she had to be in that meeting room or face Derrick's disapproving scowl. She grabbed the spreadsheet pages from the printer and stuffed them into her binder.

"Okay. Here are the coordinates." Pam rattled off the latitude and longitude of the creek. "But as I said, there wasn't anything there. Some poor old guy looking for attention, I'm sure."

"And there was no water sample taken?"

"None. What's going on, Beth?" Pam asked softly.

"As I said, I'm just trying to be thorough. My boss expects us to treat every inquiry or complaint this way. Between you and me, it's overkill. But I do what I'm told."

"Sure. But why call me?"

Now what? She couldn't tell Pam about the missing samples.

"Some of our recent sample reports are a bit suspicious. There may be a problem with the lab. I'd like to find some other water analyses for comparison."

"You too? We had some mixed up results a month or so ago, but I thought they'd fixed the problem. Listen, I'd check with the Columbia River Inter-tribal Fish Commission. I think they're doing regular water quality checks of the Columbia. I'm not sure if they're involved with the U.S. army in monitoring the Canadian side of the river, but they might get the reports. It's worth a phone call. They're way easier to talk to than the military."

"I don't think I've heard of them. Are they provincial or federal?"

"Neither. It's an American organization. Four tribes, the Nez Perce, Yakama, Warm Springs and Umatilla, have been involved in the Columbia River water management since way back in the seventies. They're fighting to have the river flow managed in a way that better suits the salmon."

"I don't understand."

"High water flows in the spring benefit the salmon run, but at that time of year electrical consumption is down, so water is typically held back by the dams. And that means low water levels for the spawning salmon."

Salmon. The Americans would be closely monitoring the river to protect this all-important natural resource. Surely they would have discovered a problem with the local water supply, if there was one. But if she doctored her results and the Americans had different numbers, she'd be caught.

"Do you have a contact there?" Beth scribbled the name and number Pam provided.

"Let me know—"

"Sorry, Pam, but I have to run to a meeting. Thanks for the info."

Through the glass, she caught Derrick's back as he left his office, headed in the direction of the boardroom. A quick glance at her watch confirmed that the meeting was about to start.

On the oversized wall map of the Kootenay region, she found the two locations Beth had given her. Between them, two monitoring wells and a third not far away, close to the creek Pam mentioned.

She could manage all of the sites in a single trip, maybe an hour's hike. And if she could collect the samples today, the results might be ready in the next forty-eight hours. Just ahead of any report the Health Authority or a private lab might deliver to the inquisitive doctor. She smiled and nodded. If there was a problem, she would be the first to sound the alarm.

But a trip out to the Valley now meant she'd be back in Nelson too late for the start of Paul's baseball game. And with Ted working until midnight at the hotel, she'd promised their son she'd be in the stands cheering.

She glanced at the framed photo on the corner of her desk, a frozen family moment from her son Paul's recent birthday party, smiling faces squeezed tight together. The nine-year-old's likeness to her handsome husband was obvious, but his green eyes were a mirror of her own. She hated to let him down.

I don't have a choice. She picked up the phone and placed a call to her friend Christine. The two young mothers had become fast friends after a chance meeting seven years ago, and to their delight, their sons, just two at the time, had followed suit. Christine was like family.

"I can't talk long," she said when Christine answered. "You're taking Jeff to play baseball tonight, right?"

"Sure. Why?"

"Any chance you can feed Paul and take him to the game? I don't think I'll make it home in time. And Ted is working the late shift."

"No problem. But you never work overtime. What's going on?"

She didn't need this.

"I've got to run. I'll see you at the game later. And thanks, Christine." And with that, she hung up without giving her friend a chance to say anything more.

Beth texted her boss with an excuse about a family emergency. Derrick would be furious at her for skipping out on the meeting, but he'd come around. She picked up her backpack, grabbed her jacket and rushed out the door.

19

NATHAN TAYLOR TRIED to decipher the name scrawled in blue ink in his notebook. Not that it would make any difference. Of the handful of people who'd been willing to talk to him after the White Building explosion, none were reliable.

At the chirp of an incoming text message, he tossed the notebook aside and picked up his cell phone. "Looks like they're finished with the investigation over at the White Building," he said after a quick read.

"That was fast. What kind of explosives?" Dave Saunders asked.

Nathan glanced over at his partner. As usual, the man was chin deep in files and pecking at his keyboard with one stubby finger.

"If you turned on your phone, you'd know," he said, expecting one of the man's witty one-line comebacks.

Dave shuffled files from one haphazard stack on his desk to another, ignoring the taunt. Only after he pulled a single sheet of paper from a manila folder and eased his bulky frame back in his chair did he answer. Even then, he didn't look up from the report in his hands.

"I get way too many calls from our friendly colonel to turn the damn thing on."

If only it was that easy. Although officially a Canadian army general headed up the Integrated Security Task Force that formed in the wake of the dam attacks, Colonel Bracken, a by-the-book career officer from his brush cut to his army-issued boxers, handled all investigations. Military and security experts from both sides of the border were at Bracken's disposal twenty-four hours a day, as were a select group of elite officers conscripted from the RCMP and the Nelson Police department. Nathan and Dave had both made the cut, a nod to their reputation as skilled investigators and their exemplary service records. But the assignment also made this irritating American officer their boss.

"You're living dangerously." Nathan slid the sleek phone onto his polished desktop.

"Why not?" Dave grinned and let the report fall from his fingers. "Now tell me what they found."

"Nothing fancy. Blast pattern looks like dynamite with a simple electrical detonator. The lab recovered some evidence they want us to see," Nathan said.

"So we were right. Same as the other Nelson bombs but definitely different from what's being used out at the dams."

Nathan nodded to a soldier who made his way past his desk. Before the military had taken over and created a bullpen of sorts to house the ISTF team, he'd had a quiet cubicle all to himself. Now, with desks crammed side-by-side in a crowded room, he could reach out and touch his neighbour.

"So why the White Building?" Nathan asked when the khaki-clad man slid into a chair two desks down.

Dave shrugged. "Could be targeting city hall, but my money's on the provincial government offices. Problem is … it doesn't make sense. You want to go after the government, you bomb the Parliament Buildings in Victoria. You don't bomb the shit out of some piddly office building in Nelson."

"Unless you're a local." Nathan reached over and grabbed the worn baseball from its wooden perch on his desk. "Lots of nice, easy targets in Nelson."

Unlike the dams, the city of Nelson itself remained relatively unguarded. Months of occupation, first by Canadian soldiers and then by the joint U.S.-Canada military force, had tamed local residents. While daytime hours were often punctuated by protests, military patrols cruised streets emptied of life at night, even now that the curfew had been lifted. It left soldiers free to concentrate their efforts elsewhere.

"Has Mercier come up with anything?"

The young Montreal-born detective, assigned to their team from the Nelson Police Department, had his finger on the pulse of the city. But Nelson was a different world from the vast Slocan Valley dotted with small communities and farms that the RCMP policed.

"Mercier's got squat. No rumours, nothing. Not even at Oso Negro. And that tells you something."

Oso Negro. Everyone showed up sooner or later at this homegrown coffee legend with its Spanish name meaning 'black bear.' People talked, and Mercier listened. But it was more than that. Built like football linebackers, Nathan and Dave intimidated people, a problem the slim-built detective didn't face. And his French accent and good looks didn't hurt.

"Well-organized. Professional." He closed his fist around the baseball. "Well, the First Nations are waging war in the courts." It was a common strategy after the historic Supreme Court case ruling in favour of the Tsilhqot'in land claims. "So, maybe one of the environmental groups."

Protests had erupted not long after the United States and Canada started renegotiating the 1964 Columbia River Treaty in earnest. Flood control, power generation and money lay at the heart of the fifty-year-old treaty, but in both countries special interest groups fiercely demanded a say in the revised treaty. Salmon. Water rights. Environmental protection. And the dams themselves. All became contentious — especially after years of devastating drought.

"Nah. The environmental groups aren't shy. They'd be shouting out their involvement in these bombings loud and clear. Gotta have something to do with the Americans," Dave said.

"Hell, we'd all like them to go home." His argument with Olivia flashed in his mind. "But setting off a bomb here in town makes no sense. We're missing something." The baseball slammed into his left palm. "Which government offices are in that building?"

"I went there with Jordan when he got his driver's license a while back. But other than that, I'm not sure." Dave pulled one file then another from a towering stack. "I've got the list here somewhere."

How the man found anything in the mess on his desk amazed Nathan. So unlike his last partner, who retired three years back. Stan Kowalski's alphabetized files had been the butt of many jokes, but the seasoned detective's ability to keep case facts and paperwork organized were legendary. Maybe it was Stan's influence, but Nathan kept only a few priority files in a neat stack next to his computer. The rest were buried in his desk drawers.

"Can't find it. But I know they handle things like liquor licenses and birth certificates. Nothing special. Otherwise the army would have it secured. The White Building, a school, a library and a clinic." Dave rapped his pencil against the stack of manila folders. "Civic buildings. Remind you of anything?"

Nathan nodded. "Sons of Freedom." He held the baseball still, fingers pressed against the stitching. "I admit there are some similarities, but I don't see that radical sect of the Doukhobors joining the fight against the dams this way."

"Why not? The Freedomites protested against the provincial government by targeting civic buildings before."

"Yeah, but that was mostly about religion ... about schooling their kids." A conflict that eventually saw one hundred and seventy-five children forced into residential schools by the government in the 1950s. A decision that affected generations. "And where would they get their hands on C-4 explosives?"

"Which leads us back to the military." Dave sighed. "We've got all these American ex-soldiers living here. You know there's a bomb expert or two in the mix."

Nathan had met many former American soldiers over the years, and most were decent guys. His neighbour, a decorated U.S. Air Force helicopter pilot with a daughter Olivia's age, was one of them. John headed up the local search-and-rescue operations when he wasn't ferrying mining equipment into the Valley. The soft-spoken man had probably saved hundreds of lives in the Selkirk Mountains since he'd settled in Nelson fifteen years back.

But there were others. At first, Vietnam draft-dodgers crossed the border to quietly settle in the Slocan Valley. Later, though, as word of this safe-haven spread, discharged soldiers who fought in Vietnam, Afghanistan and Iraq arrived, some of them emotionally scarred. These men lived in self-imposed isolation deep in the Valley, making no effort to integrate into the community.

"Saunders, we've questioned hundreds of people in the Valley, searched countless houses. And what have we found? Guns, yes. But no C-4. Not even a stick of dynamite. Farmhouse we raided last night was the same." He didn't add that his sole role in the midnight raid was to man the roadblock. An order that still rankled. With his rank and twenty-two years on the force, he should have been part of the raid, not babysitting the highway.

Dave shrugged. "Those three kids got their hands on enough C-4 to blow up the Hugh Keenleyside dam. Somebody gave it to them. Told them what to do. But maybe the guy isn't local."

"Just what we need. A whole country of suspects." Nathan shook his head. "Those kids were smart. I still don't understand how they figured a bomb would solve anything."

There was no doubt that Michael and his two companions, both from Calgary, had intended to do damage that night almost a year ago. Between them, the teens carried more than ten pounds of C-4 plastic explosives rigged with electrical detonators to the Hugh Keenleyside Dam. But if the American soldiers had arrested the boys instead of killing them, things would be different.

"Well, they're not alone. Listen to the latest post on one of the websites we've been monitoring." Dave pulled a folder from a seemingly haphazard pile and opened it. *"Good bomb at the Bonnington dam. Michael Walden would be proud!"* He handed the single sheet of paper from which he'd read over to Nathan. "And there are hundreds of websites just like it. My boys are on the Internet all the time. No way they haven't seen this crap. Scares the shit out of me."

Nathan stared at the typed message. In cities across Canada protests had turned ugly, but nothing matched the violence seen in Nelson since Michael Walden's death. He prayed Jess was right, that Liv had more sense than to get involved in this kind of thing.

He dropped the paper onto the desk. "At least with the Nelson bombings, we've got a place to start." His chair squeaked in protest as he leaned back. "The dynamite was probably stolen from a local mining company."

"Yeah, but anybody with a blasting license could have bought it legally," Dave said.

"Great. That gives us what? A few thousand suspects?"

Nathan set the baseball onto the wooden stand next to a framed photo of Jess and Olivia. There was no mistaking the resemblance between the two women, with their high cheekbones and delicate features.

"Let's go see that detonator," Nathan said.

Palms on the desk, Nathan was about to stand when his cell phone rang. He answered it and listened quietly to the voice on the other end.

"Okay, we'll check it out. Thanks for the call."

"What's up?" Dave asked.

"A report of a possible grow-op from our not-so friendly eyes in the sky. U.S. patrol flew over a couple of guys that looked like they were planting a new weed crop this morning."

Until the arrival of the unmanned aircraft patrols, the RCMP relied on the occasional tip from a hiker or prospector who chanced upon an outdoor marijuana crop. The sites, deep in the woods and often a long hike from even the most primitive road, grew Kootenay Gold, a potent marijuana plant in high demand. With medicinal marijuana dispensaries popping up across Canada and legalization of the drug in nearby Washington State, B.C. bud was more in demand than ever. But growers were vulnerable to aerial surveillance during the spring and fall when they planted and harvested their illegal crop.

"It'll be nice to do something easy for a change." Dave closed the file on his desk and reached behind him for his blue jacket. "Where are we going?"

"They're sending us the coordinates. Sounds like it's up by New Denver. We'll go and check it out after we're done at the lab."

"I say we head up the Valley and check this out first. The detonator isn't going anywhere, but those pot heads planting their weed might," Nathan said.

Dave pushed off from his desk rolling his chair back until there was enough room for him to stand. "Bracken won't be happy."

"Screw Bracken."

20

JUST SOUTH OF New Denver, Alex turned off the highway onto Four Mile Creek Road and followed the gravel road to the Bennett house. She climbed out of the 4x4 and took in the view of the Valhalla Mountains on the other side of the Slocan River. It wasn't hard to understand why Laura Bennett had chosen this ten-acre treed lot not far from Silverton.

Quick steps down a flower-lined sidewalk delivered her to the back door of the small bungalow. There, above the door frame, she found the key left there for her, as Eric had arranged. With one last glance down the driveway, she slipped the key into the lock and pushed the door open.

With the exception of a few coffee mugs in the sink, there was no evidence of everyday life in the spotless kitchen she entered. A brightly coloured tablecloth draped a table that sat in front of a large window at one end of the kitchen.

She could imagine Laura lingering over coffee at this table, admiring her garden. *Or maybe reading the paper with her husband.* The sad truth was that she knew nothing about the woman in whose home she stood. Except that Laura Bennett would never return.

On the floor next to the table sat a pair of ceramic bowls, one filled with water and the other holding kibble. A small dog or maybe a cat?

She dropped her bag onto one of the kitchen chairs and started checking cupboards until she found an open dog food sack.

"Here, pup." She shook the bag, a move she knew from experience would bring the dog running.

In her teens, a golden retriever named Sammy had been her loyal companion and she sorely missed that special relationship. But with so much time spent away from home, she knew she couldn't properly care for a dog. Even a cat would expect more time from her than she could give. For now, the occasional visit with Tracey's affectionate labradoodle, Barney, had to suffice.

She shook the bag a second time but the house remained quiet.

The dog food returned to the cupboard, she crossed to the table. She slipped two fingers into the front pocket of her jeans and pulled out her watch. In a few hours, her gear and whichever geologist Tracey had rounded up to help her would arrive at the Castlegar airport. It was tight, but if she worked quickly, the water samples might be headed to the Vancouver lab before she had to meet the flight.

A quick search of the kitchen cabinets yielded a box of preserving jars for her samples. Her luck continued when she found a roll of masking tape and a marker she could use for labels in an overstuffed drawer.

Over at the kitchen sink, she turned the cold-water tap on as far as it could go. Running water thundered against the bottom of the stainless steel sink, breaking the quiet of the kitchen. She was about to put her hand in the stream of water to check the temperature when she thought better of it.

On the windowsill over the sink, herbs their few remaining leaves yellow and brittle, were set out in matching blue-and-yellow ceramic pots. They looked like the many houseplants she'd killed due to neglect over the years, but she couldn't rule out chemical-laced water.

Hands resting on the granite counter next to the sink, she leaned forward for a look at the backyard garden that lay close to the house. Its black soil, studded with orderly rows of young leaves, stood in stark contrast to the green grass that covered most of the property. The sight of such healthy vegetation confirmed her gut feeling that the woman's lethal pesticide dose originated from something other than a contaminated groundwater supply. But the orderly vegetable garden also didn't seem like something the woman would spray with chemicals. Until a lab analysis ruled out pesticide in the water, she couldn't completely dismiss the idea.

Careful not to put her hands under the stream of well water flowing from the faucet, she filled a glass jar and capped it before placing it on the table. If there was enough pesticide in the water to kill a woman, the hospital should be overrun with victims, but the doctor had mentioned only two patients. It was far more likely that something in this poor woman's fridge held the poison.

She headed for the fridge but stopped. The hot-water tank held water drawn from the well days ago, and it might yield different results. Pivoting, she returned to the sink and cranked the hot water tap open. She grabbed a towel for protection before wrapping her hand around a glass jar, then held it under the steaming water. Even so, the heat of the rising water scalded her fingers, an unpleasant reminder of the burns on her arms.

The second water sample capped and labelled, she once again turned her attention to the fridge. A jug of iced tea, two large apple juice bottles and several cans of ginger ale dominated the near-empty glass shelves. Other than some wilted vegetables, a few eggs and cheese, there wasn't much in the way of food. Like Alex, the dead woman may have relied heavily on restaurants, but the mix of condiments and sauces in the fridge suggested otherwise. It was more likely that this woman had been too sick for anything other than soup and tea for a few days. Even so, the food needed to be tested.

Lettuce leaves, carrots, celery and cheese went into a plastic bag she found in one of the kitchen drawers. She cracked all of the eggs into one of the glass jars and threw in the shells as well.

A peek at her watch revealed a half-hour gone. With one more house to visit, she needed to speed things up.

Back at the fridge, she grabbed the opened apple juice container from a shelf and held it up to the light. Its murky brown appearance made her grimace, but it gave off a rich, sweet aroma. Turning the bottle in her hand, she found the label that described the juice as an all-natural, unpasteurized organic product from a Slocan Valley company called Tekay Orchards. Probably three times as expensive as the brand she usually bought. She poured some of the juice into an empty jar and labelled it, taking care to add the company name. Some of the iced tea, which looked homemade, went into another jar, but she ignored the canned soda. A contaminated large-scale manufactured beverage would have sounded alarms across the country long before now.

With twelve preserving jars tucked back in their box and several full plastic bags stuffed into her bag, she was finally ready to go.

A quick glance at her watch stunned her. What should have been a small favour had taken up more than an hour. *I have to move.*

She tucked the watch into her pocket and picked up the box of jars. Pain shot through her arms under its weight, and she nearly dropped the box. The box pressed against the counter, she pulled the door open, a movement that brought a fresh round of pain. Through clenched teeth, she sucked in a deep breath. With the heel of her boot, she kicked the door closed and hurried down the gravel driveway.

"Why am I doing this?" she said aloud. "Because you didn't follow your own rule. Don't get involved. Don't volunteer. How many times will I ignore my own good advice?"

She rested the edge of the box against the driver's side of the truck and opened the vehicle's back door with her free hand. She dropped the box onto the black-leather-covered seat and slammed the door shut. Once in the driver's seat, she slumped back and closed her eyes.

Her arms throbbed. It was foolish to believe she could carry on as though uninjured. Tracey had been right to insist on sending her help. But for now, she had one last stop. Walking away wasn't an option. If the doctor's suspicions proved correct these samples might keep hundreds or more people safe.

From her pocket she pulled out the piece of paper on which she had written the addresses the doctor had given her. She entered the Barlows' address into her GPS and waited for the map to come up.

Satisfied she knew where she was heading, she started the truck and turned up the radio, hoping some music or mindless chatter would help her mood.

Fifteen minutes later, she pulled into the driveway of the oversized lot just outside New Denver. Here a tangle of overgrown shrubs and weeds greeted the visitor, vastly different from the well-kept front garden she'd just left.

She slammed the truck door closed and headed for the white-trimmed house, but she'd barely taken two steps along the cement sidewalk when a petite redhead emerged from the house to stand in the doorway. *Damn.* She'd expected this place to be empty.

"Alex right? Come in, come in. Melissa called me and asked if I would drop by the house and let you in," she said. Without pausing for an answer, she ushered Alex into the living room.

So much for a quick stop.

"I'm Sarah, one of Melissa's friends. Have you seen her?" The plump woman pulled her sweater tightly across her chest. "I'm so worried about her and Gary. I'll be heading over the hospital to see what I can do to help as soon as we're done here. No, don't worry about your boots," she said as Alex reached down to untie her laces.

Alex straightened. "I'm afraid I don't know anything about what's going on at the hospital. But I promise this won't take too long." She smiled. "You'll be at the hospital before you know it. Can you point me in the direction of the kitchen?"

"Follow me," she said and turned.

Alex's boots clomped loudly against the worn hardwood floor that led past the living room to a narrow kitchen at the rear of the house. Stacks of paper were strewn over the wooden table, and a portable computer lay off to one side.

"Melissa and Gary own an organic market in town, and the kitchen has become a sort of second office for them. They're hard-working people. Can't say I've seen them take many days off. They're special. Kind and generous to their friends." Her voice cracked with emotion, and she wiped tears away with the back of her hand.

"I'm sorry." *A stupid thing to say.* She tried again. "I'm sure the doctors are taking good care of them. Right? And you'll see that for yourself soon."

Sarah's lip quivered, and Alex feared the woman would dissolve into tears. Not knowing what else to say, Alex busied herself with her bag.

"I know you're right. It's just hard."

At the words, Alex looked up. The tears had stopped. Sarah pulled a tissue from the cuff of her sweater and wiped her nose with the crumpled wad. "Is there anything you need?"

Alex smiled. "Clean jars, if you can find them. And a box to put them in. That'd be great, thanks."

"I'm sure Melissa has canning jars." Sarah crossed the kitchen and opened the door to a walk-in pantry. With the flick of a switch, shelves stacked high with a jumble of cans, jars and boxes were illuminated. "Lots of them in here. Do you want big or small ones?"

Alex stood behind the petite woman and scanned the crowded shelves. These people looked to be self-sufficient for months. Maybe that was the point. She'd met survivalists before, especially in the earthquake-prone Pacific Northwest, but here in the Kootenays she couldn't imagine anyone needing such a large emergency food supply.

Alex pointed to a small jar. "If you can find a dozen or so of these and the lids that go with them, it would really help."

"Pint jars, then. I'll have them for you in a flash. Lids should be here somewhere," Sarah said, moving even further into the pantry. A few minutes later, a set of jars, lids and screw rings were crammed onto the counter between the coffee maker and printer.

Alex would have preferred the quiet kitchen to herself, but Sarah tugged her sweater tightly closed and leaned one jeans-clad hip against the table. She squeezed past the woman and pulled open the fridge door. Like the pantry, the fridge was jam-packed with bags of vegetables and fruit, and milk, orange juice and wine stood in the door shelves. Alex reached in and released the water filter from its housing.

"Why do you need that?" Sarah asked.

"Most water filters are designed to remove organic substances such as pesticides as well as things like lead, mercury and microbes. With luck there might be something here for the lab to find."

"Do you really think there's something in the water?"

"I have no idea. I'm just being thorough," Alex said, forcing a smile. She dropped the filter into a plastic bag and reached for another bag, a move that revealed her bandaged forearm.

"What happened to your arm?"

Too many questions. It was time to get this woman out of the kitchen.

"Nothing serious. I'm a bit of a klutz, if you want to know the truth." She flashed her best smile. "Would you mind taking some hot and cold water samples from each of the bathrooms? Just run the water for a good five minutes or so and then fill a jar. And to be on the safe side, keep your fingers out of the water."

"Of course." Sarah grabbed a few jars from the table and left the room.

With two fingers, Alex plucked her watch from her pocket. A sigh escaped her lips. If she wasn't out of here in the next ten minutes, she didn't stand a chance of meeting up with the doctor before the Vancouver flight arrived.

Plastic bag in hand, she turned her attention back to the fridge. Too many fresh foods to sample, and besides, Keenan had said the wife wasn't sick.

Liquids, then. She grabbed the jug of milk and wrapped a hand around a glass bottle of pulp-filled orange juice. The unmistakable Tekay Orchards logo brought a smile to her face. Finally, a connection between the victims. She'd sample the milk just in case, but after that she was done. Her every instinct told her this juice would give the doctor his answers.

By the time Sarah returned to the kitchen with her water-filled jars, Alex was packing the last of the fridge samples into a box.

"Did you find anything useful?" Sarah asked, handing one of her sample jars to Alex.

"It's hard to say." Alex dropped the jar into the box and reached for another. She didn't need her watch to know she was running out of time. Labels could wait.

Sarah held a jar tightly between her hands. "But you'll know soon?"

"In a few days." She waited for Sarah to hand her the jar, but the woman stood unmoving, tears in her eyes. "Listen, Sarah ... I have to get to the airport, and I'm running late." Even to her own ears, the statement sounded curt.

But Sarah simply nodded. "Then let me help you. I'll finish with the box while you gather up your things." She set the jar carefully in the box and wiped a tear from her cheek.

Alex rested her hand on Sarah's arm. "I don't know if you've ever met Dr. Keenan, but believe me, he's one determined guy. I promise you ... he's going to get to the bottom of this."

An empty promise. But the only one she could offer.

21

IN THE CROWDED hospital parking lot, Alex squeezed her 4x4 into the last empty spot. Slamming the door shut, she hurried toward the emergency room entrance. With luck, she'd have Keenan's signature on the lab requisition form in a matter of minutes, and she'd be on her way. Then a quick stop at the courier, and that would be the end of it.

Get in and get out.

But once inside the busy emergency room, she heaved a sigh. Every chair in the waiting room was occupied, and more people stood crammed into the aisles of the small space. She pushed past a small group to the glass partition that served to separate nurse from patient at the triage station. But the nurse manning the station focused her attention on a computer screen and simply ignored Alex.

She glanced around. When she'd arrived here last night, a nurse had approached her in the almost empty waiting room immediately. In this crowd, she wasn't sure how the staff would even recognize a new arrival. There was no line she could join, nor did there appear to be anyone in charge. So how was she going to find Dr. Keenan?

A nurse heading back into the ER treatment area walked past her, and she jumped at the chance.

"My name is Alex Graham, and Dr. Keenan is expecting me. Can you please let him know I'm waiting out here?" she asked.

"We're very busy and—"

"I'm a friend of his, and he said he would meet me here," Alex said before the nurse could finish.

"I'll let him know. But it could be a while," the nurse said before she turned and headed off through the doors.

So much for a quick stop. *Damn.*

From a jumbled stack sitting on a small table, she pulled a magazine and found an empty spot in which to stand. Back leaned against the wall, she mindlessly flipped through the well-read pages filled with movie stars. When was the last time she had been to a movie? Probably about the same time she'd been on her last date, a failed evening with an investment banker Tracey had convinced her to meet. She was trying to remember exactly how many months ago that had been when Eric Keenan walked toward her.

"Alex. Come with me." He led her through the ER treatment room to a small room that looked like it was reserved for staff. He took one of two vacant chairs at the far end of the room.

"You look tired." She slid into the chair next to him. "Have you slept at all?"

He sighed. "Not yet. This is too important."

She pulled the requisition form from her bag and gave it to him. Several nurses were nearby, so she leaned in close.

"Well, I've got samples from both houses ready to go," she said quietly. "Now all I need is your contact information and a signature."

"I can't thank you enough, Alex." He scribbled details onto the form. "So the lab will call me with the results?"

She nodded. "This request is yours, not mine. And for what it's worth, I don't think it's in the water. I found the same brand of juice in both homes. Tekay Orchards."

His pen froze mid-stroke, and he looked up at her. "Tekay Orchards? It's a pretty popular local brand. I drank some earlier."

"Well, I'd stay away from it until you get the lab results back."

Blue scrawl filled the form he handed back to her. She reached down to pick up her bag, a move that caused her to wince.

Eric placed a hand on her shoulder. "Don't skimp on the ibuprofen. I suggested it to you for a reason."

"I'm okay. I think I just overdid it earlier with some lifting." She smiled. "I hate to admit it, but I'm actually happy my assistant is sending a geologist out with my gear, although I nearly bit her head off when she suggested it."

"Really? I would have thought you'd like some company."

"I don't mind being out there alone. And for some projects, like this one—" She caught herself before she said more. "Sometimes it's just easier." She stuffed the form into her bag and stood. "Sorry, but I've got to get moving if I'm going to make it to the airport in time."

"I'll walk out with you." He stood next to her and placed his hand on the small of her back. The warmth of his touch sent a tingle up her spine that took her breath away. But she couldn't afford this kind of distraction. Not now.

She took a quick step forward, and he dropped his hand. But she could still feel his heat as they walked down the hallway.

"When's your next shift?" she asked.

"Not until tomorrow morning. Thank god."

"So forget about this for a while. Go home, have a glass of wine or a beer." She smiled. "And get some sleep."

She blushed, suddenly aware that their conversation had turned too personal. But his broad grin reassured her.

"I'm over this way," he said and pointed in the direction of the reserved spots for doctors. "Thanks again for your help."

She dug her keys out of her pocket as she crossed the parking lot to the truck. Seated in the driver's seat, she pulled out her cell phone and called Mark Fowler at the Vancouver lab.

"There's a particularly sensitive case coming your way. You know about the American military involvement here in Nelson, right?" she asked.

"Who doesn't? And how do you always manage to find such difficult places to work in?" he laughed.

"Blame my dad," she joked. Although this time she'd put herself in this situation.

Eric drove past, giving her a wave. They'd talk again, even if it was just about the lab results. But she probably wouldn't see him again. *Too bad.*

"So what's up?" Mark asked.

"I'm just about to send off some samples to you. If anything shows up in them, it could be a big deal."

"Care to give me a hint?"

She didn't hesitate. Mark had proved himself a trusted ally time and time again. And if anyone could solve this mystery, it was this exceptional environmental chemist who ran a private lab when he wasn't teaching at the University of British Columbia.

"Pesticides. There's a doctor here who thinks two patients have been exposed. One of them is dead. We can't rule out contaminated drinking water."

Mark let out a whistle. "You weren't kidding when you said it was sensitive. All hell will break loose if the military suspects bioterrorism. I'll do the testing on this one myself."

"Good. The paperwork is in name of Dr. Keenan. I don't want any official connection to this case."

"No problem."

"But Mark, I want you to call me with the results first."

If pesticide showed up in any of the samples, the Valley would be swarming with soldiers, and she intended to be well out of their way.

22

ALEX TURNED INTO the Castlegar airport parking lot knowing the late afternoon flight from Vancouver had probably already arrived. She scrambled from the truck and headed for the terminal building, but she'd only just stepped through the door when she heard her name called.

Neil Henley, overstuffed pack riding high on his five-foot-ten frame, strode toward her. And behind him was Tim Munroe.

She sighed. It shouldn't have surprised her that Tracey sent *two* geologists to join her. It was Tracey's way of protecting her, although saddling her with inexperienced geologists wasn't exactly helpful. They were bound to slow her down.

Both men had been hired straight out of university only last summer, and while they could easily identify mineral samples and map up data-rich areas in the office, they lacked field experience. Everything out here was less than perfect, and you had to trust your gut instinct — something that only came after years of trampling through bush in search of mineral deposits.

Patience, little one. Her dad's advice, spoken too many times. He reminded her that when she'd joined his company eight years back, she'd taxed the patience of his senior geologists. How one of them, John Maxwell, had gone so far as to ask that she not be assigned to him, a brave request when talking about the boss's only daughter. But slowly, under the reluctant mentorship of geologists like John, she'd become a skilled mining geologist. Now it was her turn.

At least these two were fast learners who were quick to lend a hand and even quicker with a joke. More importantly, they treated her no differently than any of the men in the company.

"We have all of the gear you asked for and a few extras, like your favourite Scotch." Tim wore a sheepish grin that made the blue-eyed blond look much younger than twenty-two.

"Tracey thought you might not be too happy to see us," Neil added with a stroke of his wiry brown beard.

She couldn't help but laugh. "Trust Tracey ... actually, I'm glad to see both of you." Both arms held high, she added, "With my arms out of commission for a few days, I can use some help with the heavy lifting."

And if she was honest, she had to admit that she'd sleep easier with them around, knowing some lunatic arsonist was out there. While neither of the men was a big, muscular type, their very presence would be a deterrent. That and the rifles they all carried.

"Those burns must hurt like hell," Tim said.

"Yeah, but the pain meds help." She ignored the protest of her throbbing arms. "And with luck, I'll be good as new in a few days."

"Tracey said that you lost everything. The tent must have gone up pretty quick." Neil's brown eyes begged for more of the story.

The last thing I need.

Tracey had told everyone at the office the story they'd come up with: a gust of wind had carried a burning ember from Alex's campfire into the tent. It was more believable than the lantern story she'd fed the doctor, but anyone who'd spent any time in the field with her knew she was far too experienced to let something like this happen.

Still, it was the only account of the night's events that Alex was prepared to share right now. If even a hint of the real story reached her dad, he'd shut down the Tony Germaine project. She might now be a partner in the company, but her dad was still in charge. And if her cover project cratered, she'd have to come clean about the Donnovan claims, if she hoped to stay. Something she didn't want to do. *Not yet.*

But the arrival of the first of their duffels saved her from further conversation.

"Let's get the gear rounded up and get on the road," she said as their army canvas duffel bags, filled to bursting, tumbled onto the luggage carousel.

With two luggage carts piled high with base camp gear, they headed to the parking lot, where they crammed everything into the back of the 4x4 truck. She slammed the door shut, wondering just how they'd fit the groceries yet to come.

On their way out of the airport headed toward Nelson, Neil and Tim gave a rapid-fire report on life back in Vancouver. They made clear the fact that with most of the geologists off on projects in Argentina and Tanzania, the office was quiet. Too quiet for these gregarious young men.

"I was so happy when Tracey told me to pack a bag. I didn't even—"

Tim abruptly stopped talking when two uniformed men blocked their highway lane. The outstretched arm of one soldier made the order to stop clear, and their weapons made it mandatory. "Why are they stopping us?" he asked quietly.

"They don't need a reason." She rolled down her window as she slowed the vehicle to a stop. "We're in the perimeter. I'll explain later. Right now, you need to let me do the talking." She pushed the gear stick into park and tucked her sunglasses up into her brown hair. "Tim, can you hand me my bag? And both of you take off your sunglasses and dig out your ID."

Her eyes never left the approaching soldier as she reached back to take the small bag Neil handed to her. These men and women in their army fatigues, fully armed, intimidated her but they lacked the menace of soldiers she'd encountered at similar roadblocks in South America. There you could never be sure which side of the law was represented by the rifle-wielding man. But it didn't make her any less wary.

"ID." The barrel of his automatic weapon was so close to her face, she could smell the steel. His hand stayed outside of the vehicle as she passed her ID to him. A second soldier stood with his hand gripped around his weapon, his finger on the trigger. Ready to fire in an instant.

She handed her driver's license out through the window and did the same with the identification offered by the guys.

"You live in Vancouver. What are you doing here?"

"We're geologists working up in the Slocan Valley."

"How long have you been here?"

"I've been here for about two months. My colleagues have just arrived."

The hot breath of the clean-shaven man brushed against her neck as he leaned closer to the open window, his attention no doubt drawn to the gear in the back. Her breath caught high in her chest. The last thing they needed was an eager commando riffling through their belongings.

"What's in the back?"

"Camping gear. We have a house in Nelson, but we'll be spending most of the time in tents in the Valley."

"You're aware of the perimeter restrictions?"

"Yes."

"Where are you headed?"

"Up near Kokanee Glacier Park."

With one last long stare, he handed back the three driver's licenses and stepped back. "You're free to go." He turned and nodded to the soldier standing in front of the 4x4, who moved over to the side of the highway at this signal. Alex wasted no time as she put the vehicle in gear and drove past them.

Tim blew out a loud breath. "What the hell was that all about?"

"Welcome to the perimeter." She flipped down her sunglasses and in the rear-view mirror watched the distance between her and the soldiers grow.

"And they can stop us for no reason?" Neil asked.

"Yep. If you're within five kilometres of a major highway or the banks of the Columbia River you're in the perimeter. Impossible for us to avoid." She steered into a corner, the canvas military trucks dropping from view. "Helicopters, drones, vehicles. You name it, they've got it up here on patrol. Probably using technology I've never heard of too."

"Drones?" Neil craned his neck, checking the bright-blue sky for signs of aircraft. "Can you see them?"

"I don't know, to be honest. But even if you can, I bet they see you long before you spot them." Her fingers clenched the steering wheel at the sight of a Humvee racing toward them.

"How far to the campsite?" Tim asked.

"Sixty miles, give or take. About a hundred kilometres."

"And how many more times will we be stopped?" Nylon crackled as Tim turned to watch a tank-like truck pass.

"Hard to say." She loosened her white-knuckled grip. "Once we cross the bridge over Kootenay Lake and head north, we won't see too many patrols. But on this side of Nelson, we might run into another roadblock or two."

"Those guys meant business." Neil ran his hand over his beard. "What if they'd searched us and found the rifles?"

"Three rifles would definitely be suspicious. I told them about my gun once, and they had me out of the truck so fast, I thought I was going to be arrested. Interrogated me for a good half hour and searched every inch of the Rover before they let me go."

The front end of yet another Humvee rounded the curved rock wall ahead. She could see the driver's face, feel his piercing stare. "Man, they're really out in force today. Thank god we aren't doing any blasting. If we had dynamite with us, they'd really be suspicious. Especially after last night."

"Why? What happened?" Their questions collided.

"Two explosions. One in Nelson and another one out here. My guess is that one of the dams was attacked. Could have been the one coming up."

Both men stared out the right side of the truck at the massive cement Brilliant dam that controlled the spill of water from the

Kootenay River into the Columbia. But the line of army vehicles parked along the highway blocked much of the view.

Neil whistled. "Boy, talk about overkill." He pressed his hand against the window. "Is this the dam where those three guys were shot?"

"Different dam, the Keenleyside, not too far away. It's not something you want to mention around here. It's a pretty sensitive subject." Alex pushed down on the gas pedal, speeding as fast as she dared past the soldiers. "And don't mention the Columbia River Treaty either. Actually, don't mention anything to do with the river, period."

"I heard the Americans want a bigger slice of the electricity revenues in the new treaty," Tim said. "And of course the B.C. government wants the same."

"Money." Neil snorted. "Now why doesn't that surprise me?"

"There's more to the treaty renegotiation than that. There's the electricity, of course. But the dams were built to provide flood control for the United States, so water management issues are big. So is salmon. The dams are responsible for the loss of Pacific salmon in the upper reaches of the Columbia. And don't forget the environmental side. Lots of people are against the dams in principle."

"I bet the First Nations would be happy to see the dams gone too. Not just for the sake of the salmon. Some pretty important Sinixt villages and burial sites are covered in water behind the Hugh Keenleyside dam," Tim said.

Alex looked up at her young colleague's reflection in the rear-view mirror. "I'm impressed. Not many people know anything about the First Nations concerns."

"You're holding out on me, dude." Neil jabbed Tim playfully in the ribs.

Tim grinned. "Hey, I read a newspaper or two."

"Everyone wants the treaty to change, but I don't see any of them resorting to terrorism." She flipped the visor down against the blinding sunlight that flashed when the rock wall to her left all but disappeared.

"Terrorism?" Tim asked.

"Sure. What else would you call the dam bombings? They're trying to use violence to get what they want."

"Maybe, but those guys who were killed at the Keenleyside dam didn't intend to hurt anybody. They were targeting the dams," Tim argued.

"But if the dams are destroyed, millions of lives will be affected. Those dams keep floods in check, and then there's the electricity they deliver. What happens when a hospital is without power? How long will their generators supply power to ventilators and other critical equipment?" Alex felt her anger rising. The attacks on the dams had consequences that the bombers hadn't considered. Or maybe they had and they just didn't care.

"Then there's the water supply itself. No water, no crops," she said in a clipped voice. "That's a real problem with the droughts of the past few years. The dams hold back water when the river is high and then send it downstream during the drier seasons, when farmers need it to irrigate their crops."

The vehicle went quiet. She watched a military convoy rumble toward them. Her eyes darted to the dash-mounted GPS, to the edge of Nelson not far ahead. With luck, these vehicles had been part of the roadblock that had stalled her trip out to the airport, and they'd make it into town without another interrogation.

"You said there was a bombing in Nelson last night. Was anyone hurt?" Tim asked.

"I'm not sure. A building shared by city hall and the provincial government, something they call the White Building, went up in flames. I heard the blast, and I went down to take a look." She tucked her hair back behind her ears. "Dead of night, like the last bombing, so there probably wasn't anyone around."

"This wasn't the first?" Neil asked.

"No." She shook her head. "There was a school, two, maybe three weeks back. Before that, a library and a clinic."

"How do you know so much?" Tim leaned forward, one hand gripping the seat back beside her. "I thought you were up in the mountains most of the time."

"Here's an important lesson, guys. Tracey does a good job of monitoring countries we're working in, but it's not enough." She ran her palm over her faded jeans. "I've been in places where you can just tell by reading the local newspaper that it's time to get out. Police crackdowns. More violence than usual. You need to know when to high-tail it out of a country before you get stuck there. Or worse. Gold. Silver. Diamonds. They're not worth dying for."

"Man. Africa. South America." Neil tugged at his beard. "I'd have my eyes and ears open. But this is Canada."

"Right here, right now, the Slocan Valley is pretty unstable. Bombings. Protests. You could easily find yourself in the wrong place at the wrong time. And you definitely want to stay out of the way of the soldiers."

"Well, this is one road trip I'm not likely to sleep through." Tim crossed his arms over his chest and leaned back into the seat.

"I've seen you sleep through just about everything, dude." Neil grinned.

"Not this time, man. Those are American soldiers. American," he repeated loudly. "Never thought I'd see the day."

23

ALEX STEPPED THROUGH the doorway of her tent with a tightly rolled sleeping bag under one arm. A full seven inches shorter than the six-foot-high ceiling, she stood with ease in the roomy interior designed to sleep six. It was a luxury for just one person — the guys were sharing a tent of similar size. But she'd come to appreciate the extra space that made living out of a tent easier, especially given the many weeks each year she spent sleeping outdoors.

She crossed the floor to the spotless green canvas army cot and dropped her load at one end. If the guys weren't here, she'd forget about food and crawl into her sleeping bag. Simple tasks she'd done a thousand times before had taken more time and effort than she could have imagined, and every move seemed to trigger throbbing pain.

Reaching down, she untied her laces and kicked off her hiking boots. She lifted her duffel onto the cot and rummaged through its contents for a change of clothes. When she found her favourite moss-green cotton shirt amidst the t-shirts, cargo pants and other items Tracey had packed for her, she smiled. Her friend knew her so well.

It didn't take much more digging to find the bottle of Scotch nestled within the neatly folded clothes. With this treasure in hand, she strode across the tent to the piece of plywood on lumber legs that served as a desk. She filled an insulated mug with a generous amount of amber liquid before returning the bottle to her duffel. Although she didn't run a dry camp, she didn't encourage drinking either. Not since a sleepless night in an isolated camp with three testosterone-fuelled drillers who grew braver and more foolish with each drink.

She turned on her computer and settled into the canvas chair before taking a long swallow of Scotch. No doubt the doctor would have something to say about her choice of beverage, given the painkillers. But right now she didn't give a damn.

Checking her email, she scanned the subject line of each message from Tracey. Several were related to the activity back at the office, but nothing was marked urgent. And there was nothing from her dad. Either he'd bought the lie about the tent fire or he hadn't yet heard the news from anyone in the office.

From her tote bag she extracted the paper map she'd been working on last night. Sleep could wait. After another swallow of Scotch, she picked up a coloured pencil and set to work.

A rifle crack echoed through the valley. She bolted from her chair and ran out of the tent, ignoring the bite of rocks against the soles of her feet. Tim and Neil stood near the campfire, staring out into the darkening sky.

"What the hell? Which direction did that shot come from?" she asked.

"That way, I think." Neil pointed to the southwest. "Probably the next valley over."

The next valley over. Her home base for the last week, until she'd been forced out by fire. She hugged her arms to her chest and worked hard to push away the unwelcome memory of her struggle through the smoke-filled flaming tent.

Her heart raced. She couldn't let her fear take over. These men depended on her now.

Breathe.

"Hunters?" Tim quietly asked.

"Pretty early in the season for hunters," came Neil's reply in the same hushed tone.

Calmed by their voices, she managed one breath and then another. Her pounding heartbeat slowed.

Together they stood, quiet and unmoving, listening for another shot.

Smoke rose from crackling wood that burned in the fire pit. Her eyes followed the trail of grey upward into the darkening sky. So like last night. But here, outside the perimeter, aerial surveillance and patrols were unlikely.

They were on their own.

She stared at the dense forest that hugged the jagged rock wall that stood between them and the next valley. Paths favoured by elk and deer zigzagged through the thick underbrush, providing furtive access to their campsite.

A quick glance at their set-up reassured her. Their screened kitchen tent and the two sleeping tents stood close together around the campfire. At least one of the three geologists would hear an intruder's footsteps.

"Well, it's probably nothing to worry about. It wasn't all that close. All the same, I think we should have our rifles handy tonight," she said.

Their unsmiling faces betrayed their anxiety. *They need an explanation.* She swallowed hard and then plunged ahead before she changed her mind.

"That fire in my tent? Tracey and I didn't want to worry anyone, so we came up with a story. But you need to know..." She sucked in a deep breath. "The fire was intentional."

"Are you kidding?" Neil blurted.

"I wish. Some lunatic definitely wanted me out of there. My best guess is that I was too close to his marijuana crop. And my campsite was southwest of here ... in the next valley over."

"He had a gun?" Tim's words raced off his tongue. "How the hell did you—"

She raised a hand to cut him off. "Wait. That's not what I'm saying. I never saw the guy who started the fire."

"I don't get it." Neil shoved his hands deep into his pockets. "If this dude didn't have a gun, then what's the connection?"

"I'm just a little spooked, that's all." She searched their faces, trying to read the thoughts of the two men, now so quiet.

"Look. There are three of us with rifles, and we're a long way from my last campsite. There's really nothing to worry about." In the next breath, she changed the subject. "Now, who's in charge of dinner tonight?"

The question was met with silence. "Guys?"

"I'll do it." Tim turned toward the kitchen tent.

"Please tell me you've been practicing your cooking on other unsuspecting souls," Neil groaned.

Tim slapped him on the back. "Isn't that what your camp buddies are for?"

She left them, reassured by the return of their boyish humor, however hollow it sounded. Back in her tent, she sat down at the desk and took a long swallow of Scotch. Pencil in hand, she stared at the map for only a few minutes before pushing back her chair. The last thing she wanted to do right now was work.

At the cot, she pulled on her boots and slipped on a fleece jacket. She reached into her duffel and grabbed the Scotch. Mug in one hand, the bottle in the other, she headed to the campfire.

"Dump out whatever you have in your cups and have some of the good stuff." She didn't have to ask twice.

She lowered herself into a canvas camp chair pulled close to the burning logs. Staring at the flames, she touched her bandaged right arm. Last night, she'd been lucky.

"Does your arm hurt?" Neil gently tugged at his beard.

She dropped her hand to her lap. "It's not too bad."

"Do either of you know how to work this barbeque?" Tim shouted.

"Are you really telling me you don't know how to work that thing? Here, I'll show you," Neil bolted from his chair.

Sipping on her Scotch, she watched them at the nearby portable barbeque. With Neil's help, Tim lit the unit and set to work on a meal of steak, potatoes and mushrooms. But not without a few jabs from Neil.

She listened to their good-natured banter and smiled. So different from her nights alone at the campsite over the past few weeks. Work filled her evenings after long days of hiking and a simple meal. When she could no longer see the details on her maps in the dim lantern light, she'd huddle in her sleeping bag, reading the latest bestselling mystery to the music of Maroon 5 or Ed Sheeran.

The loneliness didn't bother her. In fact, she savoured this time to herself, away from the challenges of the office. But right now she hated the idea of being alone.

From her pocket, she pulled out her watch. Her fingertip circled the scratched glass crystal, settling on the predawn hour in Tanzania. Soon her dad would be up, sipping his first coffee of the day. Now that she was no longer alone and they'd settled into a new location, she might risk a call. Tell him about the fire.

"Have you made much progress here?" Tim asked.

She dropped her hands to her lap and turned to him. "Tracey gave you the project background, right?"

Tim nodded. "MTC Resources is interested in some promising silver leases that have expired."

"Right. A couple of those old leases are adjacent to freehold land, and a claim on the combined land holdings would give Tony Germaine, the owner of MTC, a pretty good-sized silver mine."

"That's what the file says." Neil grinned. "But I've been working with you just long enough to know there's more."

She laughed. "There are a few less obvious locations that have my attention."

Neither of the junior geologists would understand the significance of the mining properties they would tramp through over the next few days. And with their help, she'd be ready with an answer for Sylvia Donnovan before the deadline three days from now.

Her dad would be thrilled if the Donnovan properties proved promising, and she could snap them up. Even more thrilled if she could manage to claim any adjacent parcels that might hold silver. That would be the time to call him. Not now. When she could announce her first big silver mining project, something he'd accomplished just three years out of university.

She pushed the watch deep into the front pocket of her jeans and ran a hand over her thigh. "If we're careful, we'll have our claims locked up before the other rock hounds even know we're here."

"The chase is on!" Neil said excitedly.

She turned to the fading sun. To the majestic peaks beneath which she'd been camped last night. To the valley where a single gunshot had rung out.

A hunter's rifle seemed the most likely explanation, but a geologist or prospector, armed as they were, could also account for the gunshot.

Are we alone in the hunt?

24

RIFLE IN HAND, he sat back on his heels and stared at the blood trail forming in the shallow water. Long strands of her brown hair swayed in the current, the only movement from the body splayed face-down in the shallow creek.

She'd never looked back as he crept up behind her and took aim. He'd watched her, ankle-deep in the icy creek, bend to scoop water into a plastic cup. And when she stood, he fired a single bullet. A perfect shot that stopped her heart on impact.

The spent shell casing pocketed, he twisted back to face the ridge above the creek. For a full minute he listened to his ragged breath, searching for movement.

Nothing. At least not yet. But on a quiet night like this, hikers could be in these hills. *Witnesses.*

He eased his rifle free and carefully set it down before he stood. Cap brim rugged low, he stared up at the tree-lined ridge for one, then a second breath. Only then did he stand and drop his backpack to the rocks.

Leather gloves dug from his pocket were forced over his calloused hands. And then he grabbed the dead woman's ankles and yanked.

Rocks clattered under the weight of the limp body. His nostrils flared at the foul smell of feces and urine, emptied from her body when she died. A smell that triggered memories of far-off battlefields. Memories he'd tried hard to forget.

He shoved the dead woman onto her back. Vacant green eyes stared up at him through strands of wet hair that crossed haphazardly over a scraped and dirty face. He ground his thumb against her eyelids, forcing them closed.

On his feet, he swung back toward the ridge. From the trees on the left, a black shadow darted out. His chest tightened. Eased a moment later by the flap of a wing. A bird, nothing more.

From beside a nearby boulder, he grabbed her black backpack and dumped out its contents. Plastic bottles, white labels and a funnel lay among the jumble. Water sampling equipment.

Shit! It didn't make sense. This creek wasn't routinely monitored. He was sure of it.

He stared at the body. Good-quality hiking boots, a warm jacket. He rifled through the clutter on the rocky shore. A small first-aid kit, an emergency blanket, water purification tablets, a knife, matches and a couple of energy bars. Minimal survival supplies. Enough for a short hike. As though she had come to this creek intentionally.

Why? He dug his hands into the outer pocket of her pack. Her wallet, sunscreen and lip balm were tossed to the ground. He flipped through the pages of a hard-bound black notebook until he found the final entry. A hastily drawn map of this creek marked with two X's filled the page.

Heart racing, he searched through the plastic bottles strewn over the rocks. Four full bottles, neatly labelled. He compared the tight writing on each label to the entries in the notebook. Just one of the water samples came from this creek. The one in his hand. The others were of no consequence. Still, he emptied all four bottles into the creek before he dropped the recapped bottles into his own backpack.

He shoved the empty bottles and the rest of her equipment into her backpack. None of it could identify her.

Crouched next to the corpse, he rammed a hand into her jacket pocket. He pulled out a cell phone and tapped its dark screen. Password protected. He powered it off before dropping it into his own pocket. Arm stretched across her chest, he dug through the other jacket pocket. Faded grocery receipts, a kid's whistle, crumpled tissues. He stuffed the receipts in his own pocket and left the rest behind.

He pulled up the lower edge of her jacket and squeezed his gloved hand into a bulging pants pocket. His fingers tightened around a set of keys, and he yanked them free. Car keys.

Where the hell is it? Probably on the same gravel back road he had driven up. Too close to the perimeter not to attract attention. It had to be moved.

Keys pocketed, he stood and searched the rocks at his feet. Satisfied he'd left nothing behind, he zipped her pack closed and slung it over his shoulder. He clattered across the rocks and climbed the grassy slope beneath the ridge. Halfway up the hill, he pushed through the fragrant boughs of a stand of evergreens and dropped the bag behind one of the tree trunks. Out of sight.

Boots digging into the soft ground, he loped down the slope toward the water. He hoisted his pack onto his back and slung his rifle over his right shoulder, all while staring up at the ridge.

If the shot had been heard, he'd have company by now. *Unless.*

He raised his blue eyes to the darkening sky. Here, outside the perimeter, drones were unlikely. But a 911 call might trigger a military helicopter patrol.

His eyes darted to the trees nearest the creek. The tangled brush beneath the evergreen boughs were too dense to hike through uphill with a body. He'd be exposed, vulnerable while he climbed the slope. Only after he crested the ridge and the forest thinned could he travel beneath protective cover.

He unfolded the emergency blanket and spread the thin aluminum sheet beside the body. It was too small to cover her completely, but at least most of her torso would be covered. With one hand hooked under her shoulder, he shoved until she fell over onto the shiny blanket. And then again. The metal crunched as he wound the sheet tightly around her limp body.

He tugged his ball cap tight against his sweaty forehead and stared up at the ridge. Still no movement. His eyes dropped to the rocks where she'd lain. She'd bled out into the creek, leaving almost no trace of her fatal wound. The few blood-stained rocks would be ignored, if noticed at all.

Bent on one knee, he squeezed his arms beneath the dead woman's back and thighs. He clutched the body to his chest for an instant and then heaved her over his left shoulder.

A heavy step over the uneven rocks sent her skull crashing into his spine. His hands gripped hard against her thighs to keep from dropping her as he regained his balance. Each step deliberate and slow, he crossed the rocky shoreline, eyes on his feet. Only when he reached the grass beneath the ridge did he glance up.

Nothing. But there was no way to know what waited for him above. *No choice.*

He sucked in a deep breath and started his ascent.

25

ALEX EASED HERSELF onto a large boulder near the creek's edge and raised her face up to the warmth of the rising sun. She'd insisted on an early start this morning, although she would have happily slept another hour or two. Even with the pain meds, her throbbing arms kept her awake long into the night. Worse still, she'd found it impossible to stop thinking about the fire or last night's gunshot.

"Alex, what do you make of this?" Neil asked.

She turned to find him offering a black backpack in an outstretched hand, with Tim close at his heels.

"I found it at the base of the tree over there." Neil pointed toward the densely wooded area behind him, uphill from the creek.

Balancing the backpack in her lap, she unzipped it and pulled out a plastic bottle.

"Definitely not your usual picnic garbage. Looks like the same type of water sampling containers we use," she said. She handed the bottle over to Tim and dug into the pack again.

"Probably sampling the creek. Maybe someone from the Ministry of Environment?" Tim asked.

"I don't think so. A small creek like this isn't usually part of a monitoring program. A research project of some sort is probably more likely." She pulled a lip balm from the pack. "But even that doesn't make a lot of sense."

"Why not?"

"I can't see the ministry sending anyone out to the Valley for a research project. Between the roadblocks and the perimeter, the provincial government would probably prefer their staff stayed in Nelson." She opened the lip balm and brought it up to her nose.

"Strawberry," she said when she sniffed the waxy lip balm. "This pack belongs to a woman."

So where is she?

She stared at the creek. Although swollen with icy water from the glaciers high above, the shallow water hadn't likely taken a victim. Slowly, she scanned the tree line on the other side of the creek. Dense underbrush made it unlikely she'd gone that way.

"Something doesn't feel right about this. Guys, spread out and take a good look around."

Her young colleagues headed for the creek, but she hung back. There had to be some reason why the woman left her pack here, uphill from the water's edge. She turned away from the men and climbed the hill, searching for a break in the tangle of slim branches for a trail.

"I think I see some blood," Tim yelled.

She spun around. Neil was already on the run, fast approaching Tim's position near the bank of the creek. Arms outstretched for balance, she ran down the hill to join the two men, now crouched together staring at the ground.

"Take a look. Right here," he said pointing to the rocks at his feet.

The dark red smears on the smooth, grey rocks were obvious even to the unpractised eye. Something happened here. *A fall or maybe a serious cut?*

She searched the crevices between and under the rocks and coarse gravel near the bloodied rocks. A gum wrapper's tin foil caught the sunlight, and she bent down to pick it up. Next to it, partially concealed by gravel, lay an earring.

"Guys, over here. I think I've found something," she said.

Tim scrambled over the rocky beach to reach her first. He touched the silver hoop earring that now rested in the palm of her hand but for a moment before he stepped back.

"This can't be good," Tim said.

Alex studied her young colleague's face. His usual easy smile was gone, replaced by a tight look. Fear.

"Let's not read too much into this. We don't know how long this earring has been here. Same for the blood. And they may not be related. The blood could belong to an animal," Alex said.

"Or it could belong to the woman who owns that pack." Tim paused, his face grim. "We heard a gunshot last night, and now we've found blood. That shot could have easily come from this creek."

"Sure, but it's much more likely that this woman fell and injured herself. It happens to all of us from time to time, especially on this kind of uneven rocky ground," she said.

"Then how do you explain the pack?" Tim challenged.

"If she was injured and decided to hike out, she wouldn't have wanted to carry the pack," Alex said. "There wasn't a water bottle in with her stuff. I'd guess that she took that and left."

"Tim, we didn't find a wallet or car keys. No cell phone either. Those are the things I would have taken if I hiked out," Neil said.

"But those are also the same things you would take if you didn't want to leave any ID behind," Tim said, refusing to accept the offered story.

"You really think somebody shot this woman and took her ID? Where's the body? Did he take that too?" Neil argued.

She feared this exchange would turn into a full-blown argument between the two men. She needed to defuse it. Fast.

"Look, we don't know anything for sure except that we've found a pack and some blood."

"And an earring," Tim added.

"And an earring." She closed her hand around the polished ring of metal. It could easily belong to a woman, alone and injured. She couldn't walk away. Not yet.

"I tell you what. There's a much bigger creek less than a kilometre away that runs straight into the road." She pointed east of where they stood. "We'll hike out to the road from there. It's what I would have done if I was injured, and we'll assume this woman would have done the same. If we don't find her, we'll assume she made it out to get help. Okay?" she asked, looking directly at Tim. Alex waited for him to nod before she turned to Neil.

Neil nodded too, but he asked, "What about the pack? Do we take it with us?"

"No. Let's put it back where we found it. We may be completely misreading this situation, and the owner of that pack may come back looking for it soon," she said.

Neil and Tim repacked the bag without another word. Neither of them was happy, although whether their anger was directed at her or each other, she wasn't sure.

Neil slung the backpack over one shoulder and headed away from the creek toward the spot where he'd found the pack. As she watched his back, she felt the burden of protecting her young colleagues. While their presence made her more confident they could handle anything that came their way, they were also her responsibility.

If anything happened to either of these men, she'd never forgive herself.

26

AT THE FIRST pounding thump of Olivia's socked foot on the stairs, Jess turned to the kitchen doorway. Every morning the same. Too much time spent in front of the computer, followed by a mad rush down to breakfast.

"Just in time," Jess said as her daughter flew into the room. "Bacon's on the table, and your omelette is ready."

Olivia slid into her usual chair and reached for the paper-towel covered plate on the kitchen table. "What's the occasion?" she asked as she bit into a crisp piece of bacon.

Just three months before my little girl leaves home. But she knew better than to raise the topic of Olivia's planned eight-hundred-kilometre move to Vancouver in the fall to attend university. Not with her daughter's stress over upcoming exams.

"I need a special occasion to cook up a treat for my two favourite people?" Jess slid a perfect omelette from the frying pan onto her daughter's plate.

Olivia rolled her eyes and turned to her dad. "How come you're not at work yet? Aren't you investigating that bombing?"

One look at Nate's hunched shoulders and unsmiling face was all it took. "Liv, there has to be something else we can talk about," Jess cautioned as she eased into the empty seat next to Nate.

Olivia's eyes met hers. "I'm curious, that's all. I drove by yesterday, but it's hard to see anything with all the trucks out front. Although it wasn't hard to miss the tons of soldiers looking for the detonator." She turned back to her dad. "How much damage was there?"

"The White Building is gone," Nate answered without looking up. "The only good news is that nobody died."

He's worried. No doubt this latest bombing was responsible for her husband's fractured sleep last night. His restless movements disturbed her more than once, until finally at 5:00 a.m. she'd given up. Huddled under a quilt on the living room sofa, she'd flipped through travel brochures, waiting for the distant sound of the alarm clock.

She watched the teen dig into her eggs and grab a second piece of toast. *I'm going to miss this.* Just one of the many reasons she and Nate were planning their first trip alone in years, right after they settled Olivia into her dorm room. A transition to life without their only daughter.

"But there couldn't have been enough dynamite to take out the whole building," Olivia said between bites.

Nathan put his fork down on the blue china plate. Both elbows set on the table, he rested his chin on entwined knuckles and stared at his daughter.

"Liv, how is it that you know almost as much about the White Building explosion as I do?" The question was asked with quiet calm.

"The Internet," Olivia mumbled, eyes downcast.

Her chest tightened. Liv's refusal to look at Nate. The way her daughter stared at her plate, fork motionless in her hand. *There's more to this.*

"I don't think so. Almost nothing's been released. And there's certainly been no mention of the amount of dynamite used. Or a detonator. So you didn't read it on the Internet." Nate's voice grew cold. "Who were you talking to, Olivia?"

"No one," she quietly answered.

"Not one of your friends?"

Olivia looked up at him, her brown eyes defiant. "Just drop it."

He shook his head. "I won't drop it. You said that there wasn't enough dynamite to take out the whole building. So how do you know that?"

Olivia didn't answer. Instead she ran her fork through her eggs, her eyes downcast.

Jess turned toward Nate. She knew from the way his chest heaved with each quick breath that he wasn't about to let this go.

"Nate." Jess reached over and placed her slender hand on his arm. "I'm sure Liv just made an assumption."

But Nate ignored her. He stared across the table at their daughter, quiet and still. Like a hunting dog, he'd zeroed in on his prey, and he waited for its next move. *I have to stop this!*

"Let's—"

Nate didn't let Jess finish. "Olivia, do you know who's responsible for the explosion at the White Building?" he asked in a voice that sounded too much like a cop and not enough like a worried father.

Olivia's dropped fork cracked against her porcelain plate. "Even if I did know who was responsible, I wouldn't tell you." She thrust out her chin. "At least they're doing something. The Americans have taken over, and no one's doing anything."

"Liv, you'll be arrested," he warned. "Once they identify a suspect, they'll round up everybody who ever knew the guy. *Everybody,*" he emphasized.

Olivia's hands flew up. "So what?" she shouted.

"This was an act of terrorism. They can arrest you and throw you in jail. No lawyer. No trial. I won't be able to help you if that happens."

"Help me?" Olivia pushed her chair back hard, scraping its legs against the tile floor. She stood tall, her back rigid. "You're practically one of them!" she thundered. "Are you going to turn over your own daughter?"

"That's enough!" Jess shouted. "Your father is an RCMP officer, not a soldier. Not an American. And you won't talk to him that way." Tears spilled from Jess's blue eyes, and her voice trembled. "Please tell me you don't know anything about this explosion."

"Who else is involved in this?" Nathan demanded. "Tell me now, and maybe I can do something to protect all of you."

"I don't need your help." Olivia grabbed the back of the wooden chair and shoved it hard until it hit the table edge. "And I'm done talking."

Olivia stormed out of the kitchen. The violent slam of the back door moments later signalled her exit from the house.

In the silence left behind, she stared at her daughter's empty seat. Nate ran a hand over his brush cut and closed his eyes.

"I want to believe she's not involved, Jess, but listen to her." He turned toward her, his eyes sad. "At the very least, she knows who set off that explosion. Any idea which of her friends it might be?"

She shook her head. "They're all good kids."

"That doesn't mean they aren't caught up in the protests. Look at what happened to Michael Walden. He was a good kid too."

Michael.

She thought her heart would stop.

27

SMOKE FROM HIS clothes, burning in the rusted oil barrel, stung his eyes. His grey fleece jacket, his black t-shirt, his jeans, his gloves. He'd left nothing to chance. All of it would soon be reduced to ash in the flames.

He turned away from the barrel to read the driver's license gripped in his calloused hands. Elizabeth Chambers. A quick calculation gave her age as thirty-two. *Seventeen years younger than me.*

In the dim dawn light, he yanked items out from her wallet. Credit cards, a library card. Nothing of interest. Until he found a simple white business card. *A geologist with the Ministry of Environment.* It explained everything and nothing.

He threw the card and the wallet into the flames and picked up the small black notebook. Scrawled handwriting and crude maps filled more than half the pages. He stepped away from the barrel to sit on a wooden garden bench near the greenhouse. The morning dew still damp on the seat beneath him, he shivered and zipped his red fleece jacket closed tight against his neck.

Thumbing through the pages of the notebook, he worked back from the map of the creek. Details of visits to water monitoring stations throughout the Valley over the past two years. Spots along large creeks that crisscrossed the landscape that were routinely sampled for water quality.

The closest monitoring station, a site on a large stream that ran into the Columbia River, lay more than two miles from the creek. A site not far from where he'd finally found her white SUV.

Her GPS history showed her close to another stream more than five miles from the creek. So she'd tested two of the usual streams and then hiked to the creek. But why she'd decided to test this particular creek — this narrow side tributary of no value — remained a mystery.

He studied every notebook entry over the past two years, searching for changes, deviations from the usual routine. But she sampled only the streams that he knew were part of the monitoring network. Sometimes she didn't do them all, but she never visited any location that wasn't part of the network. Either she'd been told to check the water in this creek or she'd seen something that compelled her to do it on her own.

I have to go back.

He hammered the sole of his hiking boot into the hard dirt and hauled himself off the bench. But before he'd taken two long strides toward the driveway, he jerked to a stop.

I can't go back.

He'd covered his tracks. Police would eventually find her vehicle. But with its GPS history cleared, the SUV held nothing to indicate where she'd been. And her body, carefully hidden, might never be found.

Notebook clenched in his hand, he paced a tight line in front of the barrel.

No one had seen him. Not while he moved the body and not while he later searched for her car. He'd driven her vehicle down the sinuous mountain road onto a dark highway empty of military patrols. As fast as he dared, he sped into New Denver, where he abandoned the SUV on a deserted side street. If he'd been spotted slinking past a window at 2:00 a.m., no one called the cops.

His only close call came during the return hike to retrieve his truck. A car, its engine noise masked by a rock-walled curve in the highway, came up on him fast. He'd dropped to the ground mere seconds before the car's headlights reached him. Barely breathing, he'd lain there waiting for the screech of brakes. But the driver hadn't seen him and never stopped.

A trip back to the creek now might end differently. In the hours since Elizabeth Chambers disappeared, calls could have been made, and to assume that she'd told no one where she was going was foolish. The cops could already be at the creek. They could have found her backpack.

Shit!

He stared at the steel building that housed his workshop. One, maybe two more days of work remained. After that, nothing could tie him to the creek, but until then, interest in the creek had to be controlled. Her backpack had to be destroyed.

Twenty-four hours. He'd read that once. An angry parent complaining that the cops had done nothing for a full day after their teenager had gone missing. That gave him enough time. If it were true.

He flung the notebook into the crackling flames and grabbed his rifle.

28

ALEX WATCHED NEIL scramble up the grassy hill toward the forest of evergreens. He pushed aside heavy branches and disappeared from view for less than a minute before he loped back down the hill. From his face, she knew the answer before he spoke.

"The backpack is still there. Exactly like I left it."

This wasn't what she wanted to hear. For more than two hours, they had searched for the injured woman in the underbrush and gullies that ran alongside the creek they followed to the road. When they had finally reached a gravel road, empty of vehicles, they'd turned back. She had hoped by the time they reached the blood-stained rocks that had sent them on their unplanned hike, the pack would be gone.

"Okay. We know she's not anywhere between here, and the road and there's no car on the road. I don't know why she left the backpack behind, but she must have hiked out and driven away."

"Could she have gone in another direction?" Tim asked.

"Sure. But I still think she would have headed to the road if she was hurt," she said.

"And there aren't any other roads near here?" Neil asked.

"Not really. There's the one we came in on. But if she hiked over the ridge toward our campsite, I think we would have seen her. Don't you?" she asked.

"But if she's hurt—" Tim insisted.

"If she was seriously injured, we'd have found her already. How far could she go? And remember, we didn't find a cell phone or keys in the pack. I really think she hiked out."

"Alex is right, Tim." Neil grabbed his backpack. "We don't even know how long the pack has been here."

Tim's tight, unsmiling face warned of further argument. If she hoped to get back to work, she'd have to find a compromise.

"I tell you what," she said. "We'll start with the properties above the ridge and work our way back to the creek. If she went up that way, we'll find her. And if the pack is still here when we get back then, we'll start making phone calls."

The three of them stood in uncomfortable silence. She knew enough to wait, to give him a chance to come around.

"Okay." Tim reached down for his backpack. "Let's go."

Without a word, she slung her backpack over her shoulders and grabbed her rifle. Her arm stung with pain at the quick movement, and she bit back a curse. The pills weren't working. Not enough. She needed distraction.

"Who's got an interesting story?" Her dad's favourite question, one used countless times to break the silence.

"I've got a good one." Neil smiled. "My sister is getting married soon, right? Well, she's lost her mind." With that he launched into an animated and no doubt exaggerated report on his sister's wedding plans. And before long, he had them all laughing hard.

When they crested the ridge, she said, "The boundary of one of the claims we're looking at starts here. Spread out, and let's see what we can find. Tim, you head to the left, and when you get to the tree line, check for trails. Maybe our missing hiker worked her way back to the road from up here."

Tim gave a salute that made her smile. And with that, the two men headed off in opposite directions, their attention on the ground beneath their feet. They searched the dense underbrush for rock outcrops, their only clue to what might lie beneath the surface. With luck, one of these rocks that protruded from the earth would lead them to silver.

Time to get some work done.

Her steel-head hammer pounded against the corner of a rock wedged beneath her boot, chipping a golf-ball-sized piece to the ground. After a quick glance at an all-too-common rock, she threw it aside and stepped toward a weathered boulder. She swung around at the sound of pounding boots.

"Alex, can you take a look at this?" Neil asked.

She took the rock from Neil's extended palm. Held up to the sunlight between two fingers, the freshly exposed surface revealed tight layers of creamy white and grey.

"Argillite with bands of quartzite." She smiled and handed the rock back to him. "It's what we're looking for."

She knew which rock types were most likely to contain silver, gold and palladium, among other riches buried in the Slocan Valley. So did everyone else. Published maps built from knowledge gained over more than a century of exploration showed the extent of all of the Kootenay region rock formations.

"Bag it and label it with my initials and number …" she checked her GPS before continuing "… 164. Mark the position on your own maps too."

Tim, his eyes focused on the GPS screen in his hand, chuckled and shook his head. "Noonday and Curly. Who comes up with a name like that for a mine?"

"Nest Egg, Lucky Thought, Morning Star. I love it. Nobody gives mines colourful names like that any more." Neil scrolled through the map on his own screen. "And there's so many of them!"

"They call this place the Valley of the Ghosts. Hundreds of abandoned mines. Every one of those miners thought they'd get rich, but it's more likely that they never found more than an ounce or two. At some point they would just abandon the mine and head off to the next big strike. The next sure thing."

"Isn't that sort of like what we do?" Neil asked.

She grinned. "Sure. But at least we stack the deck with aero-mag surveys, core samples and computers. Things that weren't available in the late 1800s. And we do it quietly so the other guys don't know we're here. The last thing we want is to start a silver or gold rush frenzy like they had back then."

The competition must have been fierce. All the miners knew each other, living as they did in towns of three hundred or more that sprang up near the more profitable mines. It would have been damn near impossible to slip into the mountains alone, like she'd done over the past two months, even more so because she was a woman. She shuddered to think of what life was like for women in those mining camps more than a century ago.

"When we're next in Nelson, we'll head over to the Chamber of Mines. If we're lucky, one of the experienced local prospectors will be around. You've got to hear some of the stories about these old mines," she said.

Like the ones Baxter used to tell me. The online British Columbia mineral inventory catalogue, MINFILE, might provide a mine's history, but the local prospectors breathed life into an abandoned mine.

"I'm guessing that those prospectors have already rechecked all of these old mines," Tim said.

"Oh yeah. But that doesn't mean there isn't a good silver deposit out here just waiting to be found. Remember, back then if they found a chunk of silver or gold, they assumed they were on top of the deposit, or close to it. If the vein was even a few feet away from where they dug, or it ran in a different direction, they might miss it completely."

"But there were some big finds, right?" Tim asked.

"Sure. Sandon for one. It's north of here, not too far. A company that specializes in old claims operates a mine up there. They produce enough silver from the original vein to make the operation worthwhile."

She'd been out to the Sandon town site once before, but she found the ghost town a sad reminder of the once thriving town. More than seven hundred and fifty claims had been staked in the small, mountainous area near Sandon, the centre of the silver mining community back in its day. When the last of the big mining operations in the area had shut down, the town that had been the home of workers and a busy stop on the narrow gauge train route had simply been abandoned.

"Alex, it looks like there's an abandoned mine, maybe a half-kilo-metre up ahead," Tim said, staring down at his GPS screen.

One of Baxter's? "Does it have a name?"

Tim shook his head and said, "Doesn't seem to."

While some of the bigger mines bore labels, many more were simply locations on a map. To publicize these old mines potentially drew too many curious people, most of whom didn't understand the dangers. Cave-ins and insufficient oxygen were but two of the many risks facing those who explored these old shafts.

"Why don't you and Neil go ahead? Neither of you has seen anything of the subsurface geology yet, and there's nothing better than a mine to give you a quick overview. But don't go too far past the entrance. The mine might have a vertical shaft. It might be boarded up, but I wouldn't trust the wood to hold your weight.

"Don't worry, we know the drill. Safety first," Neil said. "We'll check the air quality and watch where we step. I have no intention of falling hundreds of feet into a pitch-black mine shaft."

"Not unless you want your obit to read 'Died in Noonday and Curly'." Tim grinned.

Neil laughed. "How about 'Thought he was lucky'."

"'Ticket to Heaven.'" Tim jabbed Neil in the ribs.

She shook her head and smiled. "The two of you are trouble. Go on and I'll meet you over there in a few minutes."

29

"ERIC, I'VE REVIEWED the case, and I can't say I would have done anything different." Dr. James Callaway smoothed his silk tie as he spoke. "Even if you'd given Ms. Bennett 2-PAM right away, you might have had the same outcome. You fought aggressively to save her life. What more do you think you could have done?"

Reassurance followed by a question designed to draw out the self-doubt. It was a tactic Eric had used with every resident he'd supervised over the past seven years. He couldn't blame the man for assuming angst over Laura Bennett's death had prompted this meeting. But the Kootenay Lake Hospital chief of staff was way off-track.

"I'm not some rookie." Eric leaned forward in his chair, his eyes locked on the deep-lined face across the desk. "Look. We have two patients with organophosphate poisoning. One's dead. We need to act. And we need to do it now."

Callaway dropped his black-rimmed glasses onto a crowded desk top. "First of all, we don't know for sure that's what happened with Bennett. We'll have to wait for an autopsy. And just because Barlow is getting better doesn't mean it was the 2-PAM."

"You can't deny that Gary Barlow's symptoms are consistent with organophosphate poisoning. The 2-PAM is the only reason he's being released from the Trail hospital later today."

"We don't know that for sure, Eric. But let's assume for a moment that you're right, and both Bennett and Barlow were poisoned. Where are the other patients?" Callaway leaned his elbows against the desk, his hands clasped. An arrogant pose from a man who thought he'd won.

Eric swallowed hard, fighting down the urge to shout, knowing that it would serve no purpose. But still, when he answered, his voice boomed.

"How many more victims do you need?" He swept his arms wide. "Two? Ten?"

Callaway sat rock-still, his steel blue eyes on Eric.

"Damn it, James, you know as well as I do that a child exposed to this pesticide won't stand a chance."

"Don't play the child card with me." Callaway dropped his manicured hands and set his open palms on the desk. "This may well be a very localized problem that affected exactly two, and only two people. Barlow could have been exposed at Bennett's house. Didn't you say he delivered groceries to her?"

"Sure, but what if it's in the water supply? We can't just ignore that possibility."

"Granted. But the Health Authority would be jumping on this thing if they thought it was in the water. It's what they do, Eric. Day in and day out. They're not convinced either."

And there it is. Eric leaned back in his chair. Even under normal circumstances, a scare over the water supply could create panic. But with organophosphates, a "boil water" advisory wasn't enough. The entire community would have to switch to bottled water until the source of the pesticide was found and neutralized. And Callaway wasn't going to take the blame for a false alarm. Not if the rumours about the ambitious surgeon's impending move to head up a Toronto hospital were true.

How to explain the fear that burned in his gut like a red-hot ember? Two patients in his ER were one too many. He couldn't let this go.

"At minimum we have to get more 2-PAM into the hospital pharmacy. Just in case," Eric argued.

"No." Callaway shook his head. "No way. If we order up a large supply of 2-PAM, the military will be notified. They'll go straight to a terrorist scenario, and the first thing they'll do is impose even tighter security. In town. Here at the hospital. And people are going to panic. Is that really what you want?"

"But—"

Callaway held up his hand. "Eric, we can get more 2-PAM when and if we need it. If we see more patients, then we'll call it in. In the meantime, you are not to share your suspicions. Have I made myself clear?" He gave Eric a cold stare before turning to his monitor. "Now. I have another meeting to prepare for."

The dismissal was certain, and Eric stormed out of the office without another word. Out in the hallway, he wove past wool-suited bureaucrats and slammed the stairwell door open. His runners pounded against the cement stairs with each swift step down to the ER.

Callaway was a fool. How many lives would be lost while they waited for proof? He shoved his fists deep into his pockets. The man had a reputation as a gifted, albeit arrogant surgeon who fought for his patients. So where was his compassion? Arthritis may have sidelined Callaway's surgical career, but even now Eric expected his chief of staff to put the people in his community above his own ambitions.

Hand squeezed around the door handle at the bottom of the stairs, he hesitated. His hand fell from the handle, and he leaned against the wall.

I have to change his mind.

Maybe another review of Bennett's and Barlow's files would uncover something useful. At least it was a place to start.

He yanked the door open and popped into the noisy hallway. As he wove past gurneys and a sea of blue scrubs, he spotted an RCMP uniform at the nursing station and heard a familiar voice.

Over the past three years, he and Constable Nathan Taylor had shared the occasional beer, especially during hockey season. The cop's arrival, here, today, presented an opportunity to quietly report his suspicions. But did he dare?

Judy glanced his way as he approached the desk. "Eric, I was just telling Nate that I was sure you were on this morning."

Nate swivelled around. "Why is that every time I'm here, you're working? You need to take some time off."

"You're one to talk." Eric grinned. "Besides, I took some time off when my brother Matt was here last month. How are you? How's Jess?"

"Good. She's busy making plans for our trip to Hawaii in the fall, after Olivia starts university." Nate shook his head. "God, it's still hard to believe Liv will be living in Vancouver in a few months."

"Vancouver's only a day's drive from here." Judy pushed her glasses up the bridge of her nose. "And let's face it, it's no picnic having a teenager in the house. I've got two of them, and believe me, I'd happily ship them off to some out-of-town university tomorrow, if I could."

"It's tougher than you think when the time comes," Nate countered before he changed the subject. "Listen, I'm looking for a woman by the name of Elizabeth Chambers who disappeared last night. She could have come in any time after…" he glanced down at his note-pad. "Three. That's when she asked a friend to take her son for the evening. When she didn't show up by midnight, the friend called the house, and Chambers' husband called us."

"I can't find her in the system." All business now, the blonde nurse's chubby fingers flew over the keyboard. "And it doesn't look like we've had a Jane Doe in the morgue in the past twenty-four hours either."

Nathan tapped his pen against the counter. "Well, she's out there somewhere."

"She might not want to be found," Judy said, twisting her own wedding band. "I mean, her husband didn't know she and the boy weren't home until her friend calls him at midnight? Come, on. There's something off about that."

Nathan shook his head. "Husband works at one of the hotels in town, and he didn't get off until midnight."

"Sure, but she wouldn't be the first woman to escape a bad marriage by disappearing," Judy argued.

Elbow propped against the counter, Eric quietly listened to their exchange, his thoughts on the pesticide. *Do I tell him?*

"Anyway, let me know if Elizabeth Chambers shows up." Nate closed his notepad and put it and his pen in his jacket pocket. "In the meantime, we'll keep an eye out for her car. Lots of patrols out because of the bombings the other night ... maybe we'll get lucky.

"Any leads yet on that last bomb at the White Building?" Judy asked.

"None." Nathan shook his head. "Makes me wish for simpler times when organizations claimed responsibility for their actions. At least you knew who you were dealing with. Now everybody's lashing out and nobody's speaking up. Makes my job a lot more difficult."

Nate was right. Fear, anger and frustration were at the root of many of the protests, both peaceful and violent, that had become a mainstay in the region. These were the kind of emotions that compelled people do things they wouldn't otherwise consider.

Am I doing the same? Eric wasn't one to play by the book, but to go around his boss directly to police wasn't just bending the rules — it was flagrant insubordination. Not a single case of suspected pesticide poisoning had come through the doors since his last shift. Maybe Callaway was right.

"I'm just glad there weren't any casualties," Judy said.

"You and me both. It's just a matter of time, though, before some innocent finds themselves in the wrong place at the wrong time." Nathan zipped up his jacket. "Well, back to the grind."

My last chance. But he had no proof of pesticide in the water — at least not yet.

"Give me a call if you want to watch a game this weekend. Should be a good one between Calgary and Vancouver," Nathan said as he turned to leave.

"Sounds good." Eric flashed a weak smile.

His stomach churned with each step the RCMP officer took toward the exit.

30

ALEX SHIVERED SLIGHTLY at the bite of a sudden gust of cold wind, a reminder that winter had not long passed. Turning her gaze upward, she could see that the sky was filling with grey clouds. The warm, sunny day enjoyed until now would soon disappear. She only hoped that another storm wasn't headed their way.

She stopped to pull her jacket out of her pack, wasting no time in putting it on. Burying her ungloved hands in her pockets, she squeezed her arms against her body. Her fingers brushed against the earring, pocketed without thought back at the creek.

A branch snapped, and she spun around to face the sound.

Downward-sweeping cedar branches formed a wall through which mere pinpoints of darkness were visible. Her breath caught high in her chest. As on the night of the fire, she was an easy target for anyone hiding beyond the greenery.

It's not the same. She wasn't alone. The guys weren't far away.

She pushed herself to move, but her body refused the request until the lowest branch of one of the giant cedars swayed.

Trembling hands reached for the rifle that rested against her back. But before she could grab the weapon, a deer poked through the cedars.

The tawny animal lifted its head and turned in her direction. Nose high, it sampled the air for her scent. She stood motionless, each breath shallow. The young doe dropped its head and chewed at the tender spring grass for just a moment before moving off in search of a less crowded place.

She shook her head at her foolishness. This was one story she'd keep to herself.

As she slung her rifle back over her shoulder, a flash of white peeking out from beneath the vegetation near her feet caught her attention. A quick strike of the hammer, and she had a small sample in hand. Soft, pure silver wove through the rock.

Yes!

A branch cracked, and she jerked her head up just in time to see a second young doe emerge from the trees. She closed her shaking hand around the piece of silver resting in her palm.

Get a grip, Alex. She'd spent far too much time in the bush alone to let her fear get the better of her. Two nights ago she was in the wrong place at the wrong time. Nothing more.

From deep within came a sudden urgency to rejoin the men, a feeling that surprised her. She dropped the rock into a plastic sample bag and updated her GPS with a few swift keystrokes. One knee on the rough ground, she stuffed everything into her pack and hefted it onto her back. The straps dug into her shoulders, and she cinched the waist belt tightly to shift the weight to her hips.

Despite the heavy load, she didn't move without her backpack. It held everything she needed to survive out here. The thought stopped her cold. So why did the pack left by the creek lack even the most basic supplies? No emergency blanket, matches, knife, water or food. No one with any sense headed into the mountains without these necessities. Especially not alone.

Maybe they were wrong about this hiker being out here alone. Her companion may have carried the gear for both of them after the woman was injured.

It was a stark reminder of how differently things might have played out if Alex had been more seriously burned. Alone, with thousands of acres of wilderness between her and help, only luck stood between rescue and a lonely death. *Except.* She stared up at the sky. The drones might spot a fire, but would they spot a dying person?

Such morbid thoughts. She needed to get out of here.

The thud of her boots against the hard ground, rhythmic under her steady stride, calmed her. But still, she moved faster than necessary, choosing a path through the least dense brush toward the mine. Toward her colleagues.

It took some effort for her to find the abandoned mine portal, partially hidden as it was beneath overgrown shrubs. Wood planks, cracked and weather-worn, once barred entry to the mine, but now they lay scattered nearby, left there by her crew or some curious hiker.

From her pack she pulled out her flashlight and ducked into the ink-black passageway.

31

ALEX FOLLOWED HER flashlight beam into the cool darkness of the narrow shaft. The yellow light bounced as she stepped carefully along the rough floor of the shaft. A few yards ahead, she saw the crouched figures of the two men she sought. *What did they find?*

Intrigued, she quickened her pace. She leaned one hand against the dirt and stone wall of the tunnel to help guide her into the depths of the mine. Although the men could not miss the echo of her boots in this confined space, neither of them looked her way. Something definitely held their attention.

Near enough to them now to add her own flashlight beam to theirs, she gasped.

A woman. Her eyes closed, and her head twisted to one side lay against the rocky floor of the mine entrance.

Neil stood and faced Alex. "We've checked, and she's dead. Looks like she took a bullet to her chest. Or maybe her back."

"There's more. She's wearing an earring like the one we found by the creek," Tim said. The young geologist sat crouched next to the body, staring down at the face of the dead woman.

Alex shone her flashlight at the woman's head and caught the glint of silver beneath brown strands of hair. She dropped her backpack and rifle and stepped closer.

"Tim." When he didn't look up, she said, "Tim, I have to get in a little closer so I can get a look at her earring."

At this, Tim finally stood. His eyes never left the body as he shuffled toward the shaft wall where Neil stood.

She squeezed past the two men and crouched down next to the woman's torso. The sickly smell of blood and flesh tightened her stomach. Lips parted, she drew her next breath through her mouth. *Better.*

Even though Tim had checked, she pressed her fingers against the woman's neck. Cold. Pulseless. She stared at the pale face of the young woman. At the silver hoop earring.

Between trembling fingers, she held the earring found at the creek next to the woman's right earlobe. There was no doubt the earrings were identical. But it was a piece of jewellery that any number of women might wear. Before she could change her mind, she gently rolled the woman's head to the right. Just enough to see her bare left ear.

"Definitely her earring." She sighed. "Can you shine your lights a bit further down?"

An unmistakable dark stain on the dead woman's chest. Blood. Alex swallowed hard and forced herself to look down at the denim covered legs.

"Good-quality hiking boots, all-weather jacket, but she's wearing jeans." Jeans, once wet, did nothing to insulate a hiker from the cold. Hypothermia, the kiss of death in unpredictable mountain weather. "No hat or gloves either, unless they're in one of her pockets. I don't think she was planning to be out here very long."

She struggled to her feet, and Tim reached out to her. With a tight grip on his hand, she hoisted herself up to a standing position next to him.

In the soft light thrown by their flashlights, the woman looked almost peaceful. Asleep.

"Did you find any personal belongings or ID?" Her flashlight swept a small arc on the rough floor just beyond where the body lay.

"Nothing," Neil said. "Not a thing. And we searched back in the mine shaft as far as we—"

"She looks a little like you," Tim blurted out.

Startled, Alex shone her flashlight on the woman's face. But she saw nothing of herself in the plump face with its sharp nose.

"The hair maybe. But that's about it." She played her flashlight beam across the woman's body. A glint of gold on the woman's left hand caught her attention. A simple wedding band. And next to it, on her little finger, a distinctive silver ring.

"Can you give me a bit more light over here?" She dropped to one knee for a closer look at the ring. The crossed hammers embossed in the metal told her everything she needed to know.

"She's wearing an Earth Ring. The kind geologists get when they graduate from an Alberta university." She eased herself to her feet. "My dad has one — I'm sure you've seen it."

"A geologist," Neil softly said. "Like us."

"The pack we found is probably hers. Same sampling equipment we have." Tim's voice cracked. "Somebody killed her at that creek."

She stared down at the woman's face. *Did we hear the gunshot that killed her?* A husband, maybe children, waited for this woman who'd never return home. *Maybe we could have saved her.* She turned away quickly.

"Let's get out of here, guys." She grabbed her backpack and rifle. "Time to call the cops."

One hand against the wall of the mine, she worked her way to the entrance without a backward glance. Outside, her eyes closed against the bright sunlight, she drew in a deep breath of fresh, cold air.

The scrape of boots behind her, she quickly wiped away the tears that pooled against her eyelashes. Before Tim and Neil emerged from the mine, she dropped her gear near a fallen log and scrambled down the hill to a clearing. She pulled out her cell phone and dialled 911, her eyes on the men huddled near the mine entrance.

"Could the gunman still be in the area?" the emergency dispatcher asked after Alex's rapid-fire report.

"I don't think so." Her eyes darted to the dark forest all too near the mine. "But there are three of us. We should be okay." She wasn't about to mention of their rifles.

"Normally I'd ask you to stay on the line, but I don't want you to drain your cell phone battery. If you hear or see anything before our officers get there, call me back immediately. Helicopter should be there shortly."

Damn. Damn. Damn. More than just local police officers were heading this way. That helicopter was likely filled with soldiers. And there was no predicting their reaction to a dead body this close to the perimeter. She and her crew would likely be transported to Nelson for questioning. Interrogated until the military were satisfied they'd done nothing wrong.

Her hand clenched into a fist. Just three days left before Sylvia Donnovan expected a decision. She couldn't afford to be detained in Nelson for any length of time.

A quick phone call to Tracey would deliver a good lawyer, someone who could get them released. But she couldn't be sure such a call would be allowed. Not with martial law in effect.

First the fire and now this. She stared back at the mine.

Two attacks on women. Both geologists. Both alone in these mountains. What were the odds? Fear squeezed her chest.

Was that bullet meant for me?

32

AT THE FIRST distinctive sound of the helicopter, they stared upward, but a low blanket of clouds obscured the machine from view until it hovered almost directly above them.

Alex walked over to stand with Tim and Neil near the mine entrance just as the helicopter descended through the clouds. With its gun-metal grey exterior and machine gun mounts, it was clear this craft was designed for war.

The pilot had barely set the chopper down when the side door slid open. Two men dressed in army fatigues jumped to the ground, their automatic rifles pointed at her. Behind them, an RCMP officer, distinctive in his working uniform, a grey shirt and dark blue pants with a yellow side stripe, eased his bulky frame from the aircraft.

She took a step forward and reached out her hand, one eye on the armed soldier who now filled the helicopter doorway. "I'm—"

"Down! Get down on your knees, hands on your head. Down!"

The geologists dropped to their knees on the rocky ground and brought their hands to their heads. A square-jawed soldier — a Sylvester Stallone clone with closely cropped black hair — took the lead. Behind him marched a tall, blue-eyed blond man with Nordic features. Neither soldier looked old enough to be out of high school, but she wasn't about to argue with them.

"Do you have any weapons?" the square-jawed soldier barked.

"Just the rifles over by the packs," Alex said.

"Are they loaded?" Another question from the same man, clearly the senior ranking officer.

"There's a bullet in the chamber of my gun. Probably the same for the other two rifles."

Boots pounded behind her, replaced by the slide of first one and then the other rifle bolts as bullets were ejected by the blond soldier.

"What happened to your arms?"

She glanced up at the white bandages that poked out from under her fleece sleeves. *Damn.* "I burned myself. An accident at my campsite."

If she had to, she'd repeat the story she'd given the doctor. Her visit to the ER could be easily checked, and she needed to keep her story consistent. She'd have to hope that neither Tim nor Neil would contradict the lie.

Her interrogator bent down and held his muscular body close enough for her to smell his musky aftershave. Every slap of his big hands against her jacket felt like a violation. When he stopped and plunged his hand into her pocket, she felt a flash of fear.

"I thought you said you didn't have any other weapons?" He held her flare gun high.

"Sorry," she said. "I don't think of that as a weapon. I carry it in my jacket pocket in case we run into a bear. A flare can sometimes scare them off."

"Bronstein." Nathan Taylor spoke his first words to the Stallone look-alike. "It's fine. Flares are common with hikers. We'd rather have them using flares than rifles." He turned to Alex before continuing. "I'm guessing you're the one who called us in. Can I see some ID?"

Alex never thought she'd be so happy to talk to a cop. She wasn't quite sure who was in charge here, but it seemed clear that Bronstein was at least listening to this RCMP officer.

"My wallet is in the front pocket of my pack. The red one over by that log," she said, gesturing with her elbow.

"I have mine right here." Tim dropped his hand down toward his back pocket.

"Keep your hands up!"

Tim jerked his hands skyward at the barked order. Nathan stepped past them and for several uncomfortable minutes she faced Bronstein's menacing stare, his rifle barrel held too close for her liking.

"She's clean. We can let them get up. They aren't a threat," Nathan said.

Alex dropped her hands to the ground, using them to help get back to a standing position. She leaned over, brushing the dirt from the knees of her pants.

"Now can I see your ID, guys?" Nathan asked. He took the wallet Tim produced from his back pocket and scribbled notes into his small black book.

"My wallet is in the front of my pack. It's the blue one next to the rock on your right," Neil said.

The blond soldier retrieved the wallet from Neil's pack and handed it not to Bronstein, but to Taylor. A clear sign that the cop was in charge.

"How far to the body?" Nathan asked.

"Just a few minutes from here." She pointed up to the shaft entrance cut into the side of the ridge.

"In the old mine shaft?" Nathan asked. Alex nodded.

The cop took up a position beside her as they climbed the uneven ground toward the mine entrance.

"Your business card says you're a geologist. Do you have a stake in this mine?" Nathan asked.

With luck I might. But she wouldn't share that information.

"No." Alex shook her head. "It was just an opportunity to see some of the subsurface rocks."

"Trespassing in these old mines is dangerous," the cop lectured.

"I know." Alex plunged her hands into her pockets. "We check pretty carefully before we go in to make sure the mine is safe." She glanced over at him. "We were just hoping for a quick look."

She turned back toward the others in the group. Tim and Neil were walking together directly behind her with the pair of soldiers not far behind. *Good.* The guys were close enough to hear her answers.

To hear how she handled questions about the perimeter, questions she knew were coming.

"So what is it exactly you're doing out here?" Nathan asked.

"Routine reconnaissance." She would volunteer nothing more.

"You're aware of the perimeter restrictions?" The question barked out by one of the unsmiling men behind her.

She wanted to roll her eyes. To tell him that no one could possibly be unaware of the perimeter. But instead, without turning, she said, "Yes. We've been working well away from the Columbia River."

She could feel the cop's eyes on her. He knew how things worked up here. In the hunt for precious metals, no one was likely to pay much attention to the perimeter boundary. So would he challenge her answer?

"Which of you went into the mine first?" Nathan asked.

A safe question. She opened her mouth to answer, but Neil beat her to it.

"Me."

Nathan stopped and swivelled to face Neil.

"And how did you find the mine? These locations aren't exactly publicized," Nathan asked.

"It's on our map," Neil said. "The government MINFILE provides the coordinates of almost all of the closed mines. Current mines too."

Damn. Their GPS units. Her sample locations, clearly shown on the maps stored in the handheld units, would reveal her work inside the perimeter. Would reveal her lie. She needed to turn this cop's attention back to her before Neil pulled out his GPS. As though in answer, the dark mine entrance came into view.

"There. Do you see it?" Alex pointed to the small rise. "The mine is just up ahead."

"Heikkinen, you stay here with them. Bronstein, you're with me."

At the order, the Nordic-featured blond stepped forward and took up a position between them and the mine. They shuffled into a tight trio under the soldier's watchful gaze while the two other men disappeared into the dark entrance.

She laid a hand gently on Neil's arm, an unspoken question. He nodded. She looked up at Tim, and he gave her a weak smile. They were okay, at least for now.

The stocky cop reappeared far sooner than she'd expected. They'd had time for a cursory look and nothing more. Keys jangled with the cop's clumsy descent down the rocky slope toward them. He'd barely stopped, directly in front of Neil, before he spoke.

"Did you touch the body?"

Tim nodded. "I checked to see if she had a pulse. I don't think I disturbed anything."

"What about the rest of you?"

"I touched her neck. And I moved her head a little." She held her questioner's gaze, knowing the cop wasn't happy about the answer. "I can explain."

Eyes locked on Heikkinen, she raised one hand. "I'm just reaching for an earring. We found it on the bank of a creek not too far from here." She slowly eased the silver hoop out from her pocket and handed it to Nathan. "The woman is wearing the same kind of earring. I moved her head so I could see if she was missing one."

Rocks crunched under Bronstein's boots as he approached and handed the cop what looked like a receipt. He held the paper carefully in his gloved hands while he scanned the faded type. Without a word, he handed the receipt back to Bronstein and then turned to her.

"Elizabeth Chambers. Does the name mean anything to you?"

"No. Should it?"

"Chambers was a geologist with the Ministry of Environment. Did you know her?"

"No." She shook her head.

"Four geologists, working up here in the middle of nowhere." The cop looked up at the snow-capped mountains. "At this time of year." His eyes locked on her. "And you don't know her. You didn't see her."

We're suspects! Her chest tightened.

Tim piped in. "We didn't see her, but I think we found her back-pack earlier. Down by the creek where we found the earring. There's some blood there too."

"And we heard a gunshot last night," Neil added in a rush. "About seven o'clock. It may have come from this direction."

"Where were you when you heard the shot?" the cop asked.

"We're camped in the next valley over," Neil pointed to the north-east.

"Take me to the creek."

33

THE TWO SOLDIERS were left behind at the mine and Constable Nathan Taylor hiked along side Alex, Tim and Neil toward the creek. He shared no further details on Elizabeth Chambers. Instead, the cop kept the focus on them, asking questions that sounded too much like an interrogation, until he learned that both she and Tim had graduated from the university his daughter, Olivia, planned to attend.

Alex breathed a sigh of relief as the conversation shifted to life on the huge University of British Columbia campus. From there, the discussion quickly devolved into a competition of sorts between Tim and Neil, each of them convinced that their alma mater was the best university in Canada.

Their banter provided a welcome distraction that continued until they started their descent from the ridge that overlooked the creek. Now, standing in front of a stand of trees that lined the grassy hill beneath the ridge, the mood was sombre.

"It was right there," Neil said, pointing to the base of a towering evergreen.

"Are you sure it wasn't another tree?" Nathan asked.

Neil shook his head. "No, I'm certain. This is the exact spot where I saw the backpack."

Nathan didn't look convinced. "And what about the blood?"

Alex pointed to the creek. "It was left of that boulder. About twenty-five yards, maybe thirty. I'll show you."

Nathan shook his head. "No. You stay here. I'll do this myself."

"It's right next to the shoreline. It shouldn't be too hard to find," Alex said.

Crowded together near the boulder, they watched the RCMP officer step carefully down the hill to the stony bank of the creek. He crouched, poking at the rocks at a spot that looked to be about the right distance away. But a moment later he rose and continued his solo walk along the creek. He bent down a few more times, but if he found anything, it wasn't obvious.

It seemed an eternity before he turned and crossed the bank back to them.

"Did you find it?" Alex asked.

He nodded. "I saw what could be blood. Not as much as I'd expect to see, and there's no way to know how long it's been here. No bullet casings either."

"But she was here! The earring proves that," Alex argued.

Nathan glanced up at the ridge. "This creek. It's two, three kilometres from the mine, maybe?"

She nodded. "About that."

"A long way to travel with dead weight. Especially when there are dozens of spots near this creek where someone could hide a body. Chambers may have lost her earring here at the creek, but I don't think we're looking at a crime scene."

"But her backpack—" Neil argued.

"Isn't here. And even if the backpack does belong to Chambers, it only proves that she was at the creek. Same as the earring."

"But if it is her pack, then how did it disappear? We saw it just a few hours ago. Maybe the guy who shot her came back for it," she challenged.

"And maybe a hiker found it and took it. You almost did that."

If only she had taken the bag with her when she'd had the chance. Eyes on the creek, she listened to the sound of rushing water.

"Look, I'll send a forensics team out here to sample the blood, but our focus will be on the mine where she was found."

She hated to give up, but she could come up with nothing to counter Nathan's logic. Gut instinct wasn't enough, not with the mine so far from the creek.

"Okay." She sighed. "So what's next?"

"I'm heading back to the mine," Nathan said. "And I'd suggest that you go back to your campsite."

"Not yet. We still have a few hours of daylight so we'll go to the mine with you and see if we can finish up there."

"Ms. Graham, you won't be able to get anywhere near that mine until the forensics team wraps up. Go back to your campsite. Get a fresh start tomorrow."

She stared up at the late afternoon sky. They'd lost almost a full day of work, but they wouldn't accomplish much near the mine, not with cops controlling access. They could stay here at the creek and check out some of Baxter's properties, but rushing through some of his most promising silver claims wasn't the best idea.

"Maybe you're right." She sighed. "We'll walk with you as far as the mine and then head for some of the properties closer to our campsite. And let's skip the formal stuff. Out here, it's Alex, Tim and Neil."

He smiled. "Nathan."

Their gear retrieved, the small group headed up the grassy hill toward the ridge. She fell behind the others, stepping slowly past the trees where Neil had found the backpack. The backpack they should have taken.

She took one last look at the creek. Elizabeth Chambers had been here, and if she didn't die here, then something — or someone — lured her to that mine.

What the hell happened?

34

THEIR SMALL GROUP crested the ridge in silence. Only when they were well beyond the creek did quiet conversation begin between Neil, Tim and Nathan. Alex kept a few feet behind them, content to listen to their voices.

"So what's it like to work with the joint military force?" Tim asked.

His bold question shocked her almost as much as Nathan's candid response. It didn't take long for her to see that he was as unhappy about the joint military force as the other residents of the Valley. The cop's comments were a reminder of just how complicated the political situation had become and how unpredictable access to this area could be.

She interrupted the men. "Nathan, how long do you think it will be before the forensic team gets to the creek?"

Nathan turned to her. "Could be tomorrow, why?"

After tomorrow, there were no guarantees they could access to the creek before Sylvia Donnovan's deadline in just three days. Even a quick look at the properties by the creek was better than nothing.

"I think I'd like to head back and try to do some work there while we still can."

She thought he would challenge her decision, but instead he just nodded.

"Let me give you my card." He reached into his pocket. "And if you find anything, take a photo of it with your phone and call me. Don't touch it."

Her face flushed at the lecture. A lecture she didn't need. She wanted to argue, to tell him that she never would have picked up the earring if she'd known a crime had occurred. But then there was her behaviour in the mine. She shouldn't have touched Elizabeth Chambers.

"I promise." She took the card from his hand and slipped it into her pocket.

"Tell Olivia not to worry. She's going to have a great time at UBC," Tim said.

Nathan smiled. "Not too good a time, I hope."

For a few minutes, the trio watched the cop hike through the valley, his pace faster now that he was alone. Alex broke the silence.

"We don't have much time, so I'd like to hit the most promising properties near the creek." She pulled her GPS from the pack, and the guys huddled around. "These ones." Her finger landed on a pair of outlined mineral claims north of where they'd found the blood.

"Same rock formations as we saw up by the mine?" Tim asked.

"More or less." She repacked the GPS. "A few important differences though." Pack slung over her shoulder, she said, "Let's go."

As they hiked, she ran through the geology with them. At the peak of the ridge, the creek in view, she abruptly stopped talking and brought her index finger to her lips.

"Guys, hold up," she said quietly. "There's a man down at the creek."

The red jacket and matching ball cap on the man were distinctive, even if his build was not. He dropped to a crouch, but seconds later he was back on his feet. Head down, he scanned the rocks as he stepped slowly alongside the creek.

She swept her gaze over the length of the creek. If the man was travelling with a companion, he wasn't nearby. As her eyes shifted back to the stranger, she saw it.

"Shit." She crouched low and headed for the cover of a cluster of chest-high bushes. A move that sent Neil and Tim scrambling behind her.

"What?" Neil said when he dropped to a crouch beside her.

"He's got a black backpack. Over by the large boulder where we were sitting earlier." She reached for her cell phone. "First guy I've seen out here in weeks, and he just happens to be at this creek with a black backpack minutes after we leave. We have to get Nathan back here."

She fished out the cop's card and punched in his number. Cell phone tight to her ear, she listened to one ring after another until Nathan's voicemail kicked in.

"Nathan, it's Alex Graham. Call me back as soon as you get this. We need you at the creek." She glanced up at Neil and Tim's unsmiling faces. "It's urgent."

"Now what?" Neil asked when she hung up.

"We wait," she said. "Nathan can't be that far."

But even as she said the words, she knew the odds were stacked against them. They'd left the cop at least fifteen minutes ago, enough time for Nathan to get to the mine and if he were inside the rock walls, he'd be without cell phone service.

She pulled her pack off and dug out her binoculars. Down on one knee, she raised her head above the bramble of branches and brought the Steiner lenses to her eyes. From his clothing, sturdy boots and day pack, the man looked like a thousand other hikers. His stance and broad shoulders though reminded her of the military men they'd just left, and the closely cropped hair visible below the back of his ball cap reinforced the thought. But he was far older than the soldiers at the mine. Too young for Vietnam, but maybe a veteran of the Iraq or Afghanistan wars.

"He just put something into the pack." Tim craned his neck. "I can't see what it is."

"Neither can I. But he's definitely collecting something. Rocks maybe?" she said.

"Maybe we should go ask him," Neil said.

"I don't think so. He's likely just some hiker, but I'm not sure I want to take that chance," she said.

"Well, we can't stay here forever." Tim dropped his pack. "Do we wait him out or go around him?"

Neither option appealed to her. She lowered her binoculars and sat back on her heels.

"I can go down. Chat him up." Neil tugged at his beard. "He's not likely to feel threatened by one of us. If everything looks okay, you guys can follow."

"Bad plan. Too easy for you to become his next victim. Remember, this guy could have a gun," she said.

"I'll take my gun." Neil wrapped his hand tightly around his rifle barrel.

"And risk a shoot-out?" She shook her head. "I think a low-key approach is better. And we should all go down together. We'll start talking loudly, make a lot of noise. If he's concerned about being seen, he'll take off."

"Okay. But the guy still might have a gun." Neil flicked off his rifle's safety. "I'm going to be ready."

The man twisted toward the ridge at the first sound of the their raised voices. They'd barely crested the ridge before he grabbed his pack and scurried off into the nearby woods.

"Well, isn't that interesting," she said. "He's definitely not happy to see us."

"I bet he's heading for the road." Tim pointed downstream. "There must be a path through the trees that we missed."

"Maybe." She stared at the forest of towering evergreens. *Too much like last night.* Her hand touched her bandaged arm. "He could be hiding in those trees, watching us."

"Then we better make this look good." Tim clutched his rifle strap.

"Make what look good?" Neil asked.

Tim turned to face his confused friend. "If we turn around now, he'll be suspicious. We need to go down to the creek."

"He's right. Let go." She dug her boot into the hill and started downward before she could change her mind.

The three of them hiked in a tight cluster, wordless. Only when they reached the bottom of the ridge did Tim shout out. "Hold up a minute. I need some water."

Tim's voice, unnatural, tense to her ears. But his quick strides toward the creek were fearless.

Neil followed a few feet behind his friend. Protective. Hand tight around her rifle strap, she hung back, putting herself between her crew and the trees.

Tim crouched on the rocky shoreline and scooped icy water into a plastic bottle. She expected him to stand, but instead he pulled a UV water purifier from his pack.

Ninety seconds. The time needed to treat the water with ultraviolet light. Every hiker out here knew the drill, knew to sterilize their drinking water. Tim was making it look good.

Her eyes darted to the forest of towering evergreens. But she just as quickly forced herself to turn away. Each breath shallow, she watched Neil nervously shift from one foot to the other. He felt it too.

She slid her hand to the rifle and eased the safety off. Fingers wrapped around the smooth stock, she hugged the rifle tight. Over the gurgle of creek water, she strained for the sound of approaching footsteps.

When Tim finally shoved the water bottle into his backpack, she forced a deep breath. She didn't waste any time.

"Okay, let's get moving." Her voice boomed.

Tim sprang forward at the command, Neil tight at his heels. She let them gallop ahead of her, watching the trees, praying that the man was more afraid of them than they were of him.

Her long legs pumped hard in her effort to catch up with the men, already halfway to the ridge. Chest heaving, she crested the ridge well behind Neil. Once on open ground, the men picked up the pace, their boots thundering against the valley floor.

She itched to glance back at the creek to see if the man stood there watching them. Instead, she sprinted to catch up with the guys.

"Hold up, guys. He can't see us from here," she said, breathless. "I want to call Nathan again."

A futile exercise.

The cop couldn't possibly get here before their mystery man disappeared deep into the mountains.

35

BACK PRESSED AGAINST the trunk of an evergreen, he yanked a large branch down until he could see the two men and a woman hike down to the creek. He'd bolted when he'd heard them, as much from surprise as fear. A stupid move. A suspicious move. At least the cop hadn't come back with them.

I should've killed her when I had the chance. But the woman had shocked him when she'd escaped the burning tent so quickly, rifle aimed in his direction. Without a weapon, he'd backed down from the challenge.

When he'd returned to the charred campsite the next day, he'd found her gone. Out of the way. It should have been the end of it. But then she showed up here with the Mountie from the roadblock two nights back. Nathan Taylor.

One of the men had led Taylor directly to the spot where the backpack had been hidden. More troubling, the woman then pointed out the stretch of shoreline where the corpse had lain. As though she knew exactly where to look.

How? No one had seen him here last night. He was sure of it.

He glared at the woman standing so casually near the creek. She'd gotten the best of him once. The bitch wouldn't do it again.

He sucked a breath through clenched teeth. These three couldn't be from the Ministry of Environment. The woman had been camped deep in the perimeter, a site no government department would authorize. And the ministry couldn't yet know their geologist was missing. Shot dead at this very spot.

His heart skipped a beat when the blond man dropped to a crouch near the water. Desperate for a better view, he pushed aside a bough and pressed forward. But the woman looked his way, and he ducked deeper into the trees.

Fists clenched, he hid in the shadows, blind to their movements. The woman's voice, loud, startled him. They were leaving after just five minutes at the creek. They had doubled-back for a specific reason.

Through the branches, he watched their backs. Saw the rifles that hung next to heavy packs. And when they disappeared over the top of the ridge, he stepped out of the trees to follow.

36

ALEX FINGERED THE zipper pull of her fleece jacket, her eyes on the map spread out over the desk. The creek lay alongside two of the more promising silver claims held by Baxter Donnovan for more than a decade. Claims that were bound to draw interest.

When Baxter died of heart failure a year ago, the grapevine buzzed with talk about the future of his properties. The rumours had died off, but there would be people watching and waiting. Elizabeth Chambers might be one of them. And so might their mystery man.

Tim and Neil's quiet voices drifted into the tent. She'd left the men by the crackling campfire, their mood sombre. Like her, they were frustrated at Nathan's refusal to order a search for the man they'd seen at the creek. "The man could be anywhere by now," Nathan had said when he'd finally called almost an hour later. Even more irritating was the cop's argument that black backpacks were common and his reminder that the creek lay almost two kilometres from the crime scene

Her cell phone chirped. She grabbed the phone when she saw the name of the caller.

"So are you camped out in the snow?" Mark asked.

The chemist's friendly voice brought a smile to her face. "Not this time. Although it's cold enough here tonight that I've put the heater on," she said. "So why are you still at the lab at this hour? Don't you ever go home?"

"I thought you might appreciate a quick turnaround on this one and I have to say, you've really managed to surprise me. Not your usual sample," Mark said.

"What did you find?" Cell phone tucked against her shoulder, she prodded a notebook out from under the stack of papers and grabbed a pen.

"Preliminary results show an organophosphate pesticide in the apple juice sample from the Bennett house. Not sure which pesticide yet, but I knew you'd want a heads-up."

That's what she liked about Mark. From their first project together more than six years back, he'd worked hard to protect her interests. In the years since, he'd become part of her most trusted circle of friends. She'd wondered once or twice why the handsome, dark-haired chemist never asked her out, but he seemed content with a professional relationship. With his first-hand knowledge of the transient life she led, she couldn't blame him.

"And the other samples?"

"Nothing. They're all clean."

"Nothing in the other juice sample? The one from Gary Barlow's house? It was the same brand. Tekay."

"No. The pesticide is only in the one sample," he said.

"But that apple juice is a local organic product. I thought they didn't use chemicals." She strummed her pen against the open notebook, the lined paper still awaiting its first entry.

"Sure, but all it takes is some fool spraying their crops on a windy day for pesticide to end up on the apples of an organic farm downwind. And if there's been a spill and the groundwater is contaminated, then pesticide could easily have been in the water used to process the apples into juice."

"But wouldn't we have more than just two victims?" She didn't wait for an answer. "And you said that the juice from Gary Barlow's place was fine."

"It could be that just a single batch of juice was contaminated. That would explain Barlow's sample coming up clean."

She dropped her pen. "So this is just the start. The rest of the pesticide-laced juice is still be on grocery shelves."

"Maybe, but the pesticide concentration in Bennett's juice is extremely high. Either we have a mega-spill out there, or someone intentionally added the pesticide to the juice."

Murder?

"Could someone have tampered with the juice in the store?" she asked.

"Anything's possible, but most products these days have safety features in their packaging. You know, plastic seals around the cap, that sort of thing."

"So there's probably a spill out there." She stared down at the map on her desk. Hundreds of fruit orchards dotted the fertile valleys in this part of British Columbia. Hundreds of farms.

"You want my opinion? Given the high pesticide concentration, I think someone deliberately poisoned Laura Bennett's juice." Mark paused. "Maybe Laura herself."

"Suicide?" She whistled. "Hell of a way to kill yourself."

"But effective."

"I don't know, Mark." She leaned a socked foot near the heater. "I think I'd find murder more believable."

"Well, it's a dangerous way to kill someone. This stuff absorbs through the skin and lungs so it's pretty easy to get a toxic dose while you're working with it unless you're careful. But it might explain the second victim, this Gary Barlow. Any history between them?"

"I have no idea. I know nothing about them but their names and where they live," she said.

"If you don't have a personal connection Alex, then why are you involved?"

She sighed at the question she'd asked herself more than once. But Dr. Eric Keenan was very persuasive.

"It's a long story." She touched her throbbing arm.

"And I bet there's a man involved." Mark's throaty laugh brought a smile to her lips. It also sparked a sudden longing for home.

"I promise to tell you everything over drinks when I'm back in Vancouver. In the meantime, keep me posted. And Mark, thanks. I owe you one."

Sitting on the edge of her cot, she stared at the cell phone in her hand. *Now what?*

Laura Bennett's death, tragic as it was, didn't point to a toxic spill. Not that she could see. But nothing Mark said had eliminated that possibility either.

To call the doctor or not? She stood and paced the nylon floor of the tent between her cot and the desk. If there was a pesticide spill, a warning had to go out. But it made sense to wait until Mark identified the pesticide and issued his report.

Waiting. She drew in a sharp breath. That's what she'd decided to do about the backpack, and that hadn't turned out well.

Perched on the edge of the cot, she dialled Eric's number.

"I always thought it was hard to get doctors on the phone, yet this is the second time you've picked up when I've called," she said when he answered after just two rings.

"I gave you my personal cell phone number, not something too many people have. So, how are you?"

"It hasn't been the best day." The words spilled out without thought.

"Are you having a lot of pain?"

His voice, coloured with concern, almost brought her to tears. She'd intended only to tell him about Mark's results, but instead the events of the day tumbled out.

"Eric, we found a dead woman in an abandoned mine up here. Her name was Elizabeth Chambers—"

"Elizabeth Chambers? Are you sure? That's the woman the RCMP are looking for!" he exclaimed. "She arranged for a babysitter for her son and then vanished."

She closed her eyes. *A young boy left motherless.*

"When did she disappear? Do you know?" she asked, dreading the answer.

"Yesterday afternoon, I think."

So the shot they'd heard could have killed Chambers. She pressed her fingers into her forehead.

"Where are you anyway?" Eric asked.

"In the mountains near Silverton. She could have been in that mine shaft for months or years if we hadn't been working nearby."

"I wonder what Chambers was doing up there."

"No idea. But the cop said she's a geologist with the Ministry of Environment, so she could have been working." She didn't mention her suspicion about the woman's interest in the Donnovan silver properties.

"Like you are." He paused before he added. "Alex, if there's a killer out there, then you're not safe."

She smiled at his concern for her. He was just one of those nice guys.

"I'm fine. I've got company, remember? Tim and Neil, a couple of geologists I work with, flew in yesterday. Besides, our campsite is a long way from the mine," she said. "Now, I called because I have some news for you."

He listened without interruption as she related the information Mark had shared with her.

"I'm not convinced this is suicide either. But I can't believe someone would want to kill Laura Bennett. She came to the ER alone, so I don't think she had a husband or boyfriend. Maybe a patient ... she was a psychologist." He sighed. "But if somebody killed her, then how do we explain Gary Barlow?"

"Mark thinks maybe he was involved."

"Gary? No way," he countered. "No, somehow he was exposed to the same pesticide. And that means there may be more of it out there somewhere. We've got to get the RCMP on this," Eric said.

"You know they'll jump to worst-case scenario, right? Bioterrorism. People will panic. Are you sure you want to do that?" Her question was met with silence. "Eric, Laura Bennett is the only victim we can confirm. And even that's not a sure thing. You said yourself that until the autopsy results came back, you won't know if Laura was poisoned. Maybe you're wrong about what made her and Gary sick."

"I could be wrong about Gary, but not Laura. Not after you found pesticide in her juice." His voice edged with anxiety. "Alex, there's a pesticide spill out there. And it has to be found."

He sounded so sure. She closed her eyes and ran her fingertips across her forehead. "You're going to need Mark's report. I'll text his home number to you."

"Thanks. Maybe he can fast-track a preliminary report. I'd rather have some proof before I call police anyway."

Their call ended, she stared off into the growing darkness outside the tent. Once Eric reported his suspicions, the military reaction would be swift and aggressive. Martial law. A lockdown of the Slocan Valley.

It's over. She'd have to use what she had to evaluate Baxter's properties to give Sylvia an answer.

It was time to get out.

37

"ALEX, COME QUICK!"

Her eyes snapped open at the frantic shout from outside her tent.

"Tim's really sick," Neil yelled. "He's vomiting, and he's having trouble breathing."

"Go get the first-aid kit from the kitchen tent!" She scrambled from her sleeping bag and jammed her bare feet into her hiking boots.

Neil's boots pounded away from her tent. Two quick steps delivered her to the tent door. Outside in the darkness, she bolted for the tent the two men shared.

The acrid smell of vomit assaulted her as she flew through the tent door. She kneeled down next to Tim's cot. In the dim lantern glow, his ghostly pale face glistened with perspiration. But it was his shallow, ragged breaths that tightened her chest.

"Do you have asthma, Tim?" He whispered a weak no to her question. "Any other medical conditions? Allergies? Anything?" Tim shook his head.

She lay her hand against his damp forehead. "When did you start feeling sick?"

"A few hours ago. My stomach didn't feel great at dinner," he paused, his chest heaving. "I didn't eat much."

"It might be an allergic reaction to something you ate." She said as she reached for a fleece jacket that lay at the foot of Tim's bed and balled it up. Not enough.

Neil plunged through the doorway, the first-aid kit in his out-stretched hand.

"Neil, grab your pillow and a sweater or something," she said as she grabbed the kit from him. "We need to get him propped up so it's easier for him to breathe."

Tim's t-shirt, wet with sweat, clung to the hand she reached beneath his back. A hard pull forced him upright. His dripping forehead rested against her chest until she could ease him back against Neil's makeshift cushion. She pulled an albuterol inhaler from the first-aid kit and shook it before handing it to Tim.

"I want you to exhale completely and then press the top of the canister at the same time you take a slow deep breath in and hold it for a few seconds."

His neck muscles tense, he struggled to push air and the life-saving medication into his lungs.

"Again."

Even a second dose wasn't likely to be enough. She plunged a syringe into a small vial of antihistamine and then injected the drug into Tim's upper arm.

"It'll take a few minutes for these drugs to take effect. Just try to relax."

She crossed the tent and set the first-aid kit on Neil's cot. *What next?* Her advanced first-aid training was better suited to broken bones than breathing difficulties. She riffled through the plastic vials and pouches in search of answers.

Tim retched and she closed her eyes. She could give him something to ease his nausea but far better for him to empty his stomach.

She turned to find Neil supporting a bucket near his colleague's contorted face. Neil's eyes met hers. Eyes filled with fear.

"Tim, I'd feel a whole lot better if a doctor took a look at you." She spoke in a low tone, trying to sound calm. "And I'd like to do that as soon as possible. So, I'm going to call for medevac."

"What can I do?" Neil asked.

"Exactly what you're doing." She placed her hand on Neil's shoulder. "Stay here with Tim and shout if you need me. I'll set up a few of the flares in the open area to the left of the tents. It should be a safe spot for a chopper to land."

She ran back to her tent, grabbed her cell phone from the desk and called 911. Pacing the floor, she gave all of the relevant details to the emergency dispatcher, who assured her that help was on its way.

Her next call was to Dr. Eric Keenan.

He owed her a favour, and she planned to collect.

38

OLIVIA EASED HER bedroom door closed. Head resting against the wooden door, she listened carefully for sounds of movement in the hall beyond. Her parents' bedroom had gone dark more than an hour before, but with her father at work, her mother would be restless, if she slept at all.

With so much at stake, Olivia had been careful. *Until today.*

How stupid to talk about the White Building bombing at breakfast! But though her father might be suspicious, he couldn't prove anything. They were safe. At least for now.

Bare feet noiseless on the carpet, she crossed the floor to the closet. Crouched inside, she threw aside an old comforter to expose a black duffel. With both hands, she carried the heavy bag over to the bed, where she dropped it onto the floral quilt.

Perched on the edge of the bed, the unopened bag next to her, she gave one last look at the door before pulling back the double zipper. She reached inside and removed the single sheet of folded white paper, jammed between bundles of dynamite and twisted detonator cord. Her elbow on the pillow, she skimmed the typewritten note under the bedside light.

Two days to work out a plan to avoid detection. Far fewer than the last job. The next words stole her breath away.

I can't believe it!

She dropped the note and grabbed the handle of the duffel. Six bombs. For the White Building, they'd used only two. The building would be destroyed.

Nicole. Kyle. They wouldn't be happy about this target, either. But the others, especially Trevor and Dylan, might see it differently. In the weeks after Michael's funeral, she'd heard them argue the merits of incendiary explosive devices, IEDs, along military convoy routes. All-out war against the Americans.

At first, she'd assumed it was nothing more than talk, but she soon realized that they were serious. She pleaded with them to find another way. Begged them to not to murder nameless soldiers. And eventually they came around.

Over endless cups of coffee, they quietly discussed car bombs and Molotov cocktails. Soon, other teens from the high school joined them. A few she knew, like Nicole, but others were just faces she'd seen at school. Little did she know that each person she met vetted her, gave their opinion, and later their vote, on her acceptance into their exclusive club.

Together the small group of eight agreed to focus on protests against their own government. The Canadian government had asked for help — agreed to help. They were the ones who could force the Americans back across the border.

They'd let me believe it was my idea.

Only after Trent revealed everything to her in a quiet conversation on a park bench near the Kootenay River did she understand. Trevor, Dylan, the others. They were hunting for people committed to their cause. People like her who would fight back against the government. And she'd willingly agreed to join them.

But this!

She paced the floor. Trent built the bombs and always had the last word on their target. They trusted this decorated American war hero, Michael's father, to guide them. But this target, this building had never been mentioned. Not once.

Her eyes darted to the computer screen. A call to Dylan asking for confirmation would be okay. She dropped into her desk chair, hands on the keyboard. But as though burned, her fingers flew to her face.

Legs tucked tight to her chest, she stared at the dark monitor. The note was crystal clear and a call now would only question her loyalty.

I have to trust Trent.

From what her father had said, the cops had few leads, and she knew the explosives couldn't be traced back to them. The dynamite, the detonators, both had come from some old army buddy of Trent's who had since died. And the ex-Marine knew exactly how to get into a building without being seen, where to leave the bombs for maximum impact.

Trent Walden knew what it took to win a war. With his help, they could continue for weeks, even months without detection. Until their government was forced to ask the American troops to withdraw. And she wanted to be part of it.

She pushed herself out of the chair and kneeled next to the bed. Her hand shook as she held it, reading and rereading the short message.

Everything about this next job was different. With the other buildings, they'd had time to learn the routine of the overnight cleaning staff. Each bomb was then detonated two hours after everyone had cleared the building. Someone could still have been in the building, but it seemed a remote possibility.

The scrape of her fingernails against the folded note edge ripped through the silence. They didn't need days or weeks to plan this job. No amount of surveillance would make a difference to the timing of the explosion.

He wants me to kill.

39

ALEX WATCHED HER breath steam in the cold morning air. Calls to Tim's parents, Tracey and the hospital had kept her up for hours. And so had the succession of unanswered calls to her dad. Exhausted, she'd tried to sleep, but her mind replayed the day's events in an endless loop. The dead woman. Tim.

Finally, she'd climbed from her sleeping bag. Elizabeth Chambers was beyond help, but if there was a pesticide spill out there, she had to find it.

But where to start?

On her knees, she scanned the topographical map spread out on the tent floor. A map studied for far too many hours. A map that refused to yield answers.

Eric insisted that Tim had been exposed to the same pesticide as the others, but she could find no connection. Neither the Barlow or Bennett house was anywhere near where they'd hiked yesterday, and thousands of acres lay between their campsite and the closest home.

She focused on the many streams that flowed through the area. But these streams started in the snowy peaks far above their campsite and carried pure, clean water down the mountain slopes. If one of them was contaminated, she was at a loss to explain the pesticide source. At those altitudes, farms were rare or nonexistent.

No doubt a few tortured souls lived in ramshackle homes hidden deep in the dense forest below the mountain peaks. Far removed from the communities that dotted the Slocan Valley, such men could live their lives without interference. It wasn't hard to imagine they might grow their own food. Or a marijuana plant or two. But it didn't seem likely they'd use pesticide.

Her knee groaned with pain when she stood. She checked her watch. Neil would be up soon, if he wasn't already.

She zipped up her jacket and grabbed a pair of gloves from the careless pile of clothing on her cot before she left the tent. Outside, a dull sky barely lit by the rising sun blanketed the quiet valley. She slowly scanned the area around the campsite as she worked her slender fingers into the gloves. Nothing moved.

Gravel crunched with each step she took toward the fire pit. From the wood piled nearby, she added new logs and kindling to the charred remains of last night's fire. Knees on the hard ground, she lit the small, dry sticks of wood with a single match. With the first spark of flame, she sat back on her heels until pungent smoke forced her away from the glowing fire.

Inside the kitchen tent, she dumped dark-roast coffee into an old-style percolator and reached for a jug of water on the table. Pain, swift and sharp, pulsed down her arm. Eyes closed, she waited for the dull ache to return before she moved again.

Tight to the table, she carefully lifted the four-litre jug in both hands before she tipped it over the coffee pot and then filled an empty glass. She fished a pill bottle from her pocket and popped two white tablets from her into her mouth, washing them down with water.

She stared down into the half-empty bottle of pills. Eric had told her it would take time for her arms to heal, but she'd never expected to need a steady diet of pain meds. And even that didn't help unless she adjusted every move, something she forgot all too often.

With a sigh, she cradled the percolator against her chest and slowly made her way back to the fire. She balanced the shiny percolator above the flames on the burning logs and then settled into one of the camp chairs.

Transfixed, she watched the flames lick at the bottom and sides of the stainless steel pot. She ran a hand along her throbbing arm. Her breath quickened as another log caught fire and the blaze grew.

The sound of a tent zipper and Neil's heavy footsteps broke the spell. She filled her lungs with cool morning air and closed her eyes. *You're not alone.*

"Coffee smells good." Neil poured coffee into a mug and handed it to her. He filled his own cup and then lowered his slender six-foot frame into the empty canvas chair beside her. "Any news about Tim?"

"I talked to Eric about an hour ago. He says that Tim is responding to the meds, and he should be just fine. I'll relax when we see for ourselves that he's okay. We'll head over to the hospital this afternoon."

"We can't go now?"

She shook her head. "No, Eric wants Tim to get some rest, so he's asked us to wait until later this afternoon to visit. It not a bad thing. It gives us time to retrace our steps. Tim must have handled something with pesticide on it, and we've got to find it."

"Do you think our food and water is contaminated?" Neil ran a hand over his bearded cheek.

"I don't think so. Unless Tim ate something we didn't."

Neil shook his head. "I made the same sandwich for all of us. I don't think I saw him eat anything else except some fruit. Maybe a chocolate bar or two."

"And we all ate the same dinner." She leaned her elbows against her thighs and stared at the flames. "Dr. Keenan thinks there's a pesticide spill out here somewhere. Tim must have touched something that was contaminated. But I don't remember him going off alone, do you?"

"Nope. Except..." His hands tightened around his mug. "He was the one who checked to see if that woman was alive. Maybe she had pesticide on her clothes or on her skin."

"Maybe. But I touched her too, remember?"

Instead of a reply, he stared down at his coffee, his thumb tracing the edge of the mug's handle. His gaze shifted from the mug to the fire pit. "I can't stop thinking about her," he said quietly. "If we'd gone out when we heard the gunshot, we might have found Elizabeth in time."

The same disturbing thought had flashed through her mind time and again. She kneeled in front of the fire pit and poked at a log, pushing it deep into the orange blaze. Wet with morning dew, the wood sizzled and spat, spewing grey smoke skyward. Her breath quickened, and she turned away from the fire toward Neil.

"Maybe we should have investigated. Arson, then a gunshot from what sounded like the same area," she said, her voice gentle. "But Neil, we could have searched for hours and never gone to that creek. Never gone into that mine. We couldn't have saved her."

Only the crackle of firewood answered. She sat down in her chair, quiet, waiting for him to speak. But he simply stared at the flames.

Finally, he broke the silence. "Deep down, I guess I know that." He turned to her, his blue eyes sad. "But she was one of us, you know? A geologist out here doing her job."

"I know," she softly said. "We half expect to fall off a mountainside or plunge to our death in a mine adit. But murder?" Her arms swept wide. "Out here? It's not something I've ever considered."

Until two nights ago. She pushed the disturbing thought away. Arms hugged tight to her chest, she turned to Neil.

"I don't know what's going on up here, but if there's a pesticide spill, we have to find it."

"What about the creek?" Neil asked. "Tim filled his water bottle there after we saw that dude. I still had a full bottle of water from camp. What about you?"

"Same, I think." She tried to remember if she had refilled one of her water bottles during their long hike out to the road. "But I didn't see Tim drink any of it, did you?"

"Only one way to find out." Neil jumped up and bolted for the tent he shared with Tim.

She scrambled to her feet and watched him duck through the yellow nylon door. Fingers tapping the side of her mug, she shifted from one foot to the other.

When Neil pushed through the doorway, he waved a blue water bottle high in the air. "His water bottle is empty," he shouted.

"Get your gear, Neil. We're going back to that creek."

40

JESS SIPPED AT her third cup of coffee rereading newspaper articles that refused to sink in. She glanced up at the clock. Eight thirty. Normally, at this time of morning, she'd be preparing for her first mortgage client of the day. But after a sleepless night, she'd emailed the bank manager, asking that all of her appointments be cancelled.

Another glance at the clock. Liv had left more than an hour ago for an early-morning volleyball practice. To delay any longer wasted precious time.

She eased her body, stiff from sitting, out of the kitchen chair and crept up the stairs to Liv's bedroom, all the while fighting the urge to retreat. Long ago, she'd promised herself that she would never invade her daughter's privacy. As a teenager, Jess had been crushed to learn that her mother had read her diary. It had tainted their relationship for years afterward, and Jess vowed that she would never do the same to her daughter.

Yet here she was in front of Olivia's closed bedroom door.

She took a deep breath and turned the door handle. The smell of Olivia's favourite cologne greeted her as the door swung open. The musky scent, a gift from a boy this past Christmas, couldn't have been more different from the light floral fragrance Jess had always given her. It was yet another signal of her daughter's all too rapid passage into adulthood.

Jess resisted the urge to pick up the dirty clothes lying on the floor as she eased into the room. She could leave no evidence of her search.

Where to start?

The empty spot on the crowded desktop meant that Olivia had taken her notebook computer with her to school. It was just as well. Although Jess took pride in her computer skills, breaking into Liv's notebook wasn't something she'd attempt. If it came to that, she'd ask Nate to find an expert to handle the job.

She opened the top drawer of the dresser feeling beside and beneath the crumpled clothing stored there. Her hand touched a small box, and she took it from its hiding spot. Inside were several pieces of jewellery Liv had inherited from Jess's mother.

Her fingers caressed the pearl brooch her mother had worn only on special occasions. Although she'd seen Olivia wear one of the necklaces from time to time, this brooch and the other antique pieces had probably never left the box.

A thorough search of the remaining drawers revealed nothing, and she turned her attention to the closet. When she saw the shelf above the clothing bar crammed with stacks of boxes, she blew out a loud breath. It would take forever to go through all of them.

Reaching up on tiptoes, she pulled down one of the boxes and took it over to the bed, where she removed the lid. A photo of Liv and one of her friends at the beach sat on top of a jumbled pile of photos and letters. She picked out an envelope, turning it carefully as she looked for a return address. But there was nothing other than Liv's name and address on the envelope, written in small, tight letters.

Her breath caught in her throat as she eased the pages from the envelope. Unfolding the crisp paper, she quickly scanned the first lines. Her body relaxed when she recognized a simple letter from a friend sent while away on holiday. An innocent keepsake. What had she expected to find? No doubt the remaining boxes held more of the same. Mementos of events important to a teenager.

Returning the box to the closet shelf, she stared at the mess of clothes and shoes on the floor. She dug her hands deep into the pile of clothes in the corner of the closet and hit something solid.

With both hands, she threw sweaters and jeans onto the bedroom floor. She grabbed the handles of the black duffel and half-dragged it onto the bedroom floor. Her heart racing, she pulled back the zipper.

A low moan escaped her lips as she collapsed onto her knees. One hand pressed hard against her mouth, she stared into the bag. Tears streamed down her face, wiped away with the back of her hand.

"No! Olivia, what have you done."

Even during her daughter's rebellious early teen years, there'd never been even a hint of underage drinking or drugs. Liv had a good head on her shoulders. Her friends seemed the same.

Except for Michael Walden.

She'd met Michael Walden only once. A polite boy, shy even. Skates slung over his shoulder by knotted laces, a hockey stick in hand, the handsome teen had stood at the front door while Liv made a dash to her room to finish getting ready. They'd chatted about his favourite hockey team and who might go on to win the Stanley Cup. With his broad smile and easy laugh, she understood why Liv liked the boy. But everything changed when she asked him about his plans after graduation. His face serious, he announced that he intended to stay in Nelson to fight against the dams.

His answer left her speechless, shocked. Nate had told her of the growing involvement of young people in the protests, but Michael was a teenager, still in high school. Just as she was about to ask how his parents felt about his decision, Liv thundered down the stairs. In another moment, they were gone and she was left staring at the front door.

She'd never mentioned the boy's comment to Nate, knowing that her husband would have overreacted. Instead, in the weeks that followed, she'd considered talking to Liv directly. A quiet conversation between mother and daughter. But Liv's focus on school work and excited chatter about university convinced her that the subject was best left alone.

And then Michael died. A life cut too short. She watched Liv closely, fearing her grieving daughter might join the new wave of

protests that surged after the shooting. But other than a certain
sadness that clouded her eyes at times, Liv seemed okay.

Through tears, she stared into the black duffel.

At the bundles of dynamite.

How could I have been so blind?

41

CROUCHED ON THE rocky creek bank, Alex scooped water into a large plastic cup. Both hands on the cup, she turned and slowly poured the water into a small sample bottle that Neil held steady. The last thing either of them needed was to get some of this water on their hands. As it was, Eric feared that she had absorbed pesticide through her skin when she touched Tim last night.

She stood and swiped her sweaty palms against her soft-shell pants before she picked up her rifle. With a tight grip on the gun barrel, she walked downstream until she found the bloodstained rocks. Forensics should have been here by now. *Were they coming at all?*

Yesterday Nathan had promised to send a team to the creek, but had it been said just to satisfy her? If only she'd taken the backpack. She glanced down. Or if she'd left the earring where it lay.

Elizabeth Chambers never stood a chance, alone up here with her back turned to her attacker. Had he watched her from the trees? *Is he watching us now?*

Hand clenched on her rifle strap, she turned to stare at the forest. And even as she did it, she knew her imagination was getting the better of her. But from the way Neil cradled his rifle, she knew that he harboured the same fear.

She dropped her hand to her pocket and pulled out her watch. Her thumb circled the scratched watch face. Eight thirty. Morning here, but already sundown in Tanzania. As soon as they got back to camp, she'd try her dad again. He needed to know about Tim, and she needed to hear his voice.

"We've got lots of time. Let's check out the area between here and the abandoned mine."

"I don't know, Alex." Neil shifted his weight and glanced around. "I don't want to end up in a hospital bed next to Tim."

"Neil, we covered the same ground yesterday, and neither of us got sick, so the pesticide is probably in the water. But maybe a second look around will give us the source. Something we didn't see yesterday."

"I think we would have noticed a patch of dead vegetation. Hell, we hiked the entire length of this creek."

"Sure, but we went downstream. If there's pesticide in the creek, the source would be in the opposite direction."

"Where do you want me to go?" he asked with a stroke of his beard.

"Start here and head upstream, then work your way up the ridge. I'll hike to the mine and work back from there. We'll plan on meeting in about two hours at the top of the ridge."

"Okay. Two hours. Then we head back to camp for lunch. Or better yet, you treat me to some fancy place in Nelson." Neil grinned and hefted his pack onto his shoulder. "And a beer."

She laughed. "Deal."

She dug her boots into the wet grass and started the all-too-familiar hike up the ridge. Her stride quickened as she passed the spot where they'd found the backpack, resisting the urge to stop, knowing that only the forensics team could hope to find anything beneath the boughs.

When she reached the top of the ridge, she turned back to Neil. For a full minute, she watched him, head down, slowly walking the rocky creek bank. She'd had her doubts about his experience in the field, but he'd proved himself already — both men had. Neil would be okay alone.

On her GPS she pulled up the map of the nearby claims. They had no idea what Elizabeth Chambers had been doing out here. Although the geologist could have been sent out here by the Ministry of Environment, her government job gave no motive for her murder. But a rich silver claim was another story.

If the geologist had been scouting out the Donnovan properties, their pesticide spill could lie in one of those claims. It was a long shot, but she cinched her waist belt tight and set off on a path that would take her through a pair of Baxter's properties. A path that would also give her what could be her only look at the old silver claims.

But by the time she neared the abandoned mine entrance an hour later, sweaty and tired, she'd all but given up on that theory. She'd seen no evidence of deadly pesticide in the healthy vegetation and underbrush. Nor had she found a single silver-bearing rock in the outcrops.

She glanced up at the yellow police tape strung across the rock slit opening. This mine wasn't one of Baxter's, but in its day, it had steadily produced silver. And this was probably her only chance to check it out.

Slowly, she climbed up to the mine. At the threshold to the mine entrance, she stared into the darkness. Before she lost her nerve, she ducked under the yellow tape and into the cool interior.

From her pocket she fished out her flashlight. In its narrow beam she saw no evidence of the police investigators who'd filled this tight space yesterday. She tried to remember how far she'd gone into the adit. Exactly where they'd found the body.

She swept the beam of light across the rocky floor. Any evidence of the woman had been taken away. Nothing remained.

Hand on the rough rock walls, she searched for ribbons of white quartzite, but she knew she'd have to go much deeper to find the silver-bearing rock the miners had followed. The vertical entrance to the mine probably wasn't much further. Likely, it had been boarded up or plugged with boulders long ago but she couldn't be sure. To fall into an open entrance in the floor would mean certain death.

The faint sound of a voice caught her ear. *Neil!*

She scrambled down the hill, back in the direction of the creek. Once on the flat, she thundered toward the creek. It seemed forever before she caught sight of the young geologist. When she was within earshot, she yelled out.

"What did you find?"

"Silver!"

42

HE TIGHTENED THE straps of the respirator that bulged from his face, sending its rubber edges deep into the skin of his forehead and cheeks. With gloved hands, he pushed the nozzle of the hose into the narrow throat of the waist-high glass container. This part of the process presented the most danger. Required the most patience.

He'd poured too fast when he'd filled one of the earliest of these carboys. The toxic chemical had spurted out of the bottle, drenching his leather gloves before it splashed against his long, rubber apron. Only pure luck had kept the poison from his skin.

One hand gripped around the hose, he cranked the handle on the rotary hand pump. Clear, amber-coloured liquid from the fifty-gallon barrel splashed against the flat glass bottom of the carboy. Each slow turn of the handle sent a stream of fluid into the jug-shaped container.

When the liquid reached the neck of the two-hundred litre bottle, he let go of the handle. He counted off ten breaths, sucked heavy and loud through the filters of the respirator. Only then, when he was sure all liquid had drained from the hose, did he pull the rubber tube from the carboy. He submerged the nozzle into a water-filled pail and reached down for the container's rubber cap.

He twisted the cap tight onto the bottle and grabbed a large label from the floor. It took three tries for him to peel the backing off the adhesive label with his gloved hands. Knees on the floor, he centred the apple concentrate label with its nonexistent fruit orchard logo onto the bottle. A computer-generated fiction that so far had passed inspection.

Bottle clutched against his rubber apron, he carried the carboy a few feet to an empty spot on the lowest shelf. Sixty bottles, filled over the past three days, stood like sentries on the steel wire shelving installed along one wall of the workshop. And there was still much work to do.

None of this would have been necessary if the pesticide, purchased in Korea, could have been shipped directly to the United States. But after weeks of discreet inquiries failed to turn up someone who could ease the banned product into the States, he'd been forced to consider other points of entry. An exorbitant fee paid to a Hong Kong man with an inside contact at the Port of Vancouver, British Columbia, solved his problem. And a shipping container filled with three hundred barrels of the hazardous concentrate quietly slipped into Canada.

But it left him with the problem of transporting the pesticide over the Canada-U.S. border. One look at a truckload of skull-and-cross-bone-labelled pesticide barrels would be enough for border agents to stop his U.S.-bound shipment. The chemical needed to be repackaged. Disguised.

He'd searched for a warehouse in Surrey, south of Vancouver, just thirty minutes north of the Peace Arch crossing into Washington State. But a cash arrangement with an unseen tenant proved impossible. And so his own farm became the only choice.

Four long, uneventful trips along the avalanche-prone highway that wound through the Rocky Mountains in an eighteen-foot cargo van. Each ending in the military-controlled Slocan Valley.

The first time he'd been forced to stop at a roadblock just outside of Nelson, he fought down panic. But the soldiers accepted his phony paperwork and gave only a cursory glance at the hazardous chemical barrels crowded into the back of his truck. In their shortsightedness, they searched only for the obvious: bombs and weapons. And so he freely passed.

Blind fools, all of them.

He rolled an empty glass container into place beside the pesticide barrel, ready to start the filling process again. With the nozzle carefully inserted into the narrow neck of the bottle, he cranked the handle on the pump. Amber liquid gushed into the clear container, splashing hard against the sides and bottom.

Gently, gently.

By tomorrow, he'd be done and this elaborate workshop would be dismantled. The cavernous space bore little resemblance to the studio in which his wife had spent so much of her time. Wooden cabinets, emptied of glass-making supplies, had been torn out to make way for an industrial ventilation system. All but two of the windows were boarded up, buried behind heavy steel shelves. Light now came solely from rows of fluorescent lights, hung on cables from the fifteen-foot-high ceilings. And the workbench where Diane had once created her small works of art now held his computer.

He jerked the pump handle, startled by the chirp of an incoming call. Pesticide splashed up from surface of the pool of liquid in the bottle. He jumped back, hand gripped hard around the nozzle. But the toxic chemical failed to reach the top of the narrow opening.

Shit!

Chest heaving, he waited for his pounding heart to slow. His eyes darted to the computer sitting on the workbench. To the distraction that could have proved fatal.

Dylan? Few others knew how to reach him here.

In the dark days after Michael's death, Dylan had reached out to him. At first, the boy had shared stories of his high-school years with Michael, but as time passed, their conversations turned to politics. And they discovered a common enemy. The Americans.

Dylan brought others to him, all of them young and foolish. They wanted to bomb more dams. Continue Michael's work. As though their puny efforts would drive the Americans across the border. They were more likely to end up dead. Like Michael. And the American soldiers would remain.

He'd finally convinced them that only their own Arab Spring would work. That protests in places like Vancouver, Calgary and Toronto did nothing to force the Canadian government to listen to their demands. They needed to up the ante. Only widespread violence would force the Canadian government to end their joint military action with the Americans.

War.

His lips curled into a tight smile. His little soldiers, so eager to fight. They had no idea they were nothing more than pawns and their attacks were a diversion for his deadly U.S.-bound cargo.

A bright blue flash of light from the computer screen caught his eye. *A message.* He stared at the half-filled bottle at his feet. The message could wait. Head down, he cranked the handle slowly.

Sweat dripped into his eyes, and he blinked back its salty sting. He shook his head to clear the tears that pooled along the inside edge of his plastic lenses and caught the flash of blue out of the corner of his eye.

He ran his tongue over dry lips. There'd been a few mistakes with the library bombing, but his minions had executed the next three attacks with military precision. Still, every mission was different. And this one was their most critical.

He forced himself to ignore the message light, instead watching the amber liquid rise inch by inch. When the poison finally reached the throat of the bottle, he jerked his hand free of the pump handle and plunged the hose nozzle into the bucket of water.

Rubber boots soundless on the cement floor, he half-ran to the workbench. One gloved hand hovered over the keyboard. It would be so easy to reach down and open the message. He yanked his hand away.

Discipline. He snatched a rubber cap and label from the workbench and hurried back to the filled bottle.

He twisted the cap tight against the glass and ripped off his gloves as he rushed back to the workbench. Bent over the keyboard, he pounded out his password and then clicked open the message. His fist slammed against the bench.

Olivia.

43

"CAN WE STOP somewhere so I can get some coffee?" Neil asked.

They'd spent far too long back at the creek, hunting for thick silver-banded rocks like the one Neil had found — especially after her GPS put the find in a mining property next to one of Baxter's, a property open for claim. And now that they were Nelson-bound, she was loathe to stop, but her need for caffeine won out.

"Good idea. There should be something along this stretch of highway. Keep an eye out."

A few minutes later, Neil pointed out a café on the other side of the road, and she turned into the crowded parking lot. They climbed the worn stairs to a glass-topped door from which an open sign hung. A bell chimed when they pushed open the door, but no one paid any attention. Instead, they were greeted by the low hum of conversation and the smell of eggs and bacon mixed with the aroma of coffee.

"Smells good. Are you sure you just want coffee?" Alex asked.

"Positive." Neil grinned and rocked back on his heels. "I'm holding out for that fancy lunch."

A lone waitress, her grey hair held in a tight bun at the back of her head, swerved between closely set tables with a pot of coffee. Only after she ducked behind the counter and plopped the half-empty empty carafe onto a burner did she greet them.

"Nothing free right now." She wiped her hands down the front of her stained apron and tucked a strand of hair into place. "A table might come open in ten minutes or so if you want to wait."

"Just some coffee to go, please," Alex said with a smile.

The woman emptied the last of her coffee into two Styrofoam cups and snapped on plastic lids. She slid the cups onto the glass counter in front of Alex.

"That'll be six dollars even."

Alex dug out a ten-dollar bill from her wallet and set it in the wrinkled outstretched hand. When the waitress stepped over to the cash register, Neil leaned in close.

"Alex, the dude from the creek," he whispered. "I think he's over by the window with his back to us. Sitting across from a girl with long blonde hair."

In an instant, she spotted the man sitting at the table near the corner of the room. The same red jacket. The buzz cut. Neil could be right. Whatever he and the young woman were discussing, it looked serious. The girl looked up at her, perhaps aware of a stranger's stare. Alex quickly dropped her head.

"It's him, isn't it?" Neil whispered.

"Maybe, but I can't be sure," she said.

And what if it is?

She grabbed the change the waitress offered and picked up the coffee cups. Turning away from the counter, she headed for the front door of the café, Neil following at her heels.

"There's something about this dude, Alex."

"Agreed. We'll wait out here until we see him leave. If nothing else, it will give us a better look at him," she said. "And I want to know that the girl isn't going with him. For all we know, he lured Elizabeth Chambers to that creek."

They sat in the truck drinking their coffee in silence, their eyes focused on the café entrance. The man they waited for pushed through the door and started down the stairs.

"There he is," she quietly said. "And he's alone. Good."

Neil jammed his coffee cup into the console holder and pressed his hands against the dash. "It's him, I know it!" he practically shouted.

The man stepped into the parking lot and headed straight for them.

"Shit. What if he's parked next to us?" She jerked her head toward Neil. "Pick up your cup! Keep your eyes on me! Please, please don't let him be parked next to us."

Would he recognize us? He couldn't have caught more than a glimpse of them before he'd disappeared into the trees near the creek. Still.

She longed to turn but didn't dare. Not until she heard the slam of a truck door. It took only a moment for her to find the man sitting in the driver's seat of a gleaming red truck parked on the other side of the lot.

"Damn. There's too much mud on the truck ... I can't get the license-plate number. I'm going to follow him." She rammed her coffee cup into the console holder.

"Are you crazy?"

"If we can give Nathan an address, maybe he'll at least check this guy out."

"Okay. I'm in," Neil said. "But we need to stay as far behind him as we can."

Her finger hovered over the ignition button. Only after their mystery man turned south onto the highway did she start her vehicle.

Several cars now stood between them and their prey. Foot hard on the gas pedal, she sped past the RV in front of her.

"Don't get too close," Neil said.

"I won't. But we can't get too far behind him either."

Up ahead, she saw the red truck turned off the highway onto a side road on the left. She slowed and then made the same turn but pulled over immediately.

"He's going to know we're following him if we head any further down this road. There isn't much out here," she said.

"Then we'll have to follow him on foot."

Eyebrows raised, she said, "Okay. That sounds like something I'd say."

He grinned. "Too much time together, I guess. But we can't quit now. This dude may have killed that woman."

"You don't have to convince me. Take your rifle and backpack, and let's go."

They set a fast pace, the crunch of gravel under their boots the only sound. On either side of the road stood massive conifers, their trunks and lower branches barely visible in the dense bramble of shrubs. They were gaining elevation, but the narrow road snaked a path that suggested it kept to the low ground below Kokanee Glacier Park.

At every curve in the road, Alex tightly gripped her rifle and pressed her back into the trees, afraid they might come face-to-face with their prey.

The greens and browns of the forest were broken by a small patch of bright blue on their left, deep within the trees. She stepped as quietly as possible toward the side of the road, Neil close beside her. The dense tree boughs offered only a glimpse of a house.

I have to get closer.

Handing her rifle to Neil, she grabbed the soft new growth of needles on a large branch of a spruce tree and pulled it hard to one side. Using her free hand, she pushed at another bough and squeezed her body into the trees. Surrounded now by fragrant spruce and fir trees, she jerked her head between the branches first one way and then another until she finally found a clear line of sight.

Twisted metal and assorted trash salvaged from a garbage dump lay next to a ramshackle shed cobbled together from scraps of wood and rusted tin. And beside it a beat-up, rusty old green truck.

Alex backed out of the trees to the road and whispered to Neil. "Not our guy."

They stepped carefully along the road side, hugging the trees. Up ahead, the trees opened up to give a glimpse of a two-storey house.

"Come on. We'll have to cross over," she said.

They scooted across the road and squeezed themselves against the trees. One careful step at a time, they inched forward until the house came into full view.

The small, tan-painted wooden house with its white-trimmed windows and door was fronted by a tidy yard protected by a line of trees on either side. Alex could see one end of a greenhouse extending out from behind the house as well as a barn.

"No sign of a truck, but I don't see a driveway either. Must be on the other side of the house," she said.

"If we take off our packs and leave the rifles, we might just be able to squeeze through the bush on this side of the road. Otherwise, we risk being seen when we cross in front of the house," Neil said.

"It's worth a try."

She set down her rifle and slipped off her backpack. It was one thing to give up her rifle to Neil, quite another to leave it behind. But as she glanced around, she knew that squeezing through the dense underbrush was their best option. The weapons would have to be left behind.

From her backpack, she pulled out her binoculars before tucking the pack and her gun underneath the bottom bough of a fir tree. They pushed their way into the thick tangle of shrubs and branches, their transit through the underbrush slow and noisy. Too noisy for her liking.

The gravel driveway came into view. A red pickup truck was parked next to the house.

Bingo.

A door slammed. She trained her binoculars on the driveway, straining to see through the trees to the front door of the house, but a large white moving truck blocked her view.

"Neil, can you see anybody?" she whispered.

"Nobody. Could be around back."

"I'm going to see if I can get in any closer."

"What? Not a good idea."

But Alex had already left the safety of the trees.

She kept low as she crossed the road and headed for the densely treed area to the right of the driveway. Dropping to one knee, she looked through her binoculars. From her new position, she could see the front half of the property, but nothing more. She caught sight of a flash of red as a man emerged from the narrow sidewalk running between the house and driveway.

He turned and stared in her direction.

Knuckles white, she gripped the binoculars hard in shaking hands.

He crossed the driveway and walked toward her.

He's seen me!

Fighting down panic, she kept the binoculars trained on his lined face. His green eyes.

The man turned and headed for a door in what looked like a garage, but it lacked the trademark vehicle-wide door. And then he was gone. Through the door and into the building.

Alex didn't hesitate. She took the opportunity to run back across the road to Neil's hiding spot.

"It's him, right?"

"I'd bet money on it." She settled into the bushes beside Neil, her breathing heavy. "Same hair. Same build. Same age."

"You're lucky he didn't see you."

"I know. But he didn't. And now we know it's him." Looking at Neil's face, she could see his fear. Fear she'd caused.

Turning away, she brought her binoculars up and scanned the area between the front door of the building and the sidewalk.

"Could you see what was in the building he went into?"

"No windows in the front of the building."

The front door to the building opened, and she ducked. She inched up enough to see the man throw a backpack into the front passenger seat before he climbed into the truck. And through the vehicle's front windshield, she could just make out the angled barrel of a rifle.

The engine roared to life.

They ducked deep into the underbrush. When he turned from the driveway onto the gravel road, dust filled her nostrils and she squeezed her eyes shut. They were too close to the road.

The truck past them and sped down the road. When the sound of his tires told them he was far from where they hid, they emerged from the bushes.

"Did you see that?" Neil asked. "He's got a rifle with him."

"I saw it." She shifted from one foot to the other. "I'd like to get a closer look at what's inside that building he went into."

"Are you crazy?" Neil gasped. "This dude could be back any time. And there could be somebody else in there."

They hadn't seen any lights or movement from the house, but that didn't mean either building sat empty.

"He wasn't in that building very long. Not long enough to talk to somebody. And we could knock on the door. Ask for directions if someone answers," she rattled on, not giving Neil a chance to argue. "If no one's home, we're fine. He'll be gone at least a half an hour, probably longer."

"What're we going to find that'll change anything?"

"If we want Nathan to bring this guy in for questioning, then we need evidence. I don't expect to find the dead woman's backpack, if that's what you mean." She stared past him at the windowless building. "But we might find pesticide."

"Pesticide? You think he poisoned the creek?"

"I don't know what to think." She turned back to Neil. "I know Nathan thinks that Elizabeth Chambers was killed near the mine, but I still believe she was shot at the creek. The same creek we suspect is loaded with pesticide. Maybe somebody else figured that out, and the ministry sent Elizabeth out to test the water."

"Man, I don't know about this." Neil tugged at his beard. "This is one dude I don't want to come face-to-face with."

"Neither do I. We'll be quick. I'll cross over and knock on the door. If there's no answer, I'll wave, and you join me with the rifles."

44

ALEX TOOK AN extra clip of bullets out of her pack, dropping it into her jacket pocket. She also pocketed her flare gun and an extra flare. Just in case.

Try to look natural, she told herself as she crossed the road to the farmhouse. She tucked her hair up under her ball cap. Two days without a shower, and she probably looked it. A fake smile pasted on her face, she slowly climbed the cement stairs and rang the doorbell.

Other than the echo of the doorbell chime from within the house, she heard nothing. She tried the bell again and waited for approaching footsteps that never came.

She signalled to Neil. He came at a run and joined her at the sidewalk that led to the greenhouse behind the house.

"I didn't hear a thing. There's no TV or radio on."

She glanced back over her shoulder. Still no one at the door.

"Any sign of the truck?" she asked in a voice barely above a whisper.

"Nope. He's long gone."

"Okay. Let's head to the back."

They crept down the narrow sidewalk. She aimed her rifle at the back door when they rounded the corner at the end of the house.

Nothing moved.

She pointed to the greenhouse, and the two of them ran across the grassy yard to the greenhouse door. Neil pulled down on the levered handle, smiling at her when it moved freely. They were in.

Rows of orderly plants greeted them. It looked like a small commercial operation, maybe a family-run business of some sort. She didn't know much about gardening. Every now and again, she'd buy a tomato plant in a container and place it out on her balcony. It would do fine for a while, but then she would be on the road again, and the poor thing would wither from lack of water.

Here, all of the plants looked well-tended. They were in various stages of development; some, like the cucumbers, looked almost ready to pick. A few of the larger plants were paired with beautiful coloured glass watering bulbs. She'd purchased a few of these for her houseplants, trying to coax them to flourish under her random watering schedule. Though similar in size and shape, these were unlike anything she'd ever seen. With their patterns of swirling colours and intricate designs, they were small pieces of art.

In the centre of the greenhouse sat a narrow wooden bench, the top of which was completely clear except for a few hand tools standing upright in a small metal bucket and a watering can. Beneath the bench stood large labelled plastic containers, each with a hinged lid.

"I've got bone meal, dolomite and alfalfa. No pesticides," she said.

"Nothing but empty pots and dirt over here."

"Let's try the other building," she said.

Through the glass, she checked the yard and the driveway as they retraced their steps to the greenhouse door.

"Anything out your side?" she asked.

"Nada. The place is deserted."

Rifle slung over her shoulder, Alex used both hands to ease the greenhouse door shut. They ran across the yard to the rear of the large wooden building that filled much of the property.

Crouched low, they inched toward the lone window centred on the back wall. When they reached the edge of the window, she raised her head just high enough to see into the dimly lit interior of the building.

Empty.

She stood and with her hand cupped above her eyes pressed into the windowpane.

"It looks like some sort of workshop, but there's not much equipment. What do you think?" she asked when Neil joined her.

"Man, this is the cleanest workshop I've ever seen. There's nothing out on the workbench except a computer. You notice all of the tools are mounted on pegboard? Who does that?" he asked.

"You see the heavy-duty wire shelving on the wall across from the kitchen? Whatever was stored there is gone. Maybe that's what the moving truck is all about."

"There's some sort of storage unit on this wall next to the window, but all I can see is the side of it," Neil said.

She turned her head, pressing her cheek to the window. "Same on this side." Her fingertips squeezed beneath the window pane, she tried to lift it. "Doesn't open. And I don't see any other windows along the other walls."

"That's weird. What do you think he uses this place for?" he asked.

"No idea. But it would help if we could get a closer look. Let's try the door out front."

Neil led the way up the sidewalk with her at his heels. When he reached the driveway, he stopped.

Without a word or a look back at her, he broke into a run. He pulled his rifle from his shoulder strap as he crossed the driveway, holding it low and close to his body.

She gripped her rifle with both hands and stepped out into the driveway after him. Her eyes darted left and right.

He saw something. But what?

Breathless at the unexpected sprint, she dropped to the ground next to their packs.

"What did you see?" she asked.

"Nothing. All of a sudden, I just got this feeling. Like we were being watched. I bolted."

She blew out a loud breath. A race for cover because he had a *feeling*? Lips pressed into a thin line, she turned away from him. She couldn't blame him. The whole place gave her the creeps, but she couldn't put her finger on why.

"Well, you scared the shit out of me."

"My bad." Neil's slender fingers pulled at his beard.

His blue eyes begged for forgiveness, and she was quick to let him off the hook. "We're both on edge. It's not like we break and enter every day." Her eyes darted to the steel building. "Can't say it's helped us figure out what's going on."

"Maybe he's growing weed. I saw an exhaust fan outlet near the back window. Looks like a heavy-duty ventilation system set-up," Neil said.

"It might explain the lack of windows. But if he's growing marijuana, we should have seen some equipment. Plant trays, grow lights. That kind of thing."

"There's lots of that sort of stuff in the greenhouse. Maybe he moves it around."

She shook her head. "It just doesn't look like the kind of set-up I'd expect from a grow-op. That workshop is definitely used for something special, though. I just don't know what." She ground the toe of her boot into the grass. "We need to get in there."

"Go back? You really want to do this again?" Fear burned in his eyes.

"It won't take long. We'll do a quick search of the workshop. Check out those storage units. Maybe get a peek at that computer."

"Alex, there's only one door. If he comes back while we're in there, we'll get caught."

"I'll go alone. You stay here and watch for him. You can signal me if he shows up."

"Don't, Alex." He shook his head. "There's something about this dude. We don't want to mess with him.

She turned back toward the farmhouse and its odd workshop. Her every instinct screamed that this man was somehow responsible for putting Tim in the hospital. And the proof was in that workshop.

But Neil is right. A search was too risky.

"Okay. Let's go."

She slung her rifle over her shoulder and turned her back on their only lead.

45

ERIC POURED STEAMING coffee into an oversized blue mug. "Coffee for you?"

Nathan Taylor shook his head. Eric added a generous splash of milk to his drink before he led the cop over to the worn leather chairs that filled more than half of the empty doctors' lounge.

"Are you going to tell me why I'm here?" Nathan asked.

Eric had been so sure that this was the right thing to do when he'd made the call. When he disobeyed a direct order from his boss. Now, as he sat in a chair across from Nate, he second-guessed his decision.

He sipped his coffee under Nate's watchful stare. The official lab report on the pesticide-laced juice would be ready later today. But there was no way to predict Callaway's reaction to this evidence. No way to know if his boss would continue to stonewall until Laura Bennett's autopsy results were in. *I won't risk it.*

"There was a young geologist admitted last night with suspected pesticide poisoning," he said.

"Where did he come into contact with the pesticide?" Nathan asked.

There was no way to keep Alex out of this conversation. He plunged ahead.

"Alex Graham, his boss, is trying to figure it out."

"Alex Graham? Short woman with brown hair?" When Eric nodded Nate continued. "I met her yesterday. Your patient was with her? What's his name?"

"Tim Munroe."

"Sure, I remember him. He looked perfectly fine when I saw him. You say you treated him. Is he going to be okay?"

"I think so. We're watching him closely, but it looks good."

Eric set his mug on the low table next to his chair. Fingers intertwined, he leaned forward and spoke in a low voice.

"The thing is, he isn't the first. Another patient, Laura Bennett, came into the ER twice this past week. First visit, she complained of vomiting and diarrhea, so I gave her fluids and treated her nausea before sending her home. A couple of days later she came back, this time with breathing difficulties too. Before I could figure it out, she died."

He stared at his hands, working one thumb over the other. He glanced up at the door as another white-coated doctor entered, and she gave him a quick nod. At least it wasn't Callaway. There'd be hell to pay if the chief of staff walked in and saw Eric here with Nate. He could lie, of course. Say that he and the RCMP constable were talking about another case, but he was sure Callaway wouldn't believe him.

"Before you figured what out, Eric?"

There's no turning back. Hands tightly clasped, he took a deep breath before he answered.

"Pesticide poisoning."

"Suicide?"

"It's a possibility. But I don't think so. And there were no pesticides at her house."

"You went to her house?"

He reached for his coffee, stalling for time, not wanting to involve Alex, but knowing he had no choice.

"Not me. Alex."

"And Alex Graham is involved in this case, how?"

"She isn't." He shook his head. "Well, she is. But only because I asked for her help."

"I don't understand."

His fingers tightened against the ceramic mug. "I needed answers fast, and she offered to take some water samples at Bennett's house. She sent everything to a private Vancouver lab she trusts."

"What not use the government lab?"

"They take forever." He set his untouched coffee on the table. "And I was reminded that the request would get the army's attention."

"I get it." Nate held up his hands. "No point inviting trouble in before you have to. So when do you expect to have the report?"

"I know they found an organophosphate pesticide in a sample of apple juice, but there's no official report yet. And until the autopsy results come back, we can't say for sure that Bennett died of pesticide poisoning."

Nathan pulled a black notebook and a pen from his pocket and flipped to an empty page. "Okay, so now, there's a second victim. This young geologist. What's his connection to Bennett?"

"That's just it. Tim Munroe couldn't be connected to Laura Bennett. He arrived here after Bennett died. But he's the third victim, not the second." He ran his hand through his hair. "Do you know Gary Barlow? He runs the Co-op." Eric waited for Nate's nod. "He came in the same morning Laura Bennett died with enough symptoms of organophosphate poisoning for me to treat him with the antidote."

"Is he okay?"

"Seems to be just fine. I sent him to the hospital in Trail, but they released him the next day. Here's the thing. His wife Melissa never did get sick, and none of the samples from their home tested positive for pesticide."

"So Barlow must have been at Bennett's house. Maybe an affair?"

He shook his head. "Gary? No way. He says he delivered some groceries to her, but that's all. He's devoted to Melissa."

"You'd be surprised at the people who cheat."

"Sure, but if Gary's covering up a relationship with Laura Bennett, it's a professional one. She was a psychologist. People don't like to admit they need that kind of help. But it doesn't explain our young geologist. He certainly didn't know Bennett."

"Was the geologist near Bennett's house? Maybe there's a local-ized spill?"

"You'd have to ask Alex to be sure, but I think she's working a long way from where Laura Bennett lived. And if there's a spill, we should be seeing more patients in the ER. To tell you the truth, I'm not quite sure what's going on here."

"If you can treat people who drink this stuff, then this isn't really much of a problem, is it?" Nate asked.

"If we know what kind of pesticide a patient's been exposed to then there are antidotes we can use. For an organophosphate, 2-PAM is the obvious treatment."

He quietly watched Nate scribble notes in handwriting that was even less legible than his own scrawl.

"Okay." Nate tapped his pen against the ink-filled page. "So as long as people get to the hospital, they'll be fine."

"Not exactly. The symptoms are very characteristic, so it's easy enough to diagnose. But we don't keep much 2-PAM here at the hospital. We had just one dose on-hand last night, and I used it on Tim Munroe."

He'd been lucky Kelly Markham had ordered a dose of 2-PAM to restock the hospital pharmacy.

"But you can get more."

He nodded. "We can get more. I had to do that once already." He drew in a deep breath. "But how much more do we get? What if these two locations are part of a large spill? Or the first wave of a terrorist attack? Even if we have enough 2-PAM on hand, children, the elderly and people with preexisting medical conditions might not recover. We're going to start seeing deaths."

"And people are going to panic," Nathan said, completing the thought.

"I hate to say it, but we might be lucky the U.S. Army is here. Not only can they help treat patients, they probably have a store of 2-PAM and the other drugs I need."

"Why?"

"Because organophosphates are nerve agents. Think sarin or Agent Orange. Chemical warfare. The U.S. Army keeps a supply of anticholinergic drugs like 2-PAM on hand to treat soldiers who may be exposed. The Canadian army too, I suppose, but the Americans will have more on hand."

"Christ. Just when I think things can't get any worse around here. We need to find out how Munroe was exposed." Nathan snapped his notebook closed and hoisted his large frame out of the chair. "Is he well enough to answer some questions?"

46

HE SLID THE box onto the only empty spot on the counter he could find. As always, the receiving area of the Sunlight Co-op was crammed with boxes of produce harvested from too many Slocan Valley farms to count. But unlike most of his visits, he stood alone on this side of the counter.

He shifted from one foot to the other, impatient for Gary Barlow to appear from behind the stacked crates.

"Trent! Didn't hear you come in." The clipboard dropped from Gary's hands onto the steel counter with a sharp clatter. "So what do you have for me this week?" The grocer peeked into the box.

"Mostly tomatoes and peppers. A few herbs." Trent Walden stared down at the cement floor. "I've got more boxes out in the truck."

"Great! I'll give you a hand."

"No, I can do it," he said.

But the broad-shouldered grocer waved away his objection and lumbered around the corner of the counter.

Just what I need. Time alone with a man who asked too many questions.

Trent lagged behind, wanting the big man get well ahead of him. But Gary stopped and turned. He waited for Trent to catch up, before they headed together out through the bay doors into the parking lot.

"Quite the thing, that explosion over at the White Building. Went by there today to check things out. The building's in rough shape."

He tuned out the tiring bore's endless report on the explosion. Until a word caught his attention.

"The hospital? It was bombed too?" Trent asked.

"No. No. I said, I was in the hospital — the ER to be exact — when the bomb went off. The one at the White Building. Didn't hear a thing."

Trent popped the tailgate free and climbed into the truck box. "You okay?" Not that he cared, but it might mean he could get rid of the man. "I can unload the truck myself."

Gary waved his hand dismissively. "Lifting a few crates isn't going to kill me. Whatever the doctor gave me worked. Eric Keenan, you know him?" Trent shook his head. "Nice guy. Anyway, I got home yesterday, and I'm supposed to be resting, but I couldn't stand sitting around. Figured I'd come in and get a few things done." Gary rested an elbow on the top of the crate. "Keenan thinks it was pesticide poisoning. Sent me over to Trail and everything."

His grip tightened against the box clutched to his chest. "Pesticide?" He forced out the question.

"Doesn't make sense, does it? Not for a guy who runs an organic grocery."

"So what do you think happened?" he asked in a voice too high. He watched Gary's upturned face, but the man seemed oblivious to his unease.

"No idea. They asked me about a customer of mine named Laura Bennett. Maybe she had the same thing. People are talking…" He shook his head and added softly, "She didn't make it."

So she's dead. He pressed his lips into a tight line, forcing back a smile. In a perfect world, he would have watched her die. *Watch her suffer.*

"She was a nice lady." Gary shoved his hands into the pockets of his jeans and gently rocked back and forth on the balls of his feet. "Came into the store once a week, every Thursday, like clockwork. Always had a smile on her face."

Trent said nothing, waiting for the man to explain how he'd been poisoned.

"Sometimes she brought her dog. Did you ever see him?" Gary didn't pause long enough for an answer. "A beautiful golden retriever. I wonder what will happen to him."

Trent wanted to scream at him. Force him to shut-up about the bitch and her dog. *I need answers!* He ran his sleeve over the sweat beading on his forehead.

"You're not coming down with something, are you?" Gary frowned.

His arm dropped quickly. "No. It's nothing. I'm just warm." He jumped down from the truck and grabbed one of the produce-laden crates from the tailgate.

Gary chuckled. "Reminds me of a joke. Have you heard about the one about the bartender, the pope and the devil?" he asked as he reached for a crate.

The grocer didn't wait for an answer before launching into a story that Trent had heard too many times before. Still, it saved him from conversation for a few minutes. He kept his pace slow and steady, allowing the distance between him and Gary to grow.

He'd followed every rule for handling dangerous chemicals. Accidental transfer of the poison to the vegetables he delivered to the Co-op was impossible.

There can't be a connection.

He stacked the crate on the counter beside the others. Hands stuffed deep into his fleece jacket pockets, he watched Gary write out the last of his receipt.

"You don't use any pesticides up at your place, do you?" Gary asked without looking up.

"No way." He swallowed hard.

"That's what I thought. 'Course, you'd be sick too if you ran into this stuff."

Gary handed him the receipt and rested his palms on the dull metal counter. "Thing is—" He sucked air through his teeth. "Cops asked for a list of our fresh produce suppliers, and your name is on that list."

The cops? Even the mere mention of his name would make him a suspect and deliver more than just cops to his doorstep. There was nothing left at the workshop for them to find, but that didn't mean he wouldn't be interrogated. And they'd definitely have him under surveillance.

"I expect they'll be showing up at your farm in the next day or two. Shouldn't cause you any trouble." Gary chuckled. "Of course, if you were still wearing your hair long and you hadn't shaved off your beard, they might figure you were growing B.C. bud."

"Any idea what kind of pesticide it was?" He tried to sound casual, but his voice, breathy and weak, drew a questioning look.

"Organophosphate. I looked it up and it's nasty stuff. Not the kind of thing an organic farmer like yourself would even consider using."

A farmer? He clenched a fist. Not any more. Not since Diane died.

"You're looking a little pale. Are you sure you're not coming down with something? Do you need some water?" Gary asked.

He shook his head. "I've got to run." A quick turn and he was headed out the door before Gary could say another word.

Almost without stopping, he slammed the tailgate of the truck shut. Hands tight on the steering wheel, his eyes darted up to the rear-view mirror. At the grocer who leaned against the open doorway, watching him.

Shoulders tense, he punched the ignition and threw the truck into reverse. He cranked the steering wheel hard to the right and leaned his foot on the gas pedal before common sense took over and he slowed the truck. He couldn't afford to give the nosy grocer any reason to be suspicious.

Eyes on the rear-view mirror, he gave a weak wave. Then, slowly, he steered the truck through the near-empty parking lot toward the highway exit.

A convoy of northbound Humvees sped past, followed by an RCMP cruiser, its lights flashing. They were headed for the Slocan Valley.

He pounded his hand against the steering wheel. Had Gary really handed over all of his suppliers? Or just one name?

Are they coming for me?

47

"NEIL, TAKE A LOOK at this." Alex pointed at the colourful glass pieces on display in a store window. Now that the creek water sample was on its way to Mark's Vancouver lab, they searched for a restaurant along historic Baker Street in downtown Nelson.

"Don't these look a little like the glass watering bulbs we saw at the greenhouse?" she asked.

"Maybe." He shoved his hands into his pockets. "I didn't pay a lot of attention to them."

"Let's go in. It's probably a wild goose chase, but who knows."

They pushed open the front door and entered a shop filled with an eclectic mix of locally made items. She scanned the shelves and display cabinets scattered throughout the spacious interior for more of the glass artwork.

On top of an antique chest, its open drawers overflowing with silk scarves and other textiles, lay a turquoise necklace that caught her attention. She fingered the blue-green pendant, admiring the silver-work surrounding it. But she pulled her hand away after a quick check of the price tag.

Turning away, she spotted Neil at a promising display near the back of the store. When she joined him, he pointed to a shelf of glass objects similar to the piece they sought. She picked up a small bowl and looked for a name on the bottom, but the scribbled signature was indecipherable.

"That's one of my favourite hand-blown glass bowls," came a voice from behind her. The girl hardly looked old enough to be out of high school, and her outfit, a thigh-skimming skirt and midriff-baring t-shirt, did nothing to convince Alex otherwise.

"I've never seen anything quite like it." Alex turned the bowl in her hand, admiring the luminescent swirl of soft colours and the feathered flow of silver. "Is it made by a local artist?"

The clerk nodded. "A woman by the name of Diane Walden. Isn't it amazing the way the piece changes as you turn it. It reminds me of water. Silver nitrate is used to create the unique colour and pattern."

Alex ran her fingers along one of the bands of colour, following it until it turned from a brilliant sky blue to a deep navy.

"If you like the piece, you should snap it up. Her stuff is pretty popular."

"Does she have a studio near here?" When the clerk bit her glossy lip, Alex quickly added, "Or maybe you have more of her art here in the store?"

"Sorry." She shook her head. "That's the only piece of Diane's art we have, and we won't be getting any more."

"And she doesn't have a studio we can visit?" Alex smiled. "I'd really like to see more of her art."

The young woman's manicured hand adjusted a vase on the shelf before she answered. "Her studio's been shut down." She dropped her gaze. "It's really sad. She committed suicide about a year ago after her son died."

Alex gasped. "How awful!"

"It really is a shame." The clerk smoothed her skirt. "Her husband brought that bowl and a couple of other pieces into the store just a couple of weeks ago. I was a bit surprised. I thought he might want to keep them, a reminder of his wife, you know?" She turned to Neil and smiled. "Men say they aren't sentimental, but deep down they are."

"We saw a plant-watering bulb that looked something like this," Neil said. "Did she make those too?"

"We've never had anything like that in the store," she said with a shake of her head. "Where did you see it?"

"Up near New Denver, at a friend's place," Alex lied. "Maybe a gift from Diane?"

"Could be, I suppose." She fingered a studded earring, barely visible beneath her curly black hair. "I think she lived up that way. Once she mentioned a clinic she worked at, and it wasn't one of the ones in town. She was a nurse, I think. This glass art was sort of a hobby."

"Any idea where the clinic was?"

The girl paused with her finger on her chin, her lips pursed. "Could have been New Denver. But I can't say for sure. I'd try the small glass studio here a few blocks from here. They're more closely connected with the artists in the community, so they might know more about Diane."

"I'll take this bowl." A small price to pay for the identity of the man they hunted. "And there's a turquoise necklace on the dresser over there that I'd like as well."

It was extravagant, especially for a piece she'd likely only wear on a date, something she hadn't had in months.

Outside the store, she said, "Did you hear that? Diane Walden lived near New Denver. I bet that farm is her place. It might explain the workshop." Her eyes shone with excitement. "We need to find out more about her. After lunch, we'll head up to that glass studio."

"This could be our guy. Forget lunch," he said. "That studio can't be too far. We'll pick up some takeout when we're done."

With its display window stocked with decorative art glass and jewellery, the studio wasn't difficult to find. She pushed open the door to the small shop, to be greeted by stifling heat and the roar of a gas/oxygen burner. Her chest tightened at the sight of a white-hot flame and its all-too-familiar smell. As though hypnotized, she stared at the tongue of fire and the man standing impossibly close to it.

"Welcome to our studio."

She spun around at the greeting shouted from the back of the shop. A tall man in his thirties, his long brown hair twisted into a braid, wiped his hands on a rag while he walked toward them.

"Have you ever seen anyone working with glass before?" he asked, smoothing down a perfectly groomed goatee.

Before she could answer, Neil said, "I did a little glass blowing in chemistry lab when I was at university, but that was pretty simple stuff. Mostly just shaping plain glass into small items we needed for experiments."

"Same principle, more or less. We heat the glass to make it fluid, and then it can be molded into just about any shape we want. You blow air into it like a balloon or stretch it thin. That's what Josh is doing right now."

They watched the aproned man in his grey t-shirt pull both ends of a long glass pipe through the glowing flame and then twist the strand of glass.

"You see, just like putty. It can be twisted and bent into just about any shape." He demonstrated with hands scarred by burns.

Her fingers touched her right arm, an arm that would probably carry the same scars. She turned away from the flame to the shelves of glass art along one wall.

"I'm trying to find a glass artist that made a plant-watering bulb I saw. A clerk at one of the downtown gift shops thought you might be able to help."

"Almost anyone who works with glass could make something like that. It's pretty simple. One end is blown into a large balloon shape while the other is left as a slim tube." He shook his head. "The only way you could identify the artist would be through the decorative details on it."

"Well, I have a glass bowl that looks like it might have been made by the same artist."

She pulled her newly purchased bowl out of her backpack. Setting it on the counter, she carefully unwrapped the bowl. The slim man picked up the piece, bringing it up to eye level. Turning it, he examined the entire surface before saying anything.

"This is Diane Walden's work. The woman had a very unique style. You see the way these colours vary and swirl?" he asked, his brown eyes on her. When she nodded, he continued. "Silver compounds in the glass create an unpredictable and most beautiful range of colours as the glass is heated and cooled."

"Silver nitrate is added to the glass?"

"One of the compounds. It makes the glass expensive to buy. Some fools have tried to create their own using leftover bits of silver they find in the mines around here. They heat the silver in nitric acid until it dissolves and then wait for the liquid to evaporate. Presto. Silver nitrate."

"More than a little dangerous," Neil said.

"No kidding. That stuff will burn your skin, and it's corrosive as hell to your eyes and lungs. Stupid to take a risk like that." He shook his head. "Anyway, you wouldn't use expensive glass to make something simple like a watering bulb. And Diane was way too advanced an artist to spend her time making stuff like that anyway."

"We were told that Diane died recently." Her voice soft, she added. "A shame to lose such a talented artist."

"She was one of those genuine people, you know?" His eyes sad, he said, "Always had a smile on her face, really cared about people she met. I guess that's why she went into nursing."

He knew her!

"Any chance you know where she lived?" she asked.

"Why do you want to know where she lived?" he asked in a voice that was no longer friendly. "Are you a reporter or something?"

She knew she'd asked a pushy question, but she didn't expect this reaction.

"A reporter? No," she said with a shake of her head. "We're geologists. I was at a greenhouse in the Valley when I saw the glass watering bulbs. I'm just wondering if she lived nearby." Even to her ears the answer was weak.

"Can't help you." He abruptly turned away and stomped to the back of the studio.

A clear message. Alex rewrapped the bowl and returned it to her backpack before following Neil out the door.

"Boy, things turned chilly in there in a hurry," he said once they were out on the sidewalk.

"You're not kidding. I wonder why he thought we were reporters."

"Must have something to do with her suicide. If there were reporters snooping around, then there are newspaper articles."

"We're close, Neil. I can feel it."

48

THE BLUE LIGHT that flashed on the computer monitor shone like a beacon in the dark workshop. More nonsense from Olivia, no doubt. He slammed the metal door shut behind him. The last thing he needed right now.

Fluorescent light flooded the cavernous space with a rough jerk of the light switch. He tore off his grey fleece jacket and flung it onto the leather chair. He'd spent more than an hour with the stupid girl just this morning. An hour he couldn't afford spent drinking bitter coffee in a crowded café. Hand-holding.

When Dylan had first suggested the cop's daughter to him three months back, he'd planned to reject her outright. But Dylan swore that she could be trusted, and so he'd agreed to meet her.

Rooted in a need to rebel against her cop father and fuelled by Michael's death, the girl's commitment to fight the Americans burned fierce. The perfect pawn, she'd proven loyal, unquestioning. Until now.

His heavy boots pounded the cement floor. *Let Dylan deal with her!* Keep her from panicking and going to the cops. Her father. And if Dylan couldn't do that, then he'd have to kill her.

He jerked to a stop in front of the computer. Blood-red letters scrolled across the locked screen. Not a missed call. A security alert. *Shit!*

His fingers flew across the keyboard, hammering out his password. He brought up the security log and raced through its latest entries.

Sensors had recorded intruders near the house, the greenhouse, and his workshop.

The cops?

Swift keystrokes revealed more details. Only the greenhouse had been breached. The police would have searched the entire property, so it wasn't them.

He ran his hand over his face. Perched on the edge of his stool, he pulled up the camera footage for the greenhouse and hit the play button.

Two people, dressed in civilian clothes, approached the door. He leaned in for a closer look, but their ball caps, pulled low, shielded them from the camera. They went through the door without hesitation. Without force. He shook his head. He'd left the door unlocked. Again.

They didn't turn on the lights, leaving him staring at nothing but their dim outlines. Until their return to the door. The shorter of the two, the one in front, looked up at the camera. He clenched his hand into a fist.

What is that bitch doing here?

Her partner had to be one of the men he'd seen her with at the creek yesterday. So where was the other one?

He pulled up the feed from the camera mounted at the back door of the house. Finger jammed on the mouse button, he sped backward through the footage until he saw them. Two of them, skulking through the yard toward the greenhouse. If there was a third person on the property, he was elsewhere. But where?

Only the woman appeared in the camera video from the front of the house. He watched her walk up to the door, ring the bell and wait at the unanswered door. A signal to her partner when she knew no one was home. *Their search was planned.* Deliberate.

Heart racing, he brought up the video feeds from the four workshop security cameras. He shifted in his chair, his eyes locked on the blur of images on the screen. He caught their cautious approach to the rear of the workshop. For several long minutes, they simply stared through the window before the woman tried to pry it open.

What did she see?

He looked around. The kitchen. The empty wire shelves. There was nothing of interest here, except maybe the computer.

When they failed to gain entry to the workshop, they scooted up the narrow sidewalk. Less than a minute later, they bolted across the driveway and were out of camera range.

He restarted the greenhouse video. The two intruders touched a few of his tools and checked under the benches. And then they left. Their entire search took less than ten minutes.

What are they looking for?

He pushed back his stool and paced the length of the workbench.

Yesterday, after following the woman to her campsite, he'd watched her and the two men for a long time. From their equipment and set-up, they looked like prospectors. No threat. He'd convinced himself that the bloody rocks or the hidden backpack had triggered their call to the cops. But the bitch must have seen more.

He'd stuffed a robin's bloated carcass into his pack just seconds before the trio had doubled back to the creek without the cop. And interrupted his search for dead wildlife along the rocky shoreline.

The narrow creek, remote and far-removed from the perimeter, seemed the perfect place to test the toxic mixture. Months ago, he had poured a small amount of pesticide into the pure, glacial-fed creek and waited.

Scores of dead fish and birds littered the creek bank over the next twenty-four hours. The stench of rotting flesh and vegetation in the days that followed confirmed a highly toxic environment. And the pesticide would continue to indiscriminately kill for a lifetime. It was the perfect weapon.

Each day, he walked the creek, scooping dead wildlife from the rocks. Enough to keep suspicion at bay. And as the carnage diminished, his visits became more sporadic. Especially after a tightening military noose forced him to accelerate his plans.

A mistake.

He replayed the greenhouse security tape. Watched the pair disappear into the darkness between the benches. He punched the pause button when the woman's face appeared.

How did she find me?

It didn't really matter.

He knew where to find her.

49

NEIL SCOOPED FOOD from aluminum containers onto a plate already piled high with a mix of spring rolls, noodles and sweet-and-sour pork.

"I can't believe you're planning to eat all of that," Alex said and took a bite of her spring roll.

"What can I say?" Neil patted his tightly muscled abdomen. "I enjoy a good meal."

"Not quite the fancy lunch I promised you, though."

"I haven't forgotten." He grinned. "But I figure now I might get lunch at the best steak house in Vancouver. We'll be heading home soon, right?"

"As soon as Tim's out of hospital, we're flying home. In the meantime, we'll stay here at the house. Tomorrow, we'll head to camp and pack up. But we're done, work-wise."

Defeated. Even with Neil's silver find this morning, she didn't yet have a clear answer for Sylvia. Now with so much money at stake and so much ground left to cover. But the pesticide had changed everything.

"So what do you think? Were we at the Walden house?" She sipped her diet soda.

"You've got me." He dug his fork into his chow mein noodles. "That building didn't have any tools like the glass studio did. It looked more like a warehouse than a workshop."

"Except for the industrial exhaust system. It's the kind you find in chemistry labs. Are the fumes when you're working with glass dangerous?" she asked.

"Not that I remember. But Alex, an isolated farm with a set-up like that? It's way more likely to be a drug lab."

"If that's the case, then we're at a dead end. But it has to be tough for a family to move on after a suicide. The clerk at that store said that her husband didn't want any of the art pieces. Maybe he cleared out everything, all of her tools, the glass."

"It's possible, I guess," Neil said. "Especially if the studio was somehow linked to her suicide or to her son's death."

"Let's see if we can find out."

She wiped her hands on a flimsy paper napkin and swivelled her laptop around so that both she and Neil could see the screen. In the search box, she typed in Diane Walden's name and 'British Columbia' and hit 'enter'. Less than a second later, a list of websites returned by the search engine filled the screen.

"Let's check out that one." He pointed to the one of the under-lined blue headings. "It looks like an interview of some sort the *Nelson Star*."

She clicked on the link, bringing up a webpage belonging to the local newspaper.

"Something about the community medical services in the Valley. I'm going to guess she's quoted here somewhere, but it isn't going to tell us anything personal," Neil said.

"Well, at least we know we might have her name right. The clerk said Diane Walden was a nurse in the Valley somewhere. Let's try just her name."

When she tried quotes around Diane Walden's name, forcing the search engine to match the entire name exactly, an obituary showed up in one of the four items listed.

"Now we're getting somewhere," she said as she pulled up the obituary and read the tightly spaced text on the screen.

"Then again, maybe not." She sighed. "This just looks like some sort of listing from one of those genealogy sites. You'd think her obituary would show up. Of course, it would depend on whether her family published one."

She strummed her fingers against the edge of the notebook computer. The information was here somewhere. They just had to figure out how to find it.

"What if the son died during a crime? Try looking for a police investigation with her last name," he said.

The screen filled with headlines. Every one of them mentioned the Hugh Keenleyside Dam explosion. And the deaths of three young men. She quickly opened one linked to the CBC news.

Neil let out a low whistle. "No wonder she committed suicide. Finding out your son is a terrorist isn't exactly a mother's dream."

"Look at this, Neil." She pointed to a line on the screen. "*Diane and Trent Walden refused to comment on their son's death,*" she read aloud.

"Okay. So we've got the father's name. Now if we can just find a photo," she said as she scrolled through the list.

"Alex, go back for a minute. What about this one here?" he said, pointing to a link on the screen. "This one is a blog of some sort on protests here in the Kootenays."

"Wow." She fell back against her chair. "There must be thousands of entries in this blog. And they're talking about bombs, arson," she scrolled down. "Everything short of outright murder."

She scrolled through page after page, searching for something posted near the date of the Brilliant Dam explosion, overwhelmed by photos of death and destruction and angry men and women.

"Neil. This photo. It's him!" She pointed to a photo of a man with his arm clutching a distraught woman to his chest.

"No way. The dude we saw didn't have a bushy beard like that, and look at the hair." Neil pointed to the shoulder-length hair clearly visible in the photo. "There's no way Mr. clean-shaven had hair that long."

Those eyes. She'd never forget them.

"Neil, I'm positive. This is the guy." Her hand reached for her cell phone. "Look, it says the photo is of Michael Walden's parents, Trent and Diane."

She punched in the Vancouver office number. Tracey picked up after the first ring.

"Have you seen Tim?" Tracey asked in a voice that made her worry clear.

"Not yet. The doctor asked us to wait until late afternoon. I promise I'll call you as soon as we've seen him. Better yet, I'll have him call you. Okay?"

"Deal. So what's up?"

She told Tracey about their run-in with Walden at the café. She ignored Neil's raised eyebrows when she skipped over their search of the farm. There'd be plenty of time later for her to give Tracey a detailed account. Right now, she wanted to avoid yet another argument about unnecessary risks with her friend.

"I got a really good look at this guy, Tracey. I'm sure he's the one in the photo. So we need everything you can find on him."

"I'm on it," Tracey said and hung up.

She stared at the photo on the screen. There was no doubt in her mind that Tracey would confirm that Walden owned the farm they'd searched. But they'd seen nothing at the farm to tie him to the pesticide or to Elizabeth Chambers.

We need more.

50

THE SIGHT OF TIM's pale face and sunken eyes as she eased her way into the private hospital room took Alex's breath away. She stopped at the foot of his bed, but Neil wove his way past a rolling table to stand next to Tim.

"Good to see you, buddy. I brought some of your stuff." Neil dropped a backpack on the only chair in the room and sat on the edge of Tim's hospital bed. "Started chasing those nurses yet?" he asked with a grin.

Instead of a clever comeback, Tim simply smiled. Eric had reassured her that Tim would be okay, but right now she wasn't convinced.

One of her geologists lay injured, a young man who trusted her to bring him home safely. When you scrambled up mountains and hiked rocky terrain for a living, injuries were inevitable. This was different.

She swallowed hard. "How are you feeling, Tim?"

"Better than I was." Tim reached for a remote and raised the head of his bed until he sat almost upright. "No more throwing up at least. But boy, am I tired."

"Dr. Keenan tells us you're going to be fine," Alex said with more confidence than she felt. "You gave us quite a scare."

"Scared me too. I guess I'm lucky that I got to the hospital so fast," Tim said. "Not something I want to do again, though. I never, I repeat never want to be in an ER again."

"Having been there myself recently, I can understand." She cupped a hand over her bandaged arm. "It's kind of a crazy place, isn't it?"

"No kidding. All those needles. And how do they expect you to sleep? It's noisy and the lights are on all the time. And don't get me started on the freaks who show up in the middle of the night."

This simple rant told her more than any test result could. *Tim will be okay.*

"I still can't figure out what happened." Tim folded his arms across his chest. "Pesticide poisoning doesn't make sense."

"We've been working on that," she said. "And we think the creek is contaminated with pesticide."

"The creek? You mean I drank this poison?" Tim's voice wavered. "Am I really going to be okay?"

"Absolutely." She locked eyes with him. "Dr. Keenan gave you an antidote. You're going to be okay. And we can't be sure about the creek, not until we see the lab results."

"Dr. Keenan said it might be something I touched." Tim shifted his legs beneath the sheets. "I figured it was something in the mine. We were in there a long time, and I did more than just touch the rock walls. I was leaning against them."

She'd been quick to write off Neil's theory of pesticide on Chambers' body, but the mine itself? That was an angle she hadn't considered.

"Dude, I'd be in the bed next to you if it was in the mine." Neil turned to Alex. "And I'm sure Alex touched the walls too."

She nodded. "And pesticide in a mine is pretty unlikely, Tim. Arsenic, I'd believe. It can naturally leach out of gold deposits over time." She pushed her hair back behind her ears. "Or maybe cyanide or mercury. If cyanide salts were used to extract either gold or silver from the ore, you might find one of these." She shook her head. "But Dr. Keenan seems pretty certain that it was a pesticide."

"Nathan wasn't convinced there was pesticide in the mine either," Tim said.

"Nathan? The Mountie?" she asked.

Tim pulled at his pillow, adjusting it behind his head. "Yeah. He showed up here a little while ago. Wanted to know where we'd been yesterday."

So Eric had called police already. He couldn't have gotten a preliminary report from Mark. Not in the middle of the night. He'd called police because of Tim. And he hadn't told her. Not once, during their many phone calls last night, had he mentioned the RCMP.

Tim's eyes closed and then fluttered open. Even this visit, short as it was, seemed to be too much for him.

"Tim, we're going to go. Let you get some sleep," she said quietly. But Tim's eyes were already closed.

When they were in the hallway outside Tim's room, Neil whispered to her.

"He doesn't look very good. Are you sure he's going to be okay?"

"We're going to ask Dr. Eric Keenan that very question. And I also want to know just how much pesticide it takes to make someone sick."

51

ALEX SQUEEZED HERSELF against the wall to avoid a chubby nurse who pushed past her in the crowded ER hallway. The clatter of metal, the cacophony of voices, the whine of a monitor. After the quiet of the mountains, it overwhelmed her. No doubt Neil, who twisted back to stare at the curtained treatment beds with each new shout, felt the same. But Eric seemed oblivious to it all.

"Tim's going to be fine," Eric said.

"You're sure," Neil pressed. "He looks just as bad now as he did last night."

"Give it a little time." Eric smiled. "He's young, strong and healthy, just like you. By tomorrow, he'll be a new man."

"And me? You said I may have been exposed because I touched Tim," she said.

"Organophosphates are excreted from the body in perspiration, so when you touched his wet skin, you absorbed some of the pesticide."

Tim's sweat-soaked forehead. His clammy t-shirt. "So I'm going to get sick too?" She clutched her stomach.

"You'd be feeling the effects by now if you'd been exposed to much of a dose. Still, if you start to feel any flu-like symptoms, I'll want to see you right away."

"How long? Before I start to feel sick?" Her eyes darted to a gurney that rolled past and the moaning patient beneath its white blankets. She folded her arms to her chest, trying to ignore the throbbing pain. The last thing she wanted was to be back here.

"Everything depends on how much pesticide you're exposed to. We see patients a few hours after they've absorbed pesticide through their skin while using spray applicators, for example." He shook his head. "They seem to think you don't need to wear gloves while handling this stuff, but all it takes is a leaking nozzle and you've got a problem."

Gloves. Had she been wearing them when she went into the mine this morning? She couldn't remember.

"What if you're exposed more than once? We think the creek is contaminated, but the pesticide could be anywhere." She glanced at Neil. "And we went back there this morning."

"Again, it depends on the dose. The pesticide you absorb stays in your system, and each new dose adds to it. It's cumulative."

Great. They might both yet join Tim in the hospital. At least Eric knew how to treat it.

"Look, I know you're both worried, but let's slow down. If you'd been exposed to a hefty dose of pesticide, you'd show symptoms by now." He turned to each of them, looking for agreement. "You know what to watch for, and I know how to treat it. You'll be okay." He flashed a convincing smile.

A metal cart pushed by an orderly loomed large behind Neil, and she grabbed his arm to pull him out of the way.

"That was a little too close. If we spend much more time in this hallway, we're likely to be your next patients!" She smiled. "I think we'll move to safer ground and let you get back to work."

"Before you go, can I talk to you alone for a minute, Alex?" Eric asked.

"I'll wait for you out in the truck," Neil said before she could react.

Neil was barely out of earshot before she locked eyes with Eric. "What's wrong? Is it Tim?"

"No. Tim's fine. I'm sorry." He dropped his gaze. "I didn't mean to scare you."

For the first time since she'd met him, Eric looked uncertain. Uncomfortable.

"So what's going on?"

He looked up at her. "I tried to keep you out of this, but I had no choice. I told the police that you collected the water samples. They're going to want to talk to you."

She sighed. "Just what I need."

Arms folded across her chest, she turned to watch a passing nurse in maroon scrubs. The tall blonde looked familiar, but it wasn't until she saw the blue plastic watch that she recognized her. But the nurse who'd taken care of her the night of the fire didn't even glance her way.

"Alex, I told them as little as possible." He placed his hand on her arm. "I did my best to keep you out of this."

She softened at his touch and twisted back around to face him.

"I still wish you'd warned me. And I should have been there when Tim was questioned by police. I'm responsible for him. He shouldn't have had to do that alone."

"You're right. I should have called you first," he said softly. "Can I make it up to you? Take you to dinner tonight?"

The unexpected invitation brought a smile to her face and with it a small flutter in her chest.

"With a nice bottle of wine?" she asked.

"Anything you want," he said, laughing.

"Then you're on."

52

NATHAN THREW HIS keys onto the small hallway table near the front door and called out his usual greeting. No answer.

Still in his jacket and rubber-soled shoes, he headed down the hall toward the sound of faint voices. Hands on the kitchen door frame, he froze.

Jess sat at the kitchen table next to Olivia, one arm wrapped tightly around their daughter's shoulders. Jess looked up at him, her face tight and unsmiling.

"What's wrong? What's happened?"

Jess turned to Olivia. "Liv, your dad can help. Just tell him everything you told me. It's okay," she said softly.

But Olivia said nothing. She stared down at her hands, her face hidden beneath strands of hair, refusing to look at him.

"Somebody tell me what's going on," he pleaded. He forced himself forward, his eyes locked on the two women. His voice soft, he tried again. "Jess?"

Jess's eyes met his. She shook her head ever so slightly, her message clear. This was Olivia's story to tell.

He clenched the back of the wooden chair with both hands. On the table, a half-empty glass of water and a pile of used tissues. Eyes down, Olivia reached for a tissue but offered no words, not even when he dragged the chair free from the table and sat down.

"Liv, you have to do this," Jess said quietly.

Olivia screamed out a gut-wrenching sob. Jess squeezed her shaking daughter to her chest and held tight. Mother and daughter entwined, as though one.

What the hell is going on? Seeing his daughter in such pain, he could hardly breathe.

"Everything's going to be okay, Liv." A mother's words of comfort, repeated like a mantra, until the sobs subsided. Until Olivia's tears were spent. Only then did Jess release her protective hold on their daughter.

Olivia dabbed at tears with a crumpled tissue and through bleary eyes finally met his gaze.

"Dad, I've really messed up," she said, her voice husky. "I don't know what to do."

He swallowed hard. *Pregnancy? Drugs?* It had to be one or the other. And the boy he'd seen on her computer screen the other night had to be involved.

"Just tell me." He reached across the table and took her hand. "There's nothing you can't tell me, Liv."

She stared down at her hands, tightly clasped around a wet tissue. "I helped bomb the White Building," Olivia whispered.

Fear crept up from deep within his gut, flooding his body. Against his tightening chest, he fought to suck in a deep breath.

His eyes darted to Jess. Her blue eyes were dark with grief, but she shed no tears. He wanted to hear his wife's voice, to hear the story Liv had told her. But Jess held her trembling lips tight. Instead, he raised his eyebrows, asking a silent question. Jess nodded her encouragement.

"Just the White Building?" Nathan asked in a tightly controlled voice.

Olivia's ragged breathing was the only sound. He sat motionless, afraid of the answer implied by her silence.

"Liv, tell him. He's not going be mad," Jess said with her gaze firmly on Nathan.

Jess was right. If his anger flared, Liv would shut down. In truth, he was angrier with himself than with her. He'd failed to see what was going on until it was too late. *I've failed her.*

"I helped with all the bombs." Head down, Olivia whispered through her tears, "There's another one planned. The dynamite's upstairs."

His heart skipped a beat. *Dynamite.* In his house. Nathan struggled to control the fear that surged over him like a wave. He forced a deep breath and then another before he spoke.

"The boy I saw you talking with on the computer, Liv ... is he part of this?" he asked gently.

Olivia nodded.

The boy didn't look much older than she was. Too young to organize and execute bombings like these without leaving evidence behind.

"But he's not the only one, right? Who's in charge, Liv?" The questions sounded harsh, even to his ear. He quickly backtracked. "I mean, there must be someone who comes up with the targets."

"We all have a say." She pulled her hand from beneath his and swiped at the tears that spilled down her cheeks.

Young and idealistic. The perfect tool for some lunatic. Beneath the table, he clenched his hand into a tight fist. He wanted the bastard that did this to her. But if he pushed Liv too hard, he'd get nothing. He tried another angle.

"So there's a group of you." He steadied his gaze on her downturned face. "Liv, do you know them all from school?"

Silence. He turned to Jess, searching her face for guidance. But he saw only her fear. Fear that their daughter might soon sit alone in a jail cell. He closed his eyes.

At least she won't be charged with murder. Each of the bombs had exploded at night, in near-empty buildings. Surely a lawyer could argue there'd been no intent to kill. But if they labelled her a terrorist?

"What about the bombs?" His voice cracked. He ran a sweaty palm over his jawline before he tried again. "Liv, where do the bombs come from?"

"We make them. It isn't hard to get dynamite." Olivia crossed her arms across her chest and looked away.

He'd seen this same posture during their many arguments, and it always meant the same thing. *She's lying.*

"It might be easy to get dynamite, but knowing what to do with it is something else," he said gently. "Who put the detonator together? I know it's not you."

"I'm not stupid, you know."

Olivia stared out into the dark hallway beyond the kitchen. She would bolt, disappear into the night, if he treated her too harshly. But he had to get at the truth.

His voice tightly controlled, he said, "I know you're not making these bombs. I need to know who else is involved."

In the silence that followed, he looked over at Jess. If he only knew what Olivia had shared with her, he might know what question to ask. Might know how to bring their daughter back to them.

Jess spoke. "Liv, you can't protect your friends. You're in serious trouble, and unless you tell your dad everything, he can't help you. You have to tell him," she said in a firm voice that demanded obedience.

He gave silent thanks for her help. For saying what he couldn't. *But would it work?*

Olivia didn't look at either of them when she finally spoke. "Trent Walden makes the bombs."

"Trent Walden?" he asked, surprised. But understanding came quickly. His voice low, he continued, "This is about Michael."

Liv worked her thumb against her hand as though rubbing out an unseen stain. She nodded. "It was my turn to pick up the bomb, and I brought it here."

He leaned back in his chair. "Do you know what the next target is?"

She finally looked up at him. In her eyes, he saw fear. Primal. Like an animal caught in a trap. He wanted to comfort her, tell her everything was all right. But in his heart he knew otherwise.

"The hospital."

Her words stabbed at his gut. "The hospital? Olivia, there are hundreds of people in that building at any given time."

"I know," she whispered.

Jess gasped, but he didn't dare look at her. He couldn't stand to see the pain caused by their daughter's simple statement. He closed his eyes.

"I couldn't do it, Dad. I couldn't. Please Dad, look at me," Olivia pleaded.

He opened his eyes to see her anguished face. And that pained him more than anything. He reached over and took her hand.

What do I do now?

53

ALEX SQUEEZED INTO a chair at the only vacant table in the All Seasons Cafe. Tucked away on a quiet alley away from the downtown core, the small restaurant was clearly a local favourite. She gazed through the window at a lovely European-style patio that sat empty on this cold spring evening. Inside, tables discreetly positioned to provide the illusion of privacy crowded what was once the main living space of a family cottage.

"It smells wonderful in here," she said.

She tugged at the zipper of her fleece, revealing a white t-shirt adorned with her newly purchased turquoise and silver necklace. Anywhere else, she might have felt underdressed, but among the jean-clad patrons of this restaurant, she felt right at home. Eric had chosen well. Still, she wished for a dab of perfume and a touch of colour on her lips.

"And the food doesn't disappoint. I come here often, and everything I've tried has been really good," Eric said.

They chatted about the menu options and listened carefully to the specials presented by their waiter. Alex settled on a lamb dish while Eric ordered a steak and a bottle of Merlot from a British Columbia winery. The wine arrived quickly, the waiter pouring each of them a glass before he set the bottle on the table between them.

Laughter from a nearby table rose over the murmur of voices that served as nothing more than background noise. Over the rim of her wine glass, Alex glanced at Eric. It was tempting to simply relax and enjoy an evening out with a handsome man. But the flame burning in the glass vase set on the table between them was enough to remind her that the events of the past few days couldn't be so easily set aside.

"I was reading a newspaper article earlier about the death of Michael Walden at the dam. Do you know much about it?" she asked.

Eric shook his head. "It was tragic. Three young men, their lives cut short. And for what? It was stupid for them to go out to the dam armed with explosives with all of those soldiers there. But nobody understands why the soldiers shot to kill. They had options. They could have arrested them or taken less lethal shots." He raised a hand. "I'm sorry, I'm ranting. Michael Walden was a local boy, and everybody including me is angry about what happened."

"Do you know the family?"

"Only the mother. Diane Walden was a nurse in one of the medical centres in the Valley. I ran into her a few times. The medical community is small here. She committed suicide not long after her son died. I'm trying to think about what the husband looked like, but nothing comes to mind. I don't think I ever met him. Why?"

How much to tell this man she barely knew? Her fingers grazed the rough gauze that clung to skin that still burned in pain. From the first night they met in his ER, Eric had shown that he could be trusted.

"You might not want to hear what I have to say."

"Now I'm intrigued." He sipped his wine, waiting for her to say more. When she didn't he added, "Look, as an ER physician I hear all sorts of things. I'm not sure you could shock me."

Alex took a sip of her wine. *Do I dare?* Even Tracey, a woman Alex trusted with more secrets than she dared remember, didn't know everything, at least not yet. Neither did her dad. She should be confiding in one of them. Not with this doctor.

Eric leaned over the table and took her free hand, his touch electric. "Alex, you can trust me."

She set down her wine glass and ran her fingers over the silver links of her necklace. It reminded her of the silver earrings worn by

Elizabeth Chambers. The woman deserved to have her killer caught, and Eric might be able to help.

The words tumbled out in a rush as she recounted their discovery of the evidence near the creek.

"So when Neil and I saw a man up by that same creek, I was suspicious. When we ran into him at a café back on the highway, we followed him—" she said.

He gasped. "You what?"

"We followed him from the café to his house. He didn't see us. We were careful. There was just something about this guy that I thought was a bit off. Anyway, we think it was Trent Walden."

She told him about the glass they'd seen in the greenhouse and their matching find at the local art gallery, as well as the Internet photo of Trent Walden.

He dropped his hands into his lap and leaned back.

"So let me get this straight. You think Trent Walden is a killer, but instead of going to the cops, you start digging around. Trying to find what, exactly?" he challenged. "You could have gotten both yourself and Neil killed!"

She stared at him, dumbfounded. He'd listened quietly, without interruption. She'd assumed everything was okay. Her face flushed with anger.

"Would you willingly go to the cops with the army here?" she demanded, her eyes blazing. "You know as well as I do that they'll be involved in this up to their eyebrows in about two seconds. I don't know about you, but I don't relish spending all of my time being interrogated."

Her hand shook as she picked up her wine glass. Staring out the window, she took a long swallow before she continued.

"And we tried to get the cops involved," she insisted. "There wasn't enough evidence, they said. Even when we saw that guy at the creek, they wouldn't follow up. So, no," she said, shaking her head. "I'm not calling the cops until I have something concrete to tell them.

"I get it. I do. I did the same thing with the pesticide. I waited until I was sure before I called the cops. And look at what happened to Tim." He sipped his wine, staring out at the patio lights.

They sat in silence amidst a swirl of voices and laughter. She fiddled with her fork, cursing herself for turning what should have been a relaxing evening into a war.

He sighed. "Alex, I'm sorry. It just that if you're right, then Walden is dangerous. And I don't want to see you back in my ER." He grinned. "As charming as those hospital gowns are, you're much prettier sitting at a table in a good restaurant."

She couldn't help but smile. "It's nice that you're worried about me, but really I can take care of myself," she said in a softer tone. "Maybe I'm too caught up in it." She sighed. "But this is personal. Tim is my responsibility."

"The cop I called about the pesticide is a friend of mine. An RCMP officer by the name of Nathan Taylor. You met him yesterday at the mine."

"Nathan? Sure, I met him and a couple of goons." She tightened her fingers around her wine glass. "And for your information, he was the one who refused to search for the guy we saw at the creek."

"That doesn't mean he isn't a good cop," he said, shaking his head. "He needs to hear what you told me about that farm. It'll make a difference."

She drew in a deep breath, her eyes on Eric. *He really believes it's that simple.* "I'll think about it, but I'm not making any promises."

"Alex, we've got to find out how three people came into contact with this poison."

"I'm not convinced there's a connection. Only the apple juice from Laura Bennett's house tested positive for pesticide. Nothing at Gary Barlow's house. And that creek is miles away from both places," she insisted.

"I know. But Alex, that's why the police need to investigate."

"You're right. But it's Laura Bennett's death they need to focus on. She could easily have committed suicide or been murdered." She leaned her chin against a folded hand. "Eric, you told me yourself that you can't confirm pesticide poisoning in any of these cases. Not without those special blood tests. So, for now the only thing we know for sure is that Laura Bennett's death is suspicious."

The waiter's appearance beside their table shut down their conversation. As though he sensed his intrusion into their private moment, he quietly refilled their wine glasses and left.

"Eric, I promise I'll talk to Nathan. Soon." His face softened, and she smiled. "Now, can we talk about something else? Just for this evening."

He reached across the table and intertwined his fingers with hers. "So what's a good topic for a first date?"

"You've got me," she said with a laugh. "You don't want to know how long it's been since I was on a date."

"Why don't we get out of here? Start over again. We'll head over to my place and see what's in my fridge. I'm a pretty good cook."

She ran her finger around the rim of her wine glass as she met his gaze. In the soft candlelight, the creases gathered in the corners of his blue eyes invited her touch. She wanted to trace a fingertip along those lines and move slowly down his face to his chest. Her cheeks flushed, and she dropped her eyes.

"A little bold, don't you think?" she asked, peeking up at him.

"Does that mean no?"

Did she dare give into her desire? *I could lose my soul to this man.* This passionate doctor she might never see beyond tomorrow.

"Actually, I like a man who's not afraid to take risks." She reached beneath the table and grabbed her bag. "Let's go."

54

TRENT WALDEN RAN his fingers over the replica Japanese fish net float balanced in the palm of his hand. Eyes closed, he could almost smell the salt air and hear the roaring surf. He'd come to Vancouver Island's west coast with several of his army buddies for the waves, expecting nothing more than a break from the dusty heat of the battlefield. But on a misty morning, on a lonely beach, he had found Diane.

He'd stopped, curious about the gnarled wood she collected from the wet sand. And from the moment her emerald green eyes met his, he was lost. Army buddies forgotten, he walked the shoreline with the black-haired beauty, searching for driftwood that she would later pair with glass. Small works of art that she sold to tourists in nearby Tofino to help pay her tuition at the University of British Columbia. But the gentle artist bristled when she'd learned he was a soldier in the U.S. Army. And in that moment he knew that he'd give it all up for her.

They wrote each other daily when he left her to return to his unit. While she finished her nursing degree and he completed what would be his last tour of duty. When she was offered a job in New Denver, they made plans to move to the Slocan Valley. And not long afterward, Michael was born. On that day, in this very room, Diane had presented him with this hand-blown glass ball. A perfect sphere made to celebrate their perfect family.

A lie.

He should have destroyed it months ago, this glass that mocked him. Glass that reminded him that he'd failed to protect his son.

Failed to save his wife. But even now, he couldn't bear to leave it behind.

From the bed, he grabbed a handful of t-shirts and wrapped the glass ball in them before he packed everything into the half-filled duffel. Then, his shoulder tight against the wall, he lifted the curtain a few inches. Since last night, too many patrols had passed this way. They drove slowly, eyes on the houses that lined this once quiet side road.

Surveillance.

When he'd left Gary Barlow yesterday, he'd half expected to be arrested. But instead he'd driven home without interference and found his farm untouched. It did nothing to quiet his fear. Not with stepped-up patrols since the night of the roadblock.

From the whispered rumours in New Denver, an ex-soldier up the road had been targeted that night. He'd warned the balding Canadian more than once that he didn't keep a tight enough circle of trust, that too many people knew about the growing munitions cache hidden in a steel-reinforced shed. But the stupid fool hadn't listened.

He'd been dragged off to some windowless cell, his weapons confiscated. By now, his interrogators had probably learned the name of every accomplice. Yet the patrols continued.

His hand reached for a revolver on the bedside table, but instead he lifted a framed photo of Michael from the dusty wooden top. The curly-haired boy grinned broadly, pointing to a fish held aloft. It was the first of many fish caught during their father-son trip on Michael's sixteenth birthday, just two years ago. Before Michael joined the protests.

They'd been proud of their young son when he marched with the First Nations people against the Columbia River dams, concrete behemoths that kept salmon from their ancestral spawning grounds. But Michael abruptly quit the cause. At the time, he'd thought a girl responsible, especially when Michael began pushing his midnight curfew.

I should have known.

Backpacks filled with bombs and a plan to blow up the Hugh Keenleyside Dam. A poorly thought-out attack by a bunch of school kids.

The American soldier's bullet barely missed his son's heart. Michael died, alone, less than an hour later in an antiseptic hospital.

He jammed the photo into the front of the duffel. He'd witnessed first-hand field medics ignoring the enemy to tend to their own. His son, the terrorist, would have been treated no differently. He balled his hand into a white-knuckled fist. No doubt the doctors hadn't even tried to save his son.

He grabbed the loaded handgun from the bedside table. The weight of the semi-automatic in his palm felt familiar even after all these years. He shoved the weapon into the front pocket of his duffel and crammed two boxes of bullets in beside it.

Curtain pulled aside, he stared out at the road. Empty.

If he'd been smart, he would have cleared out the greenhouse when Diane died. Like he'd done with her workshop. Instead, he'd foolishly continued to meet with Gary Barlow weekly to deliver the small harvest. He'd told himself that it was best to make no changes. To appear to outsiders as a grieving husband and father who struggled to continue.

A mistake.

He had to leave. Head state-side before the cops closed in. And he might never be able to come back.

Even if Gary suspected him, the cops would find no evidence. The workshop had been cleared of every barrel and carboy of pesticide. The white panel truck, parked and waiting for Nick, couldn't be traced to him. And by tomorrow night, it would be gone. Nothing linked him to the pesticide.

Except the woman. The bitch who'd dogged his every move. Violated his home.

His hands curled into fists. He had to be there. In Washington State. To drop the first bottle of pesticide into the Columbia River.

To destroy the precious river that had stolen his family. To go to war against a country he'd once sworn to protect.

I want to see it. He'd planned a quiet exit from the Slocan Valley two days from now. After the last bombing. So he could watch the hospital burn to the ground. Not this. He punched his fist into the mattress. Slinking away like a coward.

The rumble of an engine. He slipped to the window and stared through the sheers. A drab olive-green Humvee, right on time. Every hour they passed this way, no more, no less.

He shoved a handful of .22 calibre bullets into his pocket and grabbed his loaded rifle.

55

ALEX POURED HER second coffee of the morning, staring out at the soft grey sky. She'd slipped in before midnight and crept quietly past Neil's bedroom but sleep had not come easily. Lying under the cool sheets of her own bed, her thoughts lingered on Eric. The heat of his lips against her skin.

The sound of running water upstairs told her that Neil was up and in the shower. Time for one quick call to Eric before they headed back to their campsite. But as she reached for the phone, it rang. She snatched up the phone as soon as she caught a glimpse of the caller's ID.

"Mark, I didn't expect to hear from you until later today."

"This couldn't wait." His voice sounded as anxious as she'd ever heard it. "I've identified the pesticide in your juice sample. Fenamiphos. It's one nasty organophosphate pesticide. Toxic as hell. And the creek's loaded with it too," the chemist said.

"So Eric's right!" Cell phone tight to her ear, she paced in front of the table. "Laura Bennett. Tim. Probably Gary Barlow too. But how?"

"Good question. Fenamiphos isn't registered for use in Canada, so you can't buy it here. It used to be sold in the United States, but it was voluntarily taken off the market back in 2009."

She let out a whistle. "So it came from overseas."

"Probably. There are at least thirty countries where this nasty pesticide is both legal and easily obtained. But it's also possible that a local farmer purchased the pesticide in the States prior to 2009, and he's been using it ever since."

She dropped into the kitchen chair. "Mark, there are hundreds of farms in the Valley, but up near the creek there isn't anything other than a few mines. This contamination isn't coming from a farm."

"Then it's intentional. Bioterrorism. The concentration of fenamiphos in the creek is about five times the one-day exposure limit advised by the U.S. Environmental Protection Agency. That's high enough to send a whole lot of people to the hospital. Or the morgue."

"Bioterrorism? At a remote creek." She shook her head. "It doesn't make sense. Besides, most of the protestors out here are pro-environment. Protect the Columbia. Protect the salmon. I can't imagine any of them doing something like this."

"Alex, this pesticide was carefully chosen for maximum damage. It's lethal and it persists. The average half-life is just over three hundred days."

Almost a year for just half of this toxic pesticide to break down into other chemicals once it was released into the environment. And there were no guarantees that the newly formed chemicals were any less toxic than the original. Decades would pass before fenamiphos vanished from the creek.

"So let's say you're right. That the creek has been contaminated on purpose. How does that explain the pesticide in Laura Bennett's juice?"

"She could have been involved," he said.

"And she drank the poisoned apple juice afterward? I don't think so. Why go to the ER if you want to die?"

"Changed her mind, maybe. But the doctor isn't sure about the diagnosis, right? We don't know if she drank that juice. It could just have easily been intended for the creek."

She heard the thump of Neil's footsteps on the stairs. If the army restricted movement in and out of Nelson, they could be trapped here for weeks.

"Mark, I'm calling it in. They have to keep people away from that creek."

"Agreed. But this is big, Alex. I'd get out of there I were you."

"Already working on an exit plan, Mark." She smiled up at Neil as he walked into the kitchen. "With luck, I'll see you in Vancouver tomorrow."

"So we're out of here?" Neil said when she hung up. "What about Tim?"

"We're getting him out of that hospital." She punched in Eric's number. "Even if we have to airlift him to Vancouver."

They weren't leaving him here.

Not after she called in an alarm guaranteed to trigger a massive military response.

56

"THANKS," ERIC SAID as he took the key from Anne Sutton's hand. "I won't be too long. As I said, I just want to take a quick look around."

The petite woman stuffed her hands deep into the pockets of her quilted jacket. "Does this mean that you found something? You know what made Laura sick?"

He stared past her at the budding fruit trees set against a fence that separated Laura's ten-acre property from Anne's ranch-style house. If there was a nearby pesticide spill, this black-haired woman was at risk.

But what if Alex is right? Her insistence that murder or suicide explained Laura Bennett's death nagged at him. He'd been so sure about a pesticide spill, but after listening to Alex's arguments, his conviction faltered.

"No answers yet, I'm afraid." He quickly dropped his gaze, afraid his eyes would reveal the lie. "Hey fella." He patted the head of the golden retriever sitting next to Anne's feet. "He's a beautiful dog."

"Poor thing. He misses Laura. Casey likes me well enough … I always take care of him when Laura goes on vacation. Not that she did that often enough." Anne reached down and ran her hand over Casey's back. "I guess it's lucky she asked me to take him when she got so sick. Otherwise, who knows what would have happened to him."

He scratched behind the ears of the dog that leaned its soft blond fur into his leg. "Will you keep him, Anne?" he asked quietly.

She nodded. "It's the least I can do for my friend." Tears pooled in her eyes, and she turned away from him. "Just leave the key in my mailbox when you're done. You have to go 'round unless you want to climb the fence."

Anne set a quick pace away from the house with Casey trotting beside her. When the pair turned the corner for the driveway, he slipped the key into the back-door lock. He stepped into Laura Bennett's kitchen and eased the door shut.

An empty fruit bowl. A spotless counter and table. So different from his own home, where newspapers, dishes and half-filled mugs of coffee littered every surface in the kitchen.

Long after Alex had left his bed, he'd lain awake, stepping through Laura Bennett's last visit to the ER again and again. Finally, he'd given up on sleep and headed to the hospital. There, over endless cups of coffee, he searched Bennett's medical file for anything that might suggest a suicide attempt. But he found nothing.

He pushed himself time and again to remember Laura's face, her speech. She'd been anxious, a normal reaction to an ER visit, especially for someone as seriously ill as she had been. Her mental confusion, evident during her second visit, was almost certainly due to her rapidly deteriorating condition. But nothing suggested depression severe enough for Laura Bennett to take her own life. Murder seemed more likely.

But as with all his patients, he knew little about her life. There was no way to know if she'd been afraid of someone, a boyfriend or ex-husband perhaps, and kept that threat to herself. Susan had a sixth sense about these situations, but the experienced nurse noted no such suspicion in the medical file.

It left only one possibility.

The squeak of his runners announced his every move through the empty house. Past the living room, through a set of French doors that led to a sparsely furnished front entryway, he found the room he sought. Laura's office.

A few steps took him to a sleek glass desk set next to an oversized window. He dropped into the leather chair and ran his hands over a smooth desktop that held nothing but a closed notebook computer, a box of tissues and a yellow cup filled with pens. Only the impressive modern art collection on the wall across from the desk gave a glimpse of Laura's character. Everything else in the room, from the grey sofa and its matching chair to the wool rug, had been carefully selected to soothe her troubled patients.

He swivelled around to scan the framed credentials crowded onto the wall. Together, they told the story of a decade of education that led to a PhD in psychology, and the nine years of professional practice that followed.

Beneath the frames, a row of reference books held in place by an oversized globe sat on top of a lateral filing cabinet. He pulled open the top drawer and flipped through the manila folders within.

Each file label held a neatly typed last name, first name and year. If the date indicated when treatment started, some of her patients had seen her for more than eight years. So different from his own practice of medicine. He barely saw any of his patients for more than a few critical hours in the emergency room, and he knew almost nothing of their lives.

In the bottom drawer, he found more of the same, except that she'd added a second year to these labels. Closed files of past patients. This was the place to start. A threat might come from a current patient, but one who had ended treatment because of failure was more likely.

He piled a handful of manila folders on the desk and flipped through them, one at a time. As he scanned her delicate handwriting, he found that many of Laura's patients ended treatment when they relocated or transferred to another psychologist. None of them had stopped seeing Laura because they were cured. Another difference between her practice and his.

His first real suspect, a female patient who had threatened Laura over her refusal to prescribe sleeping pills, came from the next handful of files he grabbed from the drawer. He read several pages of detailed session notes before deciding that this depressed woman was more likely to hurt herself than Laura.

As he neared the bottom of the pile, he saw a name he recognized: Diane Walden. The same woman Alex asked about last night. He threw open the folder and scanned the final entry.

Damn. Damn. Damn. He reached for his cell phone but found the back pocket of his jeans empty. *The car.*

He sprung from the chair and raced out of the room. At the front door, he twisted the deadbolt in one hand, the doorknob in the other. Three steps down and he was in the driveway running toward his sedan.

Heart pounding, he yanked open the back door and grabbed his jacket from the seat. He plunged his hand into the front pocket and freed the phone.

A missed call from Alex flashed on the screen. She'd have to wait. He dialled another number instead.

"Come on. Come on. Pick up." He rapped his fingers against the hood of the car. At the third ring, the voice of Nathan Taylor broke through.

"Nate, It's Eric. You need to find Trent Walden. He had something to do with Laura Bennett's death. I know it." His words spilled out in a rush.

"Trent Walden? Eric, what are you talking about?"

He forced a deep breath and started again, slower. "I'm at Laura Bennett's house, and I've been going through her patient files. I—"

"You're looking at her files? What the hell are you thinking?"

"That a warrant takes time. And you wouldn't know what to look for anyway." He ran a hand through his hair. "Listen to me. Walden's wife Diane was a patient of Laura's when she committed suicide. Walden confronted Laura, blamed her for his wife's death. Threatened her."

"Eric, you should know better than anyone that grieving families want somebody to blame," Nate said. "I'd guess that every shrink out there has had one of those arguments."

"Sure, but Laura Bennett is dead, Nate," he said. "Not only that, Alex thinks she can connect Trent Walden to Elizabeth Chambers' murder too." The statement was met with silence. "Nate? Are you there?"

"Exactly why is Alex accusing Walden of murdering Elizabeth Chambers?" The question asked in a cold steel voice. The voice of a cop.

Damn. He could say nothing more without revealing Alex's reckless search of the farm. A search shared in confidence. A search that could get her arrested.

"I'd rather let Alex fill you in on the details. From what she told me, I think it's a real possibility. Real enough that you need to go and ask him a few questions."

"And you're really not going to tell me what Alex told you?" His voice carried an uncommon edge. "Eric, this is important," Nate insisted.

He bit down on his lip. It would be so easy to tell him everything. But he wasn't about to risk the best thing that had happened to him in years.

"No. You need to hear it from her."

"Where is Alex now?" Nathan commanded.

"She spent the night in Nelson, but she said they were heading back to their campsite this morning. I don't know exactly where that is, though."

"Eric, put everything back where you found it and get the hell out of there. Now." A click, and dead silence followed the sharp command.

Shocked, Eric stared at the cell phone in his hand. He'd known Nate a long time, and his friend had never treated him like this.

What the hell is going on?

57

ALEX SLAMMED THE rear door of the 4x4 shut.

"Well, that's the last of my gear. Before I start on the kitchen tent, I'm going to grab a quick snack and some water. Do you want anything, Neil?" she asked.

"Maybe in a few minutes, when I finish packing up my tent." Neil unclipped the last hook from the nylon shell, collapsing the tent. "How'd you manage to get yours done so quickly anyway?" he asked as he pulled one of the long fibreglass poles from its sleeve.

"Years of practice, my friend." Her eyes darted to the gravel road. "That and knowing that this whole area could be overrun by soldiers any minute now."

Bent down at the cooler next to the kitchen tent, she picked through unopened packages of cheese and meat. Food intended to cover them for the three days they should have had out here. Now, instead of investigating the Donnovan properties, they were breaking camp. And she'd have to decide whether to gamble on a single piece of silver found yesterday.

The crack of a rifle sent her scrambling for cover behind the kitchen tent. Neil threw his tent pole to the ground and sprinted over to her.

Fear filled Neil's eyes. Fear she knew matched her own.

"Where is he?" she whispered.

"Hell if I know."

She risked a peek from behind the side of the kitchen tent. Clutching the edge of the tent, she scanned the trees beyond the campsite.

A flash of sunlight bounced off the steel of a gun barrel aimed their way. Behind it, the red jacket of a man.

"Shit! It's that guy from the creek," she whispered.

In horror, she watched Trent Walden advance slowly into the open, his rifle raised.

He's hunting us! Adrenaline hit hard. Her heart pounded, and breath refused to come.

"He's heading straight for us!" She jerked her head sideways to face Neil. "Where's your rifle?"

Eyes wide, Neil whispered, "In the truck."

"Shit. Mine too."

She looked over at the 4x4, less than fifty feet away. But to get there meant crossing out into the open.

Body tense, she locked eyes with Neil. "We have to get the rifles," she whispered.

"I'll—"

She cut him off. "No. We'll go together. He can't hit both of us." She sucked in a deep breath. "Now!"

Hunched down, she darted out into the open toward the truck.

Seconds later, a rifle cracked.

She refused to look back, afraid of what she might see.

Gravel spat from beneath her boots with each frantic step. She flung herself behind the front end of the truck. Neil's arm brushed against her back a moment later. They were both safe. For now.

Neil scrambled crab-like along the side of the vehicle until he reached the back door. He wrenched the door open and grabbed the guns stored on the floor. With this precious load in hand, he rushed back and passed Alex her gun.

"I'll try to scare him off," she whispered. "Get ready, just in case."

The rifle held unsteady in her shaking hands, she pushed the safety forward. One last look at Neil, his face taut with fear. And then she stood, the rifle butt jammed hard against her shoulder.

Her finger tense against the rifle trigger, she swept the open ground in front of the truck.

Nothing.

The sharp echo of a gunshot sent her diving for cover. An instant later, she inched her head up above the truck hood. Her breath, fast and shallow, she searched for him.

A flash of red from the other side of the kitchen tent.

He's closing in!

Eyes locked on the patch of red, she eased herself up from the protective cover of the truck. Praying he wouldn't see her.

He stepped out from behind the tent, the steel barrel of his gun held high.

Now!

She swung her rifle up and aimed. In the moment between ragged breaths, she pulled the trigger.

58

ALEX AND NEIL sprinted toward Walden, who lay motionless where he fell. Close enough to hear the man's hoarse breathing, Neil slowed and aimed his rifle at the downed man. But she kept moving.

"Alex! Get back!"

She jerked her head around to see Nathan Taylor jogging toward them, his rifle clutched in one hand. *What the hell is he doing here?*

The cop stormed past them and kicked the rifle out of Walden's reach. "Are either of you hurt?"

She turned to Neil. The young geologist stood, pale-faced and silent, his weapon lowered now, but still tightly held. He stared at Walden as though he hadn't heard Nathan's question. *Shock?* Quickly she searched for blood on Neil's clothing, relieved to find none.

"We're okay," she said shakily. "We were behind the truck. I got off a shot before he could."

She watched the dark bloodstain bloom out from the centre of Walden's chest. "I thought I hit his shoulder," she whispered.

"It looks bad. Stay here. I'll get the first-aid kit from the truck and call it in," Nathan said.

"We're going to get you help." She dropped to her knees next to the man who'd tried to kill them. "Don't try to move."

A small grin appeared on his face, and he closed his blue eyes.

"*Walden!*" she shouted.

She pressed two fingers against his carotid artery. A pulse, but weak.

"Shit! Where's that first-aid kit?" she looked up at Neil and pleaded, "We need to do something. We need to stop the bleeding."

Her words jarred Neil into action. He dropped his rifle and tore off his jacket, wadding the garment into a tight ball before he crouched down next to her.

She unzipped Walden's jacket and ripped open his shirt. Blood rushed from a bullet wound centred over the heart. A shot meant to stop a man cold. Beside it, nearer the shoulder, a second wound.

Puzzled, she looked over at Neil. "Did you shoot him too?"

"That was me, Alex."

She swung around at the sound of Nathan's voice. He crouched next to her and unzipped a bulging first-aid kit.

"So then you saw what happened!"

He nodded. "You're lucky I got here when I did." He tore open a large, sterile package. "Let's get this on him."

She stared at the barely moving chest. At the bullet hole too near Walden's heart. "I aimed for his shoulder. I only wanted to wound him. To stop him."

"The shot to the heart is probably mine. Ballistics will tell us for sure." Nathan placed a compress bandage directly over the wound. "Alex, put as much pressure as you can on this bandage. I need to wrap that shoulder wound."

Using both hands, one over the other, she leaned into the wadded bandage. Walden's eyelids fluttered, and his lips moved, but no sound came out. Beneath her hands, his heart weakly pulsed.

The beat of helicopter rotors sounded just moments before a massive machine hovered near the trucks. They'd gotten here fast. *Too fast*. A chopper patrolling nearby, maybe.

Metal struts touched the ground, and fatigue-clad men jumped from the aircraft, their packs emblazoned with a red cross. Medics. Boots pounded the ground as the soldiers raced toward them.

"What have we got?" The question shouted out over the thumping rotor blades.

"Two gunshot wounds to the chest." Nathan stood back.

A medic dropped to the ground next to Walden. Two fingers on his patient's neck, he listened to the man's laboured, raspy breathing.

He pressed his stethoscope against the bloody chest and reported, "Reduced breath sounds on the left. Possible pneumothorax."

Strong hands slipped beneath hers. She stood and stared at her bloodied palms. Neil touched her elbow, easing her back.

The rip of fabric revealed Walden's tanned forearm. Chlorhexidine splashed over the crook of his arm, the second medic then jabbed a large bore IV catheter needle into the bulging blue vein.

"I'm in."

Saline flowed into their patient's vein. A blood pressure cuff inflated, and a stethoscope pressed hard against Trent Walden's skin listened for a measure of life.

"Let's move!"

Practiced hands slipped a stretcher beneath the unconscious man and buckled him down. With a nod from one of the medics, the two men rose in unison and headed for the chopper.

The whine of the accelerating rotor blades drowned out all other sound. In a swirl of dust kicked up by the blades, the soldiers shoved the stretcher through the chopper's open door and climbed in behind it.

The door barely closed, the sleek machine ascended almost vertically into the clear midday sky. And then they were gone, speeding Walden to hospital in Nelson.

The silence hit like a brick. She looked down at her feet, at the mess of paper and bloody clothing that lay there. Nausea rose up from deep within, and she swallowed hard against it.

"Now, before anyone else gets here, I want the story," Nathan commanded. "All of it."

"I don't know what happened." She clutched her arms to her chest. "He came out of nowhere and started shooting at us. No warning." Her voice broke. "I had no choice."

"And that's it?" Nathan's disbelief couldn't be missed.

Neil jumped in to defend her, in a voice too loud. "Alex had to shoot him. And if she hadn't done it, I would have," he argued. "We were defending—"

Nathan raised a hand. "Slow down. Slow down. I'll tell them what I saw. Your lawyer won't have any trouble arguing self-defence."

Her mouth went dry. *A lawyer?* Just how much trouble was she in?

Nathan turned to face Alex. "But I also know there's more going on here," he said quietly.

She met his gaze.

"I talked to Eric Keenan."

59

"ALEX! FINALLY." Eric said. "I've been trying to call you."

Nathan's cell phone held tight to her ear, Alex leaned into the side of the kitchen tent to avoid a cop who rushed past her. One of the many soldiers and police officers who had arrived by air and ground minutes after Walden had been whisked away. Since their arrival, she and Neil had stood huddled together, under the watchful stare of a humourless guard. Only when Nathan had handed her his cell phone was she allowed a few minutes of privacy.

"God, I'm so glad to hear your voice," she said. "The cops took my cell phone. Neil's too."

"Please tell me you're okay. I just left Walden. The man's got two bullet wounds in his chest. What the hell happened?"

"It's awful. I still can't believe it." Through tears, she stared down at her boots. "Walden just came at us out of nowhere. Just started shooting at us."

"What! Alex, please tell me you're okay."

"I'm fine. Neil too." She glanced over at Nathan, his booming voice commanding the frenzied activity near the bloodstained ground. "We're lucky Nathan got here when he did."

Neil had stood with her, prepared to fight. And it had given her courage. But without Nathan, they might both be lying in a morgue. *Everything happened so fast.*

"Is Walden going to make it?" She swiped a palm over her tear-stained cheek.

"It's touch-and-go. They've just wheeled him into surgery."

A shout rang out, and cops headed for a spot near where Walden had emerged from the trees. A bullet casing found, evidence to support their story.

"Look, it's crazy here, Eric. I'll come by the hospital as soon as we get out of here."

"Don't hang up," he said, his voice urgent. "Have you called your lawyer yet? Don't talk to the police without your lawyer, Alex. Not even Nathan."

She glanced over at the stocky RCMP officer. At this distance, he couldn't hear their conversation. Still, she walked a few feet further away, near the evergreens that bordered the campsite.

"I thought you said Nathan was your friend." She fingered the soft new growth of a spruce bough. "That you trusted him."

"I do trust him. That's why I called him when I discovered Diane Walden was one of Laura Bennett's patients. But he's still a cop. And he'll have the military breathing down his neck on this thing. Nate will run this investigation by the book."

"If the army lets him," she said with a sigh. "They could handle this one themselves."

"It'll be okay, Alex. Just don't say anything without your lawyer."

She turned to search for Neil, relieved to find him well away from Nathan.

"Wait a minute. Eric, you said you called Nate about Diane Walden. So why did he show up here?"

"I told him that you suspected Trent Walden and that he should talk to you."

Her hand gripped the phone. "Exactly what did you tell him?"

"Almost nothing."

I don't believe you. Eric must have repeated last night's dinner conversation to Nathan for the cop to show up here. She glanced at the gauze bandage that jutted out below her jacket sleeve. Her heart skipped a beat. *Or you told him about my burns.*

"Enough to send him out looking for me, though." She made no attempt to keep the anger from her voice. "Listen, I've got to go." Her finger punched the 'end call' button.

Eyes closed, she took one deep breath and then another to slow her racing heart. But the fragrant spruce triggered an unwelcome memory of hot flames rushing up her tent walls. *The fire.*

Neil wouldn't even be here if she hadn't been burned. She turned to find him standing near the rear of their 4x4, too near Nathan. Quick strides took back to stand between them. There's no way she'd let him get railroaded by the cops.

"Thanks for letting me take that." Her eyes on the jumble of gear plucked from their 4x4, she handed Nathan his phone. "Walden's still alive. He's in surgery now."

She watched a baby-faced soldier pull a jacket from her duffel and plunge a gloved hand into each pocket. Eric was right. This was anything but a simple shooting investigation.

"So what happens next?' She dug her hand into her pocket, her fingers searching for the watch safely tucked there.

"I've been told to deliver you both to Nelson. You'll have to give your statements to the police and probably the military too. After that, you'll be free to go."

"Unless Walden dies," she softly added. Her hand squeezed the watch tight, as though touching it could summon her dad.

"I'm probably the one who put a bullet into Walden's heart, not you," he gently said. "I was in a much better position to line up a shot than you were, and I aimed for his chest. But Alex, even if I'm wrong, it's self-defence."

"He's right, Alex. You saved us from that nutcase." Neil swept his arm up and pointed to the kitchen tent. "Look at how close the dude got to us!" He shook his head. "It took guts for you to jump up like you did and take that shot. Walden wouldn't have missed. Not from that distance." His voice trailed off as a pair of athletic soldiers pounded to a stop in front of them.

"Ready?" Nathan asked. A curt nod from the younger of the two men.

Nathan turned to Neil. "Neil, you'll go with these officers." He swivelled her way. "Alex, you'll ride with me."

Damn. There was no way to tell Neil that they were sitting on a powder keg. That their search of Walden's greenhouse tied them to their attacker. That the mention of her burns might reveal her lies about the tent fire.

"Neil, there'll be a lawyer in Nelson waiting for us." She locked her green eyes on him. "Don't answer any questions until you've talked to him. And take his advice. Every word of it," she emphasized.

Nathan steered her toward his car. He opened the back door of the cruiser. "Watch your head."

Like something she'd seen on TV thousands of times, Nathan pushed down on the crown of her head with his hand as she slid into the back seat. Though unlike the suspects in the cop shows, she wasn't handcuffed.

He slammed the door shut and climbed into the driver's seat. She expected another officer to join them, but Nathan turned the key in the ignition and started down the gravel road toward the highway.

Nathan cast a glance at her in the rear-view mirror. The Plexiglas partition that isolated her from the front seat made conversation unlikely. Still, she wondered if he wanted her alone for a reason. She rubbed her hands over her bloodstained pants.

What did Eric tell him?

Out the side window, she stared at the rushing Slocan River beneath snow-capped mountains. She found it hard to believe that Eric could have betrayed her confidence. But she'd met him at her most vulnerable. Her hand went to her bandaged arm. And she'd fallen fast for a man she barely knew. Trusted him with details she should have shared only with Tracey or her dad.

Eric couldn't have told him.

If Nathan knew that their only link to the pesticide lay on an operating table, he wouldn't be so calm. And he wouldn't have taken such a lethal shot. *Not if he knew.*

She stared at the close-cropped black hair on the back of his head. She was dying for answers. But he must be feeling the same way. After all, he'd be in the hot seat over this shooting. Surely, he wanted to know why Trent Walden had stalked her and Neil to the campsite.

He wasn't going to let this private time go to waste. They'd be in this car together for at least an hour. She leaned back into the seat and ran a hand over her bandaged wrist.

At some point, the questions would come.

She'd better be ready.

60

ALEX PACED THE scuffed tile floor like a caged tiger, each step reflected in an oversized mirror that she forced herself to ignore. When her lawyer, Murray Dodd, finally came through the heavy steel door, she heaved a sigh of relief. But her too-youthful-looking attorney had barely introduced himself before a half-dozen uniformed men filed into the interrogation room.

She and Murray huddled together in straight-back steel chairs across from a row of military officers. A mix of Canadian and American military officers from the uniforms. Only Nathan, who leaned against the back wall, wore the blue RCMP uniform.

It still surprised her that Nathan hadn't asked her a single question during their long drive into Nelson together. Had barely said a word to her when he delivered her into this windowless interrogation room that smelled of stale sweat. And he'd refused her only request — to see Neil.

"Ms. Graham, tell us what happened out there." The question asked by a broad-shouldered Canadian army officer whose nametag read "Crosby". A man who, like the others, failed to introduce himself.

Her lawyer, out of place in jeans and a denim shirt, placed a hand on her elbow. His touch a warning not to say too much. Not to incriminate herself.

"We were packing up our campsite when Trent Walden attacked us. He fired several shots. I shot once." She glanced up at Nathan. "So did Constable Taylor."

"And you have no history with the man?" Crosby asked.

"No." She shook her head. "I'd seen him a couple of times, once at a nearby creek, and another time at a café out on the highway near New Denver. But I don't know the man."

"Yet Constable Taylor informs us that you suspect Trent Walden in the shooting death of Elizabeth Chambers. Why is that, Ms. Graham?" A command from a man used to getting his way.

She swallowed hard. Eric had told Nathan everything. There was no other way they could know that she suspected Trent Walden was a killer.

"We found an earring and blood beside the creek. And a backpack filled with water sampling equipment hidden in the trees." She dug her fingers into her thighs. "The bag disappeared just before we saw Walden, and later we saw him with one just like it." Her words spilled out quickly, challenging the men who scribbled notes on yellow legal pads to keep up.

"Slow down, Ms. Graham." Crosby raised his hand. "None of this constitutes proof. It does however, suggest that you know Trent Walden enough to recognize him."

Relax, Alex. She pushed her hair behind her ears and reached for the glass of water in front of her. Pain scorched though her arm, and she squeezed her fingers tight against the glass, wishing for one of her pain pills. Pills that were probably under scrutiny somewhere in this building, like the rest of her things. At least the ibuprofen, a common enough pain medication, wouldn't draw attention to her burns. Her charred notebook, on the other hand, screamed out for explanation. As did her GPS record of forays deep into the perimeter.

A quiet knock on the door announced a khaki-clad-officer who marched over to the general and handed him a slip of paper. After Mason scanned the note, he handed it to Crosby.

Crosby read the note and then slid it under his legal pad. He scowled at her over the top of his black-framed glasses. "Let's talk about how you know where this man lives."

Eric. He must have told Nathan about the farm. About their search.

She turned to Murray, a silent plea for help. He gave a quick nod, a reassuring smile. But only because the sandy-haired attorney didn't know the whole story.

"I was suspicious of him. This guy is holding a dead woman's backpack, and he takes off as soon as he sees us. He was up to something." She squirmed in her chair under her interrogator's steady gaze. "And as it turns out, I was right. That creek is loaded with enough pesticide to land one of my geologists to hospital." She turned to Murray. "Tim Munroe. He's the other member of my crew, and he's in the hospital here, in Nelson. I called and reported the creek this morning. As soon as I found out about the pesticide."

"Ms. Graham ... Alex." The words spoken gently by a grey-haired man named Mason to Crosby's right. "That report you made about the creek came straight to me. I need to find the source of that pesticide. I need to know if there's a connection between Trent Walden and that contaminated creek."

She stared at the three gold stars on each shoulder of the man's jacket, the U.S. insignia. An American army general.

Beneath the table, she ran her sweaty palms over her bloodstained pants. "When we — Neil and I — saw him at the café, we followed him. My idea, not Neil's," she quickly added. "I wanted to be able to give the police his name and address."

"And." Crosby's single clipped word spoken in a dangerous tone.

"And we saw him drive away in a red truck not long after we got there. Other than a white panel truck, we didn't see anything."

Crosby set his pen down, manoeuvering it against the metal table until its glossy black barrel lined up perfectly with the edge of his note pad. Only then did he look up at her.

"I'll tell you what I think," Crosby said in a steely voice. "You saw something you shouldn't have when you were snooping around his place."

He paused and set his intertwined hands onto the table, staring at her. And then, like a hunter with a cornered prey, he dropped the net.

"The place had monitors everywhere. We know your every step on that property. So stop wasting time trying to cover up your search." He picked up his pen and pressed the tip against the yellow paper. "Walk me through it. Tell me what you saw," he barked.

Murray placed his hand protectively on her elbow. "Do I have your assurance that neither she nor Neil Henley will be charged with any crimes relating to what she tells you? Blanket immunity." A quick nod from General Mason. "Go ahead, Alex."

All eyes turned to her and the room went quiet.

"Yes, we searched the place," she said quietly. "We went into the greenhouse looking for pesticide. Nothing. We tried to get into his workshop but couldn't. There wasn't anything in the place anyway. Not that we could see through the window."

"Details, Ms. Graham. Every step. Everything you saw."

She swallowed hard and started from the beginning. The white panel truck. The industrial ventilation system. The empty wire racks. The glass watering bulb that eventually led them to Trent Walden's identity.

"But we headed to Nelson right after we searched his property. There's no way he followed us. So how did he know where we were camped?"

Her question was met with silence. Crosby ran his thumb back and forth over the smooth barrel of his pen, watching her with an intensity meant to intimidate. She'd met too many men over the years who'd tried that. Geologists threatened by a woman who could do the job as well as they could. Better than they could.

She straightened in her chair and faced Crosby's stare. "This is about Elizabeth Chambers. He killed her. I know it. And it has to be why he tried to kill me. It's the only thing that makes sense." She clasped her hands on the table in front of her. "He took off as soon as he saw us, but he could easily have followed us back to camp. Maybe he knew we had found the backpack. He was afraid that we could tie him to Elizabeth Chambers' murder."

"Timeline doesn't work for me. Elizabeth Chambers was found dead two days ago. Why didn't he come after you earlier?" He rapped his pen against his legal pad. "It's because you weren't even on Trent Walden's radar until you searched his farm."

"No, it has to be about the creek." She looked at each of her interrogators sitting around the table, searching for a sign that at least one of them believed her. But their faces were inscrutable.

She pressed on. "What if the Ministry of Environment suspected a problem with the creek and sent Elizabeth Chambers to check it out? If Trent Walden is responsible for the pesticide, then it explains why he killed her. Maybe he thought we worked with her. No." Her hand flew to her mouth. "He thought we were doing the same thing!"

"Why?" Crosby asked.

"Tim... my geologist. He filled his water bottle in the creek, but Walden might have thought Tim was taking a sample. If Walden killed once to cover up the pesticide in the creek, he'd do it again. Right?"

"Timeline again. Didn't you stay at the camp that night? Why did he wait?"

Damn. She slumped back against the hard metal slats of her chair. Crosby was right. They must have seen something at the farm that set Walden off. Sent him to their campsite for just one reason. To kill them.

"But we didn't see anything." She stared down at the dull metal table. "None of this makes sense."

Murray rested his hand on her arm. "Gentlemen, my client has told you everything she knows. Now unless you're charging her in what was clearly an act of self-defence, we're done."

"Trent Walden died twenty minutes ago. We could charge Ms. Graham with murder."

Murder. Nausea hit the pit of her stomach.

"But you won't," Murray insisted.

His chair scraped loudly as her lawyer pushed his six-foot-frame away from the table. She jumped up and followed him, tight at his heels, to the door. Hand on the doorknob, Murray turned back into the room.

"I want Neil Henley released. Now. And let me be clear." Murray locked eyes with the general. "You're not to talk to any of my clients. Not Ms. Graham, Mr. Henley nor Mr. Munroe. Not without talking to me first."

61

OUTSIDE THE RCMP building, Alex waited on the sidewalk for Murray to emerge with Neil. Her stomach churned as Crosby whipped open the door. His steel-blue eyes met hers, and he quickly turned away, marching down the stairs to a waiting jeep.

Only after the vehicle had roared down the street did her heart slow. She reached into her backpack for her cell phone. Murray assured her that the rest of her gear and the vehicle would be released soon, but for now the pack and this phone were enough. A scroll through her missed calls exposed several calls from Eric. She wasn't ready to talk to him. Not yet. Instead, she hit the number for Mark's UBC lab.

"You called? What's going on?" she asked when the chemist answered.

"The army showed up here a few hours back. Took everything."

Even before Crosby had started talking, the military officers in that interrogation room had known about her creek samples. Had known about Mark. Eric had told Nathan everything.

"But they didn't take you in for questioning?"

"No. Are they going to?" he asked warily.

"I don't know." Her fingers tightened against the phone. "Mark, call Tracey. She'll set you up with a lawyer. And don't say anything until you talk to him."

"Why, Alex? What's going on?"

"He tried to kill us." She stared down at her bloodstained pants.

"Who did?"

She drew in a deep breath. "Trent Walden. The guy we think dumped pesticide into the creek. He tried to kill us."

"What? Alex, are you okay?"

Am I? Her free hand closed tightly around her shoulder. She'd been ready to kill Walden. Would have killed him if the cop hadn't shown up.

"I'm fine. So is Neil. But Trent Walden's dead."

"And you're sure you're okay?"

"Yeah." She watched a pair of soldiers dressed in rifle-green push open the door to the RCMP building. "But Mark, we're caught up in something big. Trent Walden dumped pesticide in that creek. I know it. And I also know it can't be about just one creek."

"So what do you think's going on?"

"An attack on the Columbia River."

Mark whistled. "Talk about a tough target for a bioterrorist attack. It's got to be the most tightly protected river on the continent right now."

"No kidding. But if I'm right, then this creek doesn't make sense. It flows down a side valley away from the Columbia, not into it. It could be that Walden didn't know that." She shoved her hand deep into her pocket, fingering her watch. "But something tells me that this creep knew exactly what he was doing. You should have seen his workshop, Mark. Industrial ventilation, state-of-the-art security. Walden's smart. Smart enough to read a watershed map, for sure."

"Then maybe the Columbia isn't the target," Mark said. "Maybe it's the Slocan Valley. Groundwater, soil, drinking water, crops. Everything would be contaminated if Walden dumped enough pesticide into the streams and creeks. It would destroy the Valley."

She pressed her palm against her forehead. "But there'd be more people in the ER by now if that's what he did."

Could that have been why Eric was calling? Not to find out how she was but to update her on the escalating crisis in the Slocan Valley.

"Maybe he didn't do it yet," Mark offered.

"Then where's the pesticide? I was at his farm. There's nothing there." She sighed.

"The army is probably installing biodetection systems as we speak. If pesticide shows up, they'll know it."

"That assumes they believe that there's a threat. And they can't monitor every well, creek and river." She pounded the edge of a cement stair with the steel toe of her hiking boot. "They have to find that pesticide. He couldn't have done this alone. The cops need to find his partners."

"It's odd that he didn't use DDT or a more common pesticide like malathion or paraquat. Could be that he chose fenamiphos because he's had experience with it. Military experience."

"Military?" Her eyes closed, she pictured his face. "He had to be in his late forties, early fifties. Maybe the Gulf War? Lots of concern over chemical weapons in Iraq. He might have had special training."

"Alex, if there are military men behind this bioterrorist attack, then it's not over. Not just because Walden is dead. You've got to get of there. Now."

"I wish I could." Her eyes dropped to the dark stains on her jeans. "Mark, I shot him. Walden." She tightened her grip on the phone. "They're talking about a murder charge."

62

ALEX THREW BACK the covers and stared at the ceiling. A glance at the bedside clock gave the time as 2:15 a.m. Three hours since she and Neil had finally talked themselves out over a half-bottle of Scotch. When they'd climbed the stairs to their bedrooms, sleep seemed promising. But alone in the dark, the small curve of a smile on Walden's ashen face as his life drained away refused to fade. Instead of much-needed sleep, she'd lain here awake and tearful.

With a heavy sigh, she swung her legs over the edge of the bed. In the bathroom, she dropped two pain pills into the palm of her hand while cold water ran from the tap. She'd expected her burns to hurt less by now, but their ache, a constant reminder of the fire, remained strong.

Pills swallowed, she crept along down the dark hallway to Neil's partly open door. Listening to his heavy, even breathing, she smiled. At least he had managed to shut his eyes to their nightmare.

She eased Neil's door shut and quietly slipped down to the main floor. There, legs curled under her, she leaned against the padded arm of the sofa in the dark living room. Her hand reached for the cell phone on the lacquered coffee table, and she dialled a number memorized long ago.

One ring, then two. For a full minute, she listened for the sound of a voice, but the call went unanswered. Her dad could be difficult to track down, but at this time of day she'd expected him to be in his tent, out of the hot Tanzanian sun. And by now he should have heard the message she'd left earlier, asking him to call.

She stared at the phone in her hand. Eric had left four more phone messages for her since she and Neil had left the police station. Each of them the same. A plea for her to call him. Asking if she was okay. None of them contained an apology. Still, she had nearly dialled his number more than once.

If Eric hadn't called Nathan Taylor, both she and Neil might be dead. For that she was thankful. But he'd divulged their private conversation to the RCMP officer. Broken his promise. She should simply walk away. That would be her dad's advice. But she couldn't do it. Not yet.

It surprised her a little, that she wanted a relationship with this man who had revealed her secrets so easily. She'd felt the sting of betrayal once before from a man she'd loved deeply, and a painful separation had followed.

Enough.

They were stuck here in Nelson for at least another day. Until authorities decided whether to charge her in Trent Walden's murder. She wouldn't spend that time feeling sorry for herself.

She switched on the table lamp and got to her feet. From the map rack, she pulled a paper roll, which she unfurled on the dining room table and secured with heavy beanbags.

If she hoped to convince the army that Walden attacked her because of the creek, then she needed proof. She traced the fine line of the small, isolated creek. Whether Walden planned to contaminate the groundwater supply or the Columbia River, this creek didn't fit. Especially when military patrols focused solely on the threats to the dams left countless rivers and larger streams accessible from backroads and hiking trails. *No, there's more going on here.*

At the window, she stared out into the dark backyard, seeing nothing but her own reflection. She ran her fingers lightly over her bandaged left forearm. The night of the fire, she'd been quick to assume her arsonist intended only to scare her off, but he couldn't have expected her to escape the flames. And now this, a deranged terrorist hunting her down.

Eyes wide, she spun around and hurried to the table. Walden killed Elizabeth Chambers to keep her from exposing the contaminated creek. What if there was another one out there? Or worse, a pesticide-laced stream headed for the Columbia River.

On the map, she zeroed in on her burned out campsite. Although inside the perimeter, the valley surrounded by jagged peaks saw few patrols and even fewer hikers. Her finger on the contour lines, she searched for remote creeks, for streams that emptied into the Columbia. But she found only a road in the narrow valley where she had been camped.

The truck speeding down the dirt road the morning after the fire flashed in her mind. A driver hell-bent on a destination deep inside the perimeter.

A partner.

63

FROM THE MOMENT Nathan stepped into the RCMP squad room with its low murmur of conversation and almost fully occupied chairs, he knew something was up.

He walked quickly past paper-cluttered desks, nodding to the few cops who glanced up from their monitors. His own workstation, with its clear top and powered-down computer, broadcast his absence. The last thing he needed. That and Dave anxiously watching his approach.

"We found the white panel truck," Dave said when Nathan got within earshot.

"Where?" Nathan flicked the switch on the computer and yanked his arms free of his jacket.

"Parked behind the Valley Market in New Denver. Just in time too. A guy by the name of Nick Powell showed up about an hour after our guys set up surveillance," Dave announced to the beat of his pencil against the desktop.

Nathan jerked his head around to face his partner. "You've had him in custody since last night, and you're just telling me?" He dropped his jacket onto the back of the chair. "What the hell? I—"

Dave held up a hand to stop him. "Easy now. I tried to call you last night, but you didn't answer. Not like you to have your phone turned off. Where were you anyway?"

He stared down at his white-knuckled grip on the chair, unwilling to face Dave. Not with the lie to come. "Home. By the time they finally cleared me in the Walden shooting, I was beat. Turned off my phone so I could get some sleep." With the barest pause, he flipped the subject. "What happened with Powell?"

Dave dropped the pencil and grabbed a manila folder from a stack of files on the desk. "Now that was an interrogation you would have liked to see." He chuckled. "Those Homeland Security guys had Powell sweating just as soon as his ass hit the chair."

"Homeland Security? Why didn't you handle the interrogation?"

"That truck was filled with pesticide headed for the States. Scared the shit out of them. Homeland Security took over in a flash."

Pesticide. After hearing Liv's story, he'd been sure the truck would be filled with explosives. Walden had preyed on Liv and her friends, had manipulated them into setting bombs.

Sweat trickled down from his damp, sticky armpits. "And they're sure Walden is connected to the truck?"

"No fingerprints. Registration in the name of..." Dave looked down at his scribbled notes. "Jamal Farouk in Richmond, British Columbia. Clean-cut engineer, father of three. It looks like identity theft, and he's cooperating with police.

"So we've got nothing."

"Nothing but the word of our two geologists. Both Alex Graham and Neil Henley saw that truck in Walden's driveway, and they saw him at that contaminated creek," Dave said. "Same pesticide, by the way. No hard evidence, but my gut says Walden is our perp. And my money's on him for the murder of Elizabeth Chambers too."

None of the kids could have imagined they were part of a bio-terrorist attack. Liv would never have gone along with such a deadly scheme. But she'd be charged all the same.

"Guy down at the Ministry of Environment says there was no reason for Chambers to be at the creek. The only thing we can figure is that she saw something. We've sent a team back to the creek to check it out. Maybe—" The beep of his cell phone interrupted him.

Nathan shifted in his seat while he watched Dave read the text message, painfully aware of his own silent phone. Since the shooting, a wall had been erected between him and the task force. A wall that kept him on the outside, unable to protect Liv.

"We caught a break."

Nathan's heart pounded. Every muscle tense, he forced a calm façade as he waited for Dave's next words.

"There's a burning barrel in the back of the farm. Forensics are sifting through the ashes, but what they've found so far sounds like the makings of a backpack."

Elizabeth Chambers. Nathan sucked in a deep breath. As the lead investigator in her murder, that text message should have come to him. Realization hit, tightening his chest. He'd been locked out of more than just the task force. And there was no reason for it now that he'd been cleared in the Walden shooting.

Dave dropped his phone onto the desktop. "That son of a bitch. Takes a coward to shoot an unarmed woman in the back."

Nathan grabbed his baseball from its perch. If he wanted back in, he had to play the game. Take the lead.

"Doesn't fit," Nathan said. "We investigated Trent Walden after his son died." *Michael.* The start of everything. He clenched his hand around the white leather ball. "Military man if I remember correctly."

"Got his record here." Dave shuffled through a tornado of paper on his desk, pulling out a single fax. "U.S. Marines. Three tours in Iraq, five medals, honourable discharge. No job after that. Wife worked as a nurse, and he farmed."

"Any chance he sells to the co-op Barlow runs?" Nathan carefully aligned two fingers against the stitching at the top of the baseball.

"Give the man a prize." Dave grinned, his pencil pointed at Nathan. "Walden's on Barlow's supplier list, but it doesn't sound like there's anything more there. Could be that Walden tried to kill him, but it looks like an accident. Barlow remembers drinking some ice tea at Bennett's house when he delivered her groceries. Most likely that's how he got sick."

Nathan leaned forward. "Wait a minute, ice tea? I thought Bennett's apple juice tested positive."

"It did. My guess? Walden mixed pesticide into anything in her fridge that would work. She probably finished off the poisoned ice tea. Maybe made more. Did you see the lab report? Enough pesticide to kill an elephant in that juice. Walden wanted her dead, that's for sure. This was personal."

"Eric … you know him, Dr. Keenan? The ER doc?" Nathan waited for Dave to nod before he continued. "He went through Laura Bennett's patient files. Turns out that Walden blamed Bennett for his wife's death."

Revenge so personal that Liv couldn't have been involved. Not with this.

"So he's probably good for Bennett's murder." He shook his head. "I tell you, it'd make way more sense to me if this guy was targeting something up here, you know? I could see him blowing up the dam or killing a bunch of soldiers. I don't get why the pesticide is heading state-side."

"And you're sure the pesticide was headed south?"

"Positive. Powell was hired to drive the truck across the border into Washington and drop the cargo at a warehouse. Swears he didn't know the shipment wasn't legal, by the way. A loaded truck parked in a remote spot. Cash payment by a guy he's never met. And everything's on the up-and-up?" Dave shook his head. "Jesus, he's stupid."

"He must have checked out the back of that truck. No way he didn't see what he was transporting."

"Oh, he did. And that's where this gets good. Turns out this pesticide looks a lot like apple juice. So Walden filled glass bottles with the stuff, slapped a label on, and just like that." He snapped his fingers. "Walden had something he could transport across the border without too many questions."

He stared past his partner at the satellite image that filled the computer screen. "So what are you looking for?"

"The pesticide." The tip of Dave's pencil settled on a grey building on the monitor. "Powell delivered six truckloads to this warehouse near Ephrata, Washington, over the past couple months. Should be a whole warehouse full. But there's nothing there. Nada. Zilch. Pesticide's been moved," Dave said.

"Another driver," Nathan said quietly.

"Or more. No way to know how many warehouses are out there. No way to know if he dumped pesticide already, either. They're testing the Columbia River, but—" Dave pointed his pencil to a winding line east of the warehouse. "You see this line? It's an irrigation canal." His pencil moved to the right. "Here's another one. If Walden dumped pesticide into any of these canals, every farm along the route would be affected. They're scrambling to start testing groundwater and soil. But shit, we don't even know for sure if Washington State is his target."

Dave stopped short of saying it. That the only man who could tell them lay in a morgue. *Because of me.*

"Powell doesn't know anything about Walden's plan?" he asked, his voice tight.

Dave shook his head. "Nah. He spilled everything. Hell, he would have ratted out his mother. We've got the warehouse under surveillance. Border crossings into Washington, Idaho and Montana are on alert. Anybody who ever talked to Walden is being questioned. My gut tells me that Walden didn't do this alone. He's got partners. We'll find the bastards."

Nathan's chest squeezed against his pounding heart. The ball flew from his hand and smashed against the wall like a gunshot.

Every head in the room jerked up. All eyes on him.

64

ALEX CHECKED HER watch again. Five minutes past one. Maybe he hadn't gotten the text she'd sent him last night. The crunch of gravel beneath heavy tires drew her eyes to the rear-view mirror. Finally.

She climbed out of the Land Rover, and with hands deep in her pockets watched Nathan ease his truck into place behind her vehicle.

"Nathan. Thanks for meeting me here," she said when he opened his door.

"I was intrigued by your text." Hands on the door frame, he hauled himself out of the truck. "How are you and Neil doing?"

"Rough night." She stared off at the jagged mountain peaks. "Let me get my rifle, and we'll take your truck."

"Alex—"

"Trent Walden could have a partner. You might be a better shot than I am, but there's no way I'm going anywhere without my rifle."

Her words hung in the air. *Damn.* Yesterday he'd seemed so casual about the shooting. But his red-rimmed eyes told of a sleepless night much like her own. Regret over killing a man? Or fear of the consequences?

She turned on her heels and walked over to her Land Rover, grateful to escape the uncomfortable silence. Under Nathan's watchful stare, she returned to his truck with her rifle and backpack. Her gear stowed in the backseat, she slid into the passenger seat of his truck and unfolded a paper map in her lap.

"Go up the highway about three kilometres and then we'll turn off," she said.

Hands tight on the steering wheel, he kept his eyes on the road. "Tell me why we're going to this particular spot. Your message said you had a strong hunch and that you would explain all when you saw me. So?" he asked when they were underway.

She'd decided after their silent ride to the police station that he probably was one of the good guys. He played things by the book. But she still wasn't sure she trusted him.

"First, I need an answer from you."

"Alex, I don't have time for games," he said without attempting to hide his irritation.

But she pressed on anyway. "Why did you come to our campsite yesterday? What did Eric tell you?"

He sighed. "That he'd found a connection between Trent Walden and Laura Bennett. He said that you were suspicious of Walden and that I needed to hear your story."

"That's it?"

"That's it."

She turned toward the window and covered a smile with her hand. Eric hadn't betrayed her. Not if Nathan was to be believed.

"Alex, why are we here?"

He was losing patience. She took a deep breath and plunged into her story before fear changed her mind.

"Here's the thing. A few nights back before the guys joined me, I was camped out near here. In the middle of the night, my tent caught fire. That's how I got those burns on my arms," she said.

"So you lied to us," he said quietly. "Why?"

"I didn't want to have to explain. I was in the perimeter." She gave him a weak smile. "You can understand that, right?"

"I get it." He waved a hand. "I'm not happy about it, but I get it. But it doesn't explain why we're here."

"The thing is, the fire was intentionally set. I assumed at the time that I was near a marijuana grow-op, so I figured I would just move on. But what if Trent Walden set fire to my tent?"

She watched his face. But he stared straight ahead into the cloudless morning sky and refused to look at her. The grind of tires against gravel filled the silence. Finally, she turned away.

"You should have told me earlier," he said in a voice that dripped with disappointment.

Anger would have been easier to handle. Somehow knowing he'd expected more from her made her feel worse.

"I might have told you if those soldiers hadn't arrived with you when we first met. But I figured they would just make my life more difficult. Besides, as I said, I thought the fire was unrelated. It wasn't until I was looking at the map last night that I started thinking Walden might have been in the area."

"Doing what?"

"There are some abandoned mines nearby. It could be that he's storing his pesticide in one of them. There are a few that you can more or less drive up to. Not for the faint of heart, to be sure. But if you had a solid truck or a 4x4, you could do it."

"I don't buy it. Why would he risk a location inside the perimeter?"

"Don't you see? Even though technically we're allowed in the perimeter, most people are staying away from it. That means there's no one around to find his hiding spot. It's perfect."

The truck hit a rut, and her shoulder slammed into the door frame with a painful thud. Nathan swerved the steering wheel hard, forcing the tires onto the smooth, hardened gravel.

"Man, I forgot how bad this road was." She rubbed her shoulder. Nathan made no comment, his focus firmly on the road ahead of them. Gone was his friendly, easygoing attitude, so evident during their hike to the creek. A side of him that had disappeared with the shooting. Now he was all cop.

"There. That's where I was camped." She pointed to the charred remains of her tent. "We'll go about a mile further and stop."

When he eased the truck to the side of the road a few minutes later, she grabbed her pack and pulled the door open. By the time he came around to join her at the front of the truck, she already had the topographical map spread out over the hood.

"Here's where we are now. And here are the abandoned mines," she said, pointing out the location of three mines. "There are others, of course, but I think these are the most likely ones. They're accessible by road, and they're close enough to my campsite for Walden to be worried. I know it's a long shot, but you never know. He hid that poor woman's body in an abandoned mine, so he might do the same with his pesticide."

Nathan raised an eyebrow. "You're lucky you didn't get killed. Do you know that? You should have reported that fire. Involved us from the start."

"I know. I know." She raised both hands, fingers splayed. "I did what I thought was right at the time. I made a mistake."

"You sure did." He sighed. "Look. It's a wild leap between your theories and a cache of pesticide in one of these mines."

"Nathan, Walden killed Elizabeth Chambers. I'm sure of it. And he had to know about that abandoned mine. Otherwise, he would have just hidden Elizabeth Chambers deep in the trees. Right?" She didn't wait for answer before she raced on. "If he knew about that mine, maybe he knows about these ones too. Maybe like everybody else up here, he's dreamed of finding silver in one of these old tunnels. If he spent any time prospecting up here, he'd know about these mines."

"It's worth a shot," he said. "We'll start with the closest one and move out from there."

She scrambled back into the truck, relieved to be out of the hot seat and on the move. Nathan turned the truck off-road and started a bone-jarring ride up to the mine entrance.

"You did that like you knew where you were going."

"What?" He stole a quick glance at her.

"This so-called road up to the mine. It's not easy to see unless you know it's there," she said.

The truck rocked hard to the left, and she braced against the dashboard with both hands. Nathan cranked the steering wheel, barely missing a tree in his efforts to regain the rutted track.

"Thank god we don't have far to go. That's the first mine up ahead. There. On the right."

"Doesn't look like anyone's been here in a long while," he said when he stopped the truck close to the boarded-up mine entrance.

"Maybe. But people put boards back up all the time. Come on." She reached back for her rifle and backpack before she climbed out of the truck.

A steep climb delivered them to the mine entrance. Nathan grabbed the end of a cracked, grey-weathered board and yanked. The rusted nails slipped free of the rock without resistance.

"You're right. This is for show more than anything." He threw the piece of wood aside and pulled the remaining slats free.

"Wait." She put her hand on his arm before he stepped into the mine portal. "Weren't you the one lecturing me on the dangers of these abandoned mines?"

"The ceiling and walls look stable," he said. "And there seems to be plenty of air getting in."

"You can't be sure about the air. Carbon dioxide builds up as rock oxidizes in these mines. It'll kill you."

He nodded. "I remember a case some years back. Bad air killed a miner and all of the rescue workers who tried to save him."

"The Sullivan mine in Kimberly." She shook her head. "Such a shame. The original victim and all of the rescue workers suffocated. Too little oxygen and too much carbon dioxide were to blame. They were in trouble within seconds."

Crouched, she plunged her hand into her backpack. "That's why we're not going in there until we do an air quality check."

She ducked into the mine adit, a flashlight in one hand, a multi-gas monitoring device in the other. "No alarms. That's always a good sign. The readings look okay. The oxygen level is a bit less than normal, but that's to be expected. No hydrogen sulphide or combustible gases. We're good to go."

Her flashlight beam bounced off the black rock walls with each stride across the rocky floor of the mine. Nathan's boot hit hers when she stopped abruptly, her light on a black duffel bag.

Nathan dug into his pockets for a pair of latex gloves and pressed past her. Crouched over the duffel, he slipped his large hands into the protective gloves.

"Can you get a bit closer with the flashlight?" he asked.

She nodded and focused her flashlight on the duffel. When he unzipped the bag, its contents were clearly visible in the soft white light.

"Dynamite. Enough here to do some real damage," he said.

She leaned in for a closer look. "It looks like the kind of nitro-glycerine-based dynamite I use."

"Same explosive we suspect in the Nelson civic building bombings." He glanced up at her and smiled. "I'd say we found a drop-point."

Her hand gripped the flashlight. "Trent Walden set fire to my tent because I was too close to this mine. And when he saw me at his farm, he somehow recognized me. He must have thought I had found the dynamite and followed him. It explains everything, Nathan."

"Or you saw something at his farm. Or he thinks you were testing the creek water. Or … I could go on." He sighed and shook his head. "Alex, we're never going to know why he came after you. And there's no proof this duffel is connected to him. No explosives at his farm. Nothing."

"But it was him. I know it," she insisted.

"Walden's a cold-blooded killer, a terrorist. But the Nelson city explosions were carefully timed to avoid injury. One of the more misguided protest groups is far more likely to have set those bombs," he said.

"You're splitting hairs." She kicked at a loose rock. "They're all terrorists. Walden went off the deep end after his son and wife died.

What excuse are the rest of them using? They don't like the dams?
U.S. military too close for comfort?"

He turned away from her. With one gloved hand, he poked at
the contents of the duffel.

"Walden has a partner. I know it. The morning after the fire, a
truck came flying down this road. And I saw Walden with a young
woman. She could have been driving that truck. She could be his
partner," she said.

In one swift motion, he stood and turned to face her. The thin,
tight line of his mouth in a face dark with shadows betrayed his
anger.

"Another detail you conveniently left out?"

"No. I'd forgotten about it until just now. Really."

"Describe her." He demanded in a voice cold as steel.

"Pretty. Blonde. Couldn't be more than twenty."

Rock crushed beneath his heavy, rubber soled shoes as he stepped
toward her. The heat of his breath brushed across her face.

"Where did you see her?"

She shifted under his stare. "At a café up the highway near New
Denver." She shoved her hands in her pockets. "The day we followed
Walden."

"Could you identify her if you saw her again?"

"I'm not sure." She shook her head. "Maybe. But Neil caught
sight of the two of them first. He probably got a better look at her
than I did."

His sharp intake of breath echoed against the rock walls that
surrounded them. He met her gaze, his eyes black in the dim light.
Her gut tightened.

"A connection to Walden is good news, isn't it?"

He shifted his weight from one foot to another as though preparing to step forward. She leaned to one side, giving him room to
move past her. But he stood rooted in place.

Instinctively, she took a step back, fingers tightly curled around
her rifle strap. Her heart pounded as she watched his unsmiling face.

He pointed the beam of light at a spot of daylight behind her. "Let's go." Without pause, he thudded past her.

Her breath, fast and ragged, she watched his back. Only when she was alone in the dark mine did she drop her trembling hand from her rifle strap.

What the hell just happened?

65

HANDS IN A TIGHT grip on the steering wheel of the parked truck, Nathan fought the urge to go home. He stared through the windshield at the RCMP building doors. With the discovery of the dynamite-filled duffel, their first real break, the focus would be back on the Nelson civic bombings. On Liv and her friends.

He dialled Liv's number. She needed to know that she'd been seen with Walden, a warning that had to be handled carefully. But once again, his call went straight to voicemail.

Bracken pushed through the front door of the building just as he climbed from the truck. But if the lieutenant general saw him, he gave no indication. Instead, his surly boss marched over to a waiting army jeep that jerked into gear as soon as its passenger landed in the back seat. But Bracken simply turned and walked away, leaving Nathan to stare at his ramrod-straight back.

He hurried into the building and down the gleaming hallway. The place was quiet. Too quiet. Inside the bullpen, only Dave and another senior investigator were at their desks. And neither man met his gaze.

"I saw Bracken leaving. What's going on?" he asked when he reached Dave's desk. The only answer, the steady rap of his partner's pencil. "You always swing that pencil like a mad drummer when you're nervous. Out with it."

Dave held the pencil still between his fingers. "Walden's hard drive was encrypted, and it took the techies a while to crack it. When they finally did, they found a list of contacts on it. It took some effort, but they dug up his call history." The staccato beat of the pencil against the desk began anew. "Olivia was on that list."

Shit. Walden should have been more careful.

"Did you know she knew Walden?" Dave asked.

He peeled off his jacket and draped it over the back of the chair before he answered. "She went to school with Michael. Said something about a tribute to him at this year's graduation. Maybe she talked to Walden about it," he said as casually as he could manage.

"That's what she said."

"You talked to her." The statement delivered in a stone-cold voice.

"Now, before you get upset, hear me out. We were discreet. I pulled her out of class myself. Told them it was a family emergency." He spat the words out rapid-fire to the steady beat of his pencil. "I've got four kids and I took care of her like she was one of my own. And Jess was with her the whole time."

Nathan searched his partner's anxious face for more. Anything that would tell him whether they'd believed Liv.

"And that was it?"

"Homeland Security insisted on a search. They didn't find anything in her bedroom you wouldn't expect from a teenager girl."

He gripped the back of his chair. *Thank god we didn't wait.* Long past midnight, he and Liv had risked a drive into the perimeter, to Walden's drop-point. His plan was simple. Wipe her fingerprints from the duffel and return the bag to the abandoned mine. He had intended to report an anonymous tip about the mine later today, but Alex had saved him the trouble.

"They questioned my daughter. Searched my home. And nobody bothered to call me? You don't think I should have been there?"

Dave stared at the pencil, held still now between hands that hovered near the desktop. "Bracken wanted this handled quickly and you were up in the Valley. But it's probably better that you weren't there anyway. Nobody can say you influenced the investigation. It was over before you even knew about it, right? It's handled. Don't worry. They took her computer, but that's just routine."

He wiped sweat from his forehead with the palm of his hand. Liv had been careful. He'd combed through her computer searching for anything that linked her to Walden or the bombings and found nothing. But he wasn't a computer expert.

"Nate. It's okay. We brought in another kid, Dylan Carver, who was also on Walden's call list, and he gave the same story. And the high school principal confirmed that Carver approached him about a tribute for Michael. The kids are telling the truth. We sent them both home. Liv's in the clear."

At least for now. Dylan Carver couldn't be trusted not to talk if he was arrested. Neither could the rest of Liv's so-called friends. Without evidence, though, their accusations against a cop's daughter would disappear.

"We're good?"

Nathan nodded numbly and slid his bulky frame into the chair. He glanced at the corner of his desk, where Liv's newly framed graduation picture sat. Her beautiful smile. She'd been so excited about university this past year. Excited too about starting life on her own in Vancouver. *How could she risk it all?*

"Alright, on to the good stuff." Dave tapped his pencil against the desk. "We caught a break. Homeland Security arrested a guy who showed up at that Washington warehouse. He led them to a second storage site near Moses Lake." He smiled. "Place was filled with pesticide."

"So it's over." Nate heaved a sigh. "Thank god."

Dave shook his head. "Not so fast. No way to know if we've got it all. Not until we can figure out where Walden got the stuff from. Or we find his partners."

"Walden was nuts." Nate ran a hand over his cheek. "He had to be working alone."

"Maybe, maybe not. But we'll know soon enough." His chair squeaked in protest as he leaned back. "That general, Mason ... he's got some clout. Couldn't be a single soldier state-side right now who doesn't report to him. And they're hunting hard for partners.

He's got Bracken fired up about Walden's involvement in the Nelson bombings too."

"Why? I know Alex Graham thinks there's a connection, but—"

Dave held up his hand. "This doesn't come from Alex. It's the military-grade plastic explosive used to bomb the dams that has them thinking." Dave shook his head. "Can't ignore the fact that Michael was his son. The guy could definitely have been supplying locals with explosives."

How long? Liv had warned her friends to stay away from the mine. As long as they kept their mouths shut, nothing could tie her to the Nelson bombings. To Walden. Unless Alex put her in that truck headed for the drop-site. Or someone else did.

He pointed his pencil at Nate. "You okay? You're sweatin' like a pig."

"Rough night, that's all," Nate grabbed his coffee cup. "I need caffeine."

Nate scrambled from his chair and hustled through the bull pen. *It should be over.* With Walden dead, Live should be safe. He clenched his hand into a fist. But it was as though the bastard reached out from the grave.

It will never be over.

66

WINE GLASS FILLED to the brim with a California Chardonnay, Alex followed Eric to his living room. There she sank deep into the corner of the leather sofa.

"So what's next, Alex?"

"We'll spring Tim from the hospital in the morning and head straight for the airport. Tracey has us booked on an early afternoon flight to Vancouver."

His smile dropped enough for her to know her answer disappointed him. But he must have known she couldn't stay.

"I thought you'd be here for at least a few more days. I know they're not laying charges against you in Trent Walden's death, but don't the cops need you to stick around?"

She shook her head. "No. My lawyer convinced them that Neil and I could answer questions just as easily from Vancouver as we could here. Besides, there really isn't anything more I can tell them."

"You got lucky. Next time—"

She touched a finger to his lips. "There's not going to be a next time. I'm usually pretty good at steering clear of trouble, even in politically unstable countries. This is Canada, and I let my guard down. I won't do that again."

She leaned against his shoulder and drew in a deep breath that caught the scent of his freshly-washed skin.

"Will you be in Vancouver for a while?" He closed his hand around hers.

"Maybe." She sighed. "Actually, I thought about flying to Tanzania to see my dad. He's been impossible to track down by phone." She sipped her wine. "But Tracey doesn't think he's there. She hasn't been able to reach him either."

"That doesn't sound good."

"Just the opposite." She smiled. "My dad has a tendency to go off-the-grid when he's onto something big. Last time he disappeared like this, he came back with a diamond mine." Her gaze dropped to her wine. "Anyway, it's probably better if I jump into another project. Keep busy."

She ran her fingers around the rim of her wine glass. The blood. The pain on Walden's face. It was her fault.

"I shot a man. And if you hadn't called Nathan. If he hadn't arrived when he did. I might have killed Trent Walden." Eyes locked on her fingers, she continued barely above a whisper, "No, I would have killed him."

Even as she'd taken that first shot, aimed at the shoulder of his firing arm, she'd been preparing for a second, more lethal one.

"You were defending yourself, Alex. Neil too. And don't forget, it was Nate's bullet that hit Walden's heart."

A tear slid down her cheek, and she brushed it away. He wrapped his arms around her, and she pressed her back against his warm chest. "I want you to see something." She reached for the newspaper and handed it to him. "This is a photo of Elizabeth Chambers. I was pretty quick to dismiss any resemblance to her, but seeing her photo today, I'm not so sure. What if Trent Walden thought Elizabeth was me? What if I'm the reason she's dead?"

"Alex, you can't really think that. Walden killed Elizabeth Chambers because she would have discovered the pesticide in that creek. Nothing more."

She sighed. "I know you're right. But I feel responsible. For her. For Tim. I can't help thinking I messed up."

He dropped the newspaper onto the cluttered coffee table and turned to her. "I'll be the first one to tell you that you should have been honest about the fire. But it wouldn't have changed anything. Even if the cops had found the bomb, they wouldn't have arrested Walden. Elizabeth Chambers would still be dead. And your quick action saved Tim. Neil too."

She gave a weak smile. "According to Tracey, Neil's calling me Annie Oakley. I'll never live it down."

"So, focus on the good stuff. Tim, Neil. Me." He reached for her hand and brought it to his lips. "That fire brought you to my ER. Brought you into my life."

He wants more. But it was madness. She barely spent enough time in Vancouver to make relationships with men living in the same city work, and her last long-distance romance, with David, had died of neglect. Still...

"Why don't you come to Vancouver? Stay a few days," she said.

"I wish I could. But until the army gives us back our ER, my boss isn't likely to let me stray far. Of course, that assumes that I still have a job." He picked up his wine glass and settled back on the sofa.

"You really think they might fire you?" Wine glass in hand, she tucked her legs under her and leaned an arm against the back of the sofa.

"Callaway might try." He ran a hand across his cheek. "He's taking a lot of heat over the reporting delay, and he'd like to make me the scapegoat."

"Tough for him to do when you called Nathan after Tim got sick."

"Yeah, well, Callaway's even less happy about that call. 'Insubordinate' was the word he used. Not my best move, I admit." He sighed. "But it would be next to impossible for the hospital to replace me right now. Nobody's going to want to relocate to Nelson with everything going on here. So, if Callaway is smart, he'll keep me around."

She smiled up at him. "I'm not sure whether to be happy or sad about that. Lots of hospitals in Vancouver you could work at if Callaway drops the axe on you." Her hands tightened around her wine glass. "And until the army finds the pesticide, Nelson isn't the safest place."

"No new cases in the ER, and more troops are on their way. The army's taking this pretty seriously."

"Makes me glad I'm leaving." She leaned her cheek against the palm of her hand. "At least I got what I needed."

"You never did tell me what you were looking for, by the way." He traced his finger down her arm.

"Silver. And I found just enough to convince me to buy some claims that were offered to me." Her stomach fluttered at the thought of the deal she'd just closed. The money she'd promised Sylvia Donnovan in exchange for all of Baxter's properties. Without a doubt, it was the biggest gamble she'd ever taken, and with luck it would pay off in the form of a rich silver mine.

"So you'll be back."

"As if there were ever any doubt." She smiled. "The silver is just a bonus."

Author's Note

ALTHOUGH THIS NOVEL is a work of fiction, it is based on scientific and historical fact and the current political relationship between Canada and the United States.

The Columbia River Treaty at the heart of this story is real. The treaty, signed by the United States and Canada in 1961 and implemented in 1964, governs water resource development on the upper Columbia River, development that benefits both countries. Under the treaty, the Hugh Keenleyside (Arrow), Mica and Duncan dams were built in Canada, and the Libby dam was constructed in the United States. The four dams together provide flood control to the United States, and they provide hydroelectric power to the United States and Canada. As of publication, Canada and the United States are currently reviewing the terms of the treaty with the intent to renegotiate some aspects. Country-specific information about the treaty is available through the Columbia Basin Trust (Canada) and the U.S. Army Corps of Engineers (United States).

The imagined joint Canada-United States military force assembled to suppress threats to the Columbia River dams is based on The Canada-United States Action Plan for Critical Infrastructure, agreed to by Prime Minister Harper and President Obama in 2010. This document is associated with the Beyond the Border Declaration: A Shared Vision for Perimeter Security and Economic Competitiveness, an initiative agreed to by the United States and Canada. The action plan provides for an integrated response to threats to critical infrastructure and allows both countries to contribute federal-level assistance to manage threats. The definition of critical infrastructure in the agreement would include the Columbia River dams, built in

Canada for the benefit of the United States. Other Canada-United States security and defence agreements that allow for combined military action have been signed by the two countries. These include the Combined Defence Plan and the Canada-U.S. Civil Assistance Plan. What is clear from these agreements is the intent of Canada and the United States to cooperate in the security of both countries.

The Columbia River Inter-tribal Fish Commission, headquartered in Portland, Oregon, has operated since 1977. The Nez Perce Tribe, the Confederated Tribes of the Umatilla Reservation, Confederated Tribes of the Warm Springs Reservation and the Confederated Tribes and Bands of the Yakama Indian Nation are focused on restoring the Columbia River salmon runs.

The Tsilhqot'in First Nation of British Columbia were granted aboriginal title to more than 1,700 square kilometres (656 square miles) in a landmark Supreme Court of Canada case in 2012. They now have the right to hunt, trap and trade in their traditional territory, and new economic development must either have the consent of the First Nation or be substantially justified by the government.

The Sons of Freedom, or Freedomites, a small, radical sect of the Russian Doukhobors, took root in the early 1900s. For four decades, they protested British Columbia government policies through nude demonstrations, arson and the bombing of public schools, railroad lines, bridges and power stations, among others. It is important to note that almost two hundred children of this religious sect were forced into a New Denver boarding school in the early 1950s, provoking some of the worst conflict between the B.C. government and the Sons of Freedom.

Of the nearly fifty thousand Vietnam War draft resisters who moved to Canada, several hundred settled in the Slocan Valley region. About half of these resisters are believed to have returned to the United States after they were granted amnesty by President Carter.

The Slocan Valley was the centre of a silver mining boom in the late 1800s. Silver, gold, lead and copper were all mined in the Valley through the 1900s and some continue today. Hundreds of abandoned silver mines dot the Slocan Valley, as do several ghost towns. For those interested, the Chamber of Mines in Nelson is a rich source of information on the local mining industry, both current and historical.

Fenamiphos is an organophosphate insecticide classified as extremely hazardous by the World Health Organization. Research into the acceptable daily intake for humans is lacking, but a maximum acute oral dose of 0.0008 mg/kg/day, approximately 0.03 milligram for a 100 pound man, is recommended by the Food and Agriculture Organization and the World Health Organization. For this story, the average hydrolysis half-life of 301 days reported by the EPA for pH 7.0 water was used. This pH value is within the 6.5– 8.0 pH water quality guideline of both Oregon and Washington states. Both fenamiphos and the products it degrades into over time are highly toxic to fish and wildlife . It is available and in use in a number of countries.

Acknowlegements

EVERY AUTHOR SPENDS countless hours at the keyboard, putting their story to paper, but they never work alone.

Dr. Laura Lee Copeland generously supplied her time to provide detailed information on procedures and the workings of a hospital ER. Without her remarkable assistance, Dr. Eric Keenan would not have come to life. All errors in the medical procedures portrayed in this novel are my own.

Prospector R.J. (Bob) Bourdon kindly provided geological mineral maps for the Slocan Valley. Constable Dimopoulos of the Nelson RCMP Detachment provided insight into the ranks of officers and the general organization of the RCMP in he Nelson area. My use of this information in the fictitious RCMP constable and the Integrated Security Task Force is solely my responsibility.

I owe a great deal of thanks to my early readers. Kelly Pearson's thoughtful suggestions brought more depth to my characters and sparked the relationship between Alex and Eric, and her editorial assistance with the first draft pushed me forward. Don Reid, with his keen eye for detail and good storytelling, helped identify problems and suggested the illustrated map. Others who graciously commented on drafts include Margery Reid, Phyllis Seymour and Birgitta MacGilliard.

Special thanks go to my editor, Kit Schindell, who worked tirelessly with me from draft to finished story. I feel privileged to have worked with such a talented editor. Thanks also to editor Allister Thompson for his assistance with the final polish.

Finally, I have to thank my husband, Bill, for his incredible support. Without him, this book would never have been written.